CRITICS RAVE FOR MARJORIE M. LIU AND *TIGER EYE*!

"A star is born! ...Liu is an amazing new voice: ingenious, fresh and utterly spellbinding.... Everything you could want in a new book."
—*RT BOOKclub* (Top Pick)

"The romance between Delilah and Hari tantalizingly builds until it culminates in a sensual love scene.... [An appealing and] striking paranormal romance."
—*Publishers Weekly*

"The mystical meets the magical in *Tiger Eye*, and is sure to captivate lovers of paranormal romance."
—*Romance Reviews Today*

"I didn't just like this book, I LOVED this book. [Marjorie M. Liu] has a great new voice, a fresh premise, everything I love to read. Anyone who loves my work should love hers."
—*New York Times* Bestselling Author Christine Feehan

"Wow! Fans of Feehan and Kenyon will love this exceptional story. I can't wait for more from this talented author."
—The Best Reviews

A TASTE OF DARKNESS

"How much do you know?" Michael turned in her arms. "Do you know what will happen to you if the others find out? Do you know what you're risking? This can't last, Keeli. Are you willing to give up everything just for…for…"

"A fling?" She stepped away from him. Her hands curled into fists. Hurt, angry—but that was not right, that was irrational, because he was just a vampire, and she…she…

Something hard moved through his face. "Not a fling. Just…the unknown."

"I don't run," Keeli reminded him. "Not even from the unknown."

"And this is worth fighting for?" There was a terrible hunger in Michael's eyes, so much need that Keeli felt breathless with it.

"You tell me." She closed the distance between them, not touching, but close—so close that just a breath would bring her lips in contact with his throat.

"Please," Michael whispered. "I am trying to be a good man."

Keeli smiled. "You're a vampire. Don't be something you're not."

A TASTE OF CRIMSON

MARJORIE M. LIU

LOVE SPELL   NEW YORK CITY

To my grandmothers, with love.

LOVE SPELL®

August 2005

Published by

Dorchester Publishing Co., Inc.
200 Madison Avenue
New York, NY 10016

ISBN 0-505-52632-8

The name "Love Spell" and its logo are trademarks of Dorchester Publishing Co., Inc.

Printed in the United States of America.

Visit us on the web at www.dorchesterpub.com.

ACKNOWLEDGMENTS

A big thank you to Liz Maverick for letting me play in her universe—Chris Keeslar, too, for extending the invitation. Leah Hultenschmidt, you are an angel—and the same must also be said of my agent, Lucienne Diver. To Nikki and Dawn Kimberling, two lovely ladies: thank you for your wonderful advice.

This book is also for my parents, who defied pessimists and bigots, and 28 years later are still going strong. Happy Anniversary!

A TASTE OF CRIMSON

Chapter One

They are dirty beasts, but that is the way of it. We will throw the dogs a bone, Michael. Throw them a bone, and watch them lick our fingers.

"Throw them a bone," Michael murmured. He pressed his tongue against fang, tasted sweet blood. Far below him, at street level, the vampire envoys floated single file down the narrow alley, winding around Dumpsters and rusting cars. Night, a cool breeze, the scent of rain, wet concrete shining with reflected light from apartment windows—the vampires were shadows passing over slick grit and filth.

Michael scanned the path ahead of them. He sensed no movement, no scent of human or steel. Nothing of the mechs, the mechanically enhanced humans of whom the city had so recently become aware. Nothing, even, of the wolves.

They are dirty beasts. Celestine's words still whispered in his mind, her dry-silk voice soft, damning. Michael watched the top of her head, third in line behind Frederick: the envoys' leader and Dumont's hand-chosen negotiator.

1

Celestine's pale hairless scalp stood out in stark contrast to her black belted robes. Michael imagined dropping on her, dislodging vertebrae with quick fingers, immobilizing her just long enough to keep her from the negotiations with the wolves. She was a bad choice for these talks—talks that had to succeed. Michael was not a man to admit weakness, but he could eat his pride this once. The humans had proven themselves strong in their first covert offensive against the vampires, and though it had been thwarted and the man who had ordered the assassinations was dead, other enemies existed. The promise was still there, the taste of violence.

The humans know we are vulnerable, soft in our luxury and unprepared for a hard fight. Worse yet, we have proven to them that we are aware of their existence. Now they have nothing to lose. They know we will come for them.

Michael had been alive long enough to know the dangers of calculated desperation. The danger to them all would be greater than ever, and despite his mixed feelings toward his own kind, the species had to be protected at any cost.

Even if it meant an alliance with the wolves.

I would have been a better choice as an envoy, Michael thought, and almost laughed—just as Frederick had laughed outright when Michael had challenged his part of this assignment.

So, now you wish to rejoin our kind? The outsider, reclaimed? A joke, Michael. You are the Vendix, the punisher, and that is all you are good for. You are not a diplomat. You do not do well with words or tact. Simply do what is expected of you. Hunt. Watch our backs from above. Keep us safe from traps.

Be a thug. Muscle. A hired sword.

Bitterness bloomed inside Michael's mouth, down his throat and into his chest. The horrors of his past, the crimes he had committed—three hundred years later he

2

still paid. He would always pay. It might be that redemption was something he would never be allowed to find. His role in society had been burned on his body for eternity.

Michael gripped the ledge he crouched upon, then jumped. An embrace—wind cushioned his body, sheathed him tight. He floated, toes pointing downward, arms loose at his sides. Black hair fell over his eyes; he pushed it aside, brushing metal. The gold filaments laced into his thin braids felt cooler than his skin.

He flew above and ahead of the envoys, scanning the shadows. Nothing at first, just the stillness of deep night. A rare quiet for the heart of the city, without the crush of traffic and quick-paced bodies. Perfect and lovely. This was the city Michael loved best, full of peaceful solitude. It was the kind of city to get lost in, without eyes to judge or pry.

For a moment, he thought he heard singing, faraway lilting, a man's voice rimmed with shadow. Michael thought, *That does not sound human*—and then he stopped listening to the music, because less than twenty yards ahead of the envoys something large moved.

Wolf.

Michael sank swiftly, noting from the corner of his eye Frederick's slowed movement, light flickering off the lead envoy's rings. Silk flared around Michael's legs as he alighted on the ground; he brought back his right hand, brushing the hilt of his sword, and looked deep into the gloom.

"Hello," he said quietly.

He saw sleek fur, wiry legs. Golden eyes and glittering teeth. A low growl rumbled like thunder in the night air.

Michael did not respond. He waited, patient, aware of the envoys behind him, the heavy weight of their stares. He sensed their impatience. Irritation. Immortals, in a hurry. The irony was not lost on Michael, but it was troubling: a sign of nervousness that the mission—and Frederick, as its head—could ill afford. The wolves would smell weakness.

Bones crackled. The wolf's jaw shifted, receded. Fur smoothed into naked skin. Muscles rippled in forelegs, expanding, elongating; paws became sinewy, masculine hands. Michael did not avert his eyes. Vampire and werewolf locked gazes—brown to golden—until, at the very last, when the animal had become man and there was nothing left but sweat and burning eyes, a hoarse note emerged from the werewolf's throat and became, "Hello."

"We are expected," Michael said.

The werewolf's spine popped. He was tall, with pale broad shoulders. A faint scar ran up his left cheek. Silver dusted his hair, although he had a relatively young face.

"The Grand Dame Alpha is waiting. I'm supposed to lead you underground." His distaste was evident, profound.

Michael felt breath on the back of his neck. Frederick said, "We are ready."

Michael twisted sideways, stepping close to the alley wall. The werewolf frowned as Frederick passed between them, followed closely by the rest of the envoys. The vampires each floated at least six inches off the ground, giving them a secure advantage in height. Michael heard the werewolf mutter obscenities, his feet slapping hard against the pavement as he loped ahead.

Michael watched the faces of every vampire who passed, noting their focused indifference with amused detachment. The only one who met his eyes was Celestine, and her dark gaze was sly, smug. Her thin red lips tugged upwards, and then she was gone, gliding past him down the alley. The record-keeper followed, and then the seven guards, their long embroidered robes concealing more weapons than they revealed, most of which were mod rn—handguns, stun rods, small explosives.

Quaint. Not very elegant.

Michael fell into a floating step behind the last guard. He sensed a tremor run through the vampire's body, and smiled grimly. Psychopath, assassin, murderer, executioner—all of these were names other vampires had given Michael. All of these were names for their fear.

He almost touched his cheek, caught himself before he could show that sliver of weakness. The tattoo hurt. Centuries old, and still it pained him. Ink laced with gold did not heal properly, even in vampire flesh, and it would never fade or be absorbed by his body. He was marked, forever. Vendix. Punisher. Condemned to be alone.

Michael drew back, drifting higher, following the envoys at a discreet distance. No more werewolves revealed themselves. He watched as the envoys were led to a wide sewer grate. The werewolf guide leapt over the rusty steel bars and in one fluid motion swept down to yank them open. The hinges were surprisingly quiet; Michael heard only a faint squeak.

A voice rose up from the darkness of underground— hollow as a tunnel, brittle with well-worn age, feminine in a way that might have once been lovely but was now only wise.

"Welcome, vampires. Welcome to the home of Maddox."

"Thank you," said Frederick, his bejeweled hands clasped together. He bowed his head; a strand of black hair drifted over his shoulder, caressing the pale glow of his long neck. The other vampires also bowed their heads—as they had been commanded to do—though Michael did not miss the hard line of Celestine's lips, nor the arrogance that narrowed the eyes of every vampire but Frederick.

You are not a diplomat. You do not do well with words or tact.

Maybe. But at least Michael knew enough to hide his emotions for the sake of politeness. At least he still remembered humility—or as much as was necessary to pretend at compassion.

"Jas," said the voice in the darkness. The werewolf guide took a reluctant step back and gestured at the open sewer grate. His jaw was tight, his naked body rigid, coiled. Michael thought he might be shaking, and knew it for rage.

"Don't you dare try anything," Jas said. A sharp bark from underground made him flinch.

Frederick did not answer. He stepped off the alley ledge and drifted slowly down, down into the darkness of the werewolf tunnels. The other vampires followed, with more reluctance than was courteous.

Michael watched from above, waiting until the last guard descended. Jas looked up at him. The two men locked gazes and Michael felt the challenge and questions.

Just try something. And, *Who are you?*

Michael waited, silent, until Jas pulled back his lips in a silent snarl. His eyes flashed. Michael saw the hint of fur, the shift of his chin into something narrow and sharp. Then the wolf jumped down into the waiting darkness, and several pairs of hands emerged from the tunnel to pull shut the grate. Silence descended, the weight of the night bearing down into a hush. There was no singing anymore.

Alone, at last.

Michael drifted backward until his shoulders rubbed the alley wall. It was a small comfort, to be away from his own kind. He took some satisfaction in their fear, but it truly only served to heighten his isolation, the knowledge that he could never be part of them. That even if he wanted, they would never accept his presence.

6

Vampires did not easily forgive those who killed their kind—especially when the killer was a vampire himself.

His assignment was not yet over. Frederick had been very clear; Michael was to stay until the envoys reemerged. There was a three-hour deadline on the talks, enough time for the envoys to return home before sunrise. Each carried a special day-pack—enough makeup, sunblock, and shielding to protect him or her from the sun. Not that it mattered. Despite the official statements, the human offensive had begun: It was a return of the old days, if in a different fashion. There was no safety here, not when sunlight made it so difficult to pass as human.

We should have expected it. Michael tilted his head, struggling to see the stars beyond the glare of city lights and smog. *Humans have always feared us, for good reason. And now with their numbers dwindling, birth rates declining . . . they cannot risk our presence, our promises of self-control.*

Self-control. That was laughable.

He finally gave in and touched his stinging cheek, traced the hard round lines etched into his skin. No other Vendix was marked in this way. Only Michael.

For your past misdeeds, as well as the ones you will commit.

Michael pulled his hand away. He curled his fingers against the brick behind him.

Don't, he told himself. *Not now.*

He heard laughter, then, distinctly male. Raucous, drunk, wild. The kind to avoid, if he were weak and human. The kind to avoid, even if he weren't. He listened carefully, but the humans had an echo in their voices that meant distance—several blocks worth—and Michael felt little interest in investigating. As long as they did not approach the entrance to the tunnels, they could piss and vomit up their drunken stupor on any street they liked.

And then the laughter stopped. Suddenly, eerily. A curtain of silence dropped hard and fast, creating an expectant voice within the night: *Not right, not right*. Michael pushed himself away from the wall, drifting higher.

He had almost cleared the rooftops when he heard a whistle, a low catcall. Laughter, again, but lower this time. A promise. More silence . . . and then shoes slapping against concrete—hard, fast. More and more, a group of people running. Chasing.

A woman screamed.

And just as Michael shot into the sky, pursuing the sound of that terrified cry, the men began screaming, too.

Chapter Two

The Man was around, which meant that Keeli had to slip out of Butchie's through the back, leaving Shelly in the weeds with five tables, one of which whose occupants had been screaming for their fries just before that familiar starched white shirt ghosted through the front doors.

"H.I. Bob is here," Shelly whispered, and just like that, Keeli had to drop everything and dodge. Health Inspector Bob, aka The Man.

A man who had a distinct dislike for werewolves. Bob had already fined Jim Butchie three hundred dollars for keeping Keeli on as a waitress. Not that werewolves were the reason cited, but it didn't have to be. The Man had a reputation, and every other restaurant in the city—the ones that didn't discriminate—had suffered from his twitchy fingers and high fines.

Blame it on a new law from the Feds, which now required the Food and Health industry to screen all prospective employees for lycanthropy and other "aggressive" diseases. Employers weren't supposed to discriminate based on blood-test results—*that*, at least, was still illegal—but enforcement was a joke. Humans were running scared nowadays. Or at least, a little nervous.

Keeli was lucky; she still had a job. Even the most progressive restaurants fired their nonhuman servers after a run-in with the Man. Of course, most restaurants weren't owned and run by Jim Butchie, an ex-trucker who embodied the two most sacred words in Keeli's vocabulary: *fuck you.*

Butchie's was a greasy hole situated in the armpit of east downtown, the round and smelly fringe of the city. It had good cheap food, and was open twenty-four hours a day. Jim lived above his restaurant and could always be counted on to poke his nose into everyone's business, at every hour of the day. Jim didn't seem to need much sleep. One of the busboys had probably gone up to his apartment by now and told him about H.I. Bob.

Keeli crouched beside the dumpster on the other side of the restaurant's back door. The smell was overwhelming, but she didn't move. She listened to the dishwashers in the pit, young men, new to the country, chattering in a patois of Spanish, Chinese, and English that had become common in the lower classes. Keeli spoke it fluently.

She cleaned her fingernails to kill time, scraping out bits of food from beneath her long nails. She hated the feel of grease on her skin, her odor after a night on the job—the scent of wolf, drowned out by the scent of fries and hamburgers.

It could be worse. At least you have a job. You work in a place where the people like you.

Yes. She had nothing to complain about. Not like the rest of her clan, especially the men, many of whom were finding it difficult to land even grunt work. Everyone in this part of town knew each other's business—especially if you were fang or fur. And no one was hiring fur.

Stupid vampires. Word gets out on the street that they're lined up for shit, and suddenly life becomes difficult for all of us.

And it was only going to get worse. Everyone in the underground knew about the attack on the vampires. Rumor called it a rogue element of the human military, but that was shit, just some lame excuse. Keeli didn't imagine for one instant the humans wanted the vampires around. Nor did she think they would stop at just attacking the vampires. The only surprise was that the werewolves hadn't been targeted first. When it came to pure visceral reaction by humans, wolves usually got the boot up the ass before the fangs.

We just aren't sexy enough. Keeli glanced down at her striped stockings, her scuffed Doc Martens. Her torn black T-shirt barely covered her lean midriff, and her spiked hair had been dyed a fresh shade of pink just that morning. Yeah, she radiated sex appeal.

Not. Of course, that was the way she wanted it. She was sick of expectations.

She heard Jim's voice over the clanging pots and running water. Good, he was up. A moment later, H.I. Bob said something nasal, irritating. Hackles raised, Keeli edged deeper into the shadow cast by the Dumpster. The alley was poorly lit, but she always had trouble judging what humans could see or hear. *Underestimating others is a dangerous thing,* her grandmother had taught her. *Arrogance leaves you vulnerable.*

Vulnerable. Something Keeli had vowed never to let herself be.

She shifted, stretching cramped muscles. She did not like sitting still for long periods of time—it was the wolf in her, the need to run, to feel the ground beneath her feet, the rush of air in her hair, against her skin, drawing out each breath like it was her last living moment in the world. . . .

Keeli sagged against the wall, savoring the feel of the cool damp brick. Her fingernails felt too sharp. The wolf roiled within her chest, close to the surface. Too close.

Jim's voice got loud and then receded, followed quickly by H.I. Bob. Kitchen inspection was over, which meant Keeli's retreat was near an end. She'd have to go back in soon. She had responsibilities, tables waiting. Shelly needed help.

Keeli swallowed hard. It would be so easy to walk away from all this. But if she did, all her work—the slow process of proving her self-control to the clan and her grandmother—would be worth nothing. She could not allow that. She was finally making her own way, defying expectation. Nothing was worth losing that independence.

At the end of the alley, she heard a sudden burst of laughter. Men, drunk. Keeli's lip curled. There were a lot of bars in east downtown, with patrons of the human and werewolf variety. The only difference was that werewolves rarely drank enough to become intoxicated. There was too much risk. Control over the wolf could be a tenuous thing—for some wolves more than others.

And let's face it—no one likes a drunk, wolf or not.

Especially when they sounded like these guys. Keeli edged around the Dumpster, peering at the alley mouth. The back door of Butchie's was close to the main drag, so Keeli had a fine view of the sidewalk. She heard the men coming, sounding four strong. A stumbling walk, alternating pace from fast to slow. A pause; the sound of a zipper. Pissing. More laughter.

I'll have to remind myself not to walk that way after my shift. I have to deal with enough awful smells.

From the other direction came a new sound: soft soles, a light quick tread. A woman.

What timing. Keeli's stomach tightened as the woman

12

drew near. She would have seen the men by now, who were still motionless, loudly comparing the size of their dicks.

"Turn around," Keeli breathed. "Come on, lady. Common sense."

Keeli listened hard, heard a shift in the woman's gait. It faded slightly, but not enough. Not enough. The woman crossed the street; the laughter stopped.

"Shit," Keeli muttered. She glimpsed the woman on the other side of the street; walking quickly, almost stumbling over her feet, a short bulky figure wrapped in a long coat. Her curls were blond and bouncing.

Still, the men were silent. Keeli held her breath. Maybe these guys weren't shit, maybe they would let the woman go. Maybe—

The whistles began. Even as Keeli stepped away from the shadows, moving toward the alley mouth, she heard more laughter, low and hard. A growl rose up in her throat.

"Sweet," said one man, and another murmured, "Come on."

Keeli burst from the alley just in time to see the men take off after the woman. Drunk, but quick, they crossed the street in seconds and ran her down. They became a circle of arms, rough hands; she screamed. There was no question of their intent.

Then Keeli was there and the wolf was high in her throat, clawing at her skin, roping muscle and bone. She felt a terrible strength, and the fury was worse, rage seething under the shadow of righteousness, hunger. She burst into the circle of men, breaking them apart with sharp kicks, slashing nails into flesh. Close up, they smelled like the docks—fish and machine grease, mixed with alcohol. They were big men, taller than her by a foot, with shoulders thick and broad.

Keeli slammed her foot into a kneecap, savored the sharp crack, the scream torn from the man's throat. Hands wrapped around her waist. Keeli grabbed meaty fingers and yanked back; they snapped and she tightened her grip, twisting, grinding broken bone. Her assailant's screams made her eardrums vibrate. He tried to wrench free, hauling Keeli off her feet. She tucked her knees to her chest and refused to let go. When he whirled near one of his wide-eyed friends, she kicked out, landing a boot heel into the man's chin.

Fur pressed though her skin, sleek as her rage, consuming her body as she sank deeper into the fire. *Yes*, she thought. *Yes. This is what I have been pushing away.*

The man trapped against her screamed even louder. Keeli released him and fell to her feet. Her claws scraped concrete. The men ran—this time, away. But in two quick steps Keeli captured a straggler. Strong—the wolf in her was strong—she slammed him into the ground, wrenching his left arm behind his back. Canines slid gently against her lip; her jaw narrowed; her teeth jutted out, sharp. Keeli lowered her head.

She felt a presence, then, at her side. Strong hands grabbed a fistful of her hair and yanked hard. Keeli did not think; she whirled, snarling, and sank her teeth into flesh. Blood filled her mouth, hot and bitter. It tasted good.

And then—*oh, oh, shit, what have I done*—the blood turned sour and she ripped her head away, gasping.

Gone too far, too far. She had bitten a human—and oh, if not one then how about another? Because she wanted it. In that moment she wanted blood, and there was still a man beneath her, the man she had been going to kill, and the old rage felt so damn good. . . .

Keeli leaned over and vomited. Again, she felt hands in her hair, gentler this time.

"It's all right," whispered a man, in a voice so dark that Keeli shuddered. Her gaze slid sideways and slowly, slowly, up.

Sagging leather boots filled her vision, and then black silk robes reminiscent of old Asia, belted tight around a narrow waist, hugging a lean chest and bony shoulders. She saw a pale and striking face, with more bone than flesh, framed by loose black hair threaded with braids. His right cheek glittered.

And his eyes . . .

Keeli stared for one precious moment, lost in the velvet underground of that deep-set gaze. And then came a click, the recognition of Something Not Quite Right, and she realized what he was, and what she had bitten. Relief made her weak, as did humiliation, but she fought for composure, stamping down another fresh swell of inexplicable rage.

"Vampire," she growled, embarrassed at how her voice broke on that word. "Get the hell away from me."

"No," he said, so calm, so quiet. As though the warmth dripping on her hand, the blood from his torn arm, meant nothing. Her bite, meaningless. "Not until you release the human."

The human beneath her trembled. She smelled urine, sour sweat. His friends were long gone. He was all she had left, and the wolf in her still wanted him dead. One bite, a breaking of his neck. He would never hurt anyone again.

Never again. No one's ever going to get hurt again.

"You must calm yourself," whispered the vampire, as though he could read her thoughts. He bent so close they brushed noses. Keeli froze. "Please. Control the wolf. You have witnesses."

It was the "please" that finally dulled her anger—that,

and the urgency in the vampire's voice. Her gaze darted sideways.

Jim, Shelly, and a handful of strangers stood a short distance away. Everyone but Jim stared at her with eyes that seemed too full of shock, numb horror, to ever fade away into a forgivable memory. Shelly had her arms wrapped around the victim of the attempted rape, her straight red bob pressed against the woman's blond curls. Jim stood over them both. He looked worried.

Shame burned away the rest of Keeli's rage, sending the wolf in her into swift retreat. Everything she had worked for—trying so hard to fit in; to be, for once, more woman than wolf . . .

"This is not how you wish humans to remember your kind," whispered the vampire, still close. His cheek shimmered: round lines, etched in gold. For the first time, Keeli noticed his scent—dry, with a hint of wild grass, horse hair. The taint of age. "This is not how you wish them to remember *you*."

Keeli looked at her hands, still holding down her shivering captive. She was fully human again. Pink skin, clear nails. She let go of her captive and slid off his back. He continued to lie there, his eyes squeezed shut. She almost touched him—to comfort, to reassure—and then the memory resurfaced.

"He deserved it," she said. "Deserved to be scared, for what he was going to do to that woman."

"Maybe," said the vampire. "But you would have given up your own life to do it. He's not worth that."

Keeli looked at the vampire—really looked, hard—and saw nothing but calm acceptance. No anger. She glanced down at his arm.

"I'm sorry," she said, and it was one more shock to add to her collection: apologizing to a vampire. "Will you be all right?"

His mouth twitched. "I've had worse." He stood and held out his hand. Keeli refused to touch him.

Awful, disgusting. Vampires are monsters.

Monsters beneath a veneer of refinement, big money. Hypocrites and fakes. Pretending to be better, more *human* than everyone else.

Maybe this one is different.

Yeah, and maybe she hadn't just lost herself to the wolf.

Keeli pushed away, scrambling to her feet. She heard sirens and found herself saying, "You should go. The cops will be here soon. You don't want to be involved. Not with what's been going on. . . ."

The vampire hesitated. He glanced at Jim and the others, still hanging back, watching. "What of you? I can carry the both of us and fly—"

Keeli shook her head. "I don't run. Ever."

The vampire's eyes narrowed. "And will you think I'm a coward if I leave?"

"You're a vampire," Keeli retorted. "I *already* think you're a coward. Amongst other things." She wondered why the hell she was even having this conversation.

Again, that odd twitch around the vampire's mouth. "Good-bye, wolf," he said.

"The name is Keeli, fang-boy."

"Michael. And I'm not the only one with fangs." He reached out, a blur, and brushed Keeli's lips with cool fingertips.

She was too surprised to say a word—surprised at the gentleness of his touch, surprised at her reaction to it. She saw blood on his fingers; he had wiped her mouth.

"When they ask, you did not bite anyone," he added quietly, and then the vampire leapt into the air. Up and up he went, a shadow passing into shadow, into the night, until he was gone, not even an outline against the dim stars.

"Thanks for helping me," she murmured. The sirens were loud now, eardrum-shattering. She looked at Jim and Shelly, the weeping woman, her weeping attacker. Keeli squared her shoulders and prepared herself for a long and difficult night.

Chapter Three

Michael settled on a rooftop just out of the wolf-woman's sight. From his vantage point he saw flickering strobes of red and blue approaching from several blocks away. Police. The wolf was right—it was dangerous to be involved in anything these days. And the cops might have a mech with them. There had been some discussion of experimenting with the engineered oddities, getting them from the military and putting them on the force to see how they handled the street. Michael had yet to see one himself.

He gazed down and, even in the darkness, bright pink hair snared his attention. The color could have been lurid, but on the wolf-woman—with her hair already thick and wild—it fit. Fit her pale skin, with the flush of anger in her cheeks. Fit the stubborn set of her small mouth, her delicate chin. Fit the brilliant blue of her intelligent eyes.

Keeli. He rolled her name around his tongue and decided he liked it—even if it did belong to a woman who bit vampires and kicked the shit out of human men twice her size.

She wasn't herself. There was a madness inside of her.

Rage, awful and pure. He'd seen it before—in himself, no less. It was a powerful high to come down from, but the taste of his blood had smothered the unthinking nature of her anger. And for a moment—oh, the memory—the remorse in her eyes, the self-loathing, had cut him worse than her teeth. Michael knew that feeling all too well. He just had never expected to see it on the face of a werewolf.

He watched Keeli approach the humans. Some of them shied away, backing off with quick steps. Closer and closer she moved, until at last only four humans remained: a man, two women, the would-be rapist, who was still huddled on the ground. Keeli said something to them. The man nodded. The women remained very still.

Police cars pulled up, including an assault van, retrofitted for C.C.P.D.'s street-force grunts. Familiar figures poured from the vehicle, rifles raised. They had special guns, split-barrel activity, with only one button separating the different projectiles necessary against the city's paranormal populations.

"Hands up!" shouted a lean officer, sporting close-fitting armor and a blond crew cut. He aimed his weapon at Keeli's face. Jenkins always had good instincts for who was the nonhuman in a crowd—though in this case, it was self-evident.

But his intent was unjust, badly misplaced. Michael reached inside his robes and withdrew a small digi-encoder. He dialed a pager number. A moment later, everyone in the vicinity heard Jenkins's side beep.

Keeli still had her hands up. Michael could not see her eyes from his vantage, but her body was rigid. The male human who had watched her take down the rapist talked heatedly to one of the cops.

Jenkins nodded at the officer nearest him—Sheila, Michael thought—and lowered his rifle. Glancing around, he walked across the street to a nearby alley. Michael flew after him.

Jenkins waited out of sight, his hands pressed together with his fingertips touching his chin. Pensive, as always.

"This is a surprise," he said, when Michael landed. "Must be the first time you've ever paged me."

"That werewolf committed no crime," Michael said, wasting no time on pleasantries. Not that he ever did. Jenkins shook his head.

"Okay, should have expected that. You want to explain?"

Michael explained, and when he finished, Jenkins said, "It wasn't exactly self-defense." Michael's jaw tightened and Jenkins held up his hands. "Oh, and you're going to tell me that chunk outta your arm is just a scratch, huh? Yeah, didn't think so. Listen, man, you know how it is. Any of you guys show angry fangs to a human, no matter the situation, and the law is gonna come down hard. I can't change that. It was part of the truce."

"She saved that woman from being raped."

Jenkins shook his head. "How long have we worked together, Michael? How many years? In all that time, have I ever treated a vamp or wolf unfairly?"

"Not until now."

"Don't give me that. You helped make this street force what it is. Even if your name was never put to paper, you helped make the rules. And now you want me to break them for you?"

"Yes," said Michael, humbling himself. "Please."

Jenkins blinked, taken aback. "Is this personal?"

Yes. "No."

Jenkins did not believe him—his expression said it all—but he stayed quiet.

Michael didn't know why he cared. There was no good answer to his actions; this was simply instinct, inexplicable and mysterious. Keeli had to be saved—the years of incarceration the law said she deserved would kill her. Just one look in her eyes, and he knew that much. And with all that had happened in the city over the past two weeks . . .

For everything I've done wrong, if I can do this . . . just this. . . .

"All right," Jenkins said quietly. "I'll fix it. But she still has to go to lockup for the night. Processing. And there'll be a fine. A large one."

"How large?"

A look of sympathy passed over Jenkins's face. "More than you can afford on your salary, bud."

Embarrassing. Michael nodded and backed away, intent on leaving before he shamed himself any further.

Jenkins frowned. "Wait. There's something else you should hear. Another vampire was killed. And this wasn't some random skirmish or gangbang. We found the body on Fourth and Lexington about an hour ago."

Michael went very still. "How did he die?"

"How do you think? Looked like his heart was ripped out. Along with his guts. We still need to check the DNA, but it looks like our serial killer, making his rounds."

"A name?"

"Haven't made the ID yet. There wasn't much left. The body's already turning to dust, but we got to it before full decay. Looked like he was ripped into with someone's bare hands." A lengthy pause, and then, "You know what *we* think all this sounds like."

Werewolf.

Michael didn't say anything; Jenkins already knew his thoughts on the matter. Despite the enmity between their two peoples, there had been no reported skirmishes between a vampire and werewolf for years. Certainly no mass murders. But now? With tensions rising with humans, and secret negotiations beginning between their two peoples? Too much coincidence. Something odd was going on.

"Still no leads?" he asked.

"Nothing. This case is fucked up, Michael. Our killer isn't leaving behind any clues. Nothing. No DNA, no footprints, no witnesses. He's too careful."

"If you can't confirm what he is, then why are you focusing on the wolves? The killer could be human. Vampire, even."

Jenkins stared. "If you know a regular man or woman—and I'm not talking a fucking mech, here—who can pull a vampire apart like he's string cheese, then hell, feel free to let me know."

"It was that bad?"

"As bad as any typical werewolf kill."

"Have the wolves been any help at all?"

Jenkins shrugged. "We're working with their head honcho. Some old dame. She's cooperating—on the surface, anyway—but so far it's been a dead end. No one wants to talk to us."

"I wonder why."

"Funny. Thing is, there's a rumor at headquarters about another roundup. People are getting nervous, Michael. I'm worried it's gonna be Chinatown all over again."

Chinatown, over a year ago. Seven humans had been killed in a brutal werewolf attack. Every single werewolf in the city was rounded up and interned until the murderer was found. Michael thought the wolves were lucky to have been released at all. There was still talk of confinement, walled neighborhoods. Hysteria and spilled blood never mixed well.

"I need your help," Jenkins admitted.

"You have a werewolf liaison."

"Not anymore. Our last informant turned up dead. Throat kill. Vampire."

Michael shut his eyes. "This is getting out of hand."

"Michael, come on. Gimme a break. We need you on this."

He sighed. "I'll do it, but the wolves won't talk to me. I won't even get through the front door."

"You will. You're good at what you do, Michael. Just give it a shot." He looked nervous.

"What aren't you telling me?" Michael said.

Jenkins glanced around, making sure they were alone. "There's some bad shit going on in the department. No one's saying anything, certainly not on paper, but the word is that we're supposed to be completely hands off when it comes to crimes committed against nonhumans. More than usual. If a vampire or werewolf turns up dead, we're not even supposed to look into it. 'Just let it pass,' they're saying. Pass into what, I don't know. Except if we do that, we're allowing major crimes to go unpunished— and no one up top seems to care."

Michael said nothing. He was not surprised.

"Michael," Jenkins said slowly, watching his face. "What do *you* know?"

Too much. He wanted to tell Jenkins everything, but the man had a family and a career. And Jenkins was a good man; if he knew the truth, he would make a stink. He couldn't keep his mouth shut when he got upset.

Michael clapped a hand over the man's shoulder. "Nothing," he lied. "But thank you for telling me what you have."

Jenkins wasn't buying, but he nodded. A faint smile eased the hard lines of his face. "What's with the robes? You look like it's Halloween."

"Formal occasion," he replied. "Thank you again, Jenkins. For that other thing. I . . . owe you."

Jenkins muttered something under his breath, too quiet

for even Michael to make out. He raised his hand in farewell.

As Michael flew from the alley, he glanced down. Keeli was in handcuffs, being led to the police van. The rapist was also in handcuffs, but still on the ground.

Michael hovered, studying Keeli. Perhaps she felt him, perhaps he wanted her to, but she looked up at just that instant and their gazes met.

A dislocating moment—thrills in his gut, weakness. It was like being human again, racing with the wild horses on the steppes with nothing but wind against his skin, grass hot and dry beneath his bare feet. Racing for life, desire, for the pure joy of speed.

Too much—the memories were too much. Shaken, Michael tore his gaze away and shot into the sky, running, still running. But for a different reason this time.

That was bizarre. Keeli watched the vampire disappear for a second time. The memory of his eyes lingered, and she shuddered.

"Hey now," said the beefy man holding her arm. "Hold still."

"Sorry," she muttered, refraining from adding a more colorful description to her apology. She glanced at Jim, who stood on the sidelines with an expression of helpless fury on his weathered face. They hadn't said much to each other before the police arrived, only enough to reassure Keeli that Jim knew why she had attacked those men. He'd been taking up for her with the police ever since.

"S'okay," she said to him, as she was pushed into the van. She looked one last time at the woman whose life she'd saved, took in the gratitude, the lingering after-shocks of fear.

One good deed, she thought. One good deed and off to

jail. Lovely. Her life was officially ruined. She wondered how she would survive, and whether the circumstances of her attack would make a judge more lenient. She doubted it. Strangely enough, she couldn't muster much emotion about her situation—not even fear. Just a numb, hollow acceptance. Because this was what people had expected, wasn't it? All those bastards had been right, after all.

Keeli sat on a hard, narrow seat bolted to the wall. The van was cold; it smelled like sweat, gunpowder, and exposed steel. Captivity, on wheels. Fear finally threaded through her chest. She quickly suppressed it. She would handle this, no matter what. She *would*.

The officer cuffed her feet to the floor. Silver, she'd bet, though her boots kept the metal from her skin. Her wrists burned. There would be marks—scars, even. It might take an entire week to heal properly. The sign of the Man carved into her body. A bad omen, for a wolf.

Yet deep down, Keeli thought she deserved it. She would have bitten—perhaps killed—that human. She certainly hadn't hesitated when the vampire grabbed her. And that was the worst part. She had sunk her teeth into him, thinking he was human. Not caring if he were human.

That temper of hers is dangerous. You know what she's like as a wolf. Her father was the same way. Berserker. Feral. All instinct and nothing else. It's the Maddox blood. You know where that name's from, right? Mad dog. The whole lot of them, mad.

A blond man entered the van—the same one who had taken off when his pager beeped. Keeli inhaled deep. Some scent clung to him, familiar.

"I'll take care of her," he said.

The first officer followed the implicit order without comment, though Keeli noted his hesitation. The doors shut behind him and Keeli was left alone with something even worse than the Man. A true-blue C.C.P.D. accredited Officer of the Law.

"You going to strip-search me?" she drawled, when the engine started and still the blond man seated across from her had not stopped staring. The sewn-on strip above his heart said JENKINS. He looked like a professional, which was not all that reassuring.

The man snorted. "Just wondering what makes you special."

"If I were so special," Keeli said, annoyed and curious, "I wouldn't be here right now."

Jenkins smiled. "You don't know. Great, I love this."

Keeli pressed her lips together and the human shook his head. "Yeah, you're right," he said. He removed a key from his belt, and looked her hard in the eyes. Cool, assessing.

"I'm doing this because someone went to a lot of trouble for you tonight. You understand? Don't make him out to be a liar."

Keeli stared, mystified. It wasn't until Jenkins bent and unlocked her feet, and then her hands, that she understood part of what he was getting at. She rubbed her burning wrists.

"But the law . . ."

"Is being bent for you just this once." Jenkins tucked the cuffs into a deep pocket in his cargo pants. "No real jail time. Just a holding cell for the night. You go free in the morning, with a fine." He pulled a med kit from the compartment beneath his seat and removed a white tube. "Burn gel. Specially made for silver poisoning."

Keeli did not take the medicine. "What's the price?"

Because even though she was a werewolf, she was also a woman—and some men got their digs that way. Jenkins scowled. He tossed her the tube and then leaned back in his seat with his arms crossed over his chest.

"No price, as far as I'm concerned. That's between you and Michael."

"Michael?" Keeli echoed. A flurry of images tunneled through her brain: dark eyes, strong hands in her hair, the urgency of his voice. A touch, on her lips. The sight of him hovering in the night sky, staring so hard at her. And his taste, that hard swallow of his blood that had gone down hot into her belly. . . .

She recognized the scent, then—the one she had noticed on Jenkins's clothing.

"Why?" she asked, because it was the only word her voice would form.

"Don't know," he said, and Keeli sensed that he, too, was perplexed. "I've worked with Michael for a long time, and he's never pulled a stunt like this. Had plenty of opportunities, too. You're the first."

A long time with the C.C.P.D? Michael was a liaison, then. A long-term backstabber to his own kind.

Must be real popular with other vampires.

Some werewolves served the same function, running part-time with the C.C.P.D., but they never lasted long. There was too much conflict and animosity. *Clan comes first,* was the old saying. *You run apart, you stay apart.*

It had to be the same with the vampires. The fangs were even more socially unforgiving than the wolves. But what would make a vampire set himself apart like that? And why would he help her?

"This doesn't make sense," Keeli said. "I don't know this Michael. I don't *want* to know him. He's a vampire."

Jenkins shrugged, though Keeli did not miss the hard glint in his eyes. "That's your choice. I'd show a little more gratitude, though. He saved you five years hard time tonight."

More than that, Keeli thought, still stunned. If she had bitten that rapist and infected him, it would have been life in prison. If she'd snapped his neck like she wanted to? Death penalty for sure.

Jenkins peered into her face. "Isn't often people do nice things for each other."

"Vampires aren't people." She spoke without thinking, the response automatic.

He blew out his breath, annoyed. "I was talking about *you*. Shit. I don't know why Michael bothered, except you did something good tonight."

"Is she all right?" Keeli asked, quieter. She tried not to feel embarrassed.

"Yeah." Jenkins rubbed a hand over his face. "Scared shitless, but okay. She was lucky you were around." He smiled, but it was without humor. Cold, even. "You want a job?"

"No," she said instantly. "Hell, no."

His smile widened. "Thought so."

"An absolute disaster," Celestine seethed, not waiting until she was clear of the Maddox tunnel, out of earshot of the werewolves, before speaking in loud strident tones a deaf man could have heard vibrating in his chest. Frederick gave her a hard look, but did not admonish her as Michael would have.

The werewolves, a handful who had gathered to escort the envoys from the tunnels, snarled. Michael thought they showed considerable restraint. Had Keeli heard such a statement from Celestine, he had no doubt she would have leapt on the vampire with her claws out, teeth bared.

And won.

Something similar might have already happened tonight, Michael thought, remembering what Jenkins had told him. He thought of Keeli again, the look of his blood on her lips. He wondered if anything happened when werewolves drank vampire blood.

"Is there something wrong with your mouth?" Celestine snapped at Michael as she passed him. Michael raised an eyebrow, noting the shocked expressions of the other vampires. No one, not even Celestine, ever spoke to Michael in public, and certainly not like that.

"My mouth is the same as it has always been," he said, curious.

Celestine squinted. "You looked like you were smiling. It was disturbing."

"My goal, my pleasure," Michael said, and this time he did smile. Celestine looked away.

Frederick did not bid the wolves good-bye as he passed; he did not acknowledge them in any way. He did not greet Michael, either. The other envoys followed as Frederick stepped into the air, climbing stairs made of wind, a slender figure walking on shadows.

Michael did not follow. He remained by the Maddox tunnel, hands hanging loose against his thighs. He watched the werewolves. He did not know if they were negotiators, guards, or curious residents of the underground; it did not matter, either way. He was here because this was the closest clan within a fifty-block radius, and he assumed someone would know Keeli.

The sewer grate was still open; Michael sensed movement down below, the quiet hush of breathing. Jas appeared through the entrance, this time clothed in jeans and an unbuttoned denim shirt. He remained silent, as did the other werewolves. Michael raised an eyebrow. A staring contest ensued between the two men, but the vampire had eternity on his side. Jas blinked first. A low growl rumbled from his throat.

"What do you want, fang?"

Many things, Michael thought, but said, "I believe one of your wolves was taken in by the police. I made an arrangement with their chief officer. She'll be released in the morning, but there will be a large fine attached to her arrest."

Murmuring, feet shifting. Everyone looked unhappy, Jas most of all. He lowered his head, canines descending from an elongated face, inhuman muscles moving beneath his forearms. He stepped close, sniffing the air.

"Your scent," he said, rough, gritty, and strangled. "Who was the wolf?"

Something is his voice made Michael think that Jas already had a good idea whom he was going to name. Jas just needed to hear it to have his excuse. So when Michael said, "Keeli," and Jas lunged forward to grab him by the front of his robes, he was not terribly surprised. He felt the brush of claws against his chest as they pierced his clothing, heard wet cracking sounds as the other werewolves changed shape, dropping to all fours with hackles raised, heads ducked low with teeth bared. Michael did not struggle, but he did not lower his eyes, either. He was subservient to no one, especially a wolf.

Looked like his heart was ripped out. Along with his guts.

"Why did the police take her in? You have something to do with it?" Jas pressed close. His breath smelled like raw meat. His urgency took Michael aback—it was not just simple anger or hunger for a fight. This wolf was keenly afraid for Keeli.

Who is she to them?

"Enough." A familiar voice, dry with age. The same voice that had greeted the vampire envoy. All the wolves but Jas stilled, quieted. Michael tilted his head enough to see fingers emerge from the darkness of the underground. The nearest werewolves resumed human form and with great care pulled on that frail hand.

An old woman rose up from the shadows. She needed no name; Michael knew who she was, simply by the strength of her presence. Silver hair hung in loose waves around a weathered face, delicate and translucent. Bright blue eyes, keen. A stubborn mouth.

This will be Keeli. In time, this will be her. Because, despite the difference in age, it was like gazing at a mirror image. The reactions of the werewolves suddenly made more sense.

And this old woman is their leader, no less. Maddox is more unusual than I imagined.

He remembered his manners, then, and bowed his head. "Grand Dame Alpha," he murmured. "It is an honor."

"Is it now?" she said lightly. "Then you would be the first of your kind to say so." She glided forward, remarkably graceful for a woman her age.

"He smells like Keeli," Jas said. "And he's been wounded."

"I can see that," she said, looking at his arm. Michael had not wrapped his wound. The Grand Dame Alpha drew near. Her face was calm, but he sensed the urgency underlying her voice when she said, "Keeli. What trouble is she in?

Jas tightened his grip. This time, his claws drew blood.

Michael brought up his hands and in one smooth movement broke the werewolf's hold. An easy thing to do—perhaps, even, humiliatingly so. Jas snarled, the scar on his cheek prominent and pale against his flushed face.

"Jas." The Grand Dame was quiet, but even Michael heard the command. For a moment, he thought Jas would disobey, but the other wolves stared and he calmed. Sullen, angry, but obedient.

A fissure, Michael noted, as he turned to the Grand Dame Alpha with his hands loose and open. *She will need to watch this one.*

"Keeli saved a woman's life," he said.

"Saving a life is not usually grounds for arrest."

Michael hesitated. "She was not herself at the time."

The Grand Dame glanced down at his wounded arm. "Show me."

Michael held out his arm. The Grand Dame leaned close, unafraid. She sniffed his wound; her body went very still.

"Did she kill anyone?" asked the old woman quietly. "Is she hurt?"

"No," he said. He did not know what else to say. He remembered the horror on Keeli's face, and could not bring himself to betray her struggle and shame with cheap words.

The Grand Dame studied his face. Michael wondered what she saw, the story he had left untold. Her gaze was strong, sharp. He felt her take in the golden tattoo on his cheek.

"Thank you," she said. "You made an arrangement with the police?"

"They know me," he said.

"Turncoat," someone whispered.

The Grand Dame glanced sharply in the direction of that voice. A hush descended. Squaring her slim shoulders, she looked back at Michael. "We will remember your help."

"There is no debt," Michael said, turning away the precious gift of those words.

"There's always something," Jas said, and the Grand Dame Alpha did not quiet him.

"Not this time." Michael turned around and left the wolves. Glass crunched beneath his boots, a distinct cutting sound, razing the stillness of the alley. He felt the werewolves watch him, their gazes curling around his body like smoke.

He did not take to the air until he was a respectable distance away. No one liked a show-off. Especially Michael.

Chapter Four

Jail sucked. It would have sucked less if Keeli had been alone in her cell, but unfortunately, she was stuck with a persistent memory that might as well have been company, the way it consumed her thoughts.

Keeli smelled like vampire. Michael, his hand buried in her hair, his nose brushing her own—so close, so close— his scent had rubbed off on her. She hadn't even noticed until she'd finally slumped against a wall and buried her head in her arms. The scent tickled her nose—again, a reminder of dark eyes—and she knew. She *knew*.

The cell was a fifteen-by-fifteen square, with nailed-down benches against three walls and silver bars for a door. Cement, everywhere, with a public toilet and sink in the far corner. Keeli was going to have to get pretty desperate before she used that thing. It reeked of strangers and filth.

Just beyond the silver bars was the rest of the police station, lit up bright as day by fluorescent tubes. For a while, Keeli watched Jenkins at his desk, shoulders hunched over a computer keyboard. She watched officers drink coffee and talk on the phone; listened while a couple of strange werewolves were brought in for questioning, and then released. None of the wolves paid attention to her. She sat in the far corner of her cell and tried to be inconspicuous. It would be embarrassing for her grandmother and clan if word got out in the werewolf community about her arrest. Which was inevitable—she just didn't want to advertise it.

It was her first time in jail, and while she'd expected it to be frightening, after several hours her fear and curiosity waned. There was only so much energy a person could devote to analyzing uniforms and wall certificates and typing speeds. She tried very hard, though, because when she stopped for even an instant, she began thinking about Michael.

A vampire had saved her life. He had touched her and she had bitten him, and still, he had helped her. With calm strength and a low voice he had talked the rage out of the wolf, and sent the animal to sleep. Keeli did not know how or why he had done it. His bargain with Jenkins was even more baffling. What did he want from her? Or was it possible he didn't want anything?

Don't be stupid. This is big stuff. You owe this fang and you can bet he'll collect.

Keeli fingered the bandages around her wrists. Jenkins had dressed her burns on the ride back to the precinct. He was an interesting man; despite his career choice, she kind of liked him. He'd looked her straight in the eye and had a clear sharp gaze that wasn't anything but honest.

Michael had a similar way of looking at her. She wasn't so sure she liked him, though. Or at least, it seemed unnatural to have any good feelings toward a vampire.

Just wait, she told herself. *He'll show his true colors. If he wants something, you'll find out soon enough.*

She looked forward to it. Maybe then she'd be able to shake him off her mind.

"No, I won't leave," someone suddenly said outside her cell, in such an obnoxious voice Keeli peered beyond the circle of her arms to see who was talking. She immediately recognized the face and pressed up tight against the wall.

Brian O'Dell. Werewolf. Journalist—though that was a term she used loosely, considering his articles dished more gossip than news. He was someone who would surely recognize Keeli.

Shit. Is he here for me? How could he have found out so quickly?

"You know we can't give out that kind of information," an officer said to him, firm and cool. She had dark skin and fine high cheekbones, the kind of beauty that was both lovely and chiseled. Brian smiled, turning on the charm. Keeli rolled her eyes.

"Sweetheart. You know I'm a journalist. It's my job to cover all the hairy news, and my nose is telling me you've got something juicy my readers would love to hear."

The officer folded her arms and said nothing.

"See? That just confirms it. Someone got killed tonight, Sheila. I want to know who."

"Mr. O'Dell—"

"Call me Brian."

"—you have to leave. If you don't, I will be more than happy to shoot you."

"I'm planning a story on police brutality, you know. Maybe you'd like to give me an interview? Over dinner? Breakfast? The blunt end of your nightstick?"

Sheila finally smiled. "Out. Now."

Brian lifted his hands in silent surrender. His grin was anything but quiet. Keeli could almost see his tail wagging. She watched him leave, and was just about to relax when he passed Jenkins's desk and stopped cold in his tracks, gazing down. Jenkins noticed immediately and slapped closed the file he had been reading.

"What?" Jenkins said.

Brian shrugged. He glanced around the office and Keeli buried her head in her arms, willing him to pass over her. She imagined she felt him studying her; imagined, too, that he was drawing near to look through the bars, that any moment he would say her name and pressure her for an interview.

Instead, when she finally dared to look, he was gone.

"I really dislike that son of a bitch," she heard Jenkins say to Sheila. "He's too nosy for his own good."

"Free press," she replied, obviously in a much better mood regarding Brian. "He's just doing his job."

Jenkins grunted. "He get anything about the murder?"

Sheila shook her head, all business again. "No. He wanted to know why we were bringing in all those wolves for questioning. He's worried about a roundup."

"I would be, too. Doesn't matter there's no DNA linking the wolves to the crime. Cause of death was all animal. Absolutely vicious. One more murder like the one tonight, and it's not gonna matter that it's vampires dying—the public's gonna start screaming at the mayor. Once he gets involved, the wolves will be screwed six ways to Sunday. Not that they care. No one from the clans is helping worth shit."

Keeli closed her eyes. Great. Another vampire murder. Just what her people needed.

And Jenkins was right—no one would care that there was no DNA evidence to link the crimes to the wolves. Mangled bodies were enough for the public.

One problem: the only way a wolf could have killed

those vampires without leaving any trace would be to kill with the hands only, encased in gloves. Which sounded far more calculated than an enraged wolf looking to score a kill on some vampire's ass.

Unless they really did have a serial killer on their hands. A different kind of wolf.

Could be a human. A mech. But that was unlikely, after all the heat from last time. The mech program was in development, and under close scrutiny right now. And no human could kill a vampire with his bare hands. So, wolf.

Eye for an eye? Possibly. A dead werewolf had turned up only days previous with fang marks in his throat, obviously a vampire kill. Keeli didn't know the wolf personally, but he'd had a bad reputation. He'd been an unauthorized informant, spilling the beans on werewolf business to the C.C.P.D. and B-Ops alike. Keeli knew for a fact that the wolf had been close to exile—nothing less was suitable punishment for a wolf who betrayed his clan. A vampire wouldn't know that, though. A vampire who wanted to get back at the wolves for all the recent crimes.

Either way, a werewolf was dead, and so was a vampire. One more vampire to add to the list of those killed in the past month, all with superficial evidence suggesting a werewolf had committed the crimes.

The timing sucked. Or at least it was suspicious. Negotiations with the vampires had not been widely advertised between the clans, but all the wolves in the city knew what was going down in the Maddox tunnels. The Grand Dame had consulted with the lower Alphas before agreeing to speak with the vampire negotiators, and while the Alphas had tried their best not to leak the news, it was inevitable. The only difference was that the local werewolf journalists—Brian O'Dell included—were not permitted to write or speak about the subject. In fact, the Alphas had made it very clear that any wolf caught leaking information about even the possibility of a pact between vampires and werewolves would be severely punished. The kind of punishment that involved exile.

Because if the humans found out that vampires and werewolves were joining forces, shit was going to hit the fan in an ugly way. All the human hate and fear that had the vampires running scared would be turned on the werewolves, and unlike the fangs, Keeli's people didn't have the resources to get out of the city fast. The underground was more than just their home; it was livelihood and protection and safety all rolled into one. Take that away from the clans, force a mass exodus out of the city, and it would create war—or at the very least, the dissolution of current clan structures. Every major city had a werewolf population, and those wolves guarded their territories fiercely. A foreign clan in its entirety would never be adopted. Keeli had heard of uprooted wolf clans in Europe who spent twenty years wandering, losing members before finally finding cities large enough to squat in. Always in the ghettos, though. Always topside, and mixing with humans who were too poor to care that their neighbors sometimes wore fur. It was a bad way to live. Hungry, violent, and dirty.

What if these murders aren't coincidence? What if it's a deliberate attempt to sabotage our negotiations? To set us at each other's throats?

Keeli knew for a fact that there were some highly vocal dissenters, Alphas and subordinate wolves, who objected to helping the vampires. Keeli thought they were shortsighted idiots. But even one idiot could do a lot of damage if he had enough motivation. And a good old case of hate could be motivation enough in some circles.

Of course, the first of the murders had begun well before any discussion of an alliance between vampire and werewolf.

Doesn't matter who started it, or when—the result will be just the same. If this keeps up, not getting an alliance will be the least of our problems. Someone wants to start a street war between werewolves and vampires. And with certain humans on the sidelines, waiting for their moment to bring down the curtain . . . well, something had to be done.

Oh, yeah. And who's going to do it? Keeli asked herself. *Who's going to put their neck out on the line and help the cops investigate a murder against a vampire? You?*

Ha. Right.

Still, the thought gave her pause. Who amongst the werewolves would be a good liaison to the police? It was a sure bet that no one would volunteer for the job, which meant the Grand Dame would have to assign a wolf to the position—and Keeli was quite certain her grandmother would never do that. There was no love lost between the old woman and the humans. There was no love at all with the vampires, either, but the Grand Dame knew how to hold a grudge, and she had been treated badly by the police during that Chinatown fiasco. In principal, she might want to help solve the crime, but not in action. In action, the cops and their dead vamps could rot in hell.

Which was not very diplomatic at all. In fact, the only reason the Grand Dame had agreed to negotiations with the vampires was because she saw the threat, the human danger to the clans. And to keep safe the werewolf clans of Crimson City, the Grand Dame Alpha would do anything. Absolutely anything at all.

But that doesn't stop the fact that there's a murderer on the loose, and the police are itchy to pin it on a wolf. Someone needs to make nice with them. Someone who can be trusted, who can work with the police without acting like a total ass. Someone who can be a good little wolf.

Someone who was in the right place, at the right time.

"Shit," Keeli muttered, hating herself for even contemplating the possibility. If she allied herself with the police, even for something so important, she was going to make a lot of enemies. At the very least, the disapproval would be thick enough to dance on. Good deeds would kill her yet.

So don't do it. They don't need you, not really. Let the police take care of these crimes, like they're supposed to. You don't investigate your own. You don't turn over another wolf. Besides, it's not your responsibility.

Yeah, not her responsibility at all. But if the wolves didn't give the police some face-value attempt to cooperate, it might mean a whole load of trouble. The idea of another roundup chilled Keeli to the bone, a pure nausea-inducing possibility. And there was the negotiation to think of. What would be better politically than to say the Grand Dame's own granddaughter was helping solve the murders against the vampires?

Responsibility is unerring, damning. When it calls, you must answer, or else lose honor. Her grandmother's words—although until now, Keeli had never really understood their true meaning.

Yeah, well, I'm sick of caring what people think of me.

But knowing what she did, hearing those cops talk about how close the wolves were to real trouble, made it impossible not to get involved.

Okay, so do it. Now, before you give yourself time to change your mind.

Which might be at any moment, when her brain finally spun down from its current state of self-righteous commitment and thunked against the hard wall of reality.

She stood up, intent on getting Jenkins's attention, looked through the bars at the blond officer, who was sitting once again with his shoulders hunched, and then past him, at the faraway door—

The phantom taste of blood filled her mouth, a shimmering memory on her tongue. She felt it slide down her throat, into her tightening stomach, and she wondered what it meant to have vampire blood in her body, what sort of price she would have to pay, and that maybe this inability to look away from the man approaching her—so, so graceful—was the price, and oh, God, what the hell was she going to do. . . .

"Hello," Michael said, standing very close to the bars. His cheek glittered, and she realized it was a tattoo set in gold, a circle with winding lines that looked both beautiful and sinister. Much like the rest of him.

"Hi," Keeli replied, managing to shake off the spell of his eyes before she could make an idiot of herself. She forced her voice into a hard shell, readying herself for trouble. It was inevitable—she would be a fool to think otherwise. "I'm surprised to see you here," she said. "I thought you had enough class to wait at least a day."

Michael frowned. "Excuse me?"

"For payback," Keeli said. "You know, for your help. I had a feeling you'd come around eventually—although this is sooner than I thought."

Keeli didn't know him all that well, but she suspected that the sudden furrow between the vampire's eyes and the slight twist of his mouth were indications of displeasure. Either that, or he had eaten some bad blood on the way in. Maybe he had a stomachache. Did vampires get diarrhea?

"I came to see if you were all right," he explained coolly. "It's quite clear to me that you are."

"I'm just peachy," Keeli agreed, struggling to maintain her composure. "All this silver is a real turn-on."

"It could be worse."

"Well, yes," she said. There was something strange in

42

Michael's eyes—disappointment, maybe—that it pained her conscience to see. He *had* helped her, after all. Even though he was a vampire, he did not deserve cruelty. "It could be a lot worse. I appreciate what you did for me. I do. I don't know how . . . how I could have lived with myself if I'd hurt that man."

"Perhaps you wouldn't have hurt him."

Keeli shook her head, honesty surging up her throat. "You don't know my temper." She found herself reaching out to steady herself against the silver bars and snatched her hands away.

"Keeli," he said, and oh, it was strange hearing him say her name. She had not been certain he would remember it. He looked down at her hands and reached through the bars. Startled, she wanted to back away, but pride kept her feet rooted to the floor. She held herself very still and allowed him to touch her bandaged wrists. His nearness did not disgust her like she thought it would, but it did feel strange. Very strange.

"They don't hurt," she found herself saying. "How about your arm?"

"It's fine," he said, pulling back. Keeli glanced past him and found Jenkins watching with unabashed curiosity. It occurred to her that *everyone* in the room was watching, though some had the grace to pretend otherwise.

"So anyway," Keeli said, straightening up, ignoring the urge to cover her hot cheeks, "what you did for me is too big not to owe you something. I pay my debts, Michael."

He shook his head, and for just one moment, Keeli thought she glimpsed amusement in his eyes. "Debts," he said, very quietly, "don't mean much to me. There is no debt between us. You owe me nothing."

"Really. You must be some freak version of a vampire."

"A little politeness might be nice," he amended.

"Kiss my ass," Keeli said. "How would you feel if our situations were reversed?"

"Grateful."

"Wrong. You'd be wondering what the hell was going to happen next. Because let's face it: Our kind don't usually do nice things for each other."

"I don't want anything from you," he repeated.

"Uh-huh."

"Really, I *don't*."

She almost believed him. "Whether or not you want anything is beside the point. *I* feel obligated, Michael. *I* have to make things right between us."

Michael leaned close, menacing. Keeli fought not to react. He inspired a gamut of emotions: fear, anger, curiosity. She knew he couldn't hurt her—there were bars between them—but the force of his personality was almost physical, and a silver cage was no defense against that.

"There is nothing you can do, or give me, that will make me feel any different about this situation. I did not help you because I wanted something. I helped you because you needed help. So go ahead and feel obligated to pay me back. I can assure you that if you try, I will fight you every step of the way."

Up until that moment, Keeli had been dimly aware of something flickering on the edge of her vision. She now heard a faint whistle, and tore her gaze from Michael's face.

"What a way to talk to the ladies," Jenkins said, appearing beside the vampire. "No wonder you're still single."

Michael cast Jenkins such a dirty look that, if Keeli had been in the officer's shoes, she would have reached for a stake. Jenkins, however, seemed not to notice. He looked disgustingly cheerful, which made Keeli very suspicious. He had no right to be cheerful. Didn't he have a murder to investigate?

Oh. Crap. No.

"I think I know a way to clear this up," the policeman said, clapping his hand on Michael's shoulder. Keeli wondered what his balls were made of.

"If it involves whipped cream and more handcuffs, I am so out of here," she said, although she had a fairly good idea of what Jenkins was going to suggest.

Michael's mouth twitched; he briefly closed his eyes. "Jenkins, stay out of this."

"Sorry, I can't. She's offering help, Michael, and you know we need it."

"I don't know anything. I told you I would handle the investigation."

"And you think the werewolves will talk to you?" Jenkins cast a sly glance at Keeli. "I know she heard me talking to Sheila about that murdered vampire. Her ears almost grew an inch during the conversation."

Keeli scowled. "You did that on purpose."

"Yes, but it'll work out in all our favors that I did."

Michael looked like he wanted to hit someone—Jenkins, probably. "A deal is a deal."

"And she'll be getting out in the morning, just like I promised. But if she wants to help, what's the big fucking deal? Do you know who this girl is? I sure as hell do. Her fingerprints are famous. She's the granddaughter of the—"

"Stop," Keeli said, suddenly cold. "Don't bring her into this."

Jenkins's mouth snapped closed. "I'm sorry. But you have connections. Don't try to deny it."

"Connections only matter as much as a person's actions and reputation," she told him coldly. "If I help you, I'll be losing something in my clan. A little bit of respect."

"Then don't help," Michael said. "Don't turn yourself into an outsider, just for this."

Keeli glared at him. It didn't matter she had already run through these arguments, that she was ready to help all on her own. She did not like being pressured into anything. She did not like being told what to do—or what not to do.

"I'll help," she told Jenkins. She looked at Michael and said, "You know why, don't you?"

She glimpsed the surprise in his eyes, quickly swallowed by solemn comprehension. He understood. This was not just about debts. There was something bigger at stake.

Keeli felt the difference in Michael's eyes as he studied her. She did not know how to describe it, only that it felt like respect, some whisper of admiration. Either way, his sudden acceptance fascinated her.

"All right," he said quietly, while Jenkins looked on, confused.

"Did I miss something?" He glanced back and forth between the two of them. "Why are you both suddenly so agreeable?"

"It's because we love you, Jenkins," Keeli drawled. "Your needs are our needs."

Michael laughed. He had a nice laugh, short and deep. Keeli suspected he didn't laugh very much, because Jenkins stared like a wet monkey was slapping him on the ass.

"Are you sure?" Michael finally asked, his smile fading.

"Yes," Keeli lied. She wasn't sure of anything, except that someone had to do this.

"Good," Jenkins said quickly, as though he feared Michael would continue arguing. "You're officially partners."

Keeli pointed at the bars. "Does that mean I can get out of here?"

"Nope. You're stuck until dawn."

"That's lousy."

"That's punishment. You're lucky there isn't more."

"Nice to rub it in," she groused, but Jenkins had already turned to Michael and was pulling the vampire away from the holding cell. "Hey!" she called, but except for Michael giving her a quick glance over his shoulder, they ignored her. She watched them leave the room, and made herself comfortable against the wall.

Ten minutes later, Michael returned without Jenkins. Keeli did not stand up from the bench. She watched him, sullen. Michael crouched beside the bars.

"I apologize for that," he said.

"Huh. What did he want to tell you that I couldn't hear?"

Michael tilted his head; she thought he looked amused. "That you're an unknown and I shouldn't completely trust you, no matter how much you try to . . . beguile me."

"You're shitting me. He did not use the word 'beguile.'"

Michael spread his hands.

Keeli slid off the bench, intrigued. She sat cross-legged beside the bars across from him. "Are you always this blunt?"

"Are you?"

"Always. I don't see any reason not to be."

"I suppose that answers your question, then."

Keeli sighed, and glanced around the room to see if anyone was listening to them. There wasn't anyone close by. She whispered, "How bad was this murder?"

"Bad enough," Michael murmured. "The vampire was likely eaten, though the body is too much dust now for an autopsy. Jenkins is getting you a copy of the file."

"Shit," Keeli muttered. "And how much about . . . you-know-what . . . do you know about?"

"I don't think we should talk about it here." Michael leaned close; Keeli smelled his breath, light and clear. "Too many ears in all the wrong places."

Which meant he suspected the entire office, including

the holding cell, of being bugged. It wouldn't surprise her—the Man had a reputation for sneakiness. Get a confession any way possible. Nothing was illegal inside a police station.

Keeli heard a beeping sound. Michael frowned and pulled a small digi-encoder from his robes. He looked at the screen and quickly stood. Keeli scrambled to her feet.

"What is it?"

Michael slipped the encoder back into his robes. His eyes were cold, hard, and did not belong to the same man who had saved her from murder, who laughed at a stupid joke.

"Just some business I need to take care of. I'm sorry I can't stay longer to talk."

"Where should I meet you?" Keeli asked. She saw Jenkins approaching with some papers in his hands. She glanced back at Michael, and found him studying her. There was a strange look on his face.

"My place," he finally said. "Jenkins can give you the address."

"Why not you?" she asked, but Michael shook his head, already backing away.

"No time," he said. "I'll see you soon, Keeli."

He turned and was out the door before she could say a word. Vampire speed—he was nothing but a blur.

"What's up with him?" Jenkins shoved the paperwork through the bars into Keeli's hands.

"I don't know," she murmured. *But I sure do want to find out.*

Chapter Five

The stench of blood and feces overpowers, stretching his flesh full of horror as he fights not to gag and fails—his stomach turning inside out within his throat, red bile spilling through his fingers onto the red, red earth and it is ugly—the only light from fire, fueled by bodies burning while Malachai reaches close and pulls out a small charred limb, takes a bite—"tastes good," he says and laughs, and he has brought him here, led him, and blood soaks through his boots, through flesh into soul—and the children, the children are crying—he is crying— he cannot stop himself, the bleeding, the dying—and he runs— he runs—

Michael's eyes snapped open. He heard screams— shrill, tortured cries—and held himself still, trying to calm the frantic racing of his heart. Blood roared through his head; he forced himself to unclench his fingers from the bunched-up sheets.

"Dreams," he whispered, taking a deep breath. "Just dreams."

Dreams of the past, memories to be relived in the agony of the present. So much time had passed, and still the horror lived within him. It was no wonder he rarely slept.

Of course, he could also blame his restlessness on the execution he had carried out just before dawn. The message he received at the police station had contained three pieces of information—a name, a location, and a particular code known only to him.

Authorization had finally been given for the Vendix to carry out punishment against Simon Pierce, a slack-jawed asshole who had been caught draining humans to death on at least three separate occasions. And the only punishment for a vampire who repeatedly killed humans with sane, deliberate intent . . . ?

Death.

Michael closed his eyes, trying to shut out the memory of Simon's arrogance draining away into abject terror. The century-old vampire had tried to fight—he carried a gun, of all things—but when Michael had a job, nothing, not even bullets, got in his way.

The bullets were around somewhere, scattered on the floor after being removed from his body. He would have to clean them up before Keeli arrived . . . if she did. He might have presumed too much, telling her to come to his home to discuss the investigation. Of course, with Keeli he seemed to be doing a lot of things that did not make sense.

He thought of her, locked behind silver bars, stopped short by the poison that had already taken its toll on her wrists. He had not realized until that moment how sharply she had insinuated herself under his skin. Impossible. He'd known her for such a short time, and yet, to see her injured . . .

I did not mean to touch her. I did not.

But she did not pull away.

Sharp knocking, the rap of bone against wood, made

him sit up. He stared through the cracked gloom of his stained and shoddy studio, wishing he could see through doors. Was it Keeli? Had she already been released? He glanced at the window, and caught the faint rim of sunlight peeking through the bottom edge of the blind—a spot missed when he'd taped down the flimsy plastic.

The knocking continued. Michael pulled on his pants. He tucked a small shiv into one deep pocket. Three steps and he stood at the door. He leaned to one side of the battered frame and said, "Who's there?"

Quiet, and then, "Darling. Open the door."

He almost refused, but it had been a long time. Not long enough, perhaps, but there were some things within himself he could not fight. He opened the door.

Celestine stood before him, dressed in a formfitting pinstripe suit, a black wide-brimmed hat set rakishly over her brow. Sunglasses were tucked into her breast pocket. She carried a slim briefcase.

"I'm here to read you your rights," she purred.

"You're only a lawyer." Michael stood back to let her into the room. "The most you can do is take my rights away."

"Good enough." Celestine breezed past him and stopped. "Filthy," she said, staring at the studio. "You're lucky I like you enough to come to this ghetto. I swear, if any of those homeless freaks touch my Lamborghini, I'll rip out their throats."

Michael shut the door and leaned against it. "What do you want, Celestine?"

She glanced at him, and in her eyes he read the same old fear—fear masked by arrogance, conceit. Lust. How long had they known each other? And still, no change.

"I've brought your money." She tapped the briefcase with one long nail. "I'm sure you need it."

Michael gritted his teeth. "We had an appointment for the drop-off. Tonight, at the park."

"Change of plans. We have to go back to the dogs, Michael. Last night was completely useless. They won't even *consider* letting us use their tunnels. Not even in return for a sizeable sum of money." She sneered. "Dogs. That head bitch practically licked her crotch during negotiations."

Remembering his brief encounter with the Grand Dame Alpha, Michael highly doubted the accuracy of that last barb. Celestine was much more likely to commit inappropriate licking in public.

"Anything else on your mind?" Michael felt certain she must know about the latest vampire murder.

Celestine smiled; slow, seductive. "Anything and everything. You know my tastes."

Michael tried not to react. Curious. If Celestine did know about the murder, she wasn't saying anything. Michael wondered if the council were trying to keep the latest crime secret in order to aid negotiations with the werewolves. If and when the news broke, life would become even more difficult for both sides. Vampires like Celestine would surely use the opportunity to denounce the wolves and end the negotiations. Arrogance, self-reliance—taken too far.

Suicide. There weren't enough warriors left from the first war to stand up against the humans. Those who had survived that round of death were the same vampires struggling now—and unlike in the past, wits and money would not be enough. Michael knew that this time, if the humans truly set themselves to the task, they would not stop until all the vampires were gone. And after them, the werewolves would be next. Kill or be killed. Leave nothing to chance.

Leave no one alive. Because all it took was a bite . . .

Celestine tilted her head; the tip of her tongue darted

out. She swayed close. Michael stood very still, waiting, as she pressed her body against him. Soft.

"You're thinking you should kill me," Celestine said, and she was right. "Not a stretch, really. It's what you've been doing for some time now. Murdering our kind." She touched his cheek, and Michael jerked his head away.

"I control our kind," he said, the old argument coming quick to his lips. "Those I kill cannot be allowed to continue. It's because of them the humans are threatening us. Feeding indiscriminately, like animals. Humans don't deserve to be treated as cattle."

Celestine smiled. "You act so pure, Michael. But you've taken your pounds of flesh, taken them in your teeth and sucked dry the lifeblood of human after human, razing them down to husks." She nipped his chin and Michael smelled blood on her breath, fresh and sweet. She whispered, "You remember what it's like, don't you? The hunt. The *kill*."

Michael lifted his chin, breaking off another attempted kiss. Celestine laughed, low. "You should see your face! What tragedy." And then her smile faded and she leaned even closer.

"Why don't you touch me?" she breathed against his throat.

He almost did—a habit borne of loneliness—but as his gaze fell upon Celestine's pink lips, he was reminded of hair just that color, hot and wild, a riot of color surrounding a delicate stubborn face. The scent of anger, sweat. Warm skin. The memory of a memory, running wild on the steppe—

"Michael." Celestine leaned harder into his body, her breasts full against his chest. She dropped the briefcase and it hit the ground hard. Her hands drifted down his stomach, fluttered across his groin. Michael grabbed her wrists.

"You should go," he said, trying to hide the strain in his voice. "Thank you for bringing my money."

Celestine stared, her perfect oval face caught for one moment in rare surprise. And then her pink lips tightened, hard and flat.

"You refuse me?" she asked in low, clipped tones. Michael said nothing. She had a right to be shocked. He had never refused Celestine, not once during the long years they had passed in and out of each other's lives. Secret, always secret—but a respite nonetheless. Someone to be with, if only for a short time. Quick, shallow pleasure.

Celestine cared nothing for him. She had always made that clear. She came to him only because it was forbidden, dangerous. Because, long ago, they had shared a common enemy.

That no longer felt like enough.

She bared her teeth, grinding against him—violent, thrusting motions. Michael braced himself against the door. He closed his eyes, willing his body not to respond. It was easier than he'd thought.

Celestine whispered, "You're not even hard."

"I don't want you anymore," he said, and was startled at how easily the words left his lips, how good it felt to say them.

She froze, and for one moment Michael felt sorry for her. Just one moment.

Celestine raked her nails across his face—faster than he could move to block her, a cutting swipe, sharp, burrowing deep into flesh. Michael did not flinch. He savored the warm sting, tasting blood as it trickled from his upper cheek and lip into his mouth. He instantly wanted more. It was a reminder of what she was like—of what they were all like.

Michael grabbed Celestine's wrists and pushed her

away. She stumbled, but he moved with her, watching as enraged triumph quickly dulled to horror.

"Michael," she whispered.

"You forget yourself," he said, tasting her terror and savoring it as a rare moment of honest emotion. "You forget what I do."

Celestine hissed at him, but beneath her anger he felt her tremble, coil away from his body to keep him from pressing against her. *Why don't you touch me?* He remembered her words, and felt a smile rise up his throat, bitter.

"You wouldn't dare!" she cried, as he turned them both and pushed her to the door.

His smile finally emerged, humorless and cold. "I dare many things, Celestine."

Defiance rose up in her eyes, then, hardening her full lips. She twisted—once, twice—and Michael set her free. Her hat fell off and she stepped on it, one sharp heel denting the fine thick cloth. Snatching it up, she looked at him over her shoulder and bared her teeth.

"The others humor you because they think you're necessary, but you are nothing, Michael. *Nothing.* Just wasted blood in a wasted body. I hope the humans kill you."

Celestine wrenched open the door and froze.

Pink hair, a small pale face. Blue eyes bright as sky. Lips quirked in a smile or a frown. Michael felt himself go very still; a strange ache thumped against his ribs.

"I came at a bad time, didn't I?" Keeli said.

Reminder to self: bald is not a good look on a woman, even if she is a vampire.

Keeli braced herself, the wolf raising hackles beneath her skin. The woman in front of her looked ready to kill, and if the blood running down Michael's face was any indication, she'd already made one good attempt.

The woman snarled; sharp teeth glinted in the poor yellow light of the hall. Keeli's own response rose in her throat. She stamped down the growl, struggling against the wolf. She wasn't here to fight. Of course, she wasn't here to eavesdrop, either, but she had done a pretty good job of that.

Son of a bitch has no friends.

Nostrils flared; the woman's eyes shifted, a melody of uncertainty, rage—and finally, ugly comprehension. Her lips curled into a sneer. "Michael," she said, her gaze never leaving Keeli's face. "I understand now. You've decided to sleep with the dogs."

Oh. Bring on the hurt. Before Keeli could say anything, though, Michael reached past the other vampire and grabbed her hand. His was cool, electric. She was so shocked, she did not protest as he dragged her into his darkened apartment, practically throwing her behind him.

"Hey!" she gasped, but Michael ignored her, leaning close to the other vampire.

"Better a wolf than you, Celestine," he said quietly. The woman's jaw dropped. Michael shut the door in her face.

Better a wolf than you?

"You're nuts," she said, astonished. She stared at the back of Michael's head, taking in the glitter of his braids, the straight line of his back. "What the hell was that?"

He turned to meet her gaze. Dark eyes, like she remembered. Deep-set, quiet eyes. It took an effort not to flinch. Every time she saw those eyes it was difficult to speak, to think.

Vampire voodoo, she thought. But no, vampires couldn't do that sort of thing. Smoke and mirrors, lies for humans to tell each other, to make fear.

"Michael," she said, because he still had not answered her question, and she could not bear to look at him for much longer. She was afraid of herself, of her reaction to the sudden hunger in his eyes, the loose grace of his body, his sheer presence—

Celestine screamed something obscene from the other side of the door. The hinges rattled. Michael did not act as though he noticed. Blood covered half his face—scarlet, gruesome. The door shook.

"Werewolves don't heal as quickly as vampires," he said quietly, and there was something in his voice that made her heart ache. She did not like that feeling—it was too personal, something to be identified as prologue to a more intimate emotion. Wrong, wrong, wrong.

"I can take care of myself," Keeli told him. "Besides, I think it's you she's pissed at. What did you do?"

Michael glanced at the door. "I told her the truth."

"Some truth. What was it? That you're married? Gay? Got genital warts?"

Michael's gaze snapped back to her; his lips twitched. "Worse than that."

Keeli laughed out loud. "Your ass is so fried."

"Maybe." This time he did smile. "But the door isn't that strong. She's not trying very hard."

"No real conviction, huh? That's the problem with vampire chicks. All talk, no action." Keeli stopped, tapping her chin. "Or it could just be the warts. Are you that contagious?"

"I am *not* diseased."

Keeli shrugged. "Whatever you say, man. I'm sure you're all clean 'down there.'"

"Maybe you'd like to check for yourself."

Keeli's face flushed warm. So much for teasing. She stepped away, putting some distance between herself and the vampire. He was beginning to smell familiar, and that bothered her. She glanced around his apartment, thankful she could see well in poor light. It was a studio, really, with battered wood floors and cracked walls. One window with the blind taped down. An unmade bed was in the corner, and on a table shoved near the bed, an assortment of weapons. She thought she smelled roses, but this placed looked like poison to flowers. The rest of the neighborhood wasn't much better.

What is a vampire doing in a dump like this? It certainly wasn't anything she could have imagined. In fact, she'd thought Jenkins was high on crack when he'd given her the address.

The door shuddered; Keeli jumped. She had forgotten about Celestine. Crazy vampire chicks paled in comparison to being up close and personal with Michael's magnetic presence. She listened hard, and a moment later heard the fading whisper of cloth. Hoped the winos sleeping in the stairwell didn't get kicked or bitten.

"Keeli," Michael said, and she squared her shoulders against the sudden tightness in her belly, the slow stir of his voice sinking into her skin. "I'm sorry about this. That you've become . . . involved in this case. I should have argued more."

Keeli looked at him, surprised. "You couldn't have stopped me. This is what I want. Besides, no matter what you say, I do owe you."

Michael shook his head; Keeli held up her hand. "Tell me one thing," she said quickly, wanting to lay things out before she got too deep. "Tell me why you did it. I want to know why a vampire would stop a werewolf from killing a man. Why you helped me with the police."

Anger stirred in Michael's face. For a moment, Keeli thought it was directed at her. A terrible thing—the enraged woman of earlier had nothing on this man in darkness, in sheer suppressed rage—and Keeli felt herself stand on the edge of it. A muscle twitched in Michael's face, and then it was gone, calm restored. A neutral, empty mask. In a low voice, he said, "You were not yourself. I could see that. No one should be punished for the things they do in madness."

Keeli fought for her voice. "I was myself, Michael. I knew what I was doing. And I'll have to live with that for the rest of my life, that almost-murder, the taste for the kill. I wanted to kill him."

"Yes, you did," he said, surprising her. "And it made you sick afterwards. Horrified you. Don't pretend it didn't."

"How could I?" Keeli whispered, reliving that moment. "How could I live with myself if I forgot?"

"Some do forget," Michael said, and she sensed a terrible strain on his body. His cheek drew her eye—that golden glitter, duller in shadow. The tattoo looked sinister. "But you're not the kind with a bad memory. I saw that in you. It's why I helped. Your heart isn't that cold."

"You see a lot for a vampire." It was difficult to speak. Keeli had to force the words out—anything to fill the silence made heavy with his presence, the energy between them. Gibberish would be enough, though Keeli was happy she wasn't quite yet to that stage. She was an idiot, yes—standing in a darkened apartment, alone with a vampire, fit the definition quite nicely—but at least she didn't have to sound like one. She had some pride left, and maybe even enough crazy courage to follow this thing through.

"I see enough," Michael said, quiet.

She almost touched him. Appalling, crazy. Keeli balled her hands into fists. She did not understand this vampire—why he lived in a shit-hole or fought with other vampires—how he could say these things to her and act like he meant it, when really, really, he was probably just trying to use her, to make her nice and pliant. She didn't understand him—none of this—and what she didn't understand in people always made her nervous, and what she didn't understand in herself . . .

Why the hell am I here?

Because of promises and honor. Because Jenkins clearly expected her to wig out on him and Michael. Because of what the officer had told her about the crime in question.

The body was found on Fourth and Lexington, near the old bakery. Familiar territory, huh?

Yeah. Maddox territory. Double-oh-crap. Something had to be done, and fast. If Keeli had been given a chance to speak to her grandmother, the old woman might very well have agreed, regardless of the stigma attached to any liaison helping with the investigation.

But partnered with a vampire?

Keeli had no idea what Granny May would say, only that Jas had been waiting at the police station at six A.M. with money for the five-thousand-dollar fine (how Keeli was going to pay that back to the clan, she had no idea), and she had refused to go with him. That had been an hour ago: no doubt her grandmother had heard it all by now.

"I've got business to take care of," she'd said, and Jas— swearing at her—had been unable to keep up. That's what living in the underground all the time did to a wolf; made him slow. Keeli knew topside, had an unerring sense of direction in Man's world. Unnatural, maybe—it had taken long years of walking the street, seeking out every scent and nook and cranny—but it was worth it. Most wolves did not care enough—or were too scared— to go deep into the sun and moon and breeze. Not Keeli. This was her city, just as much as it was any human's or vampire's, and she meant to stake her claim, even if it were just with the soles of her boots. Until the government started locking up every werewolf behind silver bars, that was a right she was going to exercise.

In the meantime, I'll just keep digging myself deeper and deeper.

Michael continued to stare. Keeli frowned. "What?"

"Aren't you going to say something?"

"You're too deep for me. Brain cannot compute."

Michael's lips twitched; Keeli suspected that was his version of a smile. "Would you like to sit down?"

"This isn't a social call."

"We need to talk about the case."

"We can talk on the road. I promised Jenkins we'd get started on this thing, and the sooner we do, the sooner we can finish and go our separate ways."

Michael touched his face; his hand came away wet, bloody. "I need to do something about this. It will take a little time."

"Oh," she said, her defiance deflating just a little. "Yeah."

You weren't raised to be this bitchy. You wouldn't act like this if he were a human or a wolf. But hello? Vampire?

Still, guilt. Keeli scowled. "Do you have any rags? Paper towels? Antiseptic?"

Michael frowned and she fluttered her hands at his face and chest. "You need someone to look at you. I'll . . . help."

"You'll help." He drew the words out slowly, as if he didn't quite believe her. Keeli's cheeks flushed.

"Yes," she snapped, glancing around the small apartment. There was a narrow door off to her right; just beyond, a bathroom. She really had no interest in knowing whether vampires kept their toilets clean, but since she was already in, she might as well go all the way.

Keeli stalked to the bathroom and switched on the light. Standard, nothing special. Toilet, sink, shower stall.

She sniffed the air and was pleasantly surprised by the scent of disinfectant covering the faint remnant of blood-tainted urine. She turned to call Michael over and swallowed a gasp. He was right behind her.

Too close, too much skin.

You've seen men more naked than Michael. Wolves usually strip down when they shift.

Then why did this feel different? Hell, what was wrong with her?

"I can do this alone." Michael reached past her to grab a towel hanging from a hook in the wall. His powerful muscles flexed beneath pale skin.

"You look like shit."

Michael paused in his movements, effectively penning her in. Keeli forced herself to look at his face, and *only* his face. Which, in this light, was appalling. Just what had that woman done to him? And what was up with his tattoo?

"I've looked worse," he said.

"Hard to believe. You vampires aren't much for scrapping."

His eyes hardened—dangerous, cool—and Keeli clenched her jaw, steadying herself. She smelled blood, his blood, and it was not unpleasant.

"You don't know much about vampires," he said, leaning close.

"I know enough," she shot back, trying to steady her voice.

"Enough to help me solve a crime involving one? Enough to remain unbiased during the investigation? Jenkins told you, didn't he? The body was found on Maddox territory. The murderer could be a member of your own clan."

" 'Maybe' isn't the same as '*is*'," she shot back, briefly wondering who had told him she was a Maddox wolf.

"And besides, if you're worried I'll try to protect my kind or stab you in the back, don't be. I don't play that kind of dirty, even against people I don't like. If a werewolf— even a Maddox werewolf—murdered a vampire, then a werewolf will pay."

"Justice," he murmured. "You'll swear to it?"

"I already have," she said. "When I promised you and Jenkins my help."

"I want to hear it."

Keeli wanted to add more wounds to his face. "Justice," she ground out. "I swear it."

Michael nodded, though he did not move away. His gaze flickered down to her lips, back to her eyes. "You are not going to have an easy time of this. The other wolves—"

"Are my problem," she interrupted. "And considering everything else that's going on, I hope they'll understand why we have to work together." Sheer bravado. Keeli wasn't sure of anything, and it scared it. Terrified her.

Michael's mouth twisted, wry. "You give your kind more credit than I would mine."

Keeli snorted. "A word of advice. If you don't want me to insult vampires, don't give me openings like that."

This time she saw a true glimmer of a smile. Michael lowered his arm and stepped back. "If you don't want to join me in the shower, I suggest you move."

Heat filled her cheeks; she hadn't blushed this hard in years. How immature. Keeli pushed past him, hands pressed to her thighs to keep from accidentally brushing his naked torso. The back of her hand touched his hip instead; the contact was brief, but eloquent. Her skin tasted soft cotton, and beneath, so close, hard planes of muscle, bone.

Her breath caught; the door closed quickly behind her.

Standing in the middle of Michael's dark studio, Keeli

closed her eyes and focused on her breathing. Slow, calming, breaths, meant to quiet a racing heart, a flushed body.

She felt wet between her thighs.

Michael was wet all over. Shivering.

The cold shower was not working. He wondered if it was another human myth, invented by men who liked to pretend there was a cure for lust. It seemed like a myth to him. A lie. He was still hard and the cold water pounding against his body was doing nothing to drive away the throbbing ache that had begun the moment Keeli brushed against his body.

You're not even hard. Celestine's whisper haunted him. If only that were still the case.

She is a wolf, he told himself, bracing his arms against the wall. *You shouldn't be feeling this.*

Or maybe his powerful desire had nothing to do with Keeli. Maybe it was just his proximity to an attractive woman—a delayed reaction, perhaps, to his resistance against Celestine's actions. His body, finally waking up.

And refusing to go to sleep. Michael clenched his jaw. This was impossible. He couldn't stay in here forever. He thought of Keeli, waiting for him outside the bathroom, and stifled a groan as the ache in his groin intensified. He was wrong—this desire had *everything* to do with Keeli.

He turned the shower knobs; cold water changed to hot. Michael did not relax.

You can't go out there like this.

Michael touched himself. He tried not to think of Keeli. He failed.

Chapter Six

By the time Michael emerged from the steaming bathroom—clothed and slightly damp—Keeli had regained some semblance of control. She did not know what was wrong with her but it had her afraid and disgusted.

"Are you ready?" Her voice sounded unfriendly, rough.

Michael picked up a pair of mirrored sunglasses from the kitchen counter. They matched his overall look—loose black slacks, black button-up shirt. Cool, sophisticated. Keeli wondered if his archaic robes of the night before were hanging in the closet.

He put on the sunglasses and tugged a hat over his damp black hair.

"I've got sunblock on," he said, in a voice that was curiously tense. "Test me. Raise the blind."

Keeli went to the window and carefully peeled off the tape. She stuck the strips, tail-like, on the windowsill. One small tug and the blind rolled up. For a moment, as the window lay revealed, sunlight streaming warm against her face, she forgot the vampire—forgot her problems and all the shit heading toward the fan. All she could think of was color.

Just beyond the cracked glass grew a cascading riot of scarlet and tropical sunrise, canary, and mango. Thick brambling roses tumbled over a rusty fire escape, pushing through the narrow bars with thorn and stem and leaf, rubbing up against the window with petals soft as a purr.

"How?" she murmured. She raised the window. Inhaled, shuddering, as scent overwhelmed her. This was the reason she had smelled roses, but she had never imagined . . .

Remembering Michael, she whirled and nearly knocked noses with him. She felt his breath against her face, the cool pass of his skin on her own. She swallowed hard; her head felt strange. Dizzy, almost.

"My roses," Michael said, a strange expression on his face as he leaned away from Keeli. "I grow them."

"They're beautiful," she said, tearing her gaze from his covered eyes. She glimpsed her reflection in the lenses; her face looked warped, confused. She glanced at his lips and turned her head, feeling burned. What the hell was wrong with her?

Michael stepped close; Keeli stood with her back to him, gripping the windowsill so tight her knuckles turned white. He did not touch her—she did not want him to— but he was near, so near, and her body felt too warm.

"As you can tell, I have few luxuries. In my youth, before I became a vampire, I lived in a dry place. Nothing but grass and sheep and horses. I never imagined color such as this. How something could smell so soft and look so lovely, and yet be covered in thorns. I found it . . . highly appropriate."

"Beauty always hurts," Keeli said, daring to glance at him over her shoulder. "Hurts the person looking, hurts

66

the person with. The first can never have enough; the second, it's all others see."

She felt him staring at the back of her head. Her nails cracked through paint in the window ledge, dug into wood. "Are we going or not?"

Silence. Keeli took a deep breath and forced herself to turn. Michael felt too tall, too close—she craned her neck to look him square in the face, wishing she could see beyond his mirrored shades.

Vampire, she reminded herself. *Don't you forget what he is.*

Keeli pressed her palms against his chest and pushed him away from her. He stumbled backward, his hands coming up—to touch her, maybe. Frightening. She had to get away. Right now.

She did not know what she would do if he touched her. She did not want to know how it would feel.

Michael lowered his hands. Keeli squeezed past him, desperate to create space, some illusion of control.

"Are you ready?" She stood on the other side of the room, near the door. The wolf trembled beneath her ribs, but she did not rub her arms like she wanted, to check for the telltale pin-marks of dark hair through skin.

Michael glanced at the open window, sun streaming warm upon his body. He looked at Keeli and raised an eyebrow.

"All right, then." Keeli opened the door. "Let's go."

She watched him go to the table for his weapons. From her brief study of them, she knew there weren't any guns or stun rods. Just lots of sharp things. An assortment of swords, long daggers, and wicked-looking stakes. What a vampire was doing with stakes raised a lot of interesting questions. Maybe too many.

"It's illegal to carry concealed weapons," she reminded him.

Michael raised an eyebrow. "I think the simple fact of being a vampire—and werewolf—already makes us something of a concealed weapon."

Keeli flushed. "You know what I mean."

"And if something goes wrong during the investigation?"

You mean, if someone tries ripping off your head for asking a dumb question? "That's what I'm here for. I'll protect you." She smirked.

Michael did not laugh. Something hard moved through his eyes. "Maybe it will be the other way around. Did you think of that when you agreed to this?"

Yes, but she wasn't about to tell him that. She also didn't like having it thrown in her face. "Just what are you?" she demanded. "What kind of vampire works with the police, spends his mornings getting bitch-slapped and has a collection of pointy things that are death to fangs? You are too screwed up to live."

Michael glided close, and there was nothing pleasant about his gaze, the cruel warp of his mouth. His angular face lost its beauty, suddenly seemed more skull than flesh, more death than pale life.

"I am the Vendix," he said, so quiet, so dangerous. He touched his tattooed cheek. "It is Latin for 'Punisher,' and that is what I do, Keeli. I punish my own kind. I execute vampires who step outside our laws and murder humans."

"Oh," she said.

His jaw tightened. "A long time ago, it was decided that the only way to control the vampire community was the threat of death. Otherwise, it would be too easy to murder humans. To treat them as nothing more than cattle. The Primary Assembly used to carry out the law themselves, but decided that was . . . inappropriate. They passed the task on to me and a few others, all of us scattered around the world."

"How long have you been doing this?" Keeli could not imagine a life where she had to hunt and kill her own people, although this murder investigation was bringing her perilously close.

"Long enough," Michael said. His expression dared her to push him. Keeli did not feel lucky. She stepped farther into the hall. She did not know what to say to a vampire who executed his own kind. What the hell was an appropriate reaction?

He still wasn't moving. Keeli scowled, forgetting shock as her temper flared.

"Can you be any slower about moving your ass? Come on, Michael. Daylight's burning."

"Very funny," he said, rolling tension out of his shoulders. He left his weapons behind, but slipped a tiny bottle of sunscreen into his pockets.

Keeli barely waited for him as he locked the door; the moment the key turned she slipped away, stepping lightly over shattered tile, noting bullet holes riddling the corridor walls; the smells of vomit, piss. She wanted to ask Michael why he lived here when all the other vampires made their homes in downtown penthouses—the height of cool, worthy of their own documentaries on the entertainment networks—but she kept her mouth shut. Keeli had a feeling the answer, if he chose to give her one, would be too personal, and she didn't want any more of that. It was enough that he had helped her from a tough spot, enough that she was compelled to do the same. Enough, enough. She did not want to get too personal with a vampire. Especially this one.

"The vampire who was killed last night . . . what was he like?" A safe topic: completely nonpersonal and free of innuendo. She glanced over her shoulder at Michael as they walked down a set of rickety stairs.

"Did you read the file? As of last night, the police still

hadn't made an ID. Too much damage to the body. They're scanning the ashes for identifying markers."

"I know. I just thought you might have heard if someone went missing."

He did not respond, and Keeli sensed the disapproval, the heat, in his silence.

"Sorry," she said.

"It's a common misconception. I suppose I should not be surprised that you would think I'd know every vampire in this city, or that I would have my teeth on the pulse of all our comings and goings. Unfortunately, I'm just not that popular."

"Never would have guessed." Keeli refused to feel guilty. She stepped over a nest of discarded needles. "So where does that leave us?"

Another moment of eloquent silence. Keeli stopped descending the stairs. She turned around, craning her neck. Michael was one step above her, which was too tall for her tastes.

"Say it," she ordered.

"I shouldn't have to," he said. "The body was found on Maddox territory. We need to investigate your clan. Or at least, start there."

A growl rose up her throat. "Just because a vampire was found dead on our land, doesn't mean a Maddox wolf is responsible. Someone could be trying to frame us."

"Or not. But considering what else is going on at the moment, that seems like a possibility. We simply need to investigate every lead. Someone in your clan might even have witnessed the crime."

The fact that he agreed deflated her anger somewhat. She folded her arms against her chest. "It's not going to be easy. No one's going to be happy with a vampire asking questions, even if I'm there with you. And the fact that you're investigating for the Man? Worse."

"It has to be done," he said quietly. "There cannot be a true alliance between our two peoples unless we discover who is responsible for the murder. Otherwise, how can we trust each other?"

"At least we can agree on something. Any word on how the negotiations went last night?"

"Not well."

Keeli frowned. "I'm worried about what will happen when the vampires find out there's been another murder."

Michael shook his head. "I wish I could tell you how my people will react. I just hope there isn't retaliation."

"This murder might already be retaliatory. A wolf was found in the subway several days ago. Drained."

There was no faking Michael's disgust. "I had to hear that news from Jenkins. If anyone in the Council is aware of it, they're keeping quiet. Did the Grand Dame Alpha contact the vampires or police about the murder?"

"I don't think so. The victim wasn't especially loved. The Grand Dame would be reluctant to disrupt negotiations just for him."

Michael's lips pressed into a hard line. "This is unacceptable."

"No argument from me. The last thing we need is to be killing each other. Let that be a human thing. I don't want to make it any easier for them."

Keeli began walking down the stairs again. Michael easily matched her pace. She felt the long lines of his body shadow her, cool and solid. She wondered how it would feel to walk in broad daylight with him, if people would look at them funny.

And why would they? You can pass for human. So can Michael, as long as he doesn't open his mouth or do any strange voodoo. And besides, what vampire would be caught in this part of town?

True. Only Keeli and Michael would know the difference, the oddity of their situation. A sliver of excitement slid up her spine, but it was quickly dampened. Why did it matter, what people thought of a vampire and werewolf, walking together in public?

Because the wolves will know what he is, and it will matter to them. I'm just trying to prepare myself, that's all.

But why? All they were doing was investigating a crime together. It wasn't like they were having sex.

Not yet, whispered an insidious little voice. *But you want him. You want him.*

Keeli stopped on the landing, still two floors up from street level. There was a lump of a man sleeping hard against the wall near her feet: another inhabitant of this inescapable building of the damned.

"I have a question," Keeli said, turning to face Michael. "About your side of things. You know, the vampires. What will they say about you working with a werewolf on this investigation? Will *you* get in trouble?"

Michael's mouth tightened. "I don't think you understand, Keeli. I have very little contact with other vampires."

Keeli looked pointedly at the wounds on his face. "Contact enough, I think."

Michael took a step closer; she did not retreat, but it was a struggle. She felt a shift in his body, new tension, a coiled power radiating from his chest. The stillness of his arms, the movement of his throat. He opened his mouth to speak, and Keeli was ready—ready for anything— when a door slammed open somewhere below them. A shout, and then gunshots rang out. Keeli slapped hands over her ears.

"Motherfucker!" someone screamed, and there were more cries—of pain, of rage, impotent and cruel.

Michael grabbed Keeli around the waist and flung her against the wall, cushioning her in his arms, shielding her body with his tall lean strength. The floor behind him ripped open; bullets thudded into the landing above their heads. The homeless man sleeping at their feet snorted, rolled over.

"What the hell is going on?" Keeli screeched, trying to be heard over the sounds of battle playing out beneath them.

"There's been trouble between local gangs," Michael shouted back, his mouth pressed to her ear. "This is the second fight this week."

"And they think *we're* animals!"

Michael smiled—a quick flash of teeth—and warmth gathered tight in Keeli's belly. Nose to nose, suddenly the gunshots did not feel so loud, so close, the danger not so near.

Pervert, she called herself, and forced her eyes closed. She pressed her forehead against Michael's hard chest, and a moment later his hand buried itself in her hair, holding her close. He felt good, and with her eyes closed Keeli could pretend he was not a vampire and she was not a werewolf, and that this was fine, all right, *just walk on, yessiree, nothing to see, nothing to see . . .*

"We have to move," Michael said, and he was right; Keeli heard boots pounding hard on the stairs, pausing once, twice, while the air filled with quick sharp bursts. She nudged the man beside them with her foot.

"Hey!" she shouted, but he kept on sleeping, snuggling deeper against the wall. Michael said nothing. He simply bent down and picked the man up, scattering newspapers and the scent of piss. Michael slung the man over his shoulder and gestured toward an apartment door just past the landing.

"It's empty," he said, and Keeli took the invitation and kicked hard against the old wood, wolf strength flooding her muscles. Her Doc Martens broke the rusty lock on her second try, and they tumbled through as bullets strafed the hall. More shouting, most of it in mixed patois, and Michael slammed shut the door, leaning hard against it. The homeless man, finally coming out of his funk, began struggling. Michael let him slither off his shoulder, and Keeli helped him stand. She tried to ignore his smell.

"Dude," he said, gazing blearily at the two of them.

"Right back at'cha," Keeli said, giving him a gentle shove. "Now get into that bathroom and keep your head down."

"You too," Michael said, grim.

Keeli shook her head, watching the lump of beard and stained brown clothing that was the homeless guy shuffle into the bathroom. "Bullets can't kill me."

Michael looked away, as though trying to see through the door. "I always forget that part."

Keeli grinned, about to agree, but a thunderous explosion rocked the floor beneath them. She staggered, catching her balance as Michael reached out a hand to steady her. Her ears felt strange; everything sounded dull, muted.

"What the hell? They got grenades or something?"

"Something." Michael pushed away from the door, grabbing Keeli's hand and tugging her toward the bathroom. "Violence in human neighborhoods is escalating, but no one is talking about it."

"These areas are always violent."

"Not like this," he said, giving her a sharp look. "But humans take their own violence for granted, so they don't see the change. Vampires and werewolves are something else. Outside the human perception of normal. We draw attention."

Keeli heard sirens. "Police are coming."

Michael glanced into the bathroom. The homeless man was asleep in the tub. "We can't stay here. Too many questions if they find us. We don't have time to prove we're on their side."

"We didn't do anything wrong," Keeli reminded him, though she was already headed toward the window. She shoved it open and leaned out, slow and cautious.

"Firefight is dying," Michael murmured behind her.

"Good." Keeli crawled out the window to the fire escape. "Won't have to worry about our friend in the bathroom, then." She glanced up, glimpsed heavy green vines, rich with color. "Or your roses."

She stifled a gasp when Michael wrapped his arms around her waist. "Look down," he said, before she could protest. "We've run out of fire escape."

It was true, Keeli realized. The ladder below had been sawed off, leaving twenty feet of air.

It was a jump she could make, but Michael lifted her in his arms with easy grace, floating, flying, suspended light as a breeze, and Keeli could not bring herself to tell him "no." *I'm in trouble,* she thought, breathless with wonder as he brought them swiftly to the alley below. *The other stuff was child's play. I am going to hell for this one.*

Because she was beginning to like him. A vampire. Keeli shuddered.

"Are you all right?" Michael asked.

"I'll be better when we get out of here." The police were almost on top of them; the sirens hurt her ears. She'd had enough of the cops to last a lifetime. "Come on. I have a way out."

Michael frowned, but hurried to keep up with Keeli's quick strides. Instead of leading him out of the alley—and oh, God, this place smelled worse than an open sewer drain—in fact, it *was* an open sewer—she stopped after several feet, in front of a small steel door set in a wall. Unassuming, dirty, old: a round swinging door, like she had seen in pictures of submarines, dull and mean. Keeli knelt, scrabbling at the rusty grate set just below the door. She lifted it off, revealing a small keypad.

"Interesting," Michael said, as Keeli punched in a set of complicated numbers.

"Bolt-holes are all over the city, especially where there aren't other access points to the underground like dry unused sewer tunnels and drain-off grates. I think we've got three like this in your neighborhood alone."

She pushed the door open and gestured for Michael to precede her. "Hurry. I still need to replace the grate."

Car doors slammed, accompanied by shouts and gunshots. There would be police around this way any second. Michael knelt and crawled through the opening; Keeli covered up the keypad. Close . . . close . . . she finished, and threw herself after Michael into the yawning darkness, spinning on her knees as soon as she was through to shut the door behind her. Darkness swallowed them.

She stood, shoulders brushing stone walls. Penned in, caged. Her eyes adjusted enough to see Michael standing sideways in order to accommodate his wider body. Looking at him made her feel even more ill at ease.

"The bolt-holes were never meant to be comfortable," she said, sneezing as a cloud of dust entered her mouth and nose. She wiped at her watery eyes.

"Do I follow the tunnel?" Michael asked, his voice echoing softly.

"Yes, but I better lead. The door we came in through is linked to the updated security system, but before the tech was installed, we used good old-fashioned misdirection to keep the underground core safe in case someone broke through a bolt door. That hasn't changed."

Keeli squeezed past Michael, sliding tight across his body. So close to him, pressed warm and hard in the dark—truly and securely alone—and those unwanted desires she had fought to rid herself of sprang low in her belly. Keeli pushed herself free, breathing faster than she should have. She did not wait to see if Michael followed; she took off at a quick walk down the hall.

"I never imagined the wolves had such a complex infrastructure," Michael said.

A sharp response rose to her tongue, but Keeli realized at the last moment that Michael was not trying to insult her people, and so she said, "The clans have been in this city for almost one hundred years. Plenty of time to carve out everything we need to survive." Everything but acceptance. Prejudice would kill them in the long run—maybe the short run, too, if this negotiation fell apart. Werewolves simply did not have the resources to fight humanity on their own.

And why should we have to fight? We're not even the ones who started this mess. Which was a train of thought not only useless, but dangerous, as well. It was an argument Keeli remembered hearing many of the lower Alphas use as they came out of their meetings with her grandmother. *Why even bother with negotiations? Why contemplate the possibility of helping the vampires? They will just screw us in the end.*

Alpha Hargittai, one the few werewolves to initially side with her grandmother, gave what Keeli considered the best response: *The vampires only laugh at us, while the humans want to kill us. What, my dear brothers and sisters, do you prefer? What do your clans, and the children of your clans, prefer? Pride or the grave?*

The voices of dissent quieted after that.

Keeli led Michael down a ladder into another tight corridor that split off into four separate tunnels. The air felt stale, dirty. Keeli brushed her arms, trying to rub the sensation of thick dust off her skin. She wished she could do that for her burning nostrils. Her eyes watered.

Michael stood beside her, quiet and still. She tried not to look at him as she said, "The key here is scent. Follow the tunnels without one, and a silent alarm will be tripped, alerting the nearest clan—which would be mine—to an intruder."

"And what if you're a werewolf with a bad nose?"

Keeli threw him a sharp glance. "Funny."

"Actually, I was being serious."

"Any werewolf who can't smell this"—it was some awful, terrible, someone-needs-to-pay concoction—"deserves to be humiliated."

Trying to breathe through her mouth, Keeli led him down the tunnel that was second to the right. The ground was pitted with holes and broken glass, and she heard scratching sounds in the pipes that ran out and up from the wall. It was a very unpleasant place, and though the foul scent eventually dissipated, the atmosphere was depressing. It wasn't that she hadn't seen tunnels this bad before; it was just that now, with the possible end of everything the clans had fought to build, she worried this was their future. Bleak, empty, decayed—hiding like larger versions of rats in pipes, scratching out an existence that was nothing more than mere survival.

She almost said something out loud just to hear her voice—any voice—but that was silly, weak.

"This place bothers you," Michael said. Keeli stopped walking and looked at him.

"How did you know?" she asked, not bothering to lie.

His gaze remained steady. "You walk differently. You do not hold your head up. That does not seem . . . like you."

"You know me that well, huh?" She tried to sound defiant, but her gut churned. Was she that obvious? Or was he just that observant?

"I don't know anything but what you've shown me," he said.

"It's only been eight hours since we met," she replied. "I haven't shown you all that much."

She thought he smiled, but his mouth barely moved so it was difficult to tell.

"Why are you here with me, Keeli? Why do you walk here alone, with me, in this dark isolated place? I'm a vampire. You should not trust me."

"Is that a threat, Michael?"

"No, just curiosity."

He saved your life. Not just your life, but your freedom. He protected you against another vampire. He was kind.

And face it—you like him. Despite everything, you like him. Shit.

"I didn't really think about it beforehand," she said. "But thanks for bringing up the fact that it was a dumb move, and that I should be scared of you jumping my ass in this dark scary hole. You're a real nice guy, Michael. Very thoughtful."

"I won't hurt you," he said, quiet. Keeli rolled her eyes.

"You must be the most socially inept person I have ever met in my life. Dude. Do you think I would be down here in this crap hole with you if I thought I were in danger? Do you think that for one minute I would turn my back on you if I thought you were going to nix me? I would kill you first. Got that? All bets would be off, no matter how many nice things you've done for me."

He stared, and it pleased her to no end that he seemed taken aback by her words. "I thought you were just trying to be brave," he finally said, and in his voice she heard a puzzled curiosity that was touched by something soft, like wonder. "I did not want you to pretend if you were scared of me."

She *was* scared of him, but her reasons were different from his, and she had no interest in explaining why moving closer to him with her eyes intent on his pale sharp face made her want to run screaming—screaming—because her body wanted his body and she had never ever felt that way about any werewolf or human, and that was wrong. So wrong.

"Let's get something straight, Michael. I'm here with you because I made a promise, and I keep my word, no matter what. But I'm not stupid, and I don't make promises to people who I think will stab me in the back."

"So you trust me," he said.

Keeli almost found herself saying "No," but that was a lie—she wouldn't be here if she didn't trust him. Her trust, though, had come so smoothly, so naturally, that she had not even thought about it.

And *that* was terrifying. Because Keeli never gave her trust so easily, not even to members of her own clan.

"I trust you not to stab me in the back," she clarified, though she wondered if that was all, if anything else would come so easily between herself and this vampire.

"Thank you," Michael said.

Keeli's eyes narrowed. "What about you? How do you feel about me?"

"We already discussed this. You gave me your word. I trust you to keep it."

"I—" She stopped, confused. "Then why the hell are we having this conversation?"

Michael sighed. "I'm not sure anymore. I thought you looked uncomfortable. I just wanted to make sure it was not because of me."

"Oh." Keeli thought about that for a moment, trying to wrap her brain around the concept of a vampire making a werewolf feel comfortable. "Um, thanks."

She began walking again, this time more conscious of Michael's tall lean body shadowing her heels. She listened to the rustle of his clothing, and found herself concentrating more on his scent than the path.

"You smell like horses," she said.

His steps faltered. Very quietly, he said, "I was raised with them. It's the reason I'm bowlegged. I learned to ride before I could walk. But that was centuries ago. I should not still smell like home."

Keeli shrugged, trying to imagine him on horseback, wondering where that had been and when. "It's not so much a fresh scent, or even exactly the same as horse. It just has the same . . . essence."

It took him a long time to respond. The tunnel curved and the ceiling sloped lower. Keeli heard the distant rumble of the subway.

"Have you ever ridden horses?" Michael asked. The question was so surreal, she laughed.

"Horses don't like people like me. But when I was little, I always wanted to ride. I was obsessed. So when I was five my parents rented a car and took me out of the city to this place they'd heard of. A ranch. I got to stand on the fence and watch the horses."

Green grass shining with sunlight. Warm wind on her cheeks. Her mother, laughing, leaning with her arms around Keeli's waist, and around them both the arms of her father, hugging them close. A beautiful day. Safe. Loved.

Her chest hurt. She touched her breastbone, trying to feel the soft place where all her memories still lived. She hadn't thought about that day for a long time. Too long.

"That's how you know the scent, then."

"Yeah," Keeli said, still remembering her mother's hair, winding golden through her father's fingers. She caught herself drifting, and lifted her chin. "We're nearing the end of this tunnel. Pretty soon it will empty out into the main underground thoroughfare that links up the entire clan infrastructure. It's Wolf Central. Don't expect a warm welcome. In fact, you'll probably be lucky to make it through your first encounter without a matching set of scars on your face."

"Lovely," Michael said. "I'm a firm believer in the beauty of symmetry."

She smiled, and stopped to look at him. "It's going to be rough, Michael."

"For you or for me?"

Her smile slipped away, down to her toes. "Both."

She did not understand the look that passed through his eyes, but he nodded, solemn, and that quiet acceptance, the shadow of compassion, suddenly made her feel better. Like she were not alone in this strange endeavor, and that whatever happened, good or bad, she would have someone at her back. A partner. Even if he were a vampire.

"It shouldn't be that awful," she backtracked, even though Michael certainly did not look in need of reassurance. The tunnel walls vibrated, there was a loud roar, and then the noise faded, rushing into some unseen distance. They were close to the subway now. "Maddox is the largest clan in the city, and the strongest. It's the reason my Alpha is the Grand Dame, instead of just a regular clan leader. Her word is law for all the werewolves in the city, and right now she's banned any aggression between our two peoples."

"Fleur Dumont, our leader, has done the same, though I'm not sure the ban is holding. I have heard some rumors of violence, and not just the murder we're investigating."

"Gangs," Keeli said. "Yeah, I've heard the same thing. You guys are trying to ruffle our fur."

" 'You guys . . .' " he murmured. "Are vampires still all the same to you?"

Keeli glanced over her shoulder. "Don't get touchy with me, Michael. I say it the way I see it. And except for you, I don't think I've ever met a vampire who didn't automatically talk down to me. I'm a werewolf, so they think I'm dumb. They think they can call me a dog, and I'll sit up and fetch."

· "Who did that to you?" His voice was low, hard. Keeli frowned at his tone.

"Why does it matter? I don't know who they were. Crossing paths, that's all."

The tunnel ended. In front of them was another steel door with a keypad set in the wall.

"Are you ready?" Keeli typed in the access code.

"Are you?"

Keeli raised an eyebrow. "Life doesn't surprise me anymore, Michael. I'm always ready for anything."

He moved close as she prepared to open the steel door. She felt his presence wrap around her body, silent and cool. His breath stirred the hair on her neck.

She opened the door. Light and noise made her blink, duck her head in brief discomfort. She felt Michael touch the small of her back—gentle, surprising—and she stepped through the door into the sweeping cavern, fighting the urge to run, to lose herself in the crowd.

Guess who's coming to dinner? Keeli thought, and hoped it would not be her own head on the platter.

Chapter Seven

Wolf Central was the heart of the underworld, an abandoned subway station that had long ago been sealed off by humans for being too archaic and dangerous. Not too archaic or dangerous for werewolves, though, who had their own engineers, their own poor man's way of fixing things. Globe lights hung from the domed mosaic ceiling, which depicted a turquoise world of frothing seas populated by myth: mermaids and gods, shining dolphins frozen in ocean flight. Romanesque columns rose from the pale polished stone floors, which echoed dull with footfall: the click of heels, the steady tread of softer soles. Werewolves, everywhere, of every size and color, from every clan. Laughing, talking—sitting on the many wooden benches scattered through the station. No territory disputes were allowed in Wolf Central—pissing matches had to be taken elsewhere.

Keeli glanced left; far away she saw the emerald shine of leaves. Greentale Park: an artificial garden with fake towering trees and the most realistic plastic foliage money could buy, all set up on the former train tracks.

Thick, wild—Keeli remembered running small and fierce on Greentale's winding stone paths, jolting to a halt to bury her nose into thick silk rose petals. Working hard for a scent, for anything different from the other flowers, and the trees and the grass. Roses were supposed to be special; she knew that from books.

When she told her father, he went topside to find her a real rose. She still had it somewhere, pressed within a novel.

Keeli suddenly wanted to show Michael that forest. She stamped down the urge. He might laugh. If not, he would surely pity her. But then she looked up into his face and found his eyes thoughtful, distant, and he murmured, "I never imagined such a place existed. It is beautiful."

The tight knot in her stomach relaxed. Keeli smiled. "Humans cared more about things like beauty in the olden days. They did it right."

"So did the wolves," he said, turning to pull shut the door.

Keeli led Michael away, staying close to the wall. Every thirty feet they passed a door identical to the one they had just entered through. "More bolt-hole exits," she explained. "All things in the underworld lead here."

Michael's gaze roamed over the cavern. He looked out of place; tall, sharp, and pale, with an agile grace that was every bit the hunter, more so than the wolves around him. Despite his youthful face, he carried himself with the elegance of age, a marrow-deep familiarity with his body that was dangerously alluring.

He's a beautiful man. God. He's hot.

She flushed, tore her gaze away before he noticed her staring. That would not do. Not at all. She glanced around to see if anyone else watched Michael, and found they both had garnered some attention. Wolves, mostly women, studied him with narrowed, questioning eyes.

She saw some appreciation in their gazes, but mostly just hard curiosity, the kind with an instant judgment attached. It was possible they could tell he was a vampire by sight alone, but Keeli thought it more likely they believed he was a human man. She doubted anyone imagined her escorting a vampire into Wolf Central. Just wait until someone got too close, caught his scent.

"There are stores here," Michael said, examining the rows of shops set up on the opposite side of the cavernous subway station. Neat little buildings with actual glass windows to show off an assortment of wares. Mostly clothes, and things for children. Parents liked to bring their children here to shop. It felt safer than topside.

"There's a doctor's office, too. Also a free legal clinic. One of the Donovan wolves married a lawyer, so he comes down a couple of times a week to give out advice. An old subway car got turned into a small food market. More of a meat locker than anything else, since it's expensive to get good fruits and vegetables here. They go fast, though. Mothers with small children receive the first cut of what comes down."

"There is food rationing?" He sounded surprised.

"There aren't too many grocery stores topside that are within walking distance, and taxis are expensive. Werewolves don't make a whole lot of money in this city. Not anymore. The Grand Dame has had to reach into the reservoir to help the clans." Keeli steered them around a group of sullen young men loafing against a column near their path. She saw too many of these small packs lately, a product of the topside job slump. Bored young men, especially werewolf men, were never safe.

"The reservoir?"

Keeli hesitated. "Wolves who can afford it pay taxes to the Grand Dame, who holds the money in trust for the clans. When times are tough, she breaks open the bank."

And it was a large bank—a lot of money had gone into that account over the years. But the Grand Dame, and all the other Alphas before her, had a responsibility to use the money wisely. That it was being spread out now was a sign of trouble. Keeli hated that werewolves were so poor, that she had to confess such a thing, but Michael lived in a pit. If any vampire understood the concept of poverty, it just might be him.

Much to her relief, his only response was a thoughtful nod.

They had to cross the station in order to reach New Moon pass, one of the four major underground thoroughfares that led to the city's east side, and to Maddox territory. A free shuttle service ran on an automated pulley system, powered by energy siphoned off from the city—open-air carts that seated fifty people, and which ran on a one-track schedule that was a series of drop-off and pickup points, back and forth along the entire distance of each thoroughfare, twenty-four hours a day.

New Moon had two carts on a double-track pulley system, and Keeli and Michael arrived just as one of them drew up to the waiting area. Werewolves—mostly women clutching purses and small children—descended from the cart. Several of them passed near Michael. Distracted, tired—still Keeli saw their nostrils flare, their eyes change. They whirled, gasps lowering deep into growls, and Keeli stepped in front of Michael.

"No," she said. "He's not a threat."

"You're blind, then," snapped a flame-haired woman. She handed her baby to a friend. Fur flecked silver against her throat and her eyes flashed gold. She stood straight, tall, shoulders thrown back in challenge. Distinctive posture, which made her either an Alpha's mate, or someone with enough status to pull off the comparison.

Growls, everywhere, simmered low in a multitude of

throats. Keeli's gaze flickered to the other nearby were-wolves, who were responding to the threat by sinking low into the beast, even with wide-eyed children in their arms.

"Please," Michael began, but several werewolves barked—loud, piercing sounds that killed every activity in Wolf Central. Keeli bared her teeth, hissing a warning. She ran her tongue over her lengthening canines, tasting blood as her gums split with the shift.

"Escorted vampires are allowed here under protection of the Grand Dame Alpha," Keeli said, her words tumbling into a growl. "You all know why. Now leave him be."

"Or what?" snarled the woman, clenching her hands into fists. "You'll fight me? For a fang?"

"Helena," whispered her friend. She, too, showed signs of transformation, but her eyes were clear, cautious. Her arms tightened around the baby. "Be careful. She is Maddox."

Maddox. Not the clan, but the person. Mad Dog.

The change was instantaneous, a whispered ripple through the crowd. Keeli felt the other werewolves back away: slow, careful. Helena's face stilled, the wolf draining from her body. Her shoulders dipped very slightly.

"I'm sorry," she said.

"Don't be," Keeli said. "Just leave us alone."

Helena left them alone. So did the other werewolves, treating them to a studied indifference that did nothing to hide the undercurrent of fear, interest, and resentment stirring in their eyes. Tongues would be wagging today, that was for sure.

Did you expect anything less? Keeli Maddox, defending a vampire? Ready to fight for one? You'll never live this down.

Keeli lifted her chin. As if she cared what everyone thought of her. She had a job to do, promises to keep. Everyone who thought that was wrong could just go to hell.

She and Michael boarded the outbound cart. Not one person got on with them.

"I still don't have a matching set," Michael said, touching his unscratched cheek as the pulley groaned and yanked them down the corridor. Sidewalks lined the outer wall; they passed werewolves walking to and from the central station. The cart picked up speed.

"You're hilarious." Keeli studied his face. The breeze created by their movements ruffled his dark hair, the slender braids. His cheek glittered. "It could have gotten bad. You weren't scared?"

"Were you?"

"Yes." Keeli smiled. "But not so much for myself."

Michael's lips twitched. "Thank you for . . . defending me."

Her first impulse was to insult him, but instead she found herself saying, "I think you would have done the same for me." So easy—the words were easy—and much to her amazement, she believed them. She really did.

A genuine smile touched his mouth. "You know me so well? It's been little more than eight hours since we met, Keeli."

She laughed. "I know only what you show me, Michael."

"I must be showing too much, then."

Not enough. Not nearly enough.

Maybe her face revealed her thoughts; Michael's eyes darkened. He touched her bandaged wrist. Keeli glanced down at his arm. His sleeve covered the wound, but she knew it was there. She still remembered his taste.

"It was a rough night for us both, wasn't it?" She tried to smile, but his hand was too heavy, its comfortable weight scattering her thoughts. Michael said nothing. He looked like he was studying their hands. There was nothing flirtatious about his actions—just a calm inevitability, as though touching her was the most natural thing in the world. A puzzle. He seemed just as confused.

This is dangerous. Yes, maybe—but it was several minutes before she pulled away.

The cart slowed at the appropriate stops, but all the werewolves who got on caught Michael's scent and beat a hasty retreat.

"I'm sorry," Keeli said, after the last stop resulted in a gob of spit on Michael's boot. She was somewhat appalled by the behavior she saw, but not terribly surprised. Still, it wasn't fair to Michael, who was doing absolutely nothing to incite such vitriol. It made her wonder just how many of her own knee-jerk prejudices were inappropriate.

Michael stared at the spit clinging to his boot. "I've had worse reactions, usually from vampires. At least our two peoples can agree on something. There's hope for us all."

The cart's last stop was at the entrance to the Maddox tunnels. The giant gears set in the wall in front of them groaned to a halt. Keeli and Michael jumped off. There weren't many other wolves around—while the Maddox clan suffered from the same economic downturn, the Grand Dame had found jobs within clan territory for many of the men. Construction, mostly, on a pay scale that wasn't quite as high as topside work, but that still paid enough money to keep a family going. No one paid rent in the underground, but there were still utilities to chip in for, as well as food.

"Are all clan territories maintained like Maddox?" Michael asked, studying the brightly painted cement corridors, which were also decorated with the occasional large painting. Interspersed between them were framed drawings by the clan's children; there had been a school art fair only two weeks before.

"As much as they can afford to be," Keeli said. "We're

large, so we draw in more money from topside than the other clans. We also have more connections because of the Grand Dame Alpha."

Michael paused to study a crayoned interpretation of a werewolf transformation. Jagged black spikes stuck out from the contorted stick figure, which had two very long fangs hanging down to its chest.

"That's hair," Keeli said, pointing at the spikes.

"Yes." Michael smiled. "I can see that."

Two clan members walked past Keeli and Michael; they stared at Michael with hostility, but at Keeli, their gazes turned confused. She realized at the very last moment what it must look like: heads bent together, shoulders brushing. Smiling.

Keeli met their eyes, daring them to say anything. They did not. Michael watched them leave. He said, "Perhaps we should not stand so close together."

Keeli sucked in her breath. "Standing's not a crime."

His eyes flashed; hard, dark. "Your reputation—"

"Is not your concern. Just let it go."

Michael's jaw flexed. "Fine, then."

Keeli said nothing else. She led him down a network of winding corridors that alternated between stark gray walls and bursts of vibrant color. They passed large arches that led into comfortable common rooms. Keeli smelled popcorn. Teenagers slouched on battered couches reading comic books. An old television played in the background.

Past the common rooms were the residential areas. Every fifteen feet they passed heavy steel doors. Rectangular spy slots were centered at eye level in each door. Below them, numbers.

"Homes," Keeli explained. They took a left and the corridor widened. "And this is the Alpha core."

She swallowed hard as they approached her grandmother's rooms. There was no way to predict the Grand Dame's reaction to Keeli bringing home a vampire. The chances of it being a warm welcome were severely limited.

Her grandmother, however, was not home. Keeli used her spare key to open the door and led Michael inside. He made a small noise when he saw the sitting room, and Keeli smiled to herself. It was a beautiful place, the lush decorations rich with Victorian and Asian influences. Music played softly; an opera. *Aida,* maybe.

Keeli poked her head into her grandmother's darkened bedroom, calling out her name. It was empty, but she couldn't imagine the old woman would be gone for long. A hot teapot sat on her rosewood desk, along with a large pile of paperwork. Keeli glanced at the top sheet; it was a note from First Union & Trust, the largest bank in Crimson City.

Keeli's eyes widened. A fifty-thousand-dollar deposit had been made just that morning into the clan's trust account. No mention of the source, but Keeli couldn't imagine any of the wolves in Crimson City having fifty thousand dollars worth of change to plunk down for the clans.

"What is it?" Michael asked. He stood a polite distance away, not close enough to read over her shoulder.

"It's nothing," Keeli said, setting down the note in the exact same position she had found it.

Nothing normal, anyway. Maybe we've got a rich benefactor. It was Crimson City, after all, home of celebrities, movie moguls, and loaded plastic surgeons. Might be that someone with money to burn had a thing for wolves.

The gas fireplace had been left on. Keeli crouched before the flames, soaking up the gentle heat. After a moment, Michael sat beside her, his gaze still roving over the room. She felt his attention settle on her, but it was difficult to look at him, so she pretended to be engrossed by the fire.

"Your Grand Dame has excellent taste."

That made Keeli smile. "This is her sanctuary. She has many demands on her time, but this place makes her feel safe. Strong. She does most of her work from these rooms. I believe she's even holding the negotiations here."

"She trusts you," Michael said. "You have a key."

"Oh . . . well, yeah." Keeli wondered if she should tell him exactly who she was in relation to the Grand Dame. Michael ran his fingers through the thick rug covering the wood floor; she watched his hand, burnished gold in the firelight.

"About the murders," Michael said. "Do you think the Grand Dame will help us?"

"Yes," Keeli said, her gaze traveling up his wrist, his arm, to the hollow of his throat. She did this fast, hoping he would not notice, but when she looked into his eyes she found a quiet hunger that made her think he had noticed. Her cheeks warmed.

"Yes," she said again, proud of her steady voice. "The Grand Dame has no love for the police, but she does know how these murders have upset the balance between vampires and werewolves. If there isn't even an attempt to solve them, we can't expect any good faith between our two peoples. Not enough, anyway, to build an alliance on."

Keeli's words, not her grandmother's. She suspected the old woman did not give a rat's ass that some vampires were dead, but if it meant keeping the clans safe, she would pretend to care even if it killed her. *That* was something Keeli could count on, and the only reason she had taken the chance to bring Michael here without first asking permission.

"And there hasn't been any hint, not one rumor, about who could be doing this?"

Keeli frowned. "You're assuming it is a werewolf, and not just someone trying to frame us."

"True, but before the bodies turned to ash, the cause of death appeared to be consistent with an animal attack."

"You're assuming a lot, Michael."

"I'm not assuming anything, but the only evidence we have suggests a werewolf, so I am asking about werewolves."

"Fine. And the answer is no. No rumors, no nothing. The Grand Dame has had the Alphas questioning their people ever since the first death. It's bad business having a werewolf go feral, especially in this city. All of us get blamed. We're just lucky that it wasn't a human who died. No offense."

"None taken. I remember the last roundup."

The last time a werewolf went on a rampage. Keeli ground her teeth. "The police grabbed every registered werewolf, including the Grand Dame, and imprisoned them. All the unregistered wolves had to hide out in the subtunnels, or topside in abandoned buildings. We had to live like that for three months until they found the murderer. He wasn't even a member of any clan. Just an exile from another city. The city never apologized. They called it an unfortunate incident."

"Where were you?" His voice was low, almost as quiet as the flames.

"In the subtunnels for a while, and then on the street. I was seventeen at the time, so it wasn't so bad. I was old enough to take care of myself. But there were entire families put out, and that was bad. Especially during the full moon. We took to chaining ourselves in bolt-holes, or in sewer drains. Anyplace where we wouldn't be seen or heard."

"I did not know the transformation was involuntary."

"Only when the moon is full. It's the price we pay, our bargain with the wolf. One night a month the beast gets to play, and we can't interfere, just prepare. It's hell on the ones with jobs topside."

Michael looked thoughtful. "The next time could be worse, Keeli. If this trend continues, the humans won't need an excuse."

"I know." Keeli wrapped her arms around her knees. "It frightens me. All this crazy stuff happening—not just to us, but the vampires. Sometimes it feels like everyone hates us."

Michael stared into the fire. "I have seen terrible things done in the name of fear and ignorance. It seems to be part of the human condition."

"Not just humans." Her throat ached.

They sat awhile longer, quiet and still. The silence felt good. After a time, though, Keeli found herself blinking hard, struggling to keep her eyes open.

You didn't sleep last night. You've been running on adrenaline.

She swayed and her arm brushed Michael's sleeve. He said, "You're tired. You should rest."

"I can't," she said, but her eyes drifted shut and her head felt impossibly heavy. "This is ridiculous."

She fought, pinching her cheeks, digging fingernails into her palm, but she was just too tired, and here in her grandmother's rooms she felt safe. Even with a vampire at her side, she felt safe.

Michael said something, but Keeli could not keep her eyes open against the firelight, the world so heavy on her body, and she sank and sank until the last things she felt were gentle hands on her wrists, holding her upright. . . .

The next time she opened her eyes, she thought of wrists. She thought of Michael, too, because he still held her—cradling her entire body snug against his own—and it felt so good. Too good.

Keeli snapped to full consciousness and began struggling against Michael's hands. For a moment she froze inside his dark gaze; there was a story there, a new history only they shared.

And then she sensed movement, a shadow, and a dry voice said, "Well. Now this is interesting."

Both Michael and Keeli looked up.

The Grand Dame Alpha did not smile.

Chapter Eight

"Hello," said Michael, as he untangled himself. The cuts on his face throbbed almost as badly as his tattoo, though the pain was nothing to his embarrassment at being caught holding Keeli.

"Hello," echoed the Grand Dame Alpha, an odd look on her face as she watched Keeli struggle to sit up. Concern, shock, affection—Michael could not tell which was the strongest emotion on the woman's face. He was not even sure he cared. Keeli felt warm in his arms; despite the situation, it was a struggle not to keep her close, to savor her fierce heat. But that would be wrong—maybe—and they had a witness who would most certainly not approve.

Control is good. You need that. Keeli can't be allowed to suffer any sort of condemnation merely because you want to touch her.

The problem was that Michael wanted to do more than just touch Keeli. A lot more. That cheap release in the shower might as well have been a breath of air for all the good it did him. The moment he left the bathroom and found Keeli waiting for him by the window, the low hard ache had begun again, curling tight, making his fingers itch for her body.

And it was wrong. So very wrong. Especially when her grandmother was standing right there, giving him a hard look—peculiar, knowing—that made him wonder if she was a mind reader, too.

You are in trouble. Yes, and not just because of the Grand Dame. Keeli deserved better. She deserved more than Michael could ever dream of giving her, and after everything he had seen and heard, he knew he could do nothing less than preserve what she had. Keep her as safe as possible against all the terrible voices that would condemn her for even associating with him.

You should walk away now. Tell Jenkins to attach a human to the case. Give it all up and leave the city.

But as Keeli shifted against his body, he knew he would not. That despite all his silent promises, he did not have the strength to do the one thing that would keep her truly safe. He could not leave her.

Keeli defended me against her own people. A vampire. And for what? I never gave her any guarantees. She does not even know me.

All she had was the strength of her convictions, her own moral code of right and wrong. Michael had never met anyone is his life with that much honor. For the first time, someone cared if he lived or died. Someone . . . cared. It did not bother him if it was superficial or temporary.

Michael forced himself to meet the Grand Dame's gaze. It was harder to do than he imagined. There was power sleeping beneath her skin, a translucent energy masked in elegance. Vampires had all their years to accumulate knowledge, strength of character, and none could compare to the aged woman who stood above him with her keen eyes and lilting voice. Oh, what a boon if she had been an immortal. Oh, the danger.

Keeli looked dazed, flushed, her pink hair smashed flat. There was a very large tear in her striped stockings. Michael held out his hand—instinctual, unplanned—and a thrill of shock ran through his body when Keeli took it. From the look on her face, he was quite sure she didn't realize what she had done. But Michael saw the Grand Dame's eyes, sharp as dagger points, and he suddenly feared for Keeli, for what trouble might come of such a simple act. He helped pull her up, and then immediately let go.

"Would you like to explain this?" said the Grand Dame, and for a moment Michael thought she meant the brief contact of hands. But then she added, "My guests, especially vampires, usually announce themselves before entering my home. And why"—she fixed Michael with a pointed stare—"are you still concerning yourself with my granddaughter?"

Ah. He had suspected this—here, finally, confirmation of their relationship. But the tone of her voice was a clear warning: *Stay away from her. Stay far away.*

"You know each other?" Keeli stared at them both. She looked terrible, worn to the bone. Michael felt an urgent desire to find her a quiet place to curl up and sleep, to stand above and protect her precious rest.

The Grand Dame tilted her head, cool. "This vampire came to us last night with news of your arrest. He is the reason Jas was at the police station this morning, with money for your fine."

"But I thought . . ." Keeli looked at her grandmother, and then Michael, an expression of bewilderment passing over her face. "I guess I don't know what I thought. But someone should have told me."

"You didn't give Jas a chance, or so I heard." The Grand

Dame turned away and walked to the small rosewood desk, delicately carved with birds. There were papers and folders stacked in neat piles on its polished surface; a teacup perched close to the table's edge. The Grand Dame poured hot water into the cup.

A thick Persian carpet cushioned Michael's feet, the intricate designs easy to appreciate in the golden glow of antique lamps scattered throughout the room. The air was kept warm by the fire burning inside the deep fireplace. Just within the ring of flickering light sat two thick chairs, green as peas, with faded red pillows. Beyond them, to the right, an open door led to another room, where Michael glimpsed a carefully made bed. Books were everywhere.

Michael had always thought that werewolves were opposed to the aesthetic life, that they viewed luxury, and those who appreciated it, as weak and contemptible.

So much to learn, it seemed.

The Grand Dame sat down at her desk, and cradled her teacup in her palms.

"I would ask you to leave me with my granddaughter," she said to Michael, "but I don't dare let you loose in our tunnels without an escort. And right now, I don't wish to explain to my people how—or why—a vampire is in my quarters."

"Granny May," Keeli began, but stopped when the Grand Dame flashed her a hard look. A shocking thing— even Michael, with all his years and memories, felt a thrill of fear. He swayed toward Keeli, and forced himself still.

You are a guest here, and an unwelcome one at that. You are not hunter or executioner. Do not bring any attention to yourself.

The Grand Dame said, "You almost killed someone last night. A fatal breach of our agreement. You told me you could control the wolf."

"We don't have time for this," Keeli said, low.

"We will *make* time," snapped the Grand Dame. She set down her tea and curled her hands together, knuckles white. "Last night could have turned out so much worse for you. Do you understand that, Keeli? Do you?" She shook her head, mouth pressed into a hard line. "I should never have let you leave. The wolf cannot be pushed aside, not for you or me. It *must* come out, and if not in a controlled, safe environment, then out on the streets, where people can get hurt."

"She saved a woman's life," Michael said, when he saw that Keeli wasn't going to take up for herself. It pained him to see such emptiness in her face, all her vibrancy sucked away into a pale mask.

The Grand Dame's eyes glittered in the firelight. "As she should have. But that is not the point, and frankly, it is none of your business."

"It might as well be," Keeli said. Some color returned to her cheeks.

Stubborn, thought Michael.

"We're working together now." Keeli raised her chin. "With the police. A vampire's been murdered on Maddox land, and they needed a liaison."

The Grand Dame sucked in her breath. "You are working with the police? You are . . . you are partnered with this . . . this . . ."

"Michael," he said.

"Michael," she ground out. "I thought you said there would be no debt."

For a moment, Michael was unsure of her meaning, but then her gaze flickered toward Keeli and he understood.

"Keeli agreed to this of her own free will. Until late last night, I never even thought I would see her again." Which came out sounding more plaintive than he intended. He shut his mouth and glanced sideways at Keeli. She frowned at her grandmother.

"The police are beginning to blame the wolves for these murders. Someone needed to speak up for us, and I thought it might as well be me."

"Ridiculous." The Grand Dame's voice was sharp, uncompromising. "The police are in contact with me, and from what I can tell, they do not know what they have. The humans are investigating the murders willy-nilly, without any focus. The wolves have nothing to fear, not without evidence."

"Which is what we have to find, one way or another," Keeli argued. "And what about the negotiations? Do you want them to fail? Wouldn't it be nice to tell the vampires that you have someone investigating the murders? It would be a sign of good faith."

"I owe the vampires no such signs." The Grand Dame sipped her tea.

"What do you owe *your* people?" Michael asked quietly. "What do you owe them if no alliance is reached, and then later the humans strike against vampire and werewolf, and we are all weak because we are alone?"

Keeli sighed. "Please. You fought so hard to convince the other Alphas of the importance of this alliance. Don't change now. Don't let that go to waste, just because you're mad at me."

"Don't be silly." The Grand Dame grimaced, staring at the fire. "The police wish to question me. They wish to enter the tunnels and examine my wolves. Tonight, even, and I have the second night of the negotiation to think of."

"I will speak to Jenkins," Michael said. "Keeli and I can conduct the investigation."

The old woman narrowed her eyes. Keeli stepped forward.

"You don't have to say another word. I know you don't

approve. But I'm not like the other wolves, and I won't live my life in fear—"

"Stop it—"

"—of you. You raised me to speak my mind. You raised me to be strong. We both know why. So don't try to take that from me now. This is something I have to do. It's a matter of honor. Michael helped me, so now I'll do the same for him. And maybe, at the same time, I can help the clan."

"Everyone will hear of this, Keeli. It's inevitable."

"I don't care. You shouldn't, either."

"I care for you!" snapped the Grand Dame. "Already the others are saying you should be kept in the tunnels. And now this?"

Keeli's mouth snapped shut. Michael gave up on subtlety and stepped close. His arm brushed her arm.

"As Keeli already said, we do not have time for this. The police are taking these murders very seriously—as you know the vampires are. If there is another death . . ."

"The vampires cannot afford a war with us."

"Would you stake the lives of your wolves on that? Would you care to say for certain the police won't order a roundup? What if a human dies next?"

The Grand Dame set down her cup. She closed her eyes. "None of us can afford that."

Michael nodded. "So, time. We may not have enough."

The Grand Dame picked up her tea. She drank slowly, staring into the fire.

"You are a very strange vampire," she said finally. "I don't trust vampires. Just as I suspect you don't trust werewolves."

"I don't trust anyone," Michael said. "Vampires or werewolves."

The old woman snorted, her eyes keen. "Burned by your own kind, is that it?"

Michael's smile was cold. "The burning has been mutual."

The Grand Dame simply nodded, and he wondered just how much she knew about him. How much she *could* know, separated as she was from the vampires.

"Werewolves sink teeth into their own ranks," she conceded, surprising him. "But if I see *your* fangs while you are a guest in my tunnels . . ." Her eyes flashed gold and muscles rippled fine and hard beneath her delicate skin. She turned her gaze on Keeli, still with the wolf in her face.

"You take responsibility for him? And yourself?"

"I do," Keeli said, and still she did not move from Michael's side.

The Grand Dame stared at her granddaughter. "The easy life never did suit you."

"I wasn't born to ease," Keeli said flatly.

The old woman's mouth tightened, and for a moment, Michael sensed pain.

"Find the murderer," she said. "Clear the Maddox name, if you can. Do it quickly."

Michael and Keeli left the Grand Dame's small home. The empty corridor outside her apartment was made of poured concrete, well lit with industrial-sized fluorescent bulbs. The polished walls were softly curved and lined with a mishmash tangle of pipes and wires, which no doubt made sense to someone, but which to Michael looked like a fire hazard.

Michael pulled the digi-encoder from his pocket. "No reception. I need to reach Jenkins."

"You could use the Grand Dame's phone," Keeli said. "I'm surprised you didn't mention it while we were in there."

"You seemed uncomfortable. I thought we should go."

Keeli stared. Michael sensed tension in the hard line of her shoulders, her mouth. "I love her," she said.

"I know."

Keeli's jaw worked. "You'll have to use a public phone. Only the Grand Dame has direct access to the main telephone line."

Which was not a completely pleasant thought, but better than nothing at all. Better than knocking on the steel door behind his back. Vampires did not intimidate Michael. Very few had his respect. The Grand Dame had managed to do both, and it set his teeth on edge. True, he had left because Keeli was uncomfortable, and he would not return for the same reason. But he wasn't entirely innocent of feeling discomfort around the old woman.

"How long has she been Alpha?"

"Longer than I've been alive. Her husband was the Grand Sire, but he died in a challenge. She fought the wolf who made the bid. Fought and won. She's incredibly strong. Even now, at this age, there aren't many wolves in Crimson City who could take her and win."

Keeli led Michael down the corridor, which curved as if they were in the belly of a snake. He watched the doors they passed, and remembered what Keeli had told him earlier about homes.

"Who lives here?" he asked.

"No one," Keeli said.

"I thought Maddox was a large clan."

"It is. But only the family members of an Alpha are allowed to live near the central heart of the underground."

"One of these is yours."

Keeli gave him a sharp look. "You don't seem surprised. I wondered about that, back there."

"The resemblance is undeniable."

"Yeah. I get that a lot."

"You don't like people knowing?"

"It's complicated." Keeli's gaze trailed over the cold doors. Cold, so cold—a mirror of her eyes. "There's some bad history."

Michael frowned, taking in the quiet, the empty rooms. "What happened to the people who should be living here?"

Keeli's lips tightened. When she looked at him, he felt her anger, the sudden distance. She opened her mouth to speak and Michael pressed his fingers against her cheek. She froze.

"If you are going to shout at me, don't. If you feel forced to tell me the truth, don't. I ask questions because I am curious, not because I expect you to answer me."

"Okay," she whispered, after a long moment of silence. "Thank you."

Michael nodded. His fingers still lay gently on her face. "I have another question, Keeli. Why are the other werewolves afraid of you?"

Her eyes changed—not to anger, but to a quiet despair that shot straight through Michael's chest into his heart. She did not answer him.

He caressed her cheek, lightly, brushing his thumb over her softening mouth. He stepped away. Careful, restrained. *Control yourself.*

Keeli cleared her throat. She turned and began walking once again. Michael followed, silent, wondering at the secret in her eyes, the reason for such pain. It had something to do with the empty homes, the fear he had seen earlier in werewolf faces when they realized who Keeli was. He could not image the woman at his side as a frightening force.

Michael smelled the wolves before he saw them. Nothing offensive; a faint musk, the underlying odor of wet fur. Laughter, too, just as they rounded a curve in the corridor. Keeli slowed, almost to a stop.

The first person Michael saw was a tall teenage boy with thick black hair and rough sideburns. He was pressed up hard against a girl, and she was definitely not complaining.

"Oh," Keeli said. She glanced at Michael, embarrassed. "Do you know them?"

"Complete strangers. I heard some new wolves had been adopted, though. Someone said they were near feral."

Michael wanted to ask her what that meant, but the girl opened her eyes and saw them standing there. "Shit," she said, frantically pulling the young man's hand out of her jeans. She pushed down her shirt. Her boyfriend was clearly more reluctant to end his activities, but he turned away from them. Michael heard a zipper.

"Sorry!" said the girl, brushing shaking hands over her long dark hair. "Really sorry."

"You should probably use your room," Keeli said. "This corridor does get some traffic during the day."

"Yeah," said the boy, flushed. "We—" He stopped, studying Michael, nostrils flaring. A damning expression filled his eyes, disgusted and horrified and afraid. It had been a long time since someone so young had looked at him like that, and Michael felt frozen within those eyes, the echo of centuries past—the heat of flames against his cheeks, the first flush of blood, hot between teeth—and oh, the horror if it, waking in the middle of a nightmare and knowing it was real—all real—

"You smell like fang," said the boy, in a deadly quiet voice.

"I am a vampire," Michael said, and he felt as though he were confessing a sin.

The reaction was instantaneous. The boy flung himself at Michael, shifting shape as he flew through the air. Michael had never seen a werewolf transform so quickly;

when the boy hit the ground again, he looked more wolf than human, with paws and a thick tuff spiked high along the back of his misshapen head.

"Shit," Keeli muttered, lunging forward to grab the boy around the neck. His girlfriend screamed, fur pushing through her skin even as she tried to slash at Keeli with new claws. Michael grabbed her.

"Stop this," he hissed, knocking her into a hard slide along the floor. He did not give her time to reorient herself, either; he flipped the girl on her stomach and yanked her arm tight against her back. She screamed again, and this time it was all fear.

"Richard!" cried the girl, trying to buck Michael off her body. She began shifting into wolf form; he put her in a headlock. The girl thrashed against him, but Michael was stronger.

"We're not here to fight you!" Keeli shouted. "Shit! Listen to me!"

It was too late. Doors slammed open; feet pounded against cement. Men and women were pouring out of rooms, racing down the tunnels to see what could make two people scream so terribly. Michael smelled the acrid mark of something feral.

The first few werewolves hesitated when they saw Keeli, who said, "Wait, I need to explain."

"No!" shouted Richard, mostly human again. "He's gonna bite her!"

Michael felt the air change the moment he was recognized as a vampire; a crackle, the spit of electricity and fire. A shout went up, drowning out Keeli's strident pleas, an echoing cry that vibrated his bones with howls that began shrill, but shifted guttural as throats changed and thickened beneath sprouting fur.

Blasted by sound and wolf, when Keeli released Richard to step in front of Michael, he abandoned the girl and grabbed Keeli's arm to yank her behind him. She was small, so small, her pale throat too exposed, and he did not think it would matter to these wolves that she was the Grand Dame's granddaughter, that she was one of them. Only, that she stood against them for a vampire. He could not bear to see her hurt for that.

The moment Michael touched her, the wolves dashed in. He barely managed to throw Keeli behind him before the first wolf went for his throat. Teeth slid against Michael's skin but he was fast and flung the werewolf away before it could break flesh. He did not hold back his strength. He was not gentle. Pain flashed in his ribs—bright, hot.

And then Keeli was there in front of him, but she was different, sharp and wild, with the wolf riding her hard—in her face, her body, everywhere—and he felt rage pour off her in waves. It was crazy anger, the kind he had seen last night as she crouched over a man with her fangs brushing skin for blood. The werewolves faltered when they saw her face, and then they scattered as she lunged at them, howling. Michael grabbed Keeli around the waist, hauling her tight against his chest. She screamed, still fighting, mindless with fury.

"Keeli!" he shouted in her ear, uncaring what the others thought. He had to calm her. He had to make her listen before she did anything she would later regret. "Keeli, control yourself!"

The werewolves still shouted, howling; he felt them close in again, but he did not check to see if it was to help or kill. He was too busy whispering in Keeli's ear, feeling her body shudder in his arms, her heart pounding rough as her breathing slowed, slowed, slowed.

"Michael," she whispered.

"I'm here," he murmured.

A voice cut through the melee. A shouted bark of authority that was part human, part wolf—and very clearly angry.

"What is this?" snarled the Grand Dame Alpha, stalking through the wolves with a strength and poise that Michael would never have imagined, considering her age. She walked upright, completely naked, covered in thick silver fur. Her face could not have been called human, but she had not shifted enough to lose her ability to speak. The frozen state between woman and animal was monstrous in its rage; visceral. So much like Keeli, but with iron-tight control.

The Grand Dame's fists lashed out, mercilessly cuffing wolves who failed to move from her path. She kicked and clawed her way to the center of the mob, and it was a miraculous thing, seeing them cower before her on hands and knees, or with tails tucked and bellies exposed.

Michael released Keeli, who managed to stand on her own without any show of weakness. The Grand Dame came to a stop beside her granddaughter, and Michael felt power wash over him, the connection that bound the two women despite their distance in age.

"Don't I protect you?" roared the Grand Dame, spittle flying from her sharp mouth. "Don't you trust me to take care of you? Would I allow a vampire to walk our tunnels with my own blood, if I were not sure it was safe? Would I allow a vampire to live in my presence if I thought he were a threat?"

She turned slowly, every wolf touched by that hard cold gaze. "You disrespect my judgment by your actions today. You threaten my only living blood, cub of my cub. Behaving like animals. *Ferals.* All of you disgust me."

"He's a vampire." Michael turned and saw Jas sitting up from the other werewolves. "Shouldn't you be more disgusted with *him?*"

Keeli went very still. Everyone held their breath. The

old woman lifted her chin, the tips of her ears swinging forward. Tenacious, stubborn. Again, Michael sensed her power, the stain of raw untainted resolve. The years had polished her bright and hard; her body was old, but her will was not.

"I am the Grand Dame Alpha," she said, and her voice snapped out each word like the crack of breaking bones. "Do you contest my wisdom, Jas? Do you contest my authority?"

Will you fight me? Will you take what is mine? Will you kill me?

For a moment, Michael thought Jas would accept the challenge, that he would rise to his feet and meet the Grand Dame in the center of the corridor and fight her for power.

He did not. Jas lowered his body slowly until he crouched like all the others, subservient. The promise was there, though. The threat had been spoken out loud. Michael knew it was only a matter of time.

"No," Keeli breathed, and Michael realized she understood the truth of it.

Because if old age did not kill the Grand Dame Alpha, Jas most surely would.

Chapter Nine

Keeli did not pay attention to the reaction of the other werewolves. She did not look to see if they felt the same horror of anticipation, the realization of possible new leadership and challenge. Part of her was still lost to the wolf. There were moments, in the middle of the fight, when Keeli had felt herself awash in a dark sea, a cool and mindless tomb. All the anger that shifting brought to her—the rage of the wolf, uncontrolled, waiting beneath the ever-fraying seam of her human skin, waiting to spill out to sate hot fury with flesh—was too overpowering. It was the familiar danger, inherited and legendary.

And she had almost used that fury against her own people.

You will never be allowed to leave the underground. Not until you master your anger, like Granny May has.

Granny May, the Grand Dame Alpha, was beautiful, heartwarming. Her ability to make everyone cower in abject fear and humiliation was brilliant and wonderful. Everyone had listened, learned, and licked booty when her grandmother entered the fray.

And then Jas had to open his mouth and ruin it all.

Nothing lasts forever. Her grandmother's words, said to a little cub sobbing in her lap. Keeli, young and broken. *Nothing lasts forever but love and memory.*

But that's not enough, Keei told herself. She felt Michael at her side, and remembered his hands around her waist, holding her. She could still hear his voice in her ear, whispering her name over and over, bringing her back from the wolf, drawing the woman from the animal.

Keeli glanced up at his pale face and noted lines of pain around his mouth and eyes. He bled from a small wound in his ribs, his shirt torn just enough for her to see the ragged patch of flesh. Nothing lethal, but it hurt Keeli—the sight hurt her heart—because the wound was for her. He had tried to protect her.

"We need to stop that bleeding," she said.

"It's nothing," Michael replied.

"You're getting the floor dirty," she snapped, embarrassed. Her cheeks felt hot.

Michael stared at her, his expression unreadable, and said, "Keeli. I will be fine." And then, even softer, "Now is not the time."

Keeli gritted her teeth and looked away at the wolves, who were finally retreating. Anger flared in her throat. Her emotions startled her.

I almost fought my own clan. I would have fought them. For a vampire.

Maybe that was the worst of it, what still had her fuming. The actions of her clan had forced Keeli to acknowledge something about herself that she never wanted to accept.

You run apart, you stay apart.

And for a moment, while familiar faces had bared fang at her throat, tasting first the blood of the man in front of her, she had not cared. She had not cared what it would mean to make pain on members of her own clan. Only that it was right, it was just, and that she would do whatever it took. Even if that meant exile.

Michael touched her wrist. They stood so close together he only had to move his finger. His touch soothed, was warm, turned her body to liquid. She wanted to scream at herself in disgust. Was she choosing vampires over wolves?

She pulled away. Michael's gaze turned cold. So cold. Ancient and distant, and oh—it hurt. It hurt, and she could not understand why. She could not understand why she was feeling so much toward him.

He is a vampire.

But she had not been thinking of that when her clan attacked. She had not called him a vampire in her head. He had simply been a person. A man.

Perhaps, even, a friend.

"Are you hurt?" growled the Grand Dame, examining Keeli's body with her sharp gaze.

"No." Keeli looked back at Michael, and gestured to his ribs. The Grand Dame's mouth tightened into a hard black line.

"Unacceptable." She raised her voice to the retreating werewolves, most of whom had not yet reverted into human form. They hesitated, ears slicked back against their heads. "This vampire is here on important business. You will treat him with respect, or else answer to me."

No one made a sound, but there was understanding in their eyes. Understanding and resentment. It was the first time Keeli had ever seen anyone look at her grandmother that way, and it chilled her. Keeli knew dislike for vampires ran deep amongst the werewolves, but she had not realized that Michael's presence—and perhaps the negotiations—would reveal so many undercurrents of dissatisfaction with her grandmother's leadership.

But was dissatisfaction enough to commit murder, even against a vampire?

Keeli glimpsed Richard and his girlfriend. They stood off to the side against the wall, their hands linked together. They looked distraught, but when they saw Keeli watching, began sidling away. Keeli caught up with them before they could go very far.

"Are you hurt?" she asked. She had been a little rough with the boy, but he was strong and a stranger. Better safe than sorry.

"Fuck you," said Richard, though the venom in his voice was quiet, tinged with fear. "All of you are fucked up, to let vampires run around here. We thought this place was supposed to be safe. Shit. We'd be better off on the street."

Keeli was quite ready to tell them that the street would be happy to have them back, when the girl grabbed Richard's arm and whispered, "She smells just like him. A fang. He's touched her. Been all over her."

Richard leaned close, sniffing. A sneer wrinkled his mouth. "Did he pay you?"

Did he pay you for blood? Are you his whore? Is that why you smell like fang?

Keeli blinked at the insult, too disgusted to answer. Human men and women did it all the time—it was a booming business all over the city. There were even restaurants where a vampire could go and choose a pretty face, an appealing body, and order a pint of blood straight from the source. Pricy and lurid.

Keeli snarled. The girl bared her teeth in response and braced herself for another attack. Richard stepped between them.

"Suze," he snapped. "Don't waste your energy."

"She smells dirty," Suze said, butting her head against his biceps. Submissive. "She's filthy."

Keeli felt Michael draw close; she did not need to see him to know he was near. Her body felt his presence; a slow tingle drawing up her spine. The Grand Dame was with him.

"So," said the old woman, in a dangerous voice, "you've met our new additions, fresh off the street. Richard and Suze. Siblings."

Keeli almost got whiplash. She looked at Michael and found him just as bewildered. Siblings?

Holy shit.

The two teens looked extremely uncomfortable. That, and frightened. Richard stared at Keeli, a pleading gaze, and if he hadn't just called her a whore, she might have felt sorry for him.

"We had a misunderstanding," Michael said, before Keeli could confront them. He glanced at her, and then focused his attention on the two young people. His voice reflected his eyes: careful and quiet. "It won't happen again, will it?"

Suze looked so relieved, Keeli thought the girl might vomit. Keeli felt like vomiting. This was too gross. Either that, or it was the scam of the century and these two kids were totally messed up. Keeli preferred the latter, though her luck usually wasn't that good.

The Grand Dame tilted her head; there was a curious look in her eyes that made Keeli uneasy. "This is clan business, Michael. You presume too much."

"Of course. My apologies." He bowed his head, stepping back. Keeli sidled near. They shared a quick glance, and in it, a warning. A promise of words. Later, though.

Keeli saw Jas watching from the crowd. Her grandmother saw him, too. Called out his name. Gave the teens a gentle shove. They disappeared down the hall without a word, though Keeli did not miss the curious—and somewhat defiant—way they studied Michael as they left. He ignored them.

Jas was a big man, broader of shoulder than Michael, and taller by at least six inches. Second-in-command to her grandmother, he was also a star amongst the wolves; highly popular as a storyteller, leader, and fighter. His approach was slow. He glared at Keeli and Michael.

"Grand Dame," he said, trying to match the old woman's gaze. She was small—not much taller than Keeli—but she had power on her side. Jas looked away first.

The Grand Dame raised her brow—a thick line of dark silver fur—and glanced at Keeli. The corridor was nearly empty now. There was no one around close enough to hear them. "Another vampire was murdered. He was found on Maddox territory."

"We didn't do it," Jas said. He looked at Michael, as though daring him to disagree.

"It's possible you didn't," Michael said, and Keeli wondered how long he could stand there, bleeding and in pain, before he showed any kind of weakness. "But that is what we are here to determine."

"You're helping him," Jas said to Keeli. A muscle twitched in his cheek, making his scar warp.

"Deal with it," she snapped.

"You will also help them." The Grand Dame's voice was hard, rough with authority and the partial change of her fur-clad throat. It was disconcerting to see her in a twilight state, between human and wolf. Not many werewolves could hold such a shape for long. The strain on the body was too great.

"Help them implicate our own kind? Grand Dame—"

"No." The Grand Dame stepped close to Jas, and though she had to crane her neck to look him in the eyes, there was no doubt who was taller in spirit. "I know you wish to be Alpha, and when it is time, you will challenge me. That, I accept. But while I am Alpha, you will *not* question me in public. After all these years, Jas . . . how could you undermine me like that? You know better."

For the first time in her long association with Jas Mack, Keeli saw a faint flush of shame stain his cheeks. "These negotiations are a mistake," he said, glancing at Michael. "The vampires will betray us."

"The vampires will not break any treaty they sign," Michael said. "It would be considered . . . bad form."

Jas scowled. "That's no comfort, fang."

"The name is Michael. Learn to use it."

"Or what?"

"Or he'll bleed all over you." Keeli pushed between the two men. "Now stop it. This is important."

"Yes," said the Grand Dame. Her nose wrinkled. "Keeli, take Michael to your room and clean him up. Jas, I want you to spread the word. Michael is here under my protection. If there is any repeat of today—even a hint of such discord—I will hold you personally responsible."

His jaw tightened, but he nodded and backed away.

"Watch your back," Jas said to Keeli. He looked at Michael, and there was nothing friendly about that appraising gaze.

"Watch your own," Keeli replied, but he turned to stride down the corridor and did not respond.

The Grand Dame sighed. Slowly, carefully, she changed shape. It was not until she became fully human that Keeli realized how great a strain she had put on her body. The old woman swayed and Michael caught her against his hip. Blood smeared over her pale wrinkled skin.

"I'm fine," she murmured, straightening. Michael's arms fell away but he remained close; a torn shadow, long and lean. Keeli glanced around the corridor; all the doors were shut, no sounds of movement from within. No one else had witnessed her grandmother's astounding moment of weakness.

The Grand Dame took a step and swayed again. Michael picked her up.

"Stop," she said. Michael ignored her and looked at Keeli.

"Meet us in her room," he said.

And then he was gone, running faster than she could have dreamed possible. He left behind the scent of blood.

And one very confused werewolf.

Keeli ran down the hall. As she ran, her body remembered.

Hands stroke her hair, a quiet hum—sweet and pure—and "sleep" she says, and "I love you," she ends, slipping light into darkness, pulling covers tight to chin, and later, later, shouts— the scent of blood—and she looks for her mother, looks, and finds her on the floor and "mommy, please," and "mommy, no," and her father's shadow flickers, writhing beneath wolves, shouting mommy's name—her name—screaming . . .

Keeli staggered, falling hard against the wall. She scrabbled for something to hold herself up with, but the concrete was slick beneath her nails and she slumped to her knees. Tears ran down her face. Keeli pressed her forehead to the ground, rocking.

It's been so long. Images flashed through her head and she squeezed her eyes shut, trying to block out the horrible sounds of her parents screaming. The scent of their blood. The wet laughter of the men. Such a long time— she had not thought of that night for years—and now to find herself still weak with memory, still crippled by that night . . .

Tunnel air swirled, cool on her hot face. Fingers touched her cheek.

"Keeli," Michael whispered urgently. "Keeli, look at me. What happened?"

Keeli hid her face from him. "Granny May?"

"In bed. I came back to look for you." Michael's hand snaked around her waist. He swung her up into his arms. Keeli did not protest. Her legs felt like jelly and her head was aching itself into a series of lights. She could not fight even if she wanted to—and she didn't. Right at the moment, it did not matter that the man holding her was a vampire. Only that he was doing something to take care of her and she trusted him enough to do it, no questions asked.

How can you trust him? You've known him less than a day.

I don't know, she answered herself, as he ran down the hall. *I must be insane.*

And that was all right. For now, anyway.

"Your grandmother said your room was next to hers. So she could keep an eye on you."

"You shared life stories?"

"No life," he said. "Just stories."

Keeli's eyes closed. She felt Michael stop, shift her slightly in his arms. A door opened in front of them, releasing a wash of cool air. Keeli smelled books. Her own fading scent.

She felt her bed, soft beneath her back, and opened her eyes. Michael's face was only inches from her own. Her breath caught. It was good, looking into his eyes, being so close to that dark liquid warmth. Warm, not cold—the man could shift so quickly. Mecurial, Granny May might say. A mystery, Keeli called him.

Michael looked just as caught by her gaze. He licked his lips, and Keeli found her attention riveted to his mouth. She glimpsed fang.

"What happened to you?" he asked.

120

"Memory," she said, startled at how easily the truth came out. She pushed herself away from him, suddenly desperate for distance. "I need to check on my grandmother."

"She said you would feel that way. She also said not to bother."

Keeli blew out her breath. "She hates a fuss. Despises weakness in herself. To have a vampire see her in that position, and then to need his help . . ."

"I will not tell anyone," Michael said.

She hesitated. "Thank you."

"You believe me?"

"If I find out you humiliate her in anyway, I'll burn your balls off. Don't think I'm kidding."

"Why would I?" he said dryly.

Keeli scowled. "My grandmother doesn't shift as much as she used to. I guess the years are finally catching up." She studied his side, noting the rip in his shirt. "You're still bleeding."

Michael glanced down at himself. "I don't think I got much on you."

"I don't care about that." She rubbed at her eyes, smearing out the last remnants of tears. Her head still hurt but the pain was manageable. "Take off your shirt."

Michael's lips twitched.

"Just . . . shut up." Keeli pushed herself off the bed, ignoring Michael's outstretched hand. She almost took his help; her legs felt weak, tired. Keeli stumbled across the familiar threadbare rug to the small bathroom tucked at the far corner of her room, the open door barely visible between stacked books piled chest high on every available patch of floor. It was a familiar maze and she walked it without thought.

"Does all your money go into books?"

Keeli turned, a sharp comment on her tongue, words well-used from years of reacting to snide observations, but she stopped when she saw his face.

"I wasn't trying to insult you," he said quietly, somehow understanding her silence. "I was curious, that's all."

Keeli glanced around her room, taking in the stiff bindings, the hard-earned tales bought or inherited or scavenged. "Yes," she said. "Books make me feel . . . safe. Calm."

Michael followed her gaze. "I envy you. I have never stayed in one place long enough to collect books. It would not be practical. Carrying them with me each time I leave . . ."

His voice trailed off. Keeli turned away.

The bathroom was small, but clean. Keeli didn't care much about makeup or fancy lotions, so the counters were pleasantly bare. She grabbed a towel from a shelf.

"I can do this," Michael said.

"I want to see," Keeli said, meeting his gaze. "I need to know how badly you were hurt. What they did to you."

Michael's gaze flickered. Slowly, he began to unbutton his shirt. Keeli watched his face, and when that became too much for her, she watched his hands—the slow descent, gentle and careful—revealing pale flesh, the line of his chest, running lower, deeper, to his navel. Blood covered his waist. When he peeled off his shirt, Keeli sucked in her breath.

"It looks worse than it is," he said.

"I know." Keeli leaned close. "Just one bite. Shallow. Those hurt the worst, though."

"I'll heal," he said, his voice tight. "What I need now is rest and blood. Neither of which is in good supply down here."

Keeli blinked. "Blood."

Michael sighed, reaching for the towel in her hands. "Just let me clean up. The bleeding has almost stopped. You may have to begin the investigation without me while I return home for clothes and some . . . food. I'll return as soon as I can."

"Vampires eat solid, right? We've got food down here."

Michael looked uneasy. "I cannot eat solids."

"Are you sick?"

"No. Just . . . different. Not every vampire is the same, Keeli. Genetics can . . . alter the way we are made."

Keeli frowned. "I'd ask you more questions, but I'm not sure I want to hear the answers."

His lips twitched. "Fine, then." He patted his pocket, and froze.

"What?" She didn't like the expression on his face.

"My sunscreen is gone. It must have fallen out during the fight."

"Shit. It's not even ten in the morning yet. How are you going to get home? Walk? We don't exactly carry sunscreen for vampires down here, Michael."

"Is there a drugstore nearby?"

"Nothing near a manhole or sewer grate. The closest place is maybe five blocks away."

He stared at her, and there was a question in his eyes that made Keeli want to bury her head under a mountain of pillows to muffle the screams waiting so desperately to come out.

"Why don't I hate you?" Keeli asked him. "I should hate you. You're a vampire."

"You do not strike me as a bigot, Keeli. I think it is poor reasoning to want to become one."

Keeli flushed. "You know what I mean."

"Yes," he said, and there was sadness in his eyes. "I do."

Keeli sighed and patted her pockets. Maybe she still

had money in the other room. She didn't know how much that special stuff cost, but she'd bet it was expensive. "How much sunscreen do you need?"

"One bottle should be enough." Michael reached into his back pocket and removed a worn twenty. "This should cover it. Thank you, Keeli. Maybe you'll see it on the way out."

"Yeah, sure, whatever," she grumbled, taking the money and tucking it away. "You must be the most careless vampire I've ever met."

A cool hand slipped under Keeli's chin, lifting her face until all she saw and felt was Michael—pale and lean, smooth as the river stones littering her bookshelves. The cuts on his face were beginning to fade. His tattoo glittered, golden and smooth. She wanted to touch it, to ask him, "why?"

"I don't hate you," he said.

"I can tell," she answered.

"But it's strange, isn't it?"

"Very." Keeli wanted so badly to touch his skin. It was an aching need, to feel his body sliding beneath her fingers, and she thought, *No one can see me. No one will ever know.*

Slowly, carefully, she rested her palm on Michael's chest. Shivers wracked them both and Keeli gritted her teeth, desperate to hide her violent reaction. Michael's hand dropped away from her chin, slipping around her shoulders to draw her firm against his body. He covered her hand with his own, and pressed gently down.

Keeli rested her forehead against his chest, their joined hands brushing her cheek. She drew in the scent of him, wild and sweet, sharp with the taint of blood. She smelled werewolf on his body: disparate members of her clan, as well as her grandmother. She smelled herself, soaking into his skin. She thought, *maybe I don't care if they know.*

"Why is this happening?" she whispered. "It doesn't make sense. Werewolves and vampires don't mix. Ever."

"Ever?" he echoed, and his voice was thick and deep. "Perhaps they have, and no one ever spoke of it. Or maybe we are the 'ever' that proves everyone wrong."

"I don't want to prove everyone wrong," she mumbled, but still she clung to him, sinking closer into his body, as comfortable as she had ever felt in her life.

As comfortable as I've felt since I was a child, she realized.

"I need to go," she said. She needed to run. She needed to hide and never come near this man again. "Do you want me to call Jenkins while I'm topside?"

"I'll do it," Michael said. "Your grandmother said I could return to use her phone."

"I think she likes you."

"I think she's watching me, and prefers to keep her enemies closer than her friends."

"And are you an enemy?" Keeli looked straight at him.

Some terrible emotion flickered through his eyes. "I have been. To some, I still am. But not now. Not with you or your people."

Keeli pushed away from him, gentle. Michael let her go.

"Do you believe me?" he asked, and though his face was perfectly calm, she heard some subtle urgency in his voice. Or maybe that was wishful thinking on her part.

"I don't know what to believe," she lied, backing out of the bathroom. "I guess you'll just have to try harder."

Michael narrowed his eyes. He dropped the towel in the sink and moved toward her. Startled, Keeli backpedaled, knocking over a stack of books that avalanched around her legs and feet. She tripped on them, yelping as she pitched backward. Michael caught her flailing hands before she could fall and Keeli found herself pulled hard against his chest, his breath hot on her face. His mouth was even hotter on her lips.

"Umph," Keeli said, but she pressed close, opening her mouth to deepen the kiss. She'd always imagined kissing a vampire would be horrible—full with the taste of human blood, disgusting with the promise of death—yet, she tasted nothing but sweetness in Michael's mouth. His lips were firm, hard. Just like any other man's lips.

That's a lie. A lie that would be easier to believe—easier on her heart, her life—but her body would not accept it. Her body, humming with desire, refused to break contact with the man holding her tight, and she found herself clutching his tense shoulders, sliding against his cool skin, savoring the strength within his arms—a killing strength. *But he is a vampire, the Vendix, and he has murdered for his supper.* Keeli dug her nails into his shoulders, pulling herself hard against his body, grappling for more as he skimmed his tongue over her lips, drawing her tighter with a suck, a hot tug, and she wanted more. She wanted *more.*

Keeli felt his fangs brush her lips, felt the sharp tips of teeth, and then heat bloomed inside her mouth and she tasted blood.

Michael broke off their kiss, jerking away as though burned. He touched his mouth with a shaking hand. His bottom lip was wet, crimson.

"I'm sorry," he said.

Keeli ran her tongue against her lip. The tip of it stung. Michael watched her as though he expected retribution. He did not look frightened, only resigned.

But Keeli was not ready to pass judgment. She still wanted him.

You are *a pervert,* she told herself.

She stumbled backward. "I'll return soon. Be careful." The last was added as an afterthought.

"You too," he said, but Keeli didn't know what she had to be careful of, except him.

Chapter Ten

The Grand Dame Alpha was sitting at her desk in front of the fireplace when Michael knocked on the door and entered her room. She wore a silver dressing gown; the reflection of flames danced sleek against its fine silk. She was talking on the phone.

"I'll be sending it to you very soon. Yes, you can expect the courier within the hour. Just tell him to follow the instructions I've written."

She hung up, and looked at Michael, who stood back near the door.

"You may sit down," she said. "Here is the phone you asked after."

"Are you better now?" Michael settled on one of the plush green chairs placed near the fire. The warmth felt good on his body, which was covered up in a man's dark blue dress shirt he had found hanging in Keeli's closet. The discovery of such a shirt made his stomach tighten in an unpleasant manner. Or maybe that was hunger; he didn't know. He didn't want to contemplate the possibility of jealousy.

The Grand Dame Alpha eyed the shirt Michael wore. Her nostrils flared.

"I'm well enough," she said, still staring at the shirt. She tore her gaze away and looked Michael straight in the face. "Thank you for your help."

"It was nothing," he said.

"No." The Grand Dame shook her head. "It was more than nothing. How much more, I don't yet quite know."

Michael reached for the phone. The Grand Dame made as if to leave, but he waved his hand at her chair. "This isn't private. Anything Jenkins tells me you should probably hear."

"Probably," she agreed, still watching him with those sharp eyes.

Jenkins answered on the third ring. Michael heard pots banging, children crying.

"What is it?" Jenkins snapped, and Michael was not entirely sure he was speaking to him.

"It's me," Michael said.

"Oh." A moment later, the sounds of children and kitchen utensils faded. "Sorry about that. My wife is going out of town this morning and everyone is miserable."

Michael waited.

"So, um, yeah. The case. How's that little punk wolf treating you? Bet that was a surprise."

"She's a good partner," Michael said, aware the Grand Dame could hear everything Jenkins said.

"Is she now? I sort of thought—"

"Do you have any news?" Michael interrupted, quite certain he didn't want Jenkins to finish that sentence.

"Small talk is a dying art," he said. "And yes, there is news. Great news. The lab found DNA, Michael. Real fucking DNA. And it's not the victim's."

The Grand Dame stirred; a fingernail tapped her teacup.

"Was it wolf?" Michael asked, watching her.

Jenkins hesitated. "Kind of."

"Kind of? As in, kind of pregnant? Or how about kind of dead?"

"Smart-ass. The lab is pretty sure it belongs to a wolf. The problem is that there are some vampire traces, too. We got the evidence from under the victim's fingernails. Skin was whole, no signs of decay into ash."

"All dead skin cells from vampires turn to ash," Michael said. "If it were solid, then it couldn't have come from a vampire."

"I agree. The techies don't know what to make of it. Right now, their best guess is that another vampire was present at, or just before, the murder. Maybe it contaminated the evidence in some way."

Michael sighed. He felt the Grand Dame watching him as he said, "But you've confirmed some kind of werewolf involvement. Any chance it's a mistake?"

"This DNA may be screwy, but there are definite werewolf markers. Now, did a werewolf cause the death? Was a vampire involved? I can't confirm anything, Michael. But I'd bet my whole year's salary that a wolf did the deed. I can't explain the vampire DNA, though. Like the techies said, could be the victim got in a fight just before his death. If so, someone should remember."

"You have an idea of just who that 'someone' is?"

Michael could hear Jenkins smile. "We finally got an ID on the body. The fang's name was Walter Crestin. A veteran of the civil war. The *first* civil war. Favorite hang-out? The Bloody Pulp."

Michael sat back in his chair. The Bloody Pulp was a popular—but not much talked about—establishment in the Crimson Light district. Vampires only, where humans were served to the clientele from behind the bar. Michael had been there three times in the last six months, always on business.

"Michael?"

"I know the place," he said quietly. "Have you sent anyone down there yet?" But Michael already knew the answer. He wondered if his sword would be enough this time.

"You know we haven't. None of the other liaisons are willing, and even if they were, you're the only vampire we trust."

"I'm not sure that's wise."

"It's nothing to do with wisdom. It's all about gut instinct, man. Besides, they're scared of you down there."

The regulars at The Bloody Pulp would talk easier if they weren't scared, but Michael did not say that. He also did not say that he might end up dead if he walked through those doors for a fourth time. It didn't really matter in the long run. He had a job to do, and it was going to kill him eventually, whether or not he died working for the vampires or the humans—or in this case, the werewolves, too.

"I'll go, Jenkins."

"The sooner, the better. Remember, we're not even supposed to be on this case. Heat's gonna come down from above eventually, and right now, no one's responding to my questions. Vampires aren't saying a word, and the werewolves are even more tight-lipped. I want to know why this crime is so different, why I can't get answers from *anyone*. Because, trust me—this keeps up, and every wolf will be coming in for DNA tests. We've got evidence to compare suspects against now. No more excuses or stalling. So give me something, Michael. *Anything*. I need to be able to say that the wolves are cooperating, that there's progress on this case."

"I'm with the wolves," Michael said, looking at the Grand Dame. "I will get you what you need."

Her expression darkened.

"Keeli, too. Remember what we talked about, those connections of hers."

Michael felt the Grand Dame staring at him. "I would rather not talk about it. I'll call you tonight, Jenkins."

Michael hung up the phone and settled back in his chair. The Grand Dame did the same, her palms pressed together, fingertips touching her chin.

"So," she said.

"So." Michael met the Grand Dame's cool gaze. "Which of your wolves would have the strength, speed, and motivation to kill and eat a vampire?"

"You waste no time." A bitter smile flitted across her mouth. "But you have had a demonstration of all three characteristics. Would you like the names of your assailants?"

"I am not a vengeful person." Michael hardened his voice. "You know your wolves better than I do, and as I'm sure you can appreciate, time is of the essence. If you can narrow down the possibilities—"

"I understand the situation perfectly," she snapped. "But you're asking me to implicate my own people. I have a responsibility to them."

"And what's your responsibility to a murderer? There have already been six deaths. I do not know how many more can be tolerated before there is a backlash. That cannot be allowed."

Throwing the Grand Dame's words back into her face was not what Michael had planned, but he had to make her compromise on this. He did not have time to question everyone—nor did it make sense to do so. The Grand Dame Alpha knew her wolves. She knew what they were capable of. Earlier, he had planned on asking Keeli for this information, but she was not here—*don't think of her; don't think of her lips pressed tight and hot on your lips, the taste of her blood like fire, like spice, like freedom*—and he had passed all caring about politeness.

The Grand Dame stared into the fire for a long time. Finally, she said, "Very few Maddox wolves would be able to murder a vampire. Fight them, yes. Inflict deep wounds. But to consume, to plot and prey . . ." She shook her head. "It could have been in self-defense."

"We will find that out," Michael promised, though he seriously doubted her theory.

Her lips tightened into a hard line. She reached for pen and paper, and began writing. "There are over eighty wolves in the Maddox pack, but a large number of those are children and young people. It has been a good season for us." Michael heard the tight pride in her voice. "As for the adults, I can think of only three who would be capable of murdering this Walter Crestin."

She slid the paper across the table. Michael read the names.

Estella Kinsay
Jonathon Dewey
Jas Mack

"Why?" he asked, still eyeing that last name.

"Because each of them has been hurt in profound ways by vampires. Terrible things have been done to them and the ones they love, and there has been no justice. None."

"Tell me," he said, but the Grand Dame shook her head.

"They are their stories to tell. Stories, I think, you will be very interested to hear."

There was knowledge in her voice, her eyes. Michael's cheek hurt. He said, "You know what I do."

"I asked," she admitted, and pushed back her chair. She stood, and Michael rose with her. "Where is Keeli?"

"There are things I need, things only I can get. But I can't leave here during the day without certain . . . protection. She went to buy me some."

The Grand Dame did not look pleased. "You have her running errands?"

"I would do the same for her," he said, embarrassed.

Silence followed—deep, profound. The Grand Dame's gaze never once faltered as she said, "Your breath smells like my granddaughter."

Oh.

"You've touched her with your mouth."

Oh.

"And you're wearing her father's shirt."

Michael resisted the urge to close his eyes. "I didn't know this shirt belonged to her father," he said, unable to address his other business with Keeli. "My own clothing—"

"Yes," she said in a tight voice. "I remember." The Grand Dame walked past Michael and disappeared into her bedroom. A moment later she returned with a bottle of green liquid. Mouthwash. She handed it to him.

"Use this before you leave my rooms. I do not want my wolves smelling Keeli on your breath."

Her tone made him angry. "We did nothing wrong."

"Wrong?" she snapped. "There's nothing more wrong! Do you know what would happen to Keeli if the others found out? Her reputation would never survive. *She* might not survive. Such alliances are not tolerated."

"I would protect her," he said, forgetting himself, his place.

"How? By taking her away from us? From her people? And what of the vampires? What would they do if they knew?"

"Nothing," Michael said through gritted teeth. "They would assume that the humiliation of such a union would be punishment enough."

"Ah." The Grand Dame's smile was cold, mocking. "I suppose that the consequences are tolerable to you, then. Since you have already been shunned and humiliated by your own people."

Michael forced himself to take a deep breath. "I would never want that for Keeli."

"Then we have an understanding." The Grand Dame glided close, blue eyes bright and sharp. "You act like an honorable man. Make it more than an act."

He remembered Keeli's lips, the press of her body tight against his own, the comfort of holding her, like coming home. The only home, the first home.

But she is a werewolf. It will never last. You cannot allow it to last.

Michael took the mouthwash to the Grand Dame's bathroom and rinsed Keeli's taste away.

But not the memory. Nothing could take that from him.

"The things I do," Keeli muttered, stepping around some wannabe human punks who were sitting on the sidewalk in front of the drugstore. Their tattoos were cheaper than their piercings, which meant they looked like little kids who'd drawn on their arms with fat black markers and stuck aluminum foil into their eyebrows and noses. Keeli tried not to breathe as she passed through the cloud of smoke they were generating.

Those brats are smoking enough weed to give this whole neighborhood a high.

"Cool hair," drawled one girl, as Keeli put her hand on the door.

"Thanks," she said, and then: "You're gonna fry your brain, sweet cheeks."

Laughter, all around. "It's medicinal," said the girl, grinning like an idiot. She lay down on the sidewalk, propped up on one elbow, and stuck the joint back in her mouth.

The drugstore was just like any other franchise operation in the inner city—dirty, small, and dark—with only a passing resemblance to a drugstore she might see in the tamer suburbs. Both the pharmacist and the front-counter clerk were protected by bulletproof glass, which basically meant that if Keeli wanted to shoplift or rob the place, there wasn't anyone who was going to stop her. Not that she had crime on her mind. But from the looks of the bare shelves, it seemed that others did—and had.

"Sunscreen?" she asked the bored young clerk, whose long black hair was in desperate need of a wash. "Vampire variety."

He suddenly looked more interested. Keeli didn't miss the way he checked out her neck. "Far right. Back shelf, along the wall. You can't miss it."

Which, as Keeli soon found, was because it was the only area that hadn't been picked over or looted. She found a bottle of their strongest stuff, whistling at the price. Twenty bucks would cover it, but just barely. It was a good thing vampires had money.

Or at least, most of them did. Keeli thought about Michael's apartment, the simple way he lived. Like a poor man. A man used to poverty. Working class, even.

She touched her lips, remembering the taste of him.

Dangerous, a voice whispered inside her mind. *You're walking the edge now.*

Walking it, crossing it, diving headfirst over it. She didn't know what the hell she was doing.

On the way out, she passed some lycanthropy meds. Crank stuff if it was over-the-counter, but she looked anyway. None of the assorted pills and injections promised to vaccinate—most of it was just treatment of symptoms. *Live Like a Normal Human!* promised the brand Anti-Ly. *Your Friends Will Never Know.*

Yeah. Easier said than done. Infecting a human with lycanthropy—whether on purpose or by accident—was a major crime. Entire clans got punished—both with fines and by losing one of their own, usually permanently, to the legal system. And then there was the victim to deal with, who almost never wanted to leave behind his human life for the underground. It was worse if there were family involved. Kids just didn't understand why daddy or mommy had to make all those changes in their lives—or why suddenly a parent went missing, without explanation.

"Daddy had to go away," a mother might say, bundling her kids off to live in another state. "Daddy loves you, but he's different now."

Daddy can't be here. Daddy's a werewolf. Daddy might eat you for his supper.

Daddy, Keeli thought sadly. *Daddy, what happened?*

Keeli walked away from the lycanthropy meds, from the illusion of control. Control could not be bottled. Control could not be sold. Control over the wolf had to be earned, and then—maybe—you could live topside permanently. It just took time. Sacrifice.

The wolf cannot be pushed aside. It must come out.

Keeli shivered. She still tasted rage, bittersweet power, lovely and furious. So easy, to become trapped in that satisfaction. Too easy.

It's in your blood. Mad dog. Berserker. Red would be your favorite color if the others had their way. When the wolf is on you, it's the only color they think you see.

Yeah. That was the simple taunt, the most common joke. People had been telling that one for so long, it wasn't even funny to them anymore. And now what would they say, now that she was working for the Man, and her partner was a vampire? A vampire who was the best damn kisser she'd ever met.

And you still don't think your life has unraveled? That's a good one.

Keeli paid for the sunscreen. As the clerk dug around the cash register for her change, she glanced down at a pile of local newspapers stacked on the floor. Her gaze was instantly drawn to the small indie paper, *Howl*, written exclusively for and by werewolves in the city community. On the cover, inserted just below the main headline (alerting the werewolf community to the ongoing political debates about the new FDA-required employee blood tests), she read:

THE LAST SCION OF MADDOX IN JAIL—
AND MAKING DEALS WITH THE POLICE?
by Brian O'Dell

Face it, my friendly furries, there's a double standard around the town. We all know it. There isn't a one of us who hasn't been sniffed, prodded, or collared by the Man. But hey, at least it was an equal opportunity screw-down—no celebrity treatment for us wolves, right?

Wrong. Just last night, Keeli Maddox—the mysterious granddaughter of Crimson City's Grand Dame Alpha, and the sole survivor of a vicious attack that destroyed most of that infamous bloodline—was arrested for baring fang to a human. Sources verify our hotheaded Miss Maddox attacked a human man in direct response to an attempted rape. Go, girl!

That's where the story should end, right? That's where it ended for all the other wolves languishing in jail. Not so for Miss Maddox! She only spent one night in a holding cell, and then was released to her clan bright and early this morning. Oh, the shame! Was Miss Maddox the recipient of preferential treatment because of her relationship with the Grand Dame Alpha? Would our esteemed leader stoop so low?

Maybe. Little is known about Keeli Maddox, except that she has spent most of her life on the fringe of the werewolf community. Her own people have called her troubled, a reputation no doubt fostered by her family's history of violent behavior. . . .

The article went on, but Keeli stopped reading. She wanted to puke. It was highly unusual for the gossip rags to tackle her grandmother—the wolves usually had more respect, as well as a good dose of fear—but Keeli, it seemed, was fair game. And she was dragging her grandmother's good name in the mud.

Shit. It figures. Brian did see something in that file on Jenkins's desk.

But come *on*. The article practically accused the Grand Dame Alpha of violating clan trust to pull strings for her granddaughter. Keeli had expected her own reputation to go to hell for her actions, but not her grandmother's. The only thing she was grateful for was that Brian didn't seem to know about her participation in the ongoing police investigation, or her partnership with the vampire. The last thing she needed was to be called a fang-banger.

Keeli's cheeks flushed. Dammit. Maybe she already was a fang-banger. Just . . . without the banging.

She waved the newspaper at the clerk. "When did this come in?"

He shrugged. "About an hour ago."

Shoot me now.

Keeli paid for the paper and left the drugstore. The little punks were gone. Jas stood in their place. Bastard had tracked her. Perfect.

"I do not need this right now," she said, blowing past him.

"Too bad," he growled. "I want to know what the hell is going on with you and that fang."

"None of your business." Keeli marched down the street, pink hair blowing back wild from her face. People took one good look and got out of her way. She wanted to laugh. If she looked how she felt—and she probably did—then even Keeli would be making room for her on the sidewalk. Scary.

Jas caught up with her, grabbed her arm, swung her around. "Tell me, Keeli. What does that fang have on you?"

"What does he have on me?" Keeli threw up her hands. "You think I've done something worthy of blackmail? That I *could* be blackmailed? Thanks a lot, you jerk."

"Then why—" Jas stopped, abrupt. His nostrils flared. He made a strange choking sound. "You smell like him. Keeli, your breath—"

Keeli's hand flew up to her mouth.

"You *kissed* him," Jas hissed, leaning close. His hand, clamped around Keeli's arm, squeezed so hard she fought not to cry out.

"You're hurting me," she said.

He looked as though he did not care, but his grip loosened and he stood back from her. The distance did not help. His body shook, the threat of violence washing over her senses; his scent, his eyes, the wolf hair pushing through his skin. All of him, screaming.

"Are you his whore?" he whispered. His hand twitched. Keeli wanted to hit him. Instead, she bared her neck, twisting to show him her unblemished skin.

"Satisfied?" Keeli leaned close. Her canines brushed

her bottom lip. "You ever talk like that to me again, Jas Mack, and I will slap you down so hard they'll be picking you up ten years from now."

Hurt flickered in his eyes, disappearing with a blink, a breath. "How could you do this, Keeli? I thought I knew you."

"Don't give me that, Jas. You know me just fine. Don't treat me like a criminal just because of the people I spend time with."

"They are criminals. Animals. How could you treat the vampires as anything else, especially after Emily—"

"I'm sorry for that," Keeli interrupted gently. "You know I am, Jas. But Michael isn't—"

"Stop. Don't you dare." His voice broke. The scar on his face stood out in sharp relief against his red face. He breathed, "Why?"

And Keeli said, "I don't know."

Chapter Eleven

Keeli showed Jas the newspaper as they walked down the gritty sidewalk toward home. He read the article, grunted, and tossed it back at her.

"I don't feel sorry for you."

"Thanks a lot. But that's not why I showed it to you. This could get Granny May in trouble."

Jas raised an eyebrow. "What makes you think I care? I'm close to challenge, in case you hadn't noticed."

Keeli narrowed her eyes. "I've known you since you were nothing more than a scrawny pimple-faced pup on Rollerblades, trying to impress the girls. You gave me piggyback rides on those skates, if I remember correctly. You've never been cruel until now. You've never shown my grandmother the kind of disrespect I saw today. You *love* her. Or at least, I thought you did. What happened?"

"You already know," he said. "I think you're sleeping with one of my reasons."

"Screw you," she said. "Tell me the truth."

"I am. It's disgusting, these negotiations. Helping the

vampires? We should let the humans take them out if they can. Save us the trouble."

"And then what?" Keeli stopped walking, craning her neck to look him in the eyes. "You know once they're through with the vampires, they'll come after us. Probably won't even be any public opposition. At least the vampires have money and groupies on their side. We've got nothing but dirt, fur, and fang. We need this, Jas. Just as much as the vampires do. Maybe more. Shit. Even the ACLU backs off werewolf issues."

"I've heard of this Michael," Jas said, moving past Keeli. "If you think sleeping with the vampires will help your grandmother get a good deal, then you're banging the wrong fang."

"You're disgusting."

"Keep talking. The irony is killing me."

She jogged to catch up with him. "You didn't used to be like this, Jas," she repeated.

"That was before Emily."

Keeli looked away. "I heard there was some news about her, but I didn't have time to stop by."

"We're expecting our first child in May."

Her breath caught. "That's wonderful, Jas."

"Yeah," he said, swallowing hard. "But this vampire thing has gotten Emily really upset. I can't stand to see her this way, Keeli. Not after everything she's been through. I'm . . . I'm worried she's going to lose the baby."

"Maybe I could talk to her."

"You stay away. She doesn't know about your vampire yet. I don't want her to know. Emily still likes you. I want that to last as long as possible."

Hurt blossomed in Keeli's chest, along with new clarity, an agonizing understanding of the truth.

"You're doing this for her," she said. "All of it. You would kill the Grand Dame Alpha just to see the negotiations fail. You would kill the vampires too, if you could. To make Emily feel safe."

"Wouldn't you do the same," he said quietly, "if it were the person you loved?"

"I don't know what I'd do," she said, "but this isn't right, Jas. What you're stirring up with Granny May. The way you act toward me."

"And your vampire? How should I act toward him?"

Keeli sighed, gazing up at the sky, silver with smog. "He's not *my* vampire. And even I don't know how to act toward him. What I do know is that he isn't like the others. Or at least, he's different than what I expected."

"Different enough that you're kissing him? That's some difference, Keeli. How long have you known him?"

"Last night was the first time I ever laid eyes on him."

Jas looked stunned. "It took three weeks of dating before you kissed me."

Keeli just looked at him, and Jas shook his head. "You think a vampire is more attractive than a werewolf. Shit, Keeli."

"You started this."

"No. *You* did. I just hope you know what you're doing."

"Right back at you. Please, Jas. Don't challenge Granny May. Not over this."

"Will you stop kissing that vamp? Will you stop investigating our people for the murder of a vampire?"

Keeli remembered the feel of Michael's body pressed hard against her own. The liquid warmth of his dark eyes, the touch of his mouth. His courage, his comfort. So new, so dangerous. She thought of her promises.

Deeper and deeper.

Jas shook his head at her silence, lips pressed into a tight white line. "Okay, then. But if you run apart—"

"Don't you dare finish that," Keeli said.

"—you *stay* apart."

They reached the entrance to the tunnels, a steel grate door set in the ground at the end of an alley. It was placed behind a used bookstore, Share, a familiar haunt that tugged at Keeli's heart as soon as she set eyes on its weather-beaten back door. She had spent wonderful hours in that place, hidden in the embrace of old dusty books.

That had been another time, another place. Perhaps, even, another person.

Jas lifted up the grate and held it open for her. She landed light on her feet in the tunnel below. The scent of damp concrete tickled her nose. Luckily, there were no other scents. Several times a week, cleaning crews from the clan went through the exposed portions of the tunnels to pick up trash or hose down the floor with bleach and water to erase the scent of human piss. It was amazing how often humans liked to use an open grate as a toilet.

"Don't let the others smell your breath," Jas said, as they walked down the tunnel into darkness.

"I didn't think you cared." When he remained silent, she sighed. "I don't see how it matters, Jas. Their reactions can't be any worse than yours."

"They can be worse, Keeli. Just . . . don't."

She almost argued with him, but they reached the main break and took a left toward the core. There were more wolves here. Jas kept his body between them and Keeli; he refused to stop even when hands went up in greeting. More werewolves seemed to be happy to see her than not, although Keeli didn't miss several hard stares, nor could she ignore the whispers that rose behind her like a cloud of mosquitoes, out for blood.

Uneasiness filled her. Just how bad would their reactions be if they knew what she was doing with Michael, how deeply he was sinking into her life? Would they learn to accept her, or would it be too much? Did she face exile?

Do you even have to ask? You know how unforgiving wolves can be. How deep the anger runs.

Yes. She knew.

"Do you know if it's a boy or girl?" Keeli said, unable to stand the thoughts in her head, desperate for distraction.

"It's too early," Jas said, "but we're calling it a girl to make things easier. We're still trying to decide on names."

"Do you know if she'll be full wolf or mix?"

Jas shook his head. Keeli would have asked more, but shouts rang out, echoing off the tunnel walls. She and Jas broke into a run, bursting around a curve in the corridor just in time to see a tall blond woman take a swing at a very familiar vampire. Several werewolves surrounded them, cheering.

"Not again," muttered Keeli, lunging forward. Jas caught the back of her shirt, yanking hard.

"Remember what we talked about." He tapped his lips. "I'll take of this. Get that vampire out of here until things calm down."

"Thanks," she said, but Jas gave her a hard look.

"I'm not doing this for you, Keeli. Don't forget that. As long as you're with *him*, you're nothing better than a whore."

Keeli was the kind of girl who made good on her threats, but she was still taken off guard, and could do nothing more than swing away from him, stung. She turned her face so Jas would not see her reaction, and met Michael's gaze. That was enough to make her forget the pain for one precious instant. He watched her, even while dodging another blow to his healing face.

The remnants of that wound made her remember his voice, his words: *"I'm a firm believer in the beauty of symmetry."* A strange memory.

"Symmetry," she whispered, still hearing his voice inside her head. The property of being the same on both sides of a central dividing line—in this case, the line dividing their two races.

But we're not the same, she thought, forgetting Jas's advice and heading toward Michael. *And that's one big mofo of a line.*

Jas reached Michael, stepping between the vampire and the woman attacking him. When she turned, Keeli recognized her and quietly groaned.

"Estella," Jas said. "Back off."

Estella's lips pulled back in a snarl, which did nothing to ruin the perfection of her face. "I don't care what the Grand Dame wants, Jas. I won't be questioned by this . . . this *thing*. He accused me of murdering a vampire!"

"I did no such thing." Michael's voice was low, hard. "I simply wanted to know where you were last night and what you were doing."

"Knitting," the blonde drawled, then glanced over Jas's shoulder at Keeli. "Oh, *you*. Your company leaves something to be desired, Keeli."

"Take him and get out of here," Jas ordered, turning his head to look Keeli in the eye. "Do it."

"Say please," she snapped.

"You wouldn't like it if I did." Jas glanced at Michael. "Wrong place, wrong time, fang. Get out now while the going is good."

"Fine. But I will need to question Estella later. You, as well."

A muscle twitched in Jas's face. Michael stepped close. In a quiet voice he added, "We also have much to discuss about your habit of name-calling." His gaze flickered sideways to Keeli, who blinked, startled.

The two men stared at each other and Keeli wanted to say *No, stop, not now*—and perhaps they heard her. Or perhaps their own minds were thinking the same, though the rigid line of Jas's spine and the darkness in Michael's cool eyes said they were ready. But after a tense moment they stepped apart. Keeli released her breath, noticing the other werewolves, even Estella, quietly sighing too.

Michael moved away from Estella, slow and unafraid. As though he was doing her a favor. He stood near Keeli. She smelled peppermint. Antiseptic. Mouthwash.

"Later," Jas said. Michael nodded, and then he and Keeli walked away down the long corridor, from the wolves staring holes into their backs.

"Are you all right?" he asked quietly, when they were completely alone.

Keeli wanted to kick him in the balls. Instead, she said, "Fine. And you? How's your breath?"

Michael blinked. Keeli took some satisfaction in taking him off guard.

"Your . . . I . . . thought it would be best if the other werewolves didn't smell you on me. I didn't want to cause you trouble."

"I'm already in trouble," Keeli said, slightly mollified. "Jas scented you on me. We had words."

Michael tensed. "He called you a whore."

"Yeah," she said, suddenly unable to look at him. She heard anger in his voice and it made her uncomfortable. She did not want him to be angry. Not for her.

"Keeli." His fingers grazed her arm and she suppressed a shiver. "I'm sorry."

"Don't be." Keeli walked faster, trying to create some distance. Michael caught up with her.

"Did he hurt you?"

"No," she snapped, whirling on him. But Michael raised his hand, slow, and Keeli could not bring herself to move when he touched her cheek. His fingertips were cool.

"Words can be pain," he said gently. "Words can be worse."

His voice cut. Keeli struggled to control her face, but it was difficult. She was not a girl who discussed her feelings—who even thought about feelings. But here, now, with Michael—

"We should get out of the hall," she whispered.

His breath caught, hand falling away from her cheek. They started walking again. They did not touch, but touch was unnecessary. Keeli could have felt Michael beside her with eyes shut, nose, and ears plugged tight.

"Here's your sunscreen." She gave him the bag and dug his change from her pocket. She also gave him her copy of *Howl* and tapped the first page.

"Trouble," she said. "For me, anyway."

She heard voices echo off the corridor walls, and steeled herself. When they passed the werewolves, the men and women fell silent, giving Keeli—and especially Michael—confused looks that were also uneasy. Keeli greeted them, and Michael tore his gaze away from the paper long enough to do the same. Everyone was polite, distant, and then the moment passed and Keeli and Michael were alone again.

Michael touched Keeli's shoulder. "You can breathe now."

"Was I that obvious?"

He shrugged. "No one likes to fight."

"Strange. Lately, that seems to be all I'm doing."

Michael tapped the newspaper. "What does this mean to your grandmother?"

"Nothing, I hope. But the clans are equally divided on

whether we should be negotiating with the vampires. Some of the lesser Alphas have even suggested that we approach the rogue element in the government to combine forces."

"I can't imagine humans agreeing to that. And even if they did, after the vampires are gone or are under control, werewolves will be the next logical target."

"Unfortunately, not everyone thinks that'll happen. Can you believe, there're some who are saying that by attacking the vampires first, humans have declared that werewolves are . . . how do I say this . . . more 'human' than the fangs."

Michael sighed. "Vampires were attacked first because they're more powerful than werewolves, politically and economically. We're also more popular with young people."

"Old people, too, I bet. You guys may not be completely immortal, but when you can count on your youth lasting almost a millennia, who's going to care?"

Michael did not smile. "They have no idea what that means, what the price is for youth."

"There's a price for everything. For my grandmother, I think the price of these negotiations may be her leadership over the clans."

"That would be . . . shortsighted."

"The clans would call it survival. You probably already figured this out, but physical strength isn't the only thing that matters in choosing an Alpha. If a werewolf contests leadership and the majority don't believe he or she would make a better Alpha than the current one, there will be no fight. There just won't. The challenger would never be allowed to lift a hand. But if the challenger is considered a good choice for leadership, then it does come down to a fight. Winner takes all. In this case, Maddox would get a new Alpha—and Maddox, by being the strongest clan in the city, would continue its leadership over the rest."

"And if the other Alphas don't like it?"

"They don't have a choice. Not unless they want to risk a civil war. There's precedent for that, but not in a long time."

Michael held up the paper. "So the goings-on in Maddox are especially interesting for everyone."

"Unfortunately."

Michael looked displeased. "I'm going to talk to Jenkins about leaks in his department."

"Don't bother. The guy who wrote that article didn't need to talk to anyone to piss all over my grandmother's reputation."

"And yours," Michael said.

Keeli laughed. "My reputation is already shot to hell."

It was the wrong thing to say; she felt him tense, coil into something hard and still. Keeli did not know why Michael seemed to care about her reputation—why he seemed to care at all what happened to her—but it was clear that he did, that he felt responsible. Bizarre.

But she kind of liked it.

"Why did you start questioning wolves on your own?" she asked, changing the subject. "That was dangerous, Michael. You should have waited for me."

"I thought it would be better if you weren't there for the questioning. I don't want your clan to start thinking of you as an outsider or enemy. I don't want them to mistrust you, simply because of your association with me."

"I promised you I would help, Michael. We're partners in this."

"And when the partnership is over?" He took a deep breath. "I'm already an outcast amongst my people. I don't want that for you."

A sharp bark of laughter escaped Keeli's throat. "You let me worry about that."

"I forgot," he said quietly. "You never run."

"Never. Not even when I want to."

Silence, and then: "I have something to tell you."

Keeli listened to the evidence about the mixed DNA, and by the time they reached her room, she was ready to run, and run far. Life was getting way too confusing.

"Could this be a double-team?" Keeli asked, closing her door. She skirted her books and sat down on the edge of the bed. It was the only place to sit in her room. Keeli had never been one for company. If she wanted to hang out with friends, she went elsewhere. Her room was kept safe for dreams and words.

Michael remained standing. He looked uncomfortable. "I thought of that, but it's difficult to imagine a vampire and werewolf together conspiring to kill another vampire."

"What would be the motive?" Keeli wondered out loud. "I mean, we know why you and I are working together, but what else could drive our kind to cooperate?"

"Perhaps a vampire committed the murder, and the werewolf came after and fed on the body."

Keeli shuddered. "Werewolves don't eat the dead, not even when the wolf is in complete control. Wolves in the wild may go for carrion, but not us. Not ever."

"Then that means a werewolf did murder Crestin. And that he had an unfriendly encounter with a vampire sometime before—"

"Or during—"

"—his death."

Keeli leaned back on her elbows. "So what do we do? Collect DNA samples from all the wolves and match them up to what Jenkins has? That's going to be impossible, Michael." She frowned, shaking her head. "I hate to say it, but I think we're going to need more help. Can Jenkins supply extra men?"

Michael turned away from her; he looked like he was

reading the spines of her books, but Keeli knew better. There was too much tension in his shoulders, the hard line of his jaw.

"Michael," she warned. He glanced at her from over his shoulder. His eyes were dark.

"This investigation was never supposed to happen, Keeli. We're it."

"God. We're screwed."

Michael briefly closed his eyes. "Your confidence in this matter is astounding."

"You bet it's astounding. It's so astounding I'm about ready to beat your head in. What do you mean, we're all there is? What the hell is going on here, Michael?"

"Politics," he said, finally turning to face her. "There are people who no longer have a vested interest in seeing crimes against either of our kinds solved. I'm sure you can understand why."

"Shit. Michael, what if we're going about this the wrong way? What if humans murdered Crestin, and all the other vampires? What if the DNA Jenkins found was placed there deliberately?"

"It crossed my mind." He looked tired, almost haggard. "But that means they're trying to frame werewolves. I don't know why they would do that. Not unless they're trying to hide their own tracks from the media or lower police echelon."

"Or if they're trying to set up a war between vampires and werewolves. A distraction. A fight from two sides, while they move in to pick off your people."

"I wish you hadn't said that," Michael told her. He sat down beside her on the bed. "I also thought of that, but hearing it out loud . . ."

"It makes sense."

"Yes." He rubbed his face; Keeli saw his fingers linger over the gold tattoo. "All right, then. We treat it as a possibility, but not the first possibility. Let's absolve your people first, and then we go after evidence of human involvement. If I could present something to Jenkins . . ."

"You'll ruin his life if you do that."

His mouth tightened. "The walls are closing in, Keeli. I am accustomed to taking care of only myself, but in this situation, when so many are in danger . . ."

"We take care of each other," she said softly. And then, because she felt awkward, added, "All of us, vampires and werewolves. This alliance is important, Michael. We've got to make sure our sides come together, no matter what. We've got to find a way of protecting ourselves that doesn't lower us to the level of those human bastards."

"That may not be possible, Keeli." He touched her wrists, still bandaged from the silver burns. "Terrible things happen in war. And these humans who want us dead . . . they are not fighting for fun. They fight because they believe it is a matter of survival. Us against them." He paused, still touching her. "Them against us. So what will you do? What will you do to survive?"

"Fight to win," she said, feeling sick. "No matter what."

Michael nodded. For a long minute they sat in silence, until: "Your grandmother said there are very few wolves in your clan with the strength and motivation to kill a vampire. She gave me their names. There were only three."

"Estella," Keeli said, relieved he was changing the subject. "I bet Jas is on that list, too."

"And a Jonathon Dewey."

"Ah. It all makes sense now." Keeli shook her head. "I forgot about him. His mother was murdered by vampires. She was human. Wrong place, wrong time. Emily was there, too. She survived, but just barely. She's . . . never been quite the same."

"Emily?"

"Jas's human wife. Estella's best friend. And Estella, Jas, and Jonathon all know how to hold a grudge. Of course, with what happened, I can't blame them."

Shadows moved within Michael's eyes. He said, "Do they know who the responsible vampires are?"

"Never found out. It was late and everyone was walking home from dinner. Jas was running behind because he forgot to leave a tip. He heard the screams. Managed to save Emily, but got that scar on his face in the fight. The vampire had a silver knife, shaped like a crucifix. He tried to gouge out Jas's eye, but missed."

Michael looked angry. "Did they report this attack to the Primary Assembly?"

"My grandmother went in person. She was turned away. Was told that the matter would be handled."

Something very cold and cruel filled Michael's face—a mask, or perhaps the real heart of him, filling out his skin. Keeli wanted to slide away, or hide her eyes. Instead, she forced herself to watch the transformation, the brittle edge of Michael's spirit sharpening itself on fury.

"I should have been told about this, and the fact that I was not, that they kept it quiet . . ." He shook his head. "I should expect this. It should not surprise me. I do my job; I kill the vampires they want killed. I do the dirty work no one else will touch, and still . . . still . . ."

"You hate it," she interrupted, unable to bear the anger and frustration in his voice. "You hate what you do."

"The justice of it is all that matters to me," he replied, but as Keeli waited, silent, she sensed him curl up on himself, retreat, and she tried to reconcile what little she knew—roses and scars and kisses, sweet—

"Is this the reason you're an outcast?"

"One reason," he said. His voice chilled her, made her want to ask what the other reasons were. She kept her mouth shut. She did not truly want to know. Not now. She had her own secrets.

But she could not think of anything else to say, so she simply looked at him—at his face, his throat, running her gaze over his shoulders, the lean breadth of his chest. Michael looked good in blue. Very good.

Her breath caught. "You're wearing my father's shirt."

Michael rose quickly from the bed. "I'm sorry. I meant to change before you returned. I did not know it was important to you until your grandmother told me."

"It's not important," she said faintly. "I'm glad it's getting some use." Seeing the shirt outside her closet, on another man, made Keeli feel strange. Numb. She looked away.

"Keeli," Michael said, but she scooted off the bed and moved away from him.

"You said you need to get some things from your home. Or was that trip to the drugstore just a way of getting rid of me?"

"No," he said, quiet. She could not read his expression. "I need to eat. I also need weapons."

"The wolves have you running scared?" Her voice sounded rough, hard.

"Not the wolves." A bitter smile tugged at his lips. "Vampires. Jenkins said Walter Crestin liked to spend time at The Bloody Pulp. I need to go there tonight and ask some questions. Explore why there were traces of another vampire on this murder victim."

"Don't go there without me."

"No." Michael moved close. Keeli struggled not to touch him. "The last time I was there it was to enforce the law. I barely made it out alive. They're not going to be happy seeing me again."

"All the more reason to have someone watch your back."

Michael shook his head. "So stubborn."

"Yes," Keeli said. "And I keep my promises."

"Not this time." Michael took out his bottle of sunscreen and began applying generous amounts to his face, throat, and hands.

"Just try and stop me," she said, and then frowned as he capped the bottle. "What about the rest of you? That shirt isn't made to protect a vampire from UV."

"I'll make do."

Keeli hesitated. "Take off the shirt."

"That seems to be your favorite thing to say. Are you looking for excuses to see me naked?"

"In your dreams. Now do it."

"Fine," he muttered, unbuttoning the shirt. "You do realize that no one else treats me like this."

"Must be your charming personality." Her mouth snapped shut when she saw Michael's injury. The bite glared red and ugly.

"You're not healed," she said, noting how the scratches on his face had all but disappeared.

"Werewolf bites heal slow. I need blood." Michael attempted to fold the shirt. Keeli snatched it from him and dropped it on the bed.

"You take it straight from humans?" She squeezed sunscreen on her palm.

Michael touched her chin. Her gaze flew up to meet his dark eyes.

No," he said. "Not for a long time."

She had not realized how important it was for him to say that until she heard the words. Relief filled her. She pulled away from his touch, but a moment later pressed her wet palms to his chest. Michael went very still.

Keeli cleared her throat. "This won't take long."

She tried her best to smooth on the sunscreen in a detached, clinical, manner. She tried her best to ignore

Michael's long lean lines of muscle, the cool pale strength of his arms hanging loose at his sides. She tried her best to ignore his heartbeat, strong and solid beneath her sliding hands—tried also not to look into his dark eyes, dangerous with intent. She tried her best to ignore everything about Michael and found she could not.

Her hands slipped lower. Michael touched her wrists.

"Keeli." He sounded hoarse.

"I know," she whispered. "Turn around."

Michael turned. Keeli slathered on the rest of the sunscreen. It was easier when she knew he could not watch her. She did not have to hide her face. She did not have to hide what she was feeling.

Her fingers slid up his spine, flaring out to trace the sharp bones of his shoulders, dipping under his wings. He had a beautiful back, perfect in form, masculine in ways she had never seen. No gym for this man. The only thing that had sculpted his body was life.

Keeli listened to his breathing change, a perfect partner to her own as she stepped close, spreading sunscreen up his sides, rubbing the edge of his ribs with her fingertips.

"This can't go on," Michael murmured.

"I know," Keeli breathed. The sunscreen had long been absorbed into her skin and his. She had no excuse to touch him, but could not stop. Brazen, crazy, stupid.

But it was not lust. Lust was there, but stronger still was some unfathomable attraction that felt like the inevitable descent of a stone falling to earth or the tug of the tides to the moon. Keeli was not strong enough to fight the pull. In the beginning—last night, their first meeting—she could have pulled away. She could have walked from Michael without a backward glance then—though wondering, always remembering their strange encounter. The longer she spent in his company, though, the closer she felt. Bound, gently. Inexplicably.

"How much do you know?" Michael turned in her arms. "Do you know what will happen to you if the others find out? Do you know what you're risking? This can't last, Keeli. Are you willing to give up everything just for . . . for . . ."

"A fling?" Keeli stepped away from him. Her hands curled into fists. Hurt, angry—but that was not right, that was irrational, because he was just a vampire, and she . . . she . . .

Something hard moved through his face. "Not a fling. Just . . . the unknown."

"I don't run," Keeli reminded him. "Not even from the unknown."

"And is this worth fighting for?" There was a terrible hunger in Michael's eyes, so much need that Keeli felt breathless with it.

"You tell me." She closed the distance between them, not touching, but close—so close that just a breath would bring her lips in contact with his throat.

"Please," Michael whispered. "I am trying to be a good man."

Keeli smiled. "You're a vampire. Don't be something you're not."

He made a sound, low in his throat, and Keeli suddenly found herself surrounded, drawn tight against a cool hard chest. Michael buried his fingers in her hair.

They did not talk. Keeli had nothing to say that wouldn't sound trite, and really, the situation was too strange to pretend normalcy. It was like being on a roller coaster, and she remembered the only ride of her life with crystalline accuracy: stomach in her throat, heart racing, battling an uncontrollable urge to scream, laugh, and vomit.

Yup, it was the Plunge of Death all over again. But this time she wasn't ready to step off the ride.

"What am I going to do with you?" Michael stepped

back just far enough to look down into Keeli's eyes. His expression made her dizzy.

"Fight crime," she said. "I hear it makes a great first date."

He laughed, and it was strange and wonderful seeing his eyes warm, the darkness in them swallowed by something gentler, more peaceful. He brushed back her hair and pressed his lips to her forehead.

"So we'll fight crime," he said. "And then what?"

"You expect me to have all the answers?" Keeli thumped her palm against his chest. "Step up to the plate, man."

"I'm too comfortable where I am." He smiled, and the roguishness of that smile—so unexpected, so gentle in its humor—made her heart ache. Keeli raised herself up on her tiptoes and brushed her lips against his mouth. It was difficult not to do more.

"I don't understand this," she whispered. "It's freaking me out a little."

"I think it's going to freak everyone out." Seriousness crept back into his eyes. "But you're not alone. I won't leave you alone."

"You sound like a stalker."

"I sound like a man who takes care of his friends."

"Friends, are we?" she said lightly. Michael kissed her.

"Oh," she breathed raggedly, several minutes later. "Maybe just a little more than friends."

He looked just as shaken. Which was gratifying. If he had been smug, she might have had to kick his ass.

"I need to go," he said. "You should come with me."

"Just to help fetch your clothes? Nice try," she replied. "But someone needs to stay here and keep this investigation going."

Something tight moved through his face. Struggle, maybe. He said, "I don't want to leave you."

Keeli wondered how much it cost him to say those

words. She knew how challenging it would be for her to say the same thing, no matter how strongly she felt.

And admit it: you're close to that line now. Too close.

She touched his cheek, tracing the golden design inlayed into his skin. He caught her hand and pressed his lips to her palm. She shivered.

"Will you come with me?" he asked.

"I want to," she said, before she could stop herself. Truth—it was becoming the truth with this man, always. She hesitated, watching Michael's face. He nodded, gently squeezing her hand before letting go.

"But you cannot," he said. "All right, then. I will not be gone long. When I get topside I'll call Jenkins and have him send over some DNA test kits. We need to get samples from Jas, Estella, and Jonathon."

"I don't think they murdered anyone."

"Maybe not, but someone killed Walter Crestin and six other vampires. We need to find out who—or at least, rule out the wolves—before the negotiations are completely ruined."

"Maybe they already are."

"I hope you're wrong."

Michael began to reach for the blue shirt and stopped himself. Keeli handed it to him, stifling the surge of heartbreak that accompanied the feel of rough cotton in her fingers. Michael watched her carefully as he shrugged on the shirt.

"Why do you care?" she asked softly, staring at the fabric lying flush against his pale skin. "What does it matter to you if these negotiations fail? It's not like you owe anything to the vampires. Or us werewolves."

Michael stopped buttoning the shirt. "I wasn't born a vampire, Keeli. I was made one. I asked for it. I wanted a better life."

"And did you get it?" Keeli suspected it was a cruel question, but she had to ask. She had to understand him, and she sensed this might be a rare opportunity, one that might not come again.

But she kicked herself for it as all the warmth fled Michael's eyes. "I got what I deserved, Keeli. And three hundred years later, I'm still paying."

She swallowed hard. Michael stepped close. He brushed her lips with his thumb, resting his cool palm against her neck.

"I have been an outsider for my entire life," he said quietly. "Always looking in, separate and unequal. Even when I was human, I was alone. Unwanted. So I see things differently from the rest of my kind. I see the halos and the horns, the light and the dark. I see that we are all the same, none of us better or worse than the other. Humans, vampires, werewolves—it doesn't matter. In the end, it makes no difference. The only things that matter are the choices we make, the actions we build our characters on. That's why I care, Keeli. Because I am nothing more than a man who happens to be a vampire, just as you are a woman who happens to be a werewolf, and to not care, to do nothing and let there be war and death . . ." He stopped, and Keeli leaned into him.

"Tell me," she said.

"I want to be a good man," he said, an echo of his previous words to her. "Not just a good vampire. A good man."

"And that means doing the right thing, no matter what?"

"Depends on your definition of 'right,' but yes. That is it."

He looked so serious, so full of pain, and all Keeli wanted to do was smile. So she did, and held his face between her hands.

"What are you waiting for?" she asked him. "Go out and be good."

He stared at her, wonderment creeping into his eyes, and then he bent close and kissed her.

And it was good.

Chapter Twelve

The police cars were gone by the time Michael returned home, but just in case any individual cops were still in the halls, he took an alternative route up to his apartment. Broad daylight, but Michael did not worry about being seen. No one in this neighborhood cared whether a vampire lived amongst them. They had worse problems to deal with.

Up and away, he thought, floating through the air to his fire escape. He touched down, light as a breeze amidst his roses, savoring their sweet scent in his nose, the softness of petals rubbing his skin.

Keeli's skin felt softer. Her scent was even sweeter.

He thought of her as he slid through his open window, and the memory of her lips and smiling face, that tousled pink hair, was both wonderful and dissatisfying. Dissatisfying, because his apartment no longer felt like home. Not even a shadow of home. He stood in the middle of the tiny studio, and all he felt from the cracked walls was a lonely emptiness, as if everything that had allowed him to pretend this place was his—his, and enough—had been carried away by Keeli's existence.

It isn't such a bad thing to want more from life, he told himself. But how he was going to manage it, was another problem entirely. Michael sighed. Ten years in this city, the longest he had ever spent in one place. Almost one hundred years previously, he had been sent to America in the wake of a vampire migration. Sent to clean up the messes of those few who thought to make this country a feeding ground.

The prospect of another long boat ride spent cramped and starving in constant darkness had prevented Michael from returning to Europe. He did not mind. America suited the sensibilities of his youth: movement, change, unstructured borders and wild freedom.

Now, though, another upheaval.

Not that he was complaining.

He wondered how Keeli was doing—questioned his decision to leave her behind, to face all her people alone. He had promised he would not do that.

But Keeli isn't the kind of woman you protect against her will. She's strong. She's been taking care of herself long before she ever knew you existed.

It still felt like a risk, though. Michael knew how violently friends and loved ones could turn against their own. Sudden, shocking, without warning. Michael did not know much about Keeli's life, or werewolf clans, but he was certain she had been raised in a community of common bonds, straightforward action and thought. There would be very little room for deviance. For deviant behavior.

Michael sighed. In three hundred years, he couldn't remember worrying this much—if at all—about anyone but himself. The circumstances did not make it any easier, either. It was clear to him now that if he and Keeli continued doing . . . whatever . . . her people were not going to be sympathetic or disinterested. There would be a price to pay, and Michael did not want to contemplate what that might be.

So are you going to give up? Are you going to pretend there's nothing between the two of you, and just leave her when this is over?

It would be better for Keeli if he did. Better for him, too. If he could bring himself to do it.

He took off the blue shirt and carefully folded it. He did not know what had happened to Keeli's father, only that seeing the shirt had caused Keeli and her grandmother pain. He thought of Keeli, crumpled in the tunnels, sobbing and sick, and knew that whatever had happened down there to cause all those empty homes had been terrible indeed.

Keeli Maddox—the mysterious granddaughter of Crimson City's Grand Dame Alpha, and the sole survivor of a vicious attack that destroyed most of that infamous bloodline . . .

The words of the newspaper article filled his mind. So. Keeli's family had been murdered. But who would do that? Was it the humans? Certainly not the vampires. Could it be other werewolves?

She and her grandmother are the last of Maddoxes, Michael realized. *If Keeli doesn't take up the mantle of leadership—which seems likely—then Maddox will be no more. The clan will take a different name.*

Michael wondered if it would be clan Mack. Grand Sire Alpha, Jas Mack.

He did not like the sound of that.

He went to the refrigerator, pulled out two bags of blood, and put them in the microwave. Set the timer and stood back to wait for breakfast, lunch, and dinner. He was getting low on food, would have to place an order soon with the local supply chain.

The prospect of spending money reminded him of the payment Celestine had brought with her that morning. He found the briefcase right where she dropped it and carried it to the kitchen counter. He cracked it open.

Five thousand dollars in fresh crisp twenties smiled at him. Michael did not smile back. This was small change, pennies almost, to the men and women who paid him. He did not mind being poor—it was what he was used to—but every time he received payment for his work it reminded him that, in this, he was not free. That he would never be free.

Just like almost every other man and woman on this planet. You have to work for a living.

Yes. But most people probably didn't feel like killers-for-hire every time they got paid. They probably *weren't* killers for hire.

The microwave pinged. Michael closed the briefcase and set it on the ground. Wouldn't do to get anything dirty. He ate quickly, sinking his teeth into the blood packet. Warmth flooded his throat, and with it, strength.

This is what it's like for humans, for others of my kind. What it used to be like for me. Food is simply food. The same litany, chanted again and again in his mind, trying so desperately to stave off the—

Michael shuddered, squeezing his eyes shut as memory wracked him. He tore the blood packet from his mouth, spraying the floor with crimson droplets.

Remember, whispered a voice in his mind, familiar as his own, but dead. Dead.

Michael remembered. He remembered the cold chains strapping him down inside his hole in the ground, the slow torture of blood—one drop per hour—into his parched mouth. His skin, cracked and peeling with starvation, and Malachai—golden, cruel—standing above him with his long white teeth and blazing eyes, taunting him, torturing Michael into something worse than animal.

And then setting him loose. Setting him free. Starving. Frenzied. Insane.

Michael sank to the floor, sick with the taste of blood.

You have to eat, he told himself. *You have to stay strong.*

He forced himself to pick up the seeping blood packet. Michael took a deep breath, and licked the plastic clean. It helped that the blood was not straight from a human. It helped a little. He fit his teeth into the holes he had already made, and drank the packet down to the last drop. He did the same with the next packet, and after a time, his nausea subsided. He could not enjoy his meal, but at least he was able to keep it down. That was all that mattered to him. Survival. Taking in enough food to retain control.

Michael felt better, too. He glanced at his rib wound, noting the skin healing over. Keeli's bite marks were almost gone, as well. He stroked them. Werewolf bites took extra care. Nothing out of the ordinary, beyond blood and rest, but without those two things, Michael would be very uncomfortable for the next several days. He had enough on his plate without walking around in pain, half-healed. Especially for what he planned to do tonight. The other vampires at The Bloody Pulp would smell his injuries if they were too severe. And there was going to be enough trouble without anyone thinking he was in a weakened state.

Michael's shoulders tingled, a shiver of unease. He turned around. His window was still open, roses swaying gently in a breeze. He was completely alone. He slipped over to his weapons and grabbed a dagger. Held the blade flat against his thigh as he glided toward the window. When he was close, he stopped and listened. Took another step, stopped. His roses beckoned, bright as sunshine, canaries, sunsets.

He looked closer, and went completely still. A small budded stem near his window hung limp and broken from the main branch.

Michael knew his roses. He loved his roses. That little stem had not been broken when he returned to his apartment.

Which meant that someone had just been on his fire escape, watching him. Someone large and very quiet.

Michael crept close to his window, took a deep breath, and stuck out his head to look around. He did not see anyone. The sky was empty, as were the alley and fire escape. He pulled back into shadow, his skin tingling from the light. He needed to put on more sunblock.

Michael shut the window and locked it. He looked at his roses for one minute, thoughtfully tapping the dagger blade against his leg.

Who would be spying on me?

The idea of a vampire peering in through his windows was laughable. Michael couldn't imagine anyone being that stupid.

Unsettled, he returned to the table to examine his weapons: a collection of daggers, swords, and stakes. He did not use anything high tech when he killed. It seemed wrong, somehow, like he wasn't giving the other side a fighting chance. Not that he was supposed to. He was the executioner; his victims were always criminals. The most heinous kind. They were murderers, rapists—or at the worst, necrophiliacs who desecrated the bodies they drained. Even Michael thought himself an idiot, giving those rogues a chance to fight back—but he knew what it was like to be helpless, to be faced with the inescapable, and he did not wish that on his worst enemy.

Nor did he ever want himself to get used to an easy kill. Death without consequences. He remembered that, too.

Michael sorted out what he wanted to take with him: a sword, several throwing knives—two of which were tipped in oak—and several stakes concealed in arm sheaths. Collecting everything helped him focus, got his thoughts away from pink hair and soft lips. He dressed himself with a Kevlar plate over his heart and left shoulder blade, as well as a wide iron collar under his black turtleneck.

His phone rang just as he was ready to leave. He stretched out on the mattress as he answered the call. There was no greeting from the other end.

"Michael," said a deep voice. "We will need your services again tonight."

Michael closed his eyes. "I won't be available to guard the envoy, Frederick. Your own men should be enough. I don't believe the werewolves plan to ambush you."

"Are you sure of that? There's been a murder." Frederick sounded so displeased, Michael instinctively looked at his weapons.

"I heard," Michael said cautiously.

"I thought you had, working as you do with the humans." The last word was spit out. "You know, then, that the crime was committed by a werewolf."

"Maybe not just a werewolf," Michael said, deciding that this was information he could share. "A vampire could have been present, too. This is a complex situation, Frederick."

"Make it less complex," Frederick said. "You know what's at stake."

"*We* are," Michael said, unable to keep a trace of cold humor from his voice. "I'm doing my best to find out what happened. Do you know anything?"

"No," Frederick snapped. "My hands are full enough trying to keep this from destroying the negotiations. I'm only thankful the victim was Walter Crestin, and not someone of higher . . . stature."

Like one of you, Michael thought.

"I spoke with Celestine," Frederick continued, his voice changing into something even more ominous. "She told me of the werewolf at your apartment. I hope this doesn't represent a conflict of interest?"

Michael gritted his teeth. "None at all. That werewolf is my liaison to the underground. She's helping me investigate the murder."

"Ah. Fine, then. I just wanted to be clear on that point. You serve a vital function in our community, Michael. It wouldn't do to have that function sullied with . . . rumors."

"Rumors." Michael felt his heart grow hard, dangerous. "I'm already an outcast, Frederick. Everyone fears me. What could a little rumor do that would possibly be worse than that?"

Frederick laughed, and hung up the phone. Michael looked out the window and stared at the broken rose.

Chapter Thirteen

The DNA test kits arrived an hour after Michael left. Keeli read the instructions, unsure how to begin. None of the three wolves would be thrilled about giving a sample—she could imagine what Estella would say—but it had to be done, if only to clear their names. Of course, once that happened, they would be left with another problem: how to find a murderer without any real leads.

There were three hundred werewolves living in the city, and those were only the ones documented by the local government. If you never left the underground—or were just too paranoid to follow the law—then there was no need to register. What authority was going to come down into the tunnels to check your papers? Keeli guessed there might be at least two hundred wolves in that category, which didn't include everyone under eighteen years of age. That was a lot of ground to cover, and she seriously doubted anyone would be in the mood to talk. Especially with her.

And if the humans *had* murdered Walter Crestin and the other vampires? Perhaps even that werewolf found dead in the subway who everyone thought had been drained?

This was gonna be shit.

One thing at a time. Get these tests taken care of first, and worry about the rest later. Keeli thought about seeking out her grandmother's advice, but her feet refused to take her next door. It was stupid, but she couldn't help herself. She was afraid of the questions the old woman might ask. Specifically, those dealing with her and Michael.

So she went looking for Jas. There were a lot of unfamiliar wolves in the tunnels, which took her off guard until she remembered that tomorrow was the full moon. The lower Alphas always gathered the day before full shift to meet in council with the Grand Dame. Usually they held night meetings, but if another negotiation with the vampires had already been scheduled, then it made sense for the Alphas and their entourages to arrive early. Keeli had a very good idea what they would be talking about.

Good luck, Granny May. With tensions rising and vampire packs roving the streets above, just looking for a reason to retaliate against stray wolves, Keeli's grandmother would need all the skills she possessed to keep the Alphas in line with an alliance.

Keeli passed clan members involved in preparations for the vampire envoys' arrival. That mostly involved cleaning, scrubbing down the walls and floors until the cement gleamed with a dull shine. As Keeli stepped around the workers, nodding greetings, she felt a moment of heartache for her people. Why, when there was so much beauty in the world, were they condemned to live underground? Trying in vain to make *concrete* pretty?

So ironic. Because vampires, who were allergic to the sun, got to live in penthouses full of it—while werewolves, who could happily embrace the light, were condemned to live away from it.

And what were the reasons? Money? Power? Or was it just fear? Werewolves could not afford the lobbyists and PR machines that vampires invested in to keep the humans rolling happy. And the humans, who took most of the good jobs, were the teachers and cops and admissions officers. What was left for werewolves? A few got lucky and landed decent white collar jobs. But they were never the doctors and very rarely the lawyers. As a race, they were overwhelmingly poor and uneducated.

Well, at least the were-children in this city are getting an education. Thanks to the Grand Dame Alpha, anyway. She had created schools in the underground, accredited by the city government with occasional oversight from the school board. The City officials had balked at first, but it was either agree to the Grand Dame's proposal, or be accused of neglecting children—children that no one wanted in regular schools, playing with human kids. The lycanthropy virus transferred just the same, no matter how old a person was. The only difference was that the ability to shape-shift did not hit until puberty.

Separate and unequal. Even human minorities pick on us. No one gets all politically correct on their asses. And that's okay with people—no one sees the double standard—because the one thing everyone can agree on is that we're big and bad, and we scare the shit out of shit.

The vampires had it easy. No one pegged their kids, or kept them from jobs. The general human population didn't look too hard past the pretty faces and nice clothes to the monsters beneath. Celebrities. Idolizing men and women who would just as soon eat their fans as look at them.

For a moment, Keeli wondered how she could stand Michael's presence. She wasn't naïve—she knew that at least once in his life he had murdered a human for his supper. It was impossible to be a vampire and not take lives. If she let that slide—if she could forgive him for that—then wasn't her anger against all other vampires pure hypocrisy? What made Michael better than everyone else? Why did she feel differently about him?

Because he's not like the rest of them. He's not part of the problem.

As if that wasn't the lamest reason she could think of. It was like saying that Michael was good just because he didn't fit the stereotype. If someone said that about her, she'd kick some ass.

Face it. You're a racist. You've got prejudices. Accept them, and move on. Move on to someplace where you're better than all the bigots who condemn werewolves just because they're different. Don't be that ignorant or pathetic.

She had to be better than that. They all did. Wolves like Jas, who looked at the world with only resentment, would never see the light beyond the tunnels. Would never be able to lead the wolves from the underground. Even the Grand Dame Alpha lacked enough experience amongst humans to facilitate a successful transition.

A transition into what? If werewolves leave the tunnels en masse, humans will just force us—legally and without a fuss—into the ghettos.

Yeah, but it would be a start. A place in the sun that werewolves could call their own. What humans called a ghetto would not stay ghetto for long if the werewolves got hold of it. Keeli thought of the neighborhood where Michael lived, the ways it could be improved so that werewolves and humans might coexist in safety, without the threat of gang wars and drugs on every street corner.

You dream big, but none of this is going to happen when Jas becomes Alpha. He has good intentions, but the larger picture doesn't mean anything to him. Nothing will change for the wolves.

And there had to be change if werewolves wanted to

survive as more than second-class citizens, feeding on the scraps left by humans and vampires.

We are not animals.

But an animal whine suddenly echoed off the walls; pained, frightened. Another one followed, shrill, a muffled gasp. Keeli glanced at the wolves around her; they looked back with puzzled frowns. Keeli broke into a run down the corridor. All she could think of was Michael— Michael returned, attacked, perhaps the attacker—and if blood had been spilled on either side . . .

She rounded the bend and came up hard against warm bodies. Keeli did not slow down; snarling, she pressed her palms together and wedged herself into the crowd, slamming forward, shoving aside the onlookers who growled and snapped at her shoulders. When they caught her scent, recognized her face, she felt them back off. It did not hurt her feelings that they feared her anger; right now, she welcomed it.

She expected Michael, but what she found was almost worse. Richard and Suze were pinned to the ground by three larger wolves, all of them from another clan. They smelled like grease oil and fish, which meant they were from Leroux. Dock wolves. Many of them had jobs on the wharf, and guarded that employment from other clans with tooth and claw.

The three wolves looked up when Keeli burst out of the crowd. Richard raised his head, swaying. He bled from the mouth and his eye was purple. Suze curled against his side, one arm flung across his chest. Keeli could not see her face.

"What the *fuck* is going on here?" The wolf rose within her chest. Fur pressed through her skin, smooth and quick.

The largest Leroux wolf bared his teeth. He had a sharp, craggy face, with small eyes and a large mouth.

"Just cleaning the scum, pretty-pink. The girl smells like fang. Been putting out to the gangs, I think. Let me do you a favor and carve her straight from the pack. Seems to be what everyone wants."

Keeli spun around to stare at the watching werewolves. Almost all of them were Maddox, and not one looked ready to lift a finger to help Richard and Suze.

"What's wrong with you?" she said to them, appalled. "These are members of your clan! Do you hate the vampires so much that you'll toss away new family, just on the scent and say-so of a *stranger*?"

Silence greeted her; uncomfortable downward glances, the shuffling of feet. Keeli spit on the ground.

"You all disgust me. Turning on *children*. Fine, then. Let's play this for keeps. See just how far my clan is willing to go." Keeli turned to face the Leroux wolves. She spread out her arms, gliding forward on the balls of her feet. Rage poured white-hot into her limbs; her heart felt hard as diamond, bright and ready to cut. The Leroux wolves watched her, grinning. They did not know who she was.

"The girl isn't a fang-banger," Keeli said softly. She bared her teeth in a coy, cruel smile, tilting her head. "But *I* am. Oh, *yeah*." She swiveled her hips, grinding against an invisible body, all the while matching gazes with the staring men. Canines pierced her lower lip; she tasted blood. Bones popped in her arms. Claws split her fingernails. She savored the pain, used it to retain some sliver of control.

Control. Yes.

She danced closer, running her claws over her thighs. Her voice deepened. "Come on. Try to carve *me* straight."

The Leroux wolves let go of Richard and Suze. Richard

scrambled to his feet and dragged the girl away. The crowd did not part for the teens. They remained locked within the circle.

Damn it. So much for a distraction.

The three werewolves snarled. Low murmurs arose from behind her; Maddox, finally coming to life. Too late now, though. Just too damn late. Keeli was going to slam this lesson into her clan's memory, or else die trying. Prejudice had its place, no matter how much she might wish it otherwise. A person just couldn't turn away a lifetime of bad feelings overnight—but when that prejudice got in the way of honor, compassion—

"Slut," snapped the largest Leroux werewolf, already more animal than man. "Yeah, we'll carve you *fine.*"

The men attacked. Keeli let go . . . filling . . . filled . . .

Pure Maddox blood is a tricky thing—she ducked, whirling with her claws out, rushing into meaty flesh—*it is old blood, the oldest werewolf line, some say*—bone grated beneath her fingertips and she cut down, lacerating muscle—*undiluted from the first wolf, the first blood crime*—howls filled her ears and she fed on the pain she caused, twisting as she felt movement against her back, dodging a crippling strike, a long fist into her spine. *The first kill*—teeth were too slow so she used her fists, rapping blows into an exposed neck, crushing—*that first taste of blood as the wolf ate the womb of its demon mother*—and he fell, choking, and it was easy, so easy to take them down, but there was one left, the largest, and she licked the blood from her claws, shivering as she welcomed him with a smile—*infecting her descendents with rage*—he was wary now, but the beast was on his soul and he could not stop the descent of his body into her own. *So watch your control*—she sidestepped, quick—*because, Keeli*—and she wanted to taste his throat, cut his spine on her teeth—*oh, Keeli*—he turned too slow and his stomach met her claws, digging, ripping, while her mouth closed around his neck—*you are so much like your father*—she bit down—*and you know what killed him, what killed my only son*—

She stopped and all she could hear was the wild thrashing of her heart, the thick rush of gasping. Movement twitched against her body—a chest pressed hard against her own, heaving. Hot warmth spilling down her stomach. The scent and taste of blood trickled over her teeth.

Her grandmother's voice echoed inside her head.

Keeli rolled her gaze upward and saw the whites of eyes. Terror.

Kill him. Do it.

Yes. That would feel good.

But she thought of her father; remembered, too, a horrified man splayed beneath her, and the strong hand in her hair with a dark voice saying, "No."

No. You must calm yourself. Please. Control the wolf.

Slowly, carefully, she pulled her jaws from the werewolf's neck. She swallowed his blood and looked into his eyes.

"Do you know who I am now?" Her voice sounded loud in the quiet of the corridor. No one moved or spoke; even the two wounded wolves on the ground did not make a sound. Despite her reputation, her father's reputation, Keeli had never before fought in public—not with such visceral abandon, not to kill. She had unwillingly ridden her entire life on the clan's memories of her father, and now memory had become reality. All their jibes, their nervous anticipation, had finally come to have merit.

The werewolf nodded, jerky and quick.

"Then get out of here. Take your friends and go. And if you ever come back, or mark another Maddox wolf, I will finish what I started."

There was no question in his eyes. He believed her. Everyone watching believed her.

"Keeli."

She turned and found Jas directly behind her. His human wife Emily was with him, tucked tight against his side. A lovely hat covered her ravaged scalp and the remains of her face. Keeli felt her gaze, curious and green.

The Leroux wolf spoke. "Jas," he croaked. "Please give the Grand Dame my apologies. I won't be able to attend the monthly council."

Keeli barely managed to keep her face straight. The only wolves who attended the council were Alphas.

Shit, no.

No wonder the other Maddox wolves didn't attack him. They would have gotten creamed. I should have gotten creamed. She turned back to look at the Alpha. He met her gaze, but it flickered, darting sideways, away and away. She stepped forward, and felt him swing backward though his feet did not move.

"I changed my mind," she said, pressing her advantage, refusing to think of the momentous thing she had just done. "You *will* go to the council. You will go, and you will pledge your support to the Grand Dame. It is for your clan's own good, Alpha Leroux. We're not strong enough to fight the humans on our own."

"We're strong," he countered, a glimmer of defiance returning to his face.

"No," Keeli said. "You're not."

That quiet reminder of his defeat was enough. Alpha Leroux tried to take a deep breath; he clutched his bleeding stomach. "And you? Should I expect you to follow me?"

Keeli felt dizzy. By rights, clan Leroux was now hers; the wolf before her, a subordinate. He knew it—everyone knew it. What the hell had she just done?

Defended some kids. Kicked some ass. All in a day's work.

She almost laughed, and maybe the Alpha saw that, the shadow on her blood-wet lips. She smelled his fear and shame, and it was the perfect antidote to hysteria.

I am an Alpha now. I could be an Alpha if only I grabbed the claim. Her father's dream. Her accident. He had died for the thing she had done so easily, without thinking about. The irony hurt.

"I don't want your clan," she told Leroux, savoring his surprise. "I only want you to remember. I don't think that will be a problem."

Alpha Leroux would never live this down. Especially once the rest of his clan heard the story. She watched his two companions stagger to their feet. Their wounds were already knitting, but one man had trouble breathing, while the other still bled heavily from his leg. Keeli glimpsed bone.

Alpha Leroux backed away from Keeli, bowing his head. When he met her eyes again, the shame was gone, and in its place, fear and . . . respect? Was such a thing possible? Or was it just the delusion of her ego?

The crowd parted for Leroux. A wolf stepped forward to take his place. Fine weathered features, long silver hair, and clear gray eyes—Keeli knew this wolf; he was another Alpha, a friend to her grandmother. Three strangers flanked him. They carried themselves as equals, leaders.

Keeli's face grew hot as she bowed her head.

"Alpha Hargittai." She quickly bowed her head. Seeing him, a man who had known her since she was a child, made Keeli nervous in ways Leroux had not.

You respect him. There is your difference.

She respected him, loved him—in all the clans, there was no finer wolf than Hargittai. None who could compare in honesty and courage. After Keeli's father died, he had stepped in as a gentle surrogate, a bulwark against the pain of her loss.

There were those who believed Hargittai would make an excellent Grand Sire Alpha should her grandmother ever step down. Keeli agreed, but she knew Hargittai: The man had too much respect for her grandmother and the Maddox legacy. He was content with his place as Alpha of just one clan.

Hargittai bowed his head in return—as did his companions. Keeli forgot to breathe. Equals. Oh, God. These men—her elders—were treating her as equal.

"You are still wearing the wolf," Hargittai said, his deep voice soft, almost kind. Keeli looked at herself. Thick fur covered her body; her limbs looked deformed, twisted with muscle. Her claws, sharp. She had not even noticed. There was no strain, no pain. The half-state between wolf and human felt as natural as breathing.

"I didn't know," she said, struggling to change. It was difficult to revert to her human body.

Hargittai touched her chin. "Don't try so hard. Your grandmother was the same, in the beginning."

Keeli stared, and he smiled at her discomfort. "The new generation reveals itself when most needed. And now, a war leader for violent times."

"I'm no leader."

"Before the eyes of your clan, you fought an Alpha into submission. You may not have claimed his power, but it is yours, nonetheless."

Hargittai released her and looked at Jas. "I think you have met your match, Jas Mack. A stronger wolf cannot be suffered to live if you are to be the Grand Sire Alpha."

Keeli saw Emily's eyes fill with confusion, watched as those slender human hands clutched at Jas's waist.

"Wait," said Keeli.

But Jas was already nodding, his gaze hard. "The clans won't tolerate a Grand Alpha who divides her loyalties, whose breath smells like fang. They won't accept someone who takes favors for her freedom. So yes, I accept the challenge."

Every word Jas spoke cut like a dagger to the heart. His voice was cold, emotionless, but she knew him well enough to understand that the quiet man, the calm man, was also an enraged, bitterly disappointed man. Without even meaning to, Keeli had struck a blow to Jas's dreams of being Alpha.

And yet, she could not bring herself to feel sorry for that. Keeli knew what it would mean to her grandmother if Jas made his bid for Alpha. The result would be the old woman's death. Granny May was strong, but to fight someone with Jas's strength and youth? Suicide.

Which did not mean she wanted to be the next Grand Dame. Absolutely not. But if it kept her grandmother safe, if she could stand between the old woman and Jas . . . she would do it.

Emily watched Keeli, horrified. She touched her face, stroking fingers along the remains of her cheek, a tactile memory of her attack. Jas pulled her close.

I'm sorry. I'm so sorry that you're scared. Sorry if you hate me for being with a vampire.

Hargittai placed his hand on Keeli's shoulder. "The smell of one's breath should be less important than the qualities of good leadership, like courage and sacrifice. I'm sure your clan agrees. After all," and here he raised his voice, his gaze sweeping across the gathered wolves, "would you prefer a wolf who hides her true nature, who prefers politics to the protection of her clan, or one who lays her life on the line to help another, when you—all of you—are so unwilling to do the same?"

He shook his head, clearly dissatisfied with the answering silence, the expressions of uncertainty. "I'll be late to council," he told Keeli. "Perhaps you should come with me?"

Keeli shook her head. That would be too much. She had simply won a fight, not earned any rights. Nor was she ready to face her grandmother with this news. Hargittai seemed to understand. The solemn kindness in his eyes made her heart feel strange.

"Take care," he whispered. "Watch your back."

As if she could do anything else. She nodded her thanks, and turned to look again at Jas and Emily. There were things she had to say to them.

But they were already gone. Keeli glimpsed Emily's pink hat; she began to follow, but hands caught her wrists. It was Richard, his face nearly healed. "It's Suze," he said. "She's still hurt."

Most of the Maddox wolves had already dispersed, hurrying away as if they were afraid of being targeted for another demonstration of Keeli's wrath. A few others milled about, helpless expressions on their faces, as though they still could not believe what had just transpired, and were too baffled to do anything but stare and whisper. The rest, just a handful, crouched around Suze's prone body. Keeli rushed over to the girl. Sucked in her breath when she saw what had been done to her.

"We have to reset her nose before it heals that way," Keeli said, angry. She swallowed it down; easier, this time. Having someone in front of her who desperately needed help was good motivation for control.

"We were walking back to our room when they passed us," Richard said, even as Keeli and her fellow clan mates gently forced Suze to roll on her back. Her face was a mess; a large rip in her T-shirt revealed part of her bra. The Leroux wolves had been having a little too much fun, it seemed. "They smelled fang on her, from this morning's fight. It didn't matter to them the why or how, or that it wasn't sex."

"They were looking for a fight," Keeli muttered.

"You gave them one," muttered the wolf nearest her. Keeli raised her eyebrow and was given a quick sharp grin in response.

"Suze." Richard murmured, grabbing the girl's hand. "Come on."

"Are they gone?" she asked faintly. Her eyes cracked open.

"It's a good thing you're a slow healer," Keeli told her. "I have to push your nose back into a better shape. You understand, Suze? It's going to hurt, but if I don't do it now, it'll heal wrong."

"S'kay," the girl whispered, and closed her eyes.

It was not okay. In fact, resetting Suze's nose was one of the most harrowing experiences of Keeli's life. When she was finally done, and Suze had finally stopped screaming, Keeli slumped backward and lay flat on the ground, fighting for breath. She closed her eyes. Heard whispers, faint mutters, the shuffle of many feet. Richard, crooning to Suze. She smelled blood and licked her lips. Tasted Leroux.

Something brushed her cheek. It felt like hair. She opened her eyes and found Michael crouched above her. The tip of a braid tickled her skin.

"You are so much trouble," he said.

She closed her eyes again and smiled.

By the time Suze was ready to be moved, only the four of them remained in the corridor. The rest of the wolves were dispersed with a couple of careful words and some hard looks from Keeli. Yes, how lovely to act helpful when the fight was over. But to not stop the abuse while it was happening? Inexcusable. Keeli no longer cared if Leroux was an Alpha. After seeing what he and his friends had done to Suze, she was mad enough to go hunt him down a second time. The rest of her clan should have felt the same.

Times like this show you who your friends are. Throw a little vampire into the mix, and you'll get more than just a show.

Richard carried Suze back to the room they shared. Michael and Keeli followed.

The room Richard and Suze stayed in was surprisingly near the Alpha core. It had once belonged to Keeli's cousin, an older girl who was now more than fifteen years dead. Keeli couldn't remember her name anymore. The room was bare, perfectly cleaned out. All that was left were bare concrete walls, narrow beds, and a small bathroom. Nothing of comfort and home. Just four gray walls and some potential.

And a bottle of vampire sunscreen.

"Where did you get this?" Keeli asked, as Richard carefully deposited Suze on the bed.

"Um," he said.

"I picked the fang's pocket this morning," Suze said wearily. "Old habits. Sorry."

Keeli shook her head, glancing at Michael. "How long have you two been here?"

"Only three days," he said, looking warily at Michael. The vampire leaned against the wall, studying the teens with a thoughtful expression on his pale face. Suze tried to sit up. Richard grabbed her shoulders and gently pressed her back to the bed. Keeli tried not to shudder every time they touched.

"I need some water," Suze whispered. Richard jumped to his feet and padded into the bathroom. Suze watched him go, and then turned her gaze on Keeli.

"Thanks," she said. "That fucker was going to kill me."

Keeli shrugged. She wanted to say, "Maybe you would have done the same for me," but she knew what the answer to that would be, and just didn't feel like hearing it.

Richard emerged from the bathroom with a glass of water.

"You're not siblings," Michael suddenly said. Richard

stopped so fast, water sloshed over the rim of the glass. Both he and Suze stared at him with a mixture of horror and shock on their faces. Keeli turned to Michael and raised her eyebrows in silent question.

"I had eight older brothers and sisters," he said. "I can tell these things."

Which was a fascinating revelation, but there were two young werewolves watching them. Keeli tore her gaze away from Michael's face.

"I want the truth," she said flatly. "And it better be good, because the memory of you two, together, gives me nightmares."

For the first time, Suze and Richard looked at Keeli—really looked—and it was as though they saw past the scent of vampire and the Maddox name, down to the woman beneath the pink hair and striped stockings. Keeli looked right back, and wondered if she might learn to like these bold teens who stared at her so openly, without fear.

Suze said, "We act like we got the same parents because it's easier that way. We don't want anyone to separate us. That's what people do, when people think you're kids and not blood. But hell, we weren't sure it would work. We don't look anything alike."

Keeli begged to differ. "You're not siblings?"

"Not unless someone important is asking," Suze said. "You're dirty for thinking that way."

"Yeah, I'm dirty in the best possible way. You two are idiots, acting like you're siblings and then doing each other in public. That's . . . that's so gross! What the hell were you thinking?"

"We love each other," Richard said, crouching protectively at Suze's beside.

"That explains everything," Michael said.

Keeli frowned. "You sure you're not siblings? I think I want blood tests."

"Bitch."

"That's Miss Bitch to you. And while you're here, no more pretending to be kin. Now *that* is dirty."

"We did it to—"

"I know why, but I promise that no one is going to separate the two of you just because you're not blood-related. You're safe, understand? Jeez, I mean it. You're both safe."

Richard and Suze looked at each other. Some tension left their shoulders.

"It's been a long time," said the teen, gazing around the room like it was something from the Ritz, instead of just old concrete.

Michael squatted. "How long were you on the street?"

"Years," said Suze, looking at the ceiling. "We were too afraid to approach any clans for help. Had some bad experiences."

"We were going to steal a car," added Richard. "Sell it, get enough cash for over the border. Take us to the new underground."

Mexico. An easy place to get lost in if you were a werewolf. The new underground for those who wanted to live in relative freedom, where humans were so poor they didn't care if you wore fur or fang, just as long as you didn't bite the hand paying the check, or take the blood or flesh of family. Farther south into Brazil, life got better—or so rumor said. Werewolves in places like Rio de Janeiro lived above ground, no room in the sewers to carve out new clan homes. Human children occupied those places.

"What's the name of your old clan?" Keeli asked.

"We come from different clans. They can go fuck themselves." Suze's mouth twisted. "We wouldn't have come here, but there was some bad shit on the streets. Real bad. Killing-kind bad. We saw it ourselves, and were afraid it would get us."

"What did you see?"

"Blood," Richard whispered. "Lots of it. On a man. On his face and body. Like he rolled in it. You don't get that wet unless you've been in it real hard."

"Was this a human bad or vampire bad?" Keeli asked. "Werewolf?"

Richard and Suze looked at each other.

"Was it something else? A mech, maybe?"

Richard shook his head. "No. But we've seen those, too. We know what those smell like. They look human, but smell . . . wrong. No. This was different. A little bit of . . . everything."

"He saw us." Suze's voice was low; Keeli had to lean close to hear. "I looked right into his eyes. He had a funny voice."

"He sang a song," Richard said.

"What else did he do?" Michael looked troubled.

"He told us to run," Suze whispered. "We did."

"When did this happen?"

"A week ago. We started knocking on doors right away. Maddox was the only clan to take us in."

"My grandmother must have been the one who interviewed you. Did you tell her this?"

They nodded, and all the bravado and punk-wit was gone. Richard and Suze looked like two scared children. Richard said, "She told us it was a demon."

"Maybe," Michael said, though Keeli heard the doubt in his voice. She wondered why the Grand Dame had not mentioned it to them. A man covered in blood when there was a serial killer on the loose seemed like a significant piece of information to give to the two people who were supposed to be investigating the crime.

They left the teens to recuperate—and from the way Richard looked at Suze as they closed the door, have some really good sex. The corridor outside was empty, quiet except for the distant banging of pipes and sledge-hammers. The clan was growing so fast that the Grand Dame had authorized funds for renovations. More homes, more rooms to spread out. The werewolves who would benefit from the expansion were still children, barely teenagers, but Keeli's grandmother liked to think long-term.

Michael wrapped Keeli in a tight embrace. Warmth flooded her body, lingering even when he released her.

"Are you all right?" he asked.

"How did you know?"

He touched her jaw, feather soft. "I looked at your face."

She closed her eyes, pressing her forehead against his chest. "I beat the crap out of an Alpha and two of his men. I've been declared Jas's challenger in any future fight for leadership. And I still haven't gotten all that DNA I promised you. I want to run away, Michael."

She heard the smile in his voice when he said, "Where would you go?"

"Where were you born?"

He stilled. "Central Asia. The high steppes, just below what is now Russia."

"Is it beautiful?"

"Very."

"How long since you've been back?"

Michael touched Keeli's cheeks, lifting her chin so he could gaze into her eyes. She sensed his pain, discomfort, and was instantly sorry she had asked.

He said, "It's been a long time, Keeli. For good reason. But one day, maybe, it will be time to go back. When I do, we'll go together."

Her breath caught. "You mean that."

"I would not say it if I didn't."

They heard footsteps in the hall. Michael began to pull away, but Keeli grabbed his hand, entwining their fingers.

"Keeli," he said.

"Let them look," she said. "I don't care."

She might have punched him for the breathless way he stared at her; agony and pain and troubled darkness swirled through his eyes, only to be mixed with awe. Sweet—his lips were sweeter, and she pressed upward into his gentle kiss, wanting the world to see how much she cared about the man, how much she did not care about the *what* or the *how*, but instead the simple lovely *who*, the who touching her shoulder, drawing her into a cool strong embrace.

"Cold showers do not work for me," he murmured in her ear, and she laughed out loud, turning as she did to see who had passed them in the hall. Two wolves, their backs turned, spines ramrod straight. *Fine, then. Fine.*

"They don't work for me, either," she told him, her body shifting into something warmer and more delicious than the wolf. She felt wet, ready.

They did not run back to her room, though it was only a corridor and a twist away. They walked at a normal pace, Keeli's hand locked in Michael's, and it was a game, a test, to see who had the most self-control. She felt tension running through his arm; she brushed her breast against his bicep and savored his shudder. Fought down her own, as well.

But the moment Keeli opened her door and they stepped into her room, control became a myth, an absolute mystery. Michael slammed shut the door, crashing back against it hard. He grabbed Keeli tight against his chest as she grappled with his pants. Her limbs banged up against multiple solid objects. She peeled back his coat and saw steel, wood.

"Wow," she said, but then his hands were on her and she forgot his weapons.

"Kiss me," he said, and she did, swallowing his gasp as

she ripped open his top button and plunged her hand down, down, wrapping fingers around his hard hot length, stroking quick with her thumb. She pulled away from his kiss, sliding down his body, dragging her nails across his chest. She licked the front of his pants, nuzzling, and then in one quick movement yanked them down to his ankles. Michael did not have time to react; Keeli ran her tongue up his entire length, swirling her tongue around the seeping tip. She sucked gently. Michael buried his hands in her hair, jerking.

"No," he gasped, sinking to the ground, grabbing Keeli's T-shirt and pulling it over her head. He unsnapped her bra. "You're too quick for me."

"I like it fast," she said.

"Not *that* fast." He smiled, and she laughed as he took her breast into his mouth. Laughed, and then moaned, arching her back when his teeth—sharp, good—tugged. His hands moved under her skirt; she felt her stockings rip, and then his fingers were inside her, moving and pressing and—

She cried out, bucking against his hand as he shifted rhythm, faster, harder, his teeth tugging, tongue licking, pulling, while her hands reached down to his hair, his face—

She came and it was good, so good, but even before the last shudder was done she felt him, the hard hot length of him, and he kissed her on the mouth, his tongue ducking light against her own, and he slid in and in and in, pushing deeper than anyone had ever gone, and she was still coming down from the last high, the last big wave, and the feel of him so large and thick, the first thrust, made her senseless all over again so by the second thrust she was a goner, shaking, her body clenching tight—so tight—and he called out her name and pounded her hard, hard, hard, her head banging into a pile of books that toppled down on top of her and she did not care—barely noticed that *Moby-Dick* was lying open on her face, though she had enough sense to think *how ironic* before she was hit for a third time—the charm—because Michael came with her, and . . .

It was difficult to breathe. Michael, shaking, with his mouth pressed to her ear, whispered her name. In his voice: respect, admiration, relief, and exhaustion. Contentment.

And more—so much more that Keeli did not dare name. "Yeah," she breathed, her voice floating, curling. "I feel the same."

Chapter Fourteen

He wanted to drown himself in her salty sweet scent, the soft creamy warmth of her pink skin, drown himself in sleep, dream away his life, free of nightmare and pain and sorrow. He pressed his lips to her neck, tasting her hot pulse, licking the sweet spot of her throat.

"You going to bite me?" Keeli asked drowsily. There was no rancor in her voice, no fear or recrimination. Just a question. Simple. Michael ran the tips of his fangs over her skin. She shivered.

He pulled away, suddenly uneasy. Keeli opened her eyes, looking him full in the face. Her eyes were strong, clear, blue as crystal sky. She touched his face, fingers tracing the tattoo in his cheek. "What's wrong?"

He began to shake his head, but stopped. "I haven't taken blood from a person for a long time. It feels . . . wrong to me. Dangerous."

She studied him, with her fingers still dancing, whirling lovely patterns. "Why?"

"Why?" It was difficult talking to her like this; it was more intimate than he could have imagined, as though his soul were laid open, his pain and insecurity tangible enough to taste. He did not pull away, though. He controlled his terror of her deep-seeing eyes, and said, "Because there was a time when I took too much, when I was not . . . myself. People died."

Her eyes did not change. "Are you sorry?"

"Yes," he breathed. Sorry was inadequate. Sorry would never be enough.

She said nothing, and Michael waited, locked tight within her gaze, desperate for some answer, even more desperate for silence. Better that, than hearing words that would kill.

In the end, Keeli gave him silence; but it was not what he expected. She wrapped her arms and legs around his body, drawing him into a tight, soul-reaching hug that did not ease in potency or strength, even after long minutes passed into the quiet rhythm of their beating hearts.

"Who would have thought?" she finally whispered. She brushed her fingers through his hair.

"Thought what?" he murmured, savoring her gentle touch. In all his life, all the centuries left dull and dead behind him, he had never felt so comfortable, so at ease. So at home.

"This," she said. "All of this. I never imagined."

Michael wrapped his arms around her body and turned them. Books scattered, pressed hard into his side. He ran one hand up her thigh, caressing the crease of her backside. Keeli smiled, snuggling closer. His hand trailed into her bunched-up skirt, which rode up her waist, bumping her breasts.

"You do like it fast," he said.

"I like it slow too," she said.

He laughed, and she kissed him. "I like that even better," she breathed against his lips. "Do it again."

He laughed, low, and it was easy. Easy, because it was Keeli in his arms, that smile on her pink mouth. He slid out of her body, and she looked down between them. She stilled, her smile fading.

"You didn't use a condom."

Michael blinked. Did he even carry them? "I—no. I forgot."

"So did I."

"I'm not sick," he said.

"That's not what I'm worried about."

They stared at each other.

"It's not possible. It can't be," Michael said.

"Yeah, but how often has it been tested? Can you say for certain?"

"No." Michael propped himself up on his elbow. "It just seems outside the realm of possibility. A child who is both vampire and werewolf?"

"A child is a child," Keeli said thoughtfully. "But yes. That would be . . . different."

"Some might call it an abomination."

Keeli gave him a sharp look and he shook his head. "Not me."

"Good," she said, fierce.

He wanted to ask her why she cared—why the possibility of such a child would make her so protective—but he said nothing. In a way, he felt the same—or at least, he thought he did. But it was so far outside the realm of possibility, as to be a dream. An odd one, at that.

Someone knocked on Keeli's door; hard raps that echoed like dull iron chimes.

Michael stared at Keeli, frozen.

"Keeli!" A woman's voice. "Please, are you in there?"

"Shit." Keeli scrambled out of Michael's arms. She hiked down her skirt and grabbed her T-shirt off the floor.

Michael pulled up his pants. His shirt was still on. His body suddenly hurt from all the places his weapons had jabbed him.

"Who is it?" he asked, as Keeli ran fingers through her hair.

"Emily. How do I look?"

"Like you've had sex."

Keeli grinned, which made him feel better. He still wasn't sure she would make it another day without regrets.

Appreciate the little moments, he told himself. *Make them last.*

Michael stood behind Keeli as she answered the door, and it was good he'd had centuries to practice hiding his emotions, because the woman who appeared before him stirred every instinct, every ounce of sympathetic agony.

Emily wore a pink hat with a wide sweeping brim. It did not hide her ravaged face. A full mask would still have revealed tragedy; the energy sweeping off the young woman was all sweet pain, desperate desire.

The left side was the worst: a gutted cheek, a scarred nose thick with ridged flesh that arced high into her torn brow. No hair spilled out from beneath her hat. Her left ear was gone. A delicate golden earring spun from her right ear.

A vampire did this to her. A vampire who went unpunished.

"Keeli," Emily said, breathless. She looked up at Michael and her green eyes grew large, dewy. Beautiful eyes, almost lovely enough to make a person forget her monstrous face. Michael watched fear enter her gaze, the first mark of panic, and he did not know what to do—how to calm a woman who had been so ruined by his own kind. He did not blame her for being frightened of him, and finally—finally—Jas's unreasoning hatred made sense. The entire clan's prejudice made sense.

Keeli grabbed Michael's hand. Emily watched, blanching.

"He's safe," Keeli said. "Please don't be afraid. He won't hurt you. I promise."

"They lie," Emily whispered, beginning to shake. "Please don't touch him, Keeli."

Michael carefully disengaged himself. He took a step back, deeper into the room. "I would never hurt Keeli," he promised, trying desperately to be gentle. "I would never hurt you, or anyone else in this clan."

Emily took a deep, shuddering, breath. "You're the first vampire I've seen since . . ." She touched her face. "You frighten me. I'm sorry, but you do."

"I understand." Michael looked at Keeli. "Perhaps I should leave while the two of you talk."

He could see the apology in her eyes as she nodded. Emily had been hurt too badly for him to expect her to embrace his presence with any degree of calmness. He slid past Keeli out the door, pretending he did not notice the corridor-wide berth Emily gave him. She dashed into Keeli's room as soon as he was a good distance away. Michael met Keeli's gaze. Her smile was rueful, gentle. Michael wondered if it would always be so, if they would always be separated by the fear of others.

He watched her shut the door.

Emily perched on the edge of Keeli's bed, rubbing her arms. Convulsive, mindless. Keeli wrapped a blanket around her friend's shoulders and sat beside her— surveyed the mess, just as Emily was doing. She wondered if her friend would come to the right conclusion.

"I'm sorry," Emily said. "I'm so sorry, Keeli. I acted like an idiot."

"You were afraid," Keeli said gently. "You had a right to be."

"No, I didn't. You vouched for him. I trust you. It's just . . . he was the first. The first I've been close to, and I just couldn't think straight." Emily began to rock. Keeli placed an arm around her slender shoulders and drew her close. "All those memories," Emily whispered. "I can't ever get away from them. Not looking like this, anyway."

Not looking like this. Not with her face a constant reminder. Jas and Emily had no mirrors in their home, but it was enough that Emily could see her disfigurement in the faces of every person she passed. She knew what she looked like. The only miracle was that she had not managed to push Jas away. Keeli knew Emily had tried—that at first she believed he deserved someone less broken, someone who wouldn't turn his stomach—but Jas, with careful patience and love, had convinced her that he didn't care about her appearance, that he still adored her with the same passion he had felt the first time he laid eyes on her. Keeli wanted to cry every time she thought of it.

I'll never be able to hate Jas. Even if I don't agree with him, I know why he's doing this. And maybe . . . maybe I would do the same if I were in his position.

Maybe. Probably. Keeli and Emily were friends, but still, she had only been hurt in a peripheral way by Emily's attack. Nor had her judgment of vampires ever turned to hate. It had been frustration, anger, and an awareness of the atrocities they were capable of.

She still felt the frustration and anger, the wary distrust, but Michael—Michael, somehow, by some slip of a miracle, had managed to make her see the bigger picture with nothing but his example: that vampires and werewolves were not so different, and that to dehumanize one would be the same as dehumanizing herself.

But would she ever be able to convince anyone else of that?

"Jas told me about the baby," Keeli said. "I'm so happy for you, Emily."

That made the woman smile, and for a moment, Keeli glimpsed her friend's old beauty, ethereal and golden. "It's wonderful, Keeli. I can feel her inside me, growing. And Jas . . . Jas is so excited. He keeps asking me if we should start buying clothes and toys. He's going to redecorate the guest room soon."

Emily touched her stomach. Keeli could not see any sign of her pregnancy, but she imagined a tiny life turning warm in the womb.

"About Michael," she began.

Emily glanced up, quick. She said, "I can think more clearly when he's not around." She smiled, wry. "I used to believe I was so tough. So brave. Funny how that can change. But if you trust him, Keeli, I'll do my best to feel the same. I'll try."

Keeli's eyes felt hot. Prickly. "Thanks, Em."

Emily shrugged. "Everyone is talking about him and you. They want to know what's going on, what got into you."

"It's complicated. Do you . . . do you hate me for it? For the investigation, for bringing him down here?"

Some of the old tartness touched Emily's lips. "Do you think I would be here if I hated you?"

Keeli flushed. "I just thought . . . You know. . . ."

"I think you're smart, Keeli. I think you know what the vampires are capable of. I think you know what you're doing." Emily touched Keeli's hand. "I also think you're insane." She glanced around the room, at the scattered books. Her gaze fell upon the black bra lying twisted on the ground. "Very insane." Emily hesitated. "You know I don't like the idea of this alliance. It scares me, opening ourselves to vampires. I don't trust them."

"I don't trust them, either," Keeli confessed. "I trust

Michael, but that's it. He says that once the vampires sign the treaty, they'll abide by it, but he doesn't speak for everyone." She frowned, thinking. "Though I suppose if anyone breaks the truce, they'll answer to him."

"What do you mean?"

"He punishes vampires who breaks their laws. He executes them."

Emily blinked, taken aback. "He kills his own kind?"

"Yes." Keeli frowned, thinking of the way he lived, the scratches the female vampire had left on his face. "It hasn't made him very popular."

"I can't imagine it has. I didn't know vampires did that. Murdered their own kind." There was an odd light in her eyes; speculation, perhaps. Hunger, maybe.

"He doesn't enjoy it," Keeli said carefully, watching her friend.

"Of course," Emily agreed, distracted. "Oh, I can see why you find him attractive."

"Excuse me?"

"He's better than the others. He's not like them."

Which was true, to some extent, though Keeli sensed that Emily had another meaning, and it bothered her. Made her uneasy.

"I'm not with him because he kills his own kind," she said.

Emily did not seem to hear. She stood up, rubbing her arms. The room was not cold; Keeli sensed the shivers were from excitement. Her eyes were bright. "I came here because of the challenge. I didn't know Jas was making a bid for Alpha, Keeli. I really didn't. But I was there when you fought those wolves today. I saw, and I know . . . I know . . . Jas can't beat you. He can't. And I just wanted . . . wanted to ask you to please, please . . ."

"I don't want to fight him," Keeli said.

"I know, I know. Maybe now you won't have to. Jas is

doing this for me, because I'm afraid of the vampires. But it's really only one who scares me. Just the one." She raised a hand to her face; her fingers trembled. "If Michael could . . . get rid of him . . . maybe I could convince Jas to lay off the bid. Maybe I could convince him to support the alliance."

Keeli stood up. "Do you realize what you're saying? You want Michael to kill someone."

Emily's eyes hardened; her mouth twisted. Just that, and her face—which seemed so unchangeable in its wounded agony—shifted into something truly monstrous. Ugly. "I want *justice*, Keeli. I want him nailed to the floor with his head in my lap, so I can do the same thing to his face that he did to mine." She pulled off her hat. Keeli barely kept from flinching. It had been a long time since she'd seen up close Emily's scalp. Or rather, what was left of it.

"Yes," Emily hissed, her raw pink head bobbing like a slick beach ball, or the torso of a skinned whale. "Yes, you understand. You have to. Do you know what it's like to be scalped alive, Keeli? Can you imagine?"

"No," Keeli breathed. "I can't."

"Then don't judge me. I want this. I want to stop jumping at shadows, wondering when that freak fang will come and finish the job. He told me he would, Keeli. He whispered it my ear. Called it the foreplay of his class act event. And I believed him. I still do."

"Emily," Keeli said, stricken.

The door opened. Nerves strung tight, Keeli crouched instinctively into an attack. Emily gasped.

Michael did not intend to seek out Jas, but he heard the werewolf's voice shouting orders, and curiosity dragged him down the corridor. He had the DNA kits; it might be a good time to press for Jas's cooperation in at least one small thing.

The werewolf was not hard to find. He stood in the middle of exposed piping, heavy corrugated steel piled around his legs. Men worked near him; the air smelled damp. New waterlines, it seemed.

"Hello," Michael said, over the dull clang of pounding steel. "I need to talk to you."

"You and everyone else." He raked the vampire with a cool gaze. "Where's your fang-bang?"

Michael's mouth twisted. "You will speak about Keeli with respect."

"Or what?" Jas sneered. "Are you going to be her hero?"

"If I have to," Michael said quietly. "If she'll let me."

Jas looked away. He watched the other werewolves hammer and weld pipes into the wall. Michael noticed soft plugs stuck into their ears. Good. The sound hurt.

"What do you need?" asked Jas.

Michael showed him the kit. Jas shook his head.

"Shit. You pulling the Man down on me?"

"Keeli doesn't think you did it. I trust her. But I need the sample to prove it to the police."

"Who else is on your list?"

"Whom do you think? I've been told there aren't many people in this clan with the strength and motivation to kill a vampire."

"Yeah." For a moment, Michael thought Jas looked tired. "I can only think of a couple."

"Estella," Michael said.

"I guess Jonathon, too. Considering our history and all."

Michael held up the test kit. "Let's make this easy."

Jas snorted. "Easy. Shit." He took the kit, but grabbed Michael's wrist with his other hand. He whispered, "I don't trust you. I'm just doing this so I don't make waves with the Grand Dame. I'm a good little wolf."

"Sure you are," said Michael easily. "That's why you're planning on murdering her and fighting Keeli."

Jas sucked in his breath. "You don't understand our ways. You never will. You're a vampire."

"Your wife is human," Michael said, "but she could have been a vampire. What would you have done then, Jas? What would you have done if her attacker turned her? Would you hate her, just because she drinks blood? Would you hate her, even if it were the same woman in a different skin? You tell me, Jas. How much do you love your wife, and would it matter to you if she weren't human anymore?"

Jas shoved Michael away from him. "Don't you dare talk to me about Emily. You have no right."

"Pushed a button, didn't I?" Michael raised an eyebrow. "Think about it, Jas. Think hard. I'm sure Emily will."

Jas straightened; his fists curled hard and tight against his thighs. "What do you mean by that?"

"Emily and Keeli are together. Talking. It's why I'm here, to give your wife space."

Construction had stopped. Jas snarled at the men, some of whom had pulled out their earplugs. "Get back to work!"

"Yes, let them work," Michael said, sweeping his gaze over the watching werewolves. They were all strangers, but he knew that to Keeli they were family, friends. Clan. He felt their uncertainty, confusion, and knew that such emotions could lead so easily to fear, and then hate. Hate for him, and by extension, Keeli.

Are you going to be her hero?

"None of you know me," he said, turning in a slow circle. "None of you know the kind of person I am. Only, *what* I am. And that is fine. That is all I can expect. But you

203

do know your Grand Dame Alpha, and what she is trying to accomplish by negotiating with us vampires. You know that, because she has told you, and you trust her with the truth. There might be a war coming, and no matter how much you wish it otherwise, all of us—vampires *and* werewolves—are involved. We need this alliance. This new waterline you're building? The expansion of your clan? It won't mean anything if the humans come after you. They will take it all, drive you out of the city. Or worse, just kill you. They have already started on my people. What makes you think you wolves won't be next?"

Michael looked at Jas. "You're angry at Keeli. I understand why. But she is still a good woman. She does not deserve your contempt. Not when she is sacrificing so much to make sure this alliance is a success."

Jas said nothing, but Michael felt the other wolves stir within their ranks, tasting the echo of his words.

"Let's go," Jas said, gruff. "I want to get Emily." He threw a warning glance at the staring wolves. They went back to work.

The two men walked down the corridor, side by side.

"Nice speech," Jas said.

"I thought so," Michael agreed.

Jas grabbed his arm, swung him around. "I'll do what I have to, to keep Keeli safe from you. She doesn't know what she's doing. You've . . . brainwashed her." He sniffed. "And you're having sex. God. Everyone must have smelled her on you."

"Brainwashed her?" Michael shrugged off his hand. "You don't know Keeli at all if you think she could be . . . brainwashed by someone like me."

"I know Keeli better than you," Jas growled, "and this isn't her."

"Maybe it is." Michael leaned close, savoring the anger

seeping through his fraying patience. "Maybe you never looked deep enough to see it."

Jas's eyes flashed into the wolf, his lips darkening, stretching back over sharp teeth. A thin sheen of sweat slicked his forehead.

"Save it," Michael snapped, baring his own teeth. "You can piss at me all you want, Jas, but not on my time. I have better things to do than listen to you *whine*."

Michael was glad of the iron collar he wore. He had used it in the past to deflect attempts to cut off his head, but it was just as good a defense against werewolves who wanted to rip out his throat and run away with it.

Heartbeats passed; Jas settled back on his heels, his features smoothing into something more human. Michael did not relax. The immediate danger might be over, but not the anger, resentment. Jas had a vendetta without bounds. It was only a matter of time before it erupted into physical violence.

They reached Keeli's door; surprisingly, Michael heard the faint hum of voices through the steel. He wondered how much of their own recent activity had been audible to passersby outside her room. Jas froze, his hand poised to knock. Michael stepped close, listening hard.

He heard Emily, her voice desperate, hard. Her desire. Her ultimatum—for him to kill the vampire who'd maimed her. Jas looked stricken. He glanced at Michael, and the men shared a moment of perfect unity. Perfect pain; helpless, horrified. Michael tried to imagine Keeli in Emily's place, her vibrancy stolen away by one violent act, and felt his heart grow hard and cold.

Jas opened the door. Michael watched Keeli spin; their eyes met and then he gazed past her to the disfigured woman gleaming pink and raw. Raw to the heart, raw to the bone. She gasped.

"I'll do it," he said, without thought. Committing himself to the execution, to the death.

"Michael," Keeli breathed.

"I will bring him to you," Michael promised. "And then you can make him pay."

"No," Jas murmured. "Emily, no."

Emily's startled gaze turned to Jas. Her lips tightened. "I want this, Jas."

"The baby . . ." he began.

"The baby will be as strong as his mother, and he will never *ever* live with my fear." Emily carefully replaced her hat, fingers sliding over the wide pink brim. She kissed Keeli on the cheek, and then walked up to her husband, hands outstretched. He caught them without hesitation, though his conflict remained clear. Emily held his gaze, and then looked past him to Michael. "Thank you," she said. "If you do this, things will be different. I promise."

Jas began to protest. His wife cut him off with a look.

Michael stirred. "I am not doing this for payment. I am doing this for you."

Emily studied his face; slowly, she nodded. "Still," she said quietly, ominously, "you'll get what you deserve."

She began to leave. Michael touched Jas's shoulder. The werewolf merely looked at him; there was no anger in his face, just resignation: startled and sad. Michael handed him the DNA test kit. Jas took the device and pressed the flat end against his arm.

"Thank you," Michael said, when Jas handed back the sampler.

Again, silence. The werewolf held his wife's hand and drew her away, down the corridor out of sight.

Michael turned. Keeli watched him, her face tight and closed.

"Keeli," he said, but she turned away. He followed her, closing the door behind him. She sat on the edge of the bed, her arms wrapped around her stomach. He sat beside her.

"It doesn't seem right," she finally said. "You can't do this. Emily is the gentlest person I've ever known."

"She's changed. Anyone would, under her circumstances."

"But Michael, if she does this—"

He silenced her with a kiss. Keeli broke away and leaned her head against his shoulder. Michael's chest relaxed, his muscles unfurling into easy warmth.

"I like it when you do that," he said quietly. "I keep thinking you will reject me."

"If I were going to reject you, I wouldn't have had sex with you on my floor."

Michael began to laugh, but sobered almost instantly. He thought of Emily, and the way Jas looked at her. Like there was nothing to see but beauty. "How did they meet?" he asked.

He felt Keeli's sad smile. "Emily was a student at the local community college. Jas was there to get a degree in business management. It was love at first sight, though Jas waited forever to tell her he was a werewolf. She took it really well. They got married a week later."

Michael stared at his hands. "Has she ever thought about reconstructive surgery?"

"It's too expensive. They tried approaching some foundations, but the work that needs to be done is so extensive, no one is willing to do it pro bono. Being married to a registered werewolf doesn't help her case, either. The doctors are afraid of catching something."

"Jas must be extremely careful with her."

"He is. He worships the ground she walks on."

Michael touched Keeli's face. He kissed her mouth, gentle.

"Trust your friend," he said softly, against her lips. "Revenge may not be the best answer to her fear, but that's something only she can learn. Otherwise, she will continue living her life through other people."

"You think you're so smart," she muttered, but without malice.

"I'm a very old man." He kissed her. "And you are so very young."

"Oh?" She smiled against his lips. "What is it with old men and their young girlfriends?"

"They are sick." Michael's fingers moved under her shirt, tracing a path up her ribs. "Very sick."

"Sick is good," she murmured, touching him through his pants. He began to reach under her skirt and she stopped him.

"Not without a condom."

He blinked. "What if I pull out early?"

She hesitated. He touched her breast, rubbing her nipple through the thin T-shirt. "That is so unfair," she said, shuddering. "And this is stupid. Oh, boy, it's stupid."

She unzipped his pants. He pulled off her skirt.

Chapter Fifteen

This time, they took it slow as they made love. When Keeli finally came, writhing naked and sweaty beneath his body, Michael increased his rhythm—tight, hard, fast—savoring the quick build. At the last moment, he pulled out. Keeli sat up, a blur, and then—shocking, unexpected—her mouth engulfed him, hot and wet, and he was still thrusting, and her hands brushed his balls.

He came in her mouth and she did not pull away. Her nails dug into his hips, holding him to her as he poured himself down her throat.

"Bet that was new," she said. She grinned, wiping her glistening lips with the back of her hand. Michael could not answer her; he was still breathing too hard.

They got dressed in increments, helping each other with bits and pieces, touching and kissing. Michael savored the intimacy, drew it in with each careful breath. He had never been so close to anyone—had not even imagined that a person could feel so much for another. It baffled him, but that was good; he could take confusion, as long as it kept him near Keeli.

When they were finally presentable—or at least, as presentable as two people could be, smelling of sex in a den full of werewolves—Michael pulled out the remaining two DNA kits. Keeli sighed. Michael felt the same. This was not going to be easy.

They went to Estella's home, the last door at the end of a canary yellow hall. She answered on Keeli's third knock. Her sparsely furnished home was filled with werewolves. Everyone looked very uncomfortable.

Estella frowned. "You're interrupting something."

"Too bad," Keeli said. "This will only take a minute."

Estella's eyes narrowed. She glanced over her shoulder at her guests. "All of you out. Jonathon, stay."

"You sound like you're teaching an obedience class," Keeli remarked, as werewolves shuffled past her out the door. Michael smelled the faint odor of musk, wet fur. Watched how the men and women avoided looking Keeli in the eyes. Paid attention to the flare of their nostrils, the careful neutrality of their faces. And yet, not one person showed disrespect, disgust, or scorn. Keeli noticed—he saw it on her face, the tentative surprise. The distrust.

One person did not leave Estella's home: a young man, tall and lanky, with a narrow pinched face. He looked like a scholar, but his hands were wiry and strong.

"Jonathon," Keeli said.

"Is it true?" he asked quietly. He looked at Michael. "Are you going to find my mother's murderer?"

Word traveled fast in the underground, it seemed. Michael nodded and Jonathon sighed. He ran his hands over his face. "I don't want to see him. Please. Whatever Emily has planned, don't involve me."

"No stomach," Estella muttered. Michael gave her a sharp look.

"Don't measure courage in terms of revenge," Keeli said harshly. "The math will come out all wrong."

Estella snorted. "You don't scare me, Keeli Maddox. You may have beat the crap out of Leroux's Alpha, but that doesn't make you strong enough to be our Grand Dame. Takes more than a little bloodlust to lead the clans."

"I agree," Keeli said. "I don't want to be the Grand Dame. On the other hand, I don't want Jas to snuff my grandmother. I'm not in a very good position, Estella."

"You've made it worse with him." Estella pointed at Michael. "You smell like you've been screwing each other's brains out."

Michael frowned. "Keeli, did you see any brains?"

"No, Michael. But then again, I was too busy being screwed to notice."

"Ha." Estella stepped aside. "Come in. I don't want anyone to see you lingering at my door."

"Why the hell not?" Keeli walked past her. "The entire clan was packed in here just a minute ago."

Estella did not answer Keeli's question. Jonathon also said nothing. He studied Michael, and Michael studied him back.

"Why are you different?" asked Jonathon. "I'm not scared of you."

It was the first time anyone had ever said that to Michael, and it took him off guard. "Thank you," he said. "I do not want to be frightening."

"Isn't that sweet?" Estella crossed her arms. "You're like Ferdinand the Bull, or Casper the Friendly Ghost. The most snuggly little vampire in all the world."

"Yes. Snuggly." Keeli pulled out the DNA kit and stuck it in Estella's face. "Don't argue with me about this. Just do it."

"Or what?"

"Estella." Jonathon gave her a hard look. The blond woman blinked, startled. Without another word she took the kit. Keeli stared.

"What the hell was that?" she asked.

"Respect," Jonathon said, low and hard. "You've earned it, Keeli. You did the right thing today, taking down Leroux's Alpha. You did better than any of us." He reached for the other DNA kit. "That's what everyone was talking about when you got here. What we should have done—how far we let Leroux go in abusing our own, just because of a scent. You shamed us, Keeli, even the wolves who weren't there."

"She didn't shame me," Estella muttered, giving back her tissue sample.

Jonathon looked at Michael. "Thank you. I don't agree with Emily, but that doesn't mean I don't want this . . . vampire . . . off the street. No one else should lose family to him."

"I am the Vendix," Michael said. "This is what I do."

"Yeah?" He stuck out his hand. Michael, taken aback, shook it.

"Wasn't so bad," murmured Jonathon, a half-smile on his face.

"No," said Michael. "I just hope the rest of the negotiation goes as smoothly."

"Maybe it will." Jonathon turned to Keeli. "Good luck on your investigation. I'll . . . see you later."

Estella stared at him, her mouth hanging open. Jonathon grabbed her hand and pulled her away until Keeli and Michael left the apartment.

"That was strange," Keeli said, when the door shut behind them. "Strange, but good."

"I agree," Michael said, watching her. "But we have the DNA now. Let's call Jenkins."

They went topside to use Michael's digi-encoder. They waited in an alley, in the shadows, and watched the sky darken into evening, the oncoming sunset. Keeli's mood

212

soured; it was clear to Michael that patience was not her strength.

A patrol van finally pulled in. Jenkins was at the wheel, and he was alone.

"I hate you," Keeli said, when he got out of the car.

Jenkins glanced at Michael. "Good evening to you, too. Not getting any sleep last night really caught up with you, didn't it?" he asked her.

Michael briefly closed his eyes as Keeli said, "No offense, but your idea of pleasant conversation makes me want to drive a power drill into my ears."

"Why would I be offended?" Jenkins smiled. "You have the kits?"

Keeli tossed them into his outstretched hands. Jenkins glanced at the packets and withdrew a small white box from the deep pocket of his navy cargo pants. "DNA reader," he said. "The latest tech. Those tissue samples you got started breaking down the moment they came into contact with the sampler. Now I just have to insert them in this thing and we'll see if there's a match with the werewolf markers we found on Crestin."

The first sample tested was Jonathon's. He came up clean. Michael stepped closer as Jenkins inserted Estella's sample. He glanced up and down the alley, but they were alone except for pigeons plodding on the ground near a pile of garbage. He smelled old vomit and car oil. Maybe some pizza on Jenkins's breath.

"Is there a reason for the personal visit?" Keeli asked. "You could have sent someone else. Or did you just miss us that desperately?"

Jenkins placed a hand over his heart, though his eyes never left the DNA reader's screen. "It's true, kid. I can't live another minute without you."

"Smart-ass."

"Punk."

"Weevil."

"Weevil?" He shook his head. "You can do better than that."

"I'm trying to be respectful."

"Yeah. I can tell." He removed Estella's sample. "She's clean. Maybe third time will be the charm."

"That's not funny."

"Murder never is."

But Jas was clean. Jenkins gathered up the tissue samples and gave them back to Keeli. "I'm supposed to keep those, but this investigation is already playing under the radar, so the rules are mine."

"Thank you," Michael said. He studied Jenkins's face as Keeli took back the kits, juggled them in her hands. Shadows and wrinkles lined the skin beneath the cop's eyes. The corner of his mouth sagged. Jenkins caught Michael staring, and raised his brow in silent question.

"You look terrible," Michael said. "Are things that bad?"

"You tell me," Jenkins said. "I want to know what's going on, Michael."

"You'll have to get more specific than that."

Jenkins shook his head. "I can see right through you. Something isn't right. Not with my bosses and the government brass, and not with you guys. All of you know something big. Shit, I'm lying awake at night, scared that the middlemen like me and my people are gonna get screwed."

"We're all screwed," Keeli said. "In various, increasingly unpleasant ways. We might as well tattoo it on our foreheads."

"You gonna tell me why?"

"No," Michael said. "This is for your own good, Jenkins. There are things going on that could destroy your career. Just leave it alone."

"Right," he said. "Like I should leave alone all those UV lights that were installed last week, huh? The ones that got destroyed almost the same day they appeared? Or how about those two vampires who got gunned down by that mech? Or the mech itself? Don't try to con me, Michael. I may not know everything, but the clues are there. I just want to hear it from you. The straight, honest truth. Between friends, no less."

Michael stepped close. "Friends protect each other, Jenkins. That's what I'm trying to do for you and your family."

"Bullshit."

"Please." Keeli touched both their shoulders. "Don't fight over this. We'll tell you eventually, Jenkins, but not yet. We can't."

He looked like he wanted to argue—pigheaded, stubborn—but he swallowed hard, sucking down his words. "I'll take that for now, but not much longer. I can't afford to."

"I understand," Michael said, relieved. "Thank you."

"Don't." Jenkins began to walk back to his car. "The only way you can thank me is with the truth."

The truth? Easier said than done.

They took a walk around the neighborhood and looked at the graffiti. The artists, along with their usual scrawled insults and concrete poetry, had managed correct and succinct depictions of current affairs in the city.

"We think we're living such secret lives," Keeli said, looking at a mural that showed some rather bloated wolves sucking vampire cock.

"Hm." Michael pointed at another, smaller, picture that illustrated humans ramming a wooden spike down a vampire's throat.

"Wrong spot," Keeli said, tilting her head. "They need to go for the heart."

"It's art, Keeli. Allow them their drama."

"I'm just saying."

But the one that disturbed Keeli the most, which kept them both standing still for much longer than was wise, was a rough drawing of a werewolf and vampire feeding, together, on a human.

"Is it possible they know what's going on?" Keeli wondered. "About the possible alliance? Or did the humans anticipate an alliance all along? Is it them doing this, trying to frame a werewolf for murdering vampires, keeping us from banding together before we're destroyed?"

"Anything is possible," Michael said, tearing his gaze away. "But don't forget that traces of vampire DNA were found under Walter Crestin's fingernails. This could be a different kind of setup."

"You really think there are vampires so hot against this alliance they would kill their own kind just to frame us?"

An odd expression passed over Michael's face. "Some, yes."

Darkness pressed gently down on the streets; headlights flashed in their eyes. Cigarette tips flared bright in shadows. Keeli and Michael could see just fine; they were the only ones on the sidewalk who managed to avoid the piles of broken glass, used condoms, discarded needles. Prostitutes eyed Michael and Keeli but kept away, giving them wary looks while shaking their backsides at drivers.

"How do they know what we are?" Keeli asked Michael.

"Good survival instincts," he said. "When you're always prey, you learn to spot the predators."

Keeli shook her head. "It shouldn't have to be that way."

"But it is. In all my years, I have never seen anything

different. The cities may change, as well as the clothes and customs, but the people don't. People don't ever."

"I changed," Keeli said quietly. "I changed fast."

Michael said nothing for a moment. He picked up her hand and cradled it in his elbow. Keeli felt like an old-fashioned girl being walked to dinner, a dance.

"I stand corrected," he said, his voice dark and lovely.

"Of course you do," she said.

He laughed, low, and it was strange—strange and wonderful—being normal and easy with a man, someone so different from Keeli and yet so similar.

And those differences should have been overwhelming—*were* overwhelming to everyone else—but Keeli could no longer give them any real meaning. Just a day—oh, God, a day—and she felt like she knew this man. All the essentials that mattered, and she was crazy—so crazy . . .

Michael stopped walking. "Do you hear that?"

Keeli listened hard. She heard car tires on pavement, the jeers of prostitutes. She heard men and women talking, cursing, the chatter of train tracks from far away. And above it all, light and lilting, came a man's lovely voice, floating desperate melodies in shadow.

Keeli grabbed Michael's shoulder. "Could that be the same person Richard and Suze talked about? He sounded dangerous."

"I have heard that voice before," he said. "Last night, just before the envoys entered the underground."

"He must have been near Maddox territory. Do you think . . . do you think he was involved with Crestin's death?"

"There's only one way to find out." Michael pulled her into an alley.

"Wait," she said, but he kissed her hard and jumped into the air.

"I can fly faster than you can run," Michael said. "Please do not be angry, Keeli. I'll meet you back at the tunnels."

And then he was gone, zipping into the darkening sky.

"Hey!" Keeli shouted after him. "Hey, you stinky bastard! Come back here!"

Which did not bring him back, but did gather some very appraising looks from several nearby junkies who were jacking needles into their legs. Keeli scowled at them and trudged back home to the tunnels.

Walking helped her nerves, her irritation at being left behind. She worried about Michael, too. Of course, it wasn't like he didn't know what he was doing. He'd been alive a lot longer than Keeli—and she could certainly understand his reasoning. Flying was faster.

It was just . . . she wanted to help. She'd always been one to take care of herself first, but now she had this desire to do the right thing, to spread herself out in a way that did something for other people. That did something for her clan. For Michael.

She thought about this, letting her instincts guide her down the dirty sidewalks. The neighborhood got better. Less broken glass and broken people; cleaner buildings with actual business, and customers who looked askance at her pink hair and rough clothes.

Keeli moved down old Smokehouse Street, past the rows of underground clubs, which even at the dinner hour were already adding a *thump-thumping* to the air. Their long lines were filled by the early birds—young sharp kids with sharper eyes, who also judged her hair and clothes and attitude like it meant something, as if it were currency or power instead of just fun.

She walked past them to the calmer joints, the simple blue-collar bars with motorcycles and floozy women hanging out the door, talking shit about their bosses. They looked at her funny too, but their eyes were less feral, more tired. Nothing to prove. Just a hankering for a drink and some talk and maybe a soft bed or body to share it with. Keeli would not have minded a drink, but now was not the time—there might never be a time, certainly not to loosen control. Not here. Not with strangers.

Maybe with Michael.

Maybe. Maybe she trusted him that much. Maybe, yes. Maybe, definitely. Maybe she was insane.

You already covered that, she told herself. *And there are worse things than being crazy.*

Yeah, like being dead. Or living like an uptight asshole.

Raucous laughter made her veer down a side street. The men were far away, but Keeli had too many uncomfortable memories from the night before. Just because she could protect herself did not mean she wanted to go out of her way to find situations where she had to.

Keeli walked faster. The street was unlit except for the dim glow of light streaming down from several apartment windows, but even that did little to cut into the hard black shadows. She had no trouble seeing, but something about the darkness made her uneasy. The back of her neck prickled. She turned, walked backward for a moment as she scanned the street that had been behind her. Nothing. Everything was very still. Quiet.

Movement flashed at the corner of her eye, a lifting of shadow from shadow. Keeli whirled, crouching low. Barely breathing, she searched the narrow alcove where darkness seeped like oil.

She heard humming, then, so out of place it took her breath away. She listened, resisting the urge to take off screaming, Richard's voice running a litany through her mind about blood and song and other, more frightening things. The humming was from a lovely voice, soft and eerie.

Very slowly, Keeli said, "Come out, come out, whoever you are."

The humming stopped. The silence was almost worse. Keeli heard a deep voice, quiet and masculine and strained, say:

"I like that. You're different from the others. The wolves. I think I like you."

"Yeah?" Claws pushed through Keeli's fingernails. Her muscles tightened. "Why the hell should that matter to me?"

"It means you should go now. You should run. Please."

Shit, yes. But Keeli did not run. She said, "Who are you to tell a werewolf what to do?"

"I'm no one," said the voice. "No one. Or everyone. I don't know. Please. I'm not supposed to hurt you. Just watch, just watch, but I'm so hungry, too hungry to watch."

Keeli edged down the alley, taking deep even breaths. Her heart felt like it was going to pound right through her ribs. "So find something to eat. There's a restaurant right down the street."

"It's wrong to eat humans. It's wrong to eat wolves."

Keeli froze. She stared hard into the shadowed alcove and thought she saw a hand, pale and large.

"Go," he said. "Please. There's someone else I need to find, but I just had to see you close. I had to see your eyes."

"Come closer," Keeli said, tasting blood as her canines pushed into her bottom lip. Her claws felt sharp, tight. She glanced down the alley; it looked empty. No witnesses. No one else to get hurt. "Come on," she said, taking a step toward the alcove. "Show me *your* eyes."

"No," he breathed. "I'm not right; I'm not good. I'll hurt you."

"Yes," Keeli said. "You can try."

His answering cry nearly deafened her. Heartrending, terrible, the sound cut through her ears and heart. Keeli staggered as something large flew out of the alcove—man-shaped, but so fast that all she could do was raise her hands before it slammed into her chest, knocking her to the ground. Breath left her lungs and she arched upwards, scrabbling for flesh. She tried to see—to smell—but the darkness pressing down on her was too thick, blinding, and she felt cloth, and—*he is hiding his face*—he was strong—*oh God, he's strong*—and she dug her claws into where his eyes should have been, digging deep, screaming, screaming . . .

He rolled off her body, clutching his face. Keeli smelled blood. She scrambled to her feet, breathing hard.

"Come on," she snarled, the wolf raging inside her chest, howling for release. She tore into her T-shirt, ripping it off. Her ribs began to shift. "Let's try this again."

The mask he wore had a tear in it now, a gaping hole that revealed blood on pale skin, a high cheekbone. She did not recognize his scent, which tasted strange, familiar yet alien.

"I'm so sorry," he whispered, still covering his eyes. She heard shame in his voice and it made her gut twist.

"Sorry," she hissed. "What good does that do me?"

He shook his head, backing away. "I'm sorry," he murmured again, and he looked at her—looked—and Keeli saw blood and the glitter of impossible eyes, eyes as bright as fire, even in the darkness shining—and she stepped closer, all of the sudden unmindful of danger. The man shook his head.

"No," he said in a strangled voice.

He looked up at the sky, and then he was gone. Shooting up, flying away into the night. A blur, swallowed by the sky.

Keeli was left alone, shivering and half-naked. She stared at the sky, watching the retreat of violence, and felt very, very, afraid.

Chapter Sixteen

Keeli jumped down the first tunnel entrance she found and raced through the wide corridors so quick she almost dropped to four legs instead of two. She fought to keep the wolf at bay—she was already running on instinct, but it was tempered with humanity. If she went to the beast, she might lose that. She might get everyone in a stir, when what was needed now was calm.

The werewolves she passed shouted after her—"*What is wrong, do you need help?*"—but Keeli ignored them. She had no time. She had to find her grandmother. Michael.

Please let him be here. Please, oh God.

She reached the Alpha core, turned a corner, and found the Grand Dame standing in the doorway of her brightly lit home. She held herself straight, clad only in an elegant silk robe that draped around her bare feet. Lower Alphas surrounded her, keeping a respectful distance. Leroux stood in the back, shoulders hunched, the front of his shirt covered in blood.

Jas was there, too. He noticed Keeli and glanced quickly away. He seemed tired.

Hargittai touched the Grand Dame's shoulder and gestured at Keeli. The Grand Dame pretended not to notice. She continued speaking to the other wolves, some of whom gave Keeli and her grandmother curious looks. It was quite apparent that none of them missed the old woman's slight against her granddaughter.

Keeli's cheeks warmed; her pounding heart tightened into an unbearable ache. She knew her grandmother very well, and it was clear that the woman was angry.

I don't have time for this.

She approached slowly but with intent, throwing confidence into her every step. If she were the challenger, an Alpha in principle, then it was her right—though it pained her to use that against her grandmother, especially now.

"Grand Dame Alpha," she said, lowering her chin. "I need to speak with you. It's very urgent."

"Later," said the old woman, without sparing Keeli a glance. She continued talking with a skinny red-haired Alpha, whose gaze flickered past the Grand Dame's shoulder to Keeli and her dirty, nearly naked, body.

"Grand Dame," Hargittai murmured. "You should at least look at her."

"She is being disruptive," growled the Grand Dame. "Now be silent."

Hargittai blinked, as did everyone else. Keeli gritted her teeth.

"Fine. Ignore me." Keeli gestured at the other Alphas, who *were* paying attention. "All of you need to keep your wolves off the street tonight. There's something—"

The Grand Dame snarled, whirling with claws outstretched, teeth sharp. She faltered when she saw Keeli's body, the signs of a fight, but then her eyes hardened and she stalked forward with vicious intent. Keeli felt slapped upside the head by her grandmother's anger, but she steeled herself past the pain and held her ground.

"It is not your place to give orders," snapped the old woman.

"You wouldn't listen to me," Keeli replied, trying to keep her voice steady, quiet. "There is something out hunting wolves tonight. Hunting vampires. It almost killed me."

"It obviously didn't try hard enough." The words came out fast, angry; Keeli stifled a gasp, and for a moment imagined she saw regret in her grandmother's eyes. But it was too late for that. Keeli's heartache turned to anger.

"Fine then," she spat, backing away. "Don't listen to me. But if a wolf is found dead in the morning, you'll only have yourself to blame."

The Grand Dame threw back her head and barked— sharp, and piercing. The Alphas backed away. When there was a respectable distance separating the Grand Dame from her subordinates, she approached Keeli. Gold flecks blazed within her blue eyes. Keeli felt trapped by that gaze, by the unfamiliar rage that for the first time— awful, stunning—was directed at her alone.

"How dare you," whispered the Grand Dame. "How dare you come here and undermine me like that. In public, no less."

"Jas did it earlier," Keeli said, licking her dry lips. "You were not so angry at him."

"Despite what I told him, I expected it. I've known for some time he would make a bid. But this, from you . . ."

"What has you so mad?" Keeli asked, desperate. She could not stand this. "If it's because of the bid, I'm sorry! I had no idea who Leroux was when I fought him, and he was hurting—"

The Grand Dame bared her teeth. "No excuses. You

made your bid, Keeli. You made your bid for Alpha, just like your father did all those years ago. They killed him for that. For his temper. They called him unstable, because he could not control himself, even against other wolves. A threat. A mad dog. Your poor mother tried to protect him, and they . . ." She shook her head and leaned close. "They will do the same to you, Keeli. You with your temper. And your vampire." Her nostrils flared. "Everyone can smell you. Smell his seed on your body. It's sick. *Disgusting*."

"You're disgusting," Keeli said, fighting back tears. "To use my father's death against me like this. I know why he died, and maybe the same thing will happen to me, but I don't care. *I don't care*."

The Grand Dame moved so fast Keeli barely had time to gasp. Hands pressed down on her shoulders; her heart clutched, twisting. Voice breaking, her grandmother whispered, "I won't lose you. I won't take the risk."

"Don't," Keeli breathed. "Don't do this to me."

"It is too late. Everyone knows. Brian O'Dell was here, asking questions. He is going to write about your fight with Alpha Leroux. He is going to tell *everyone* what you are doing with—with *him*."

"Good," Keeli spat. "I want everyone to know."

"Idiot." The Grand Dame's lip curled. "You are just like your father. Brash, impulsive. Arrogant. *So* arrogant. He thought he could claim leadership of any clan he wanted."

"I am not him." Keeli shook with anger. "But I loved him, and he loved us. Don't you dare speak badly of your son."

"I dare what I like! You are *my* blood, *my* wolf. I cannot make you give up your bid—that would go against all our laws—but you and the vampire are *done*. Do you understand? He is dead to you. He is *dead*."

"No," Keeli breathed.

"You had your chance to prove control, but in every way you have failed me. After the negotiations are over, I will abdicate to Jas. Until then, you will remain in your room. I am ashamed of you, Keeli. I am so disappointed. You smell like trash."

Keeli snarled, breaking her grandmother's hold. The Grand Dame's hand shot out and slammed into Keeli's breastbone. A crack, and pain made her blind. She fell hard to her knees, unable to breathe. She heard shouts. Hargittai, maybe. More than one wolf; a clamor of voices.

The Grand Dame knelt close and brushed cool fingers against Keeli's flushed cheek.

"Forgive me," she whispered. "I do this because I love you."

Keeli would have laughed, except she thought it would make her faint. Instead, she choked out, "Love's not . . . supposed to hurt . . . this much."

The Grand Dame's sorrowful eyes turned cool. Keeli felt a moment of fear, and it was horrible, terrible, being afraid of her grandmother. All those soft memories of warmth, safety—gone.

"I thought you knew, Keeli. Love *is* pain. Perfect love kills."

Her grandmother rose, elegant and distant. Keeli heard quick footfalls, and then Jas said, "Grand Dame?"

"Put Keeli in her room. Do not let her out until I give you permission."

Jas picked Keeli up, cradling her against his chest. He turned away from the Grand Dame and carried her down the hall. Keeli tried not to cry, but tears raced down her cheeks, hot and salty. She watched Jas's face, and clutched his shirt.

"Don't," she gasped. "Please."

Jas's neutral expression cracked. Compassion filled his eyes.

"I'm sorry," he whispered. And that was all he said, even when he set Keeli down on her bed with a blanket pulled over her body, and locked the door behind him.

It was a bad night to be on the street; Michael felt it in his bones, in his ears with that elusive song soft like a lure. He thought he came close once or twice, but the music eventually stopped and the trail went cold.

He hung high in the sky, savoring the wind rushing tight around his body. For a moment, his heart thrilled hard with joy—the first time in ages—and he knew it was because of Keeli. He wanted to see her so badly, to be reminded again and again of her light, quick voice and searching eyes. Being with her took away the loneliness of exile, the poison of his people's contempt for him. The torment of his actions and past. With her he felt new. He felt . . . good.

Oh, Keeli. I don't deserve you. He did not deserve much of anything at all. And if she knew what he had done, the atrocities he had committed with his own two hands . . .

She will hate me. She will kill me.

But maybe that would be preferable to keeping the truth from her. She certainly deserved the truth. Tough, strong, compassionate Keeli—who could take her hate for vampires and still find it within herself to hold one, kiss one.

Perhaps even love *one.*

He launched himself into movement with just a thought, riding the air currents—*riding, riding into the blue sky horizon, away and far*—feeling for a moment the past upon his soul, the peace before blood and dark. Or at least, now, it felt like peace. In the days before his transformation into vampire, nothing had felt peaceful about his life. It was only hunger and poverty and disdain.

Nothing had changed. Nothing.

I was such a fool. A fool to believe anything that Malachai told me.

Well, Malachai was dead now. No more words, ever again, would pass through those lips. Michael had made sure of that. Burned the body and scattered the ashes.

His tattoo throbbed. He rubbed the hard gold.

An unnatural shift in the wind caught his attention. He whirled, glimpsing something large and dark at the corner of his eye. It moved incredibly fast, staying just out of Michael's line of sight until he felt like a top spinning round and round, and it was too much—Michael shot up, so fast his eyes watered.

Hands grabbed his neck. Michael struggled to break free but the creature holding him was incredibly strong and supple. It moved as Michael moved, fluid and graceful, smelling strong of blood.

"I'm sorry," whispered a low voice. Hot breath swept over his neck; teeth scraped against his iron collar. Leather-clad fingers slipped beneath, pressing hard on his throat, puncturing skin. Killing him.

His attacker stopped—still, so still. Hushed.

"You carry her scent," he whispered, and with those words, Michael stopped thrashing. Terror filled him, hot and biting—so unfamiliar that at first he had no name for it. That blood he smelled . . .

"Wha—" Michael tried to speak, but his vocal cords were held too tight. He wanted to scream with frustration, and in his mind he did, again and again, howling.

"She told me it was impossible," said the creature. "Told me never, not ever, not even in a dream." He released Michael.

Michael spun around, reaching for his sword. He glimpsed red eyes in a torn mask.

"Did you rape her?" asked the creature, shaking. "She did not look raped, but I don't know about those things. Did you hurt her? Did you? Is that why you have to die?"

"What do you want?" Michael rasped. His throat hurt.

"You've had sex with a werewolf," said his attacker—a man, a creature—some strange mystery. "A vampire and a werewolf. You smell so strong of her."

Michael lashed out, dancing on air, his sword flickering quicksilver in the moonlight. The creature whirled, turning against the blade, cutting his clothing on the razor edge. Michael plummeted feet first to the earth. The creature followed; when they were less than twenty yards from concrete, Michael threw himself flat and shot sideways, up. His pursuer barely managed to stop himself. Michael fell on him, stabbing. He reached for the mask.

The creature caught Michael's hand and tossed him away. Michael skidded into a dumpster.

"I thought she smelled strange," said the creature, breathing hard. "Strange, familiar. It's why I followed her. I . . . I wasn't supposed to."

"Did you hurt her?" Michael staggered to his feet. Wildness spun through his heart, biting, hard.

The creature touched his eyes. "I didn't mean to."

"I am going to kill you," Michael said, raising his sword. "I don't care how strong you are. I will kill you for that."

"Please," said the creature, and something in that voice made Michael hesitate long enough to hear, "Do you love her?"

Michael stared.

"Please," said the creature again, floating closer.

"Please tell me. Do you love her? Is it possible for a vampire to love a werewolf? Please."

If Michael held any doubts about the *her* his assailant was referring to, they were completely erased by that one question.

"Who are you to ask such a thing?" Michael asked, so quiet he was not sure the creature would hear him.

"I . . ." He stopped, and those red eyes became so anguished Michael felt the creature's pain as surely as if it was his own. "I . . . don't know."

"Fight me, then," Michael said, gliding close. "Fight me, and maybe you will remember."

Because he wanted a fight—oh, he wanted blood from the man who had tried to hurt Keeli. Nothing less would satisfy.

The creature backed away. "You don't want me to fight you. I'm too hungry. It will end badly. It is supposed to end badly. You are supposed to die tonight."

Memory stirred in Michael's heart, centuries old, of a moment when conscious thought penetrated the fog of savage hunger that had clouded his mind for months, and he stopped—stopped before the kill, and the ragged man beneath him still wanted to fight. *I am so hungry,* Michael whispered. *Please, don't. It will end badly. It will end—*

Michael looked hard at this new creature—*no, no, not another mirror, not another Malachai*—and swallowed his terrible desires as he had done so long ago. Familiar dread filled his heart as he said, "Who is hurting you?"

The creature made a low sound.

Michael glided forward. He lowered his sword. "It was done to me," he said, as though they were holding a normal conversation that had nothing to do with death and torture. "My master put me in a hole where he starved me until my body shriveled, until my mind held nothing more than instinct. No thought, except for hunger, for survival. And when I was near death, but still strong enough to kill, he released me in the middle of sleeping families, to watch me feed. It was his sport, his entertainment, and I was helpless to that game for a very long time."

"There is no entertainment," said the creature. He touched his neck, and Michael noted a bulge beneath the tight outline of his dark clothing. "But she does watch me. She has always watched me."

"Who are you talking about? Who did this to you?"

The creature shook his head, backing away. "No, I can't. This is wrong. You're the enemy. You're *food*. You don't talk to food." His voice broke. "Please, go. Just get away from me."

"Why were you going to kill me? Who told you vampires were food?"

"Reversal of fortune," whispered the creature, floating off the ground. "Karma."

And then he shot up into the air. Michael tried to follow, but the creature quickly lost him amidst the tangle of city buildings. Lost him so easily, in fact, that Michael wondered if he'd had training. No one ever had escaped him like that; Michael was too fast, too skilled at the hunt.

Please tell me. Do you love her? Is it possible for a vampire to love a werewolf? Please.

He remembered that pleading voice, asking the one question Michael could never have foreseen.

And then he remembered the scent of blood.

Werewolves guarded the first tunnel he tried to enter. They held sharpened wooden pikes, guns holstered to their sides. It was the first time Michael had ever seen the werewolves arm themselves, and he thought it was bad timing, considering the second negotiation with the vampires was scheduled for that night.

He tried to pass them and they blocked his path.

"The Grand Dame is restricting all access to the tunnels," said the shorter werewolf, all muscle and beard. The taller held his pike loose, ready to stab.

"The Grand Dame knows me. I am helping her granddaughter investigate a murder."

A tight grin passed over the short wolf's face, though his companion remained tense. Worried, even. "Yeah, we can smell all the help you've been giving Keeli. You've been doing a real good job, haven't you?"

"Dan, stop that," said the tall wolf. He looked at Michael and lifted the pike, aiming the point at his heart. "You better go. We have our orders."

Michael held out his hands. "I do not want to fight. Please, where is Keeli? Did anything happen to her?"

The second wolf began to answer, but Dan lashed out, stabbing at Michael's chest. Michael blocked the pike and twisted it out of the werewolf's hands. He broke it over his knee and tossed the pieces away.

"Where is she?" he shouted, advancing on the two werewolves. Dan pulled out his gun, while the other wolf lifted his pike—warier now, with a tight grip on the wooden shaft. Michael smelled their sweat, heard the racing thrum of fearful hearts—and underneath it all, the hot promise of blood.

But if he fought these wolves—if he hurt them in any way—Keeli would be the one to suffer. He had already made her a target, without inciting even more resentment and rage. Michael backed away. He left the tunnel entrance and took to the air.

He found another entrance, and the result was the same:

armed werewolves, with orders to keep him—and it was only him, he was sure of that—out of the underground.

What happened? What changed in the Grand Dame's heart to make her do this?

Or was it Keeli herself who had begged for the order? Had she changed her mind about him? Was this what her rejection looked like?

No. He did not doubt the possibility of her rejection, though it was not something he wished to contemplate, but he could not believe she would do it like this. Keeli was too straightforward. She would never ask anyone else to fight her battles.

Which meant that something was very wrong.

He was turned away at the third tunnel, and it was difficult—almost impossible—not to knock aside the wolves and run rampant through the underground, searching and screaming her name.

Enough of this. Forget control. Do you think Keeli would apologize for being tactless? No.

He unsheathed his sword, preparing to jump back down into the tunnel he had just left.

Someone whistled.

Michael glanced over his shoulder and saw a familiar face peering out from behind a dumpster. Suze gestured furtively and pressed a finger to her lips. Michael glided close, ducking into the shadows beside her. Their shoulders pressed together; he did not miss the way she shuddered, but for once, he didn't care.

"Keeli," he whispered.

She refused to look at him. "There was a fight between her and the Grand Dame. Keeli got knocked flat and locked in her room. You're bad guy numero uno."

"I need to get her out."

"Sure, fine. That's why I'm here. We got word that you

tried to get into the South Street entrance, and guessed you'd end up here eventually if you didn't lose your cool. Richard is looking for another way in."

Michael stared. "You hate me. Why are you doing this?"

Suze finally looked him in the eye. "Because Keeli took up for me. She slammed an Alpha and his goons, for Christ's sake, just because he was beating on me. Your fault, don't forget."

"I haven't," he said grimly.

"Yeah. Well, Richard and I remember when people do good things for us. When you've got nothing, a little something becomes real important."

"If the others find out—"

She cut him off. "They can't do anything worse to us than what's already been done. Richard and I will just stick with the original plan. Go to Mexico or something."

Michael shook his head. "Do you have a good memory?"

Suze gave him a strange look, but nodded. Michael gave her his address and made her repeat it back to him.

"There's a briefcase with five thousand dollars in it. I've got it at my apartment. If you and Richard get into trouble and I'm not around, the money is yours."

Her mouth fell open. "You're fucking nuts."

"Yes," he said. "That's why Keeli likes me."

"I'm cool with that," Suze said, still looking dazed. They heard a scuffling sound and Richard appeared. He frowned when he saw Michael sitting so close to Suze, but only gestured for Michael to follow him. He had some papers stuffed in his hand.

Michael, Suze, and Richard jogged down the alley, turning out on the street with headlights flashing bright in their eyes. They walked for two blocks in complete silence, and then Richard dragged Michael down a series of steps that led to the front door of a basement business, closed for the evening. There was a drainage grate in front of the door. Richard pointed at it.

"There's your door. It's not guarded."

"How did you find it?"

Richard grinned. "When you live rough, you learn to play rough." He held up the papers in his hand. "The first thing I did when Suze and I moved in was find the clan's blueprints of the place. Told them I didn't want to get lost." He sneered. "Made sure I found all the back holes, the ways in and out. Made drawings. I don't trust anyone."

"Except for Suze," Michael commented, lifting the grate free. The hole smelled wet and dirty. Out of the corner of his eye, he saw Richard snag Suze around her waist and pull her close. Michael thought of doing the same thing to Keeli. He sat down on the edge of the hole and dangled his legs in the darkness.

"Thank you," he said, looking up at the two teens. They shrugged, but it was enough.

Michael dropped through the hole, scraping the sides of his arms. He did not hit the ground, stopping mere inches above it so he would not make a sound. Michael saw the rough outline of pipes, the accumulated debris. This place was very old.

"It'll run out three tunnels over from the Alpha core," Richard whispered, replacing the grate. "There shouldn't be too many wolves in the halls. The fangs are supposed to arrive soon."

Earlier than what Michael had expected. *Frederick must be feeling pressure to get this resolved.*

Michael almost felt sorry for the elder vampire; the Grand Dame was not going to be in a pleasant mood tonight. An alliance between their two peoples was looking less likely, and this time, the blame could be put squarely on his own shoulders. Michael did not doubt he was part of the reason Keeli and her grandmother had fought.

Do you know what would happen to Keeli if the others found out? Her reputation would never survive. She might not survive. Such alliances are not tolerated.

Or maybe such alliances were not tolerated by certain individuals. It was clear to Michael that every werewolf near them had smelled the sex on their bodies, and only a handful had made an issue of it. Perhaps that had to do with respect for Keeli's position and her temper, or maybe the werewolves—even if they were disgusted— were far more polite than Michael had ever given them credit for.

Or maybe this was the consequence the Grand Dame had spoken of when she begged Michael to do the honorable thing. A promise Michael had found impossible to uphold.

Please forgive me, he begged Keeli, flying through the tunnel, watching the shadows for movement.

The tunnel narrowed. The smell of dirt and damp disappeared, and everything, even the pipes, looked cleaner. Michael glimpsed light, and slowed his approach. The main corridor was empty. Michael took his chance and flew down the hall. He heard a rustling sound just before he turned a corner, but he could not stop—did not want to stop—and he ran into a werewolf who barked sharply as Michael tackled him to the ground. They tumbled over each other, grappling, punching, and he heard the wolf say, "Michael, it's me."

Michael bared his teeth. "I know. Don't stop me now."

Jas hissed. "I thought you'd manage a way in. How did you do it?"

"I have my ways."

"The Grand Dame wants you dead."

"I suspected that."

"I'm of two minds, believe it or not."

"Since you haven't tried to kill me yet, I also suspected that to be the case."

Jas snorted. "I hate your guts, but Keeli . . . likes you, and Emily wants to use you. You have my ass over a barrel."

"Thank you," Michael said.

"Don't. Really. I'll puke if I hear it."

Michael smiled. "Thank you for helping me, Jas. You're an inspiration. Watching you I am overcome with the urge to do greater things with my life."

Jas took a swing at Michael's face. Michael caught the werewolf's fist in his hand and held him there.

"I'm going to kill you," Jas growled.

"But not today." Michael released him and stepped back. He watched the conflict in Jas's eyes—hate and uncertainty and confusion—and waited. Waited for the next move.

Jas sucked in a deep, shuddering breath. "I don't know what she sees in you."

Michael briefly closed his eyes. "I wish I knew."

Jas opened his mouth, hesitated. A moment later, he turned and walked away. Michael followed him. They did not speak again.

Keeli healed. Thirty minutes after her grandmother left and Jas locked the door, the pain was gone. Or at least, her breastbone stopped hurting. There was still a lot of pain.

Keeli just wished she could stop crying. There was something broken inside the soft part of her chest, buried deep beneath the bone. She scrabbled at the flesh, digging her nails into the yielding bits, trying so hard—*so hard, and oh my God what just happened, what did I do, this is my fault and I hate her, I love her and*—to touch that broken piece and hold it tight, safe. She hadn't felt this way since her parents died.

All I wanted to do was help someone. Help the clan.

Yeah.

Keeli staggered to her feet, knocking over books. She kicked them aside, but that wasn't good enough so she picked up some of the heavier ones and threw them at the door. She threw herself next, screaming, her throat raw with sound as she punched and kicked at the metal, abusing it almost as much as she was abusing herself, and she did not care—she did not care—because it felt too damn good and when she got free, oh, God, when she got out of this trap she was going to kill her. She was going to kill her with words. She was going to make her grandmother's heart break and die, and it would feel so good. So good she would do it and smile.

Stop. Stop this now. Granny May was trying to protect you. You know why. She has a good reason to be afraid.

Because she'd thought the clans would do the same thing to Keeli as what had been done to Keeli's father, all those years before: a slaughter in the night.

But that had been different. Keeli was not her father. She was not Mad Dog Maddox, who had been so sweet to his family, but addicted to the ring, to the werewolf games, who'd had to find some outlet for the temper always raging beneath his skin. Better a strange wolf than a familiar one, she remembered him saying, always with that grin, that white smile, and she never knew until it was too late, never knew the injuries he caused, the anger he stirred with just one fight, because no one liked a constant winner—no one liked a man with a temper who lost himself in a fight and beat a wolf into a coma, and then acted like it was just blood, just—*"In my nature,"*—and then with that smile and that charm made a bid for Alpha of a different clan. A strange wolf with a bad reputation, marking territory where he had no business. Arrogant.

No, Keeli was not her father, though the temper was the same, and the reputation only slightly better. Granny

May had the same rage, but she had learned to control it at an early age, used it in her prime to make her bid and win. It was a powerful thing, the Maddox temper. Keeli's father had misused his, while Keeli had tried to bury it.

Not anymore.

Exhausted, Keeli slumped against the door and slid down to the hard cold floor. She hugged her knees to her chest and sat, angry and dozing. An hour passed. She thought of Michael, alone and looking for a creature that hunted werewolves, who might hunt vampires. And didn't *that* raise some interesting questions?

I need to get out of here.

Keeli tested the door, but except for some dents and scratches, the hinges still seemed strong. They were hidden behind a metal frame so she couldn't unscrew them. She tried banging on the door again, lighter this time, and calling out for help. She heard people pass her room, but no one responded. Probably too frightened of getting in trouble. That, or they were happy Keeli was finally getting her comeuppance.

She was just about ready to light fire to her room—maybe that would get someone's attention—when the lock turned. The door opened.

"Michael," Keeli breathed, startled, and then he was there, pulling her into his arms for a hard tight embrace that left her breathless. She clutched at his back, drinking in his wild sweet scent. Just beyond Michael, she heard boots scuffing the ground. She tore herself away, ready to fight. Jas held up his hands.

"What the hell are you doing here?" she asked.

"I have too much pride to answer that question," Jas said. "Now get out of there."

Michael snatched a black sweater from Keeli's closet and gave it to her. "Is there anything else you need?" he asked, as she covered herself. Keeli's breath caught. She knew what he was really saying.

You may not be here again. You may never be able to come home again.

Jas stepped into the room. "Do what you have to, Keeli. Stay or go."

"Will I be welcomed back?" She felt proud that her voice did not break.

"Don't ask stupid questions," he said, rough. "Now, hurry."

It was not an answer, but it was not an outright rejection, either. It was the best Keeli could hope for, given the circumstances. Michael grabbed her hand and led her out of the room. Jas closed the door behind them and locked it. His face was hard, but calm; the key turned steadily in his hand.

"The vampire envoys arrived five minutes ago," Jas said.

"You'll be missed," Keeli said.

Jas shook his head. "They came early, which gives me an excuse." He pointed down the corridor. "You know the way out, right? They'll be coming this way any minute. The negotiations are being held in your grandmother's rooms."

Keeli nodded. She began to thank Jas, but he held up his hand. "Later," he said. "I'm fucked sideways to Sunday if I'm caught."

"You're the only one who can lead the clan after she's gone," Keeli said sadly. "She won't exile you."

"I disagree," he said. "On both counts."

He did not give Keeli a chance to respond. They all heard footsteps; Jas turned and jogged down the corridor, toward the sounds of approach.

Keeli tugged on Michael's hand. "Come on."

He did not run. He touched her cheeks. "You've been crying."

"I'll keep crying if we're caught," she said, swallowing hard. His eyes were soft, dark with compassion. Her throat hurt, looking at him.

They padded down the corridor at a careful run, listening hard.

"They have all the exits guarded," he told her.

"I know another way," she said.

"There's someone coming."

"We're close."

Just outside the Alpha core, Keeli took a left down a narrow unlit corridor. It was a maintenance hall, nicknamed the Tunnel of Love because so many people took advantage of the shadows for some heavy make-out sessions. She hoped it would be empty tonight, and her wish almost came true; after a minute she heard heavy breathing, the wet smack of a sloppy kiss. Michael squeezed her hand; Keeli glanced over her shoulder and mouthed the word "speed." He understood instantly and picked her up.

Michael ran fast. Keeli sucked in her breath at the rush, the terrible wonder of life passing in a blur. He blew past the engrossed couple leaning up hard against the wall. Keeli heard a gasp, but was reassured by the embarrassed giggling that followed. And then she and Michael were completely alone, running, running. . . .

Near the end of the maintenance tunnel, Keeli told Michael to stop.

"How did you know this would be unguarded?" he asked, his hands moving on her back as she slid down his body.

"You'll see in a minute." She walked to a rusty ladder screwed into the wall and began climbing the ten-foot distance. Michael, his arms folded against his chest, floated upward beside her.

"Funny," she said. He smiled, and then blinked, looking up. Keeli heard cars roar above her head.

"I see," he said quietly.

"Bad access," she added. "No one ever uses this place to come in or out. It's a death trap."

"I came in a safer way."

"One I'm sure you would have mentioned, if there hadn't been an ass-load of vampires and werewolves in that direction."

"You're a mind reader now," he said, wrapping a strong arm around her waist. The iron manhole cover was heavy and smelled dirty. Keeli and Michael listened for silent intervals between cars. Some were short, others long—there just wasn't a way to know which they would catch.

"The next one," Michael whispered. He kissed Keeli, and she pushed against him, hard. His teeth scraped her bottom lip.

Michael shoved upward with one strong hand. The cover popped free and he pushed it aside. They heard a car and froze, helpless, as the chassis sped over their heads in a dark blur. Another car followed, and then another. Sweat rolled down Keeli's back.

Michael pulled her off the ladder and shot upward. Headlights bore down on them—*fast, fast*—but he kept moving and Keeli felt the rush of cool air as the car passed beneath, horn blaring. Adrenaline rode her hard; she felt like she had wings, that if Michael let go she would float beside him and it would be like that scene in *Superman*, the one where Lois flew by her fingertips beside the Man of Steel.

She threw her head back and laughed. Michael stared at her upturned face like she was insane, but a moment later a smile touched his lips. He whirled her around in a tight circle, and Keeli threw out her arms, trusting him to hold her tight, to keep her safe.

"Dance with me," she said. "I want to dance on a cloud."

"It's not safe," he said, but rose higher, past the apartments, past the sharp edges of business buildings, past the safety net of steel and glass and light. The city sat beneath their bodies, a delicate web.

A trap, Keeli thought, *with the spider sleeping, invisible until it needs to feed.*

The air cooled as they rose, higher and higher. Keeli did not notice the temperature change, though her breath left her mouth in white puffs. She watched clouds, tinted by city light, resting low to hug the sky. Closer, so close, and her mouth went dry with wonder as Michael carried her into the soft embrace of her first cloud.

"Oh," she sighed, surrounded by mist. The city disappeared—the world, gone—and the only person left was Michael, holding her tight. Clouds suddenly seemed less important than his eyes, the line of his mouth, the hard strength of his arms. Their white breath mingled.

"Thank you," Keeli said, awed by the moment. Michael pressed his cool lips against her forehead.

"Put your feet on top of mine," he said, and she did.

They danced.

Chapter Seventeen

They left the cloud, shivering and soaked from water vapor, cold, uncomfortable, but smiling so bright—so hot—that Michael felt burned by joy. Dancing within the clouds, Keeli laughing in his arms, had been a miracle. To have the power to give her such a gift made him happy to be a vampire.

He could not remember ever feeling that way before.

As they made their descent, he watched the smile slip from her face. Her gaze sharpened; she scanned the skies with an urgent concentration matched only by Michael's own sudden unease.

He alighted on the roof of a skyscraper. Gravel crunched beneath their feet. Keeli swayed unsteadily, and Michael caught her waist. He held her close, drawing in the scent of her hair, the press of her warm body against his own.

"He said he tried to hurt you." Michael did not need to identify that particular "he." Keeli shuddered; her mouth tightened into a hard pink line.

"You fought him, too." Her voice wavered. "I was

scared he would find you, but I didn't know what to do, how to track you down. So I went home to warn my grandmother." Her voice wavered. "She refused to listen to me."

"She blocked all the entrances to the tunnels. Richard and Suze helped me find a way in. They said she hurt you."

"Yes," Keeli whispered. "She said you were dead to me."

Michael pressed his lips to her brow. "No," he murmured, fierce. "Never."

"But almost," she pressed. "If you fought that creature, it must have been close. He was so strong, Michael. I was lucky to get away. Or maybe not. He kept saying he didn't want to hurt me, that he wasn't supposed to. It was almost like he didn't have control over his actions."

"He was covered in blood," Michael whispered. "I thought it was yours."

"I'm sorry," she murmured, and then, "What was he?"

Please tell me. Do you love her? Is it possible for a vampire to love a werewolf? Please. "Keeli," he said, hesitant. "He wanted to know about us. Our relationship. He smelled you on my body and it shocked him into letting me live."

"That doesn't make sense."

Michael looked out at the city below them, the wide sweeping expanse of light and steel and heartache. Nothing about their lives made sense. "He was hungry when he left me. He was distraught."

She sucked in her breath. "Michael."

They went looking for their attacker. Michael spiraled into a wide descent, a twisting path that brought them into Maddox territory. They searched the skies, the streets, listening to the breeze for a song. Nothing, just the city.

Under the hush of the sky, Michael told Keeli about his strange battle. When he was done, Keeli did the same. She also told him of her fight with the Grand Dame. She was oddly dispassionate at first, but towards the end, her voice broke.

"This is my fault," Michael said, aching for her. "If I had left you at the beginning of the investigation, or just refused your partnership, none of this would have happened."

"It would have happened. I owed you. I would have tracked you down."

"But this, Keeli. Us—"

"It was inevitable," she said. "Spending any time with you at all made it inevitable."

Michael briefly closed his eyes, savoring the delicious sweetness of those words. "Jas accused me of brainwashing you."

Keeli laughed. "Of course. Because I'm just that easy."

He tried not to smile. "I did wonder."

She laughed and he clutched her tight, whirling, until something below caught his eye, something familiar and impossible. They were almost five hundred feet above the ground, passing between office towers with careful ease, and Michael watched the flash of a bald head, moving deep within shadow. He went very still.

"What is it?" Keeli asked, gazing down.

Michael frowned, shaking his head. What was Celestine doing, walking alone in Maddox territory? Why wasn't she at the negotiation? Michael drifted closer. He tracked the vampire, and knew she was not aware of his presence because she constantly stopped to look over her shoulder as she glided quickly over the ground. If Celestine really thought anyone were following her, she would have kept her gaze straight on her path; she would have moved with confidence, without slowing. In preparation of attack.

But this was a more furtive Celestine, a less confident woman than Michael was accustomed to seeing.

She finally stopped. In front of her, movement. A man. He had long silver hair.

Keeli sucked in her breath. "Hargittai."

The werewolf and vampire stared at each other.

"Hello, dog." Celestine's voice wavered.

"Celestine," said Hargittai, quiet. "You're looking well."

"You've aged."

"It was bound to happen." He smiled gently. "It's why you left me, if I remember correctly."

Celestine said nothing. Michael could not believe what was unfolding beneath him. Celestine had taken a werewolf as a lover? This, from the woman who called werewolves dirty beasts, who took every opportunity to insult them?

"I was surprised to see you," Celestine said.

"I became the Alpha of my clan," Hargittai said, and there was pride in his voice—that, and a strange longing. "It was my right to be there. But I was equally shocked to see you. I thought you had left the city."

"I changed my mind." Again, that quaver in her voice.

They said nothing else, still standing, watching each other. Keeli stirred against Michael's chest. He glanced down at her face; she watched the werewolf with large eyes. He remembered that she had named him; this was someone she knew, and he could not imagine her shock.

And I thought we were the only ones.

"I need to go before I am missed," Celestine finally said. "I told Frederick I needed air, that the smell of dog was sickening me."

Hargittai laughed out loud. "You were always good at pretending."

She lifted her chin. "Who said I was pretending?"

Hargittai took a step toward her. Celestine's hands flew up.

"Please," she said. "Not again."

"I still miss you," he said. "I never took a mate, Celestine."

She shook her head, backing away. "Don't."

"Just tell me why you left, and not that old lie. I know you too well. You *loved* me."

"I did not!" she gasped. "And I should not have come here. It was wrong."

"It's not wrong anymore." Hargittai darted forward. He grabbed Celestine's hands. "There are others, now. My Grand Dame's own granddaughter has taken a vampire for her lover, and they are not hiding."

"They should be," Celestine snapped, though she did not wrench herself free. "Who is the vampire?"

"He calls himself Michael."

Celestine froze, and then threw her head back in a sharp burst of laughter. "Of course. I knew there was something between him and the pink-haired bitch."

Hargittai frowned. "Don't speak of her in that way. She could be our next Grand Dame."

Celestine bared her teeth. "Not with Michael as her lover. He is a murderer of the worst kind, Hargittai. It is why he is an outcast, why his face has been branded. Ask him, if you ever meet, what a *child* tastes like. He is only one of a few who could tell you."

Keeli twitched. Michael could not bring himself to meet her gaze, to see the expression in her eyes when she realized it was the truth.

Hargittai stared. "You're lying."

Celestine pulled away. "I only ever lied to you about one thing. The rest . . . the rest was always the truth."

He lunged after her, but she slapped him away, the sound of her palm striking his face ringing dull in the night air. It was the last word; Celestine turned and walked away. Hargittai watched her go.

Michael rose into the air. Keeli said, "Is it true?"

"It's complicated," he said.

"Tell me," she said, and there was steel in her voice, daggers in her eyes. *Danger,* his heart whispered, but it was too late. She needed the truth.

"Let's get you dry and warm first," he said, stalling.

They did not talk as he flew them back to his apartment. The silence hurt. All the warmth between them had fled, and he felt like screaming.

He landed in the middle of his roses and set Keeli gently on her feet. He made her wait while he jimmied his window open and climbed inside. He checked the closet and bathroom. The apartment was empty; his belongings undisturbed. The briefcase full of money was still where he had left it.

"Can I come in?" Her voice was cold, distant.

"Yes."

As she climbed through the window, he added. "Someone watched me today from the fire escape. I don't know who, but I felt him there. He broke a rose."

He was talking to fill the silence, but Keeli paused, and shut the window behind her. She locked it and pulled down the shade. Turned around, her arms wrapped around her stomach, her face too pale beneath the shock of pink hair.

"Now," she said. Her eyes were liquid and huge.

"I was alone," he said immediately. "I was hungry and tired. My family no longer welcomed me. One more mouth to feed and I was almost grown, so they sent me out. I traveled for years, looking for odd work. Traveled north, into what is now Russia, and from there I wondered into Europe. A lone, lost, starving oddity. And then one night a man came to me. He called himself Malachai. He was rich and he gave me food. And when I was sated and ready to listen, he told me how I could be just like him. Wealthy. Powerful. Immortal." Michael swallowed hard, trying to speak in a voice louder than a whisper. It was difficult. "Malachai told me he was a vampire, and that it was an easy thing to become. So easy. So I did it. I had nothing to lose."

Keeli sat down on Michael's bed. After a moment, she rubbed the space beside her. He hesitated, but finally sat on the edge of the sagging mattress. He could not bring himself to look at her.

"I don't remember much of what happened after he made me. I do know that I spent a very long time chained inside a hole. Buried alive. Malachai starved me, and when I was almost past the point of no return, he started feeding me blood in miniscule amounts. Not enough to give me strength, but more than enough to drive me into a frenzy."

"He turned you into an animal," Keeli said quietly.

"Yes," Michael said, sinking back into memory. "And when he was ready to be entertained, he released me in the middle of solitary families. Sometimes, even, villages. I could not be fought or reasoned with. I was insane."

"So you . . . ate children."

"I did." Michael forced himself to look at Keeli. There was no pity in her gaze, but no hate, either. "I make no excuses for my crime."

"Good." She wrapped her fingers around his hand and squeezed. "How did you escape?"

Michael forced himself to breathe. "I finally remembered who I was, and when I remembered, I found my control. I turned on Malachai and killed him."

She touched his cheek, the golden tattoo. "What happened afterward?"

He covered her hand. "Elders found me. I told them everything. Everything that had been done to me, everything I had done to others. I knew nothing about being a vampire, except how to kill, but they . . . forgave me my crimes. Malachai had a reputation for cruelty, and there were those—including Celestine—who also suffered under him."

"And no one ever punished him?"

"At that time, vampires rarely punished their own. And . . . Malachai was old. Older than most. Everyone was afraid of him."

"And this?" She looked at the tattoo.

"My punishment. If I had not killed Malachai, perhaps things would have been different. Perhaps they would have . . . accepted me. Like they accepted Celestine, and the others he made and then abused. But I did kill him, and after he was gone, the elders had no excuse to give themselves when vampires went out of control and killed indiscriminately. So they marked me as a reminder to everyone else, and then they made me Vendix, the first Vendix. They said I was well-suited to it."

"Well-suited." Keeli shook her head. Michael watched her hands, small and white, clench into tight fists. She bounced them on her thighs. "How could they do that to you?"

"They were right," he said, catching her hand. He slid down to the floor, and she slid with him, leaning hard against his shoulder. "I blamed them all for what was done to me. I looked for any excuse to punish. I was . . . cruel."

"And now?" She pressed herself closer.

"I'm older," he said quietly. "And I got tired of hating everyone."

Keeli sighed. She wrapped her fingers tight around his hand. "I'm glad you told me."

"I knew I would have to, eventually. I was afraid of your reaction."

She smiled bitterly. "If you had told me when we first met, we wouldn't be here right now."

"What changed?"

"I have no idea," Keeli said. "I don't know how I got to this point. When I'm with you, my heart feels bigger. I think I could forgive you almost anything. Or maybe I'm just fucked up." She gave him a hard look. "Don't push your luck."

"I would not dream of it." Michael smoothed back her damp hair, looking deep into her eyes. "And you? How are you, Keeli?"

She lowered her gaze. "I'm bad, Michael."

"You are spoiled," he said lightly, though his heart tightened, aching for her. Keeli stared, and he could tell she was trying to decide whether or not he was teasing. He added, "Your grandmother raised you gently, with love. That is what you expected. You've been spoiled on that love. So, the one time when she is not gentle—when she loves you with pain—it hurts more because it is not what you are used to."

"Michael, the woman brutalized me. She broke my breastbone. She locked me in my room. She was going to keep me from you."

"I'm not defending her," he said. "I just . . . I do not want you to hold on to your anger or your hurt. I understand those things and they won't help you, Keeli. They will only damage you."

Her eyes narrowed. "I don't need a lecture."

"I'm not giving you one," he said, hardening his voice. "But what your grandmother did to you was gentle. When I was a child and disobeyed my father, he took a whip to my back until I bled, and then made me sleep outside in the snow without a blanket. I would spend the night freezing, terrified that not only would I die from the cold, but that the wolves would smell my bleeding back and try to eat me."

"I don't feel sorry for you," Keeli half-joked. "You probably deserved it."

Michael didn't laugh. "Maybe. But don't you think your grandmother's actions should be forgiven? Didn't you tell me she had a good reason to be afraid for your safety?"

Keeli was quiet for such a long time, Michael was not entirely sure she would tell him. But then she rubbed her arms and said, "When I was a child my father made his bid for Alpha of another clan. You have to understand, that was highly unusual, but not unheard of. The problem was that my father had a lot of enemies. He was a gambler, of sorts. With his body."

"I don't understand."

"He liked to fight. Cage games. He was a betting man, and he almost always won. Made people angry. Jealous. My grandmother tried to rein him in—his actions reflected badly on her—but Dad liked the money. He liked being able to buy my mom and I nice things. He liked that he could make us secure. I think, sometimes, that his bid for Alpha was just another way for him to do that. To keep us safe with power instead of money."

"It did not work," Michael murmured.

"They came for us," Keeli whispered. "The Tepper wolves. Their Alpha and his men. There was already bad blood, but making that bid was more than they could take. So they came, and there were no guards or locked doors because we were supposed to be safe, all of us in the underground, safe from each other, and at first they just wanted to talk, and then that was not enough, and so they killed. They killed everyone, Michael. I was the only one who survived. My grandmother saved my life."

Michael fought for his voice. "What happened to the murderers?"

"They were executed," she said softly. "They were not even given the dignity of their human bodies in death. My grandmother said that as they killed, so should they die. As animals."

"That bothers you."

"*Everything* about my family's death bothers me, but yes. Yes. At the time I didn't know any better, but when I got older I decided it was wrong. Wrong that those men should have died that way."

"Why?"

"Because that could be me." She turned her stricken gaze on him. "When I lose myself to rage, to the wolf, I am just like those men. Worse, even."

"No," Michael said, pulling her tight against him. "No, you are not. I have not known you long, Keeli, but there are truths I can see, and one of them is your strength. Your sense of right and wrong. You are too strong to ever lose yourself like that, to ever submit so completely to the wolf that those around you become nothing more than food."

"You had to stop me from killing that rapist."

"But you knew what he was," Michael reminded her, desperate for her to understand the distinction. "You were *aware*, and when you had to, you stopped. You stopped, Keeli. And not just then. I heard your clan talking. I know you could have killed that Alpha. You did not."

"I got lucky. So did Leroux."

"It has nothing to do with luck. You do not embrace your rage. You use it as a tool. There is a difference, Keeli."

She sagged against him. "Maybe. I don't want to think about it anymore, though. I'm so tired."

"You've barely slept since we met," he said, rising to his feet. He dragged Keeli up with him and began undressing her. "To be warm and clean. That is what you need."

"I need you," she said, reaching for him.

"You have me," he said.

They did not talk again for quite some time.

Keeli fell asleep in Michael's arms. She dreamed of wolves wearing vampire skins, zipping on flesh like a coat, or armor. She dreamed she wore Michael's body, and that it felt good and warm. She woke with his arms still curled around her body, her back tucked against his stomach. His lips brushed her neck.

"Hargittai," she said, after a moment.

"Celestine," he answered, following her thoughts.

Keeli tasted the memory. "That was . . . bizarre."

"Yes." Michael tugged Keeli around so she faced him. "I've known Celestine for a very long time. She has never spoken a kind word about werewolves. I thought she was a terrible choice for these negotiations."

"She's the one who beat you up, right?" She smiled when Michael grimaced. "It's okay, you know. Getting beat up by girls."

Michael closed his eyes. "Perhaps you would like to knock me around some more?" His hands trailed down her back and he cupped her tight against his body. Keeli reached down between them, slowly brushing her fingers through thick curls until she found him. Michael sighed.

"So we're not alone in this," Keeli whispered. She kissed his neck.

Michael's fingers trailed fire along her hip. He worked them up her inner thigh, into her soft cleft. "Perhaps not," he said, as Keeli clenched her teeth. "Though I would like to believe we will do better than Celestine and Hargittai."

"Much better," Keeli promised. "I won't abandon you, Michael."

His eyes darkened, became gentle, soft. Hungry. He removed his hand and pressed his body against her. She felt him, hard, and she guided him all the way, sucking in her breath at his still-new weight and size. Yet, when she was full and ready, he did not move. He wrapped his arms around her shoulders, simply holding her—inside and out—as they rested on their sides, embraced by the moment and each other.

"I am going to take care of you," he promised, and she felt his words thrill through her body. She had never wanted anyone to take care of her, but with Michael it felt safe, right and good. She took in those words and did not want to cringe.

"I love you," she said, because it was time, and she could not deny it to herself any longer.

"Keeli," sighed Michael. "Do you remember that moment, when you were in handcuffs and I was in the air above you? Our eyes met."

"I remember, but I hope that's not going to be your only response to what I just said."

"That is when I fell in love with you. That moment."

"Oh," she breathed, and Michael began moving, rocking within the cradle of her arms and legs. Exquisite agony; making love with Michael was like building a mystery within her body. She did not know herself until that moment, and with each touch, every stretch and pull, she learned more, more—

"Taste me," she gasped, looking deep into his startled eyes. "I want to know what it feels like."

He was so close; she could feel it in the rock-hard tension of his shoulders, the careful strain of his hips. She guided his head to her neck and felt his mouth press hot against her skin. "Please," she whispered. "Trust yourself."

He bit her. At first there was pain—bright, quick—but Keeli made no sound as she sank into the sensation of his mouth softly pulling on her body. And then he shuddered, thrusting hard, harder, again and again, and he pulled his mouth away from her neck to gasp her name. She clutched him tight against her body so he would not slip away, her legs winding like snakes. She felt his seed, wet on her thighs, and remembered, once again, that they had forgotten to use a condom.

"I'm sorry," he mumbled, stirring against her.

"For what?"

"You didn't . . ." His voice trailed off.

His consternation made her laugh. "Great sex doesn't always have to end in an orgasm, you know."

"It seems unfair," he said, though his mouth hinted at a smile. His lips were stained red.

Keeli touched them. "How was I?"

She saw the answer in his dark eyes, heard it in the shallow quick breath. She touched her neck and felt the puncture wounds. Her fingertips came away clean.

"My saliva coagulates the blood," he said softly. He licked his lips. "You tasted good, Keeli. Maybe too good."

"You going to start taking midnight snacks?" she said lightly. He did not smile.

"Your blood is in me now. It will be hard to resist."

"I love it when you talk dirty."

He rolled his eyes. She laughed, and kissed him.

Someone knocked on the door. Keeli froze against Michael's body. The lock jiggled. The bolt slid back.

Michael sprang out of bed, a blur. He reached the door just as it opened and then there were bodies on the ground; shouts and cries, and Michael standing with a dagger in one hand and a head full of hair in the other.

"Fuck," Richard groaned, his throat exposed to the blade.

Keeli flopped back on the bed, burying her face under the pillows.

Michael released Richard. Suze climbed to her feet.

"You scared the shit out of me," she said, breathing hard.

"Good," Keeli said, her voice muffled. "Why are you here and how did you find us?"

Richard and Suze glanced at each other. Keeli heard Michael sigh, and she watched him get a briefcase from the kitchen. He handed it to the teens.

"This is a lot of money," he said, "but it will go fast. Try to spend it wisely."

Richard and Suze looked at each other again. Suze said, "You're really going to give us five thousand dollars? You look like you need it more than we do."

"I'm old. I have unique skills. You're young and uneducated. Trust me, *you* need it more."

Keeli sat up. "How much money are you giving them, and why?"

"We helped," Richard said, but he still had not touched the briefcase. He looked embarrassed.

"Oh. Thank you," Keeli said, suddenly remembering what Michael had told her. "I . . . I really appreciate it."

Suze stared at her feet. "Yeah, whatever."

Michael still held out the money. "Do you want this?"

Suze's head flew up. "Well, duh. But we didn't come just for the money. We thought you guys might be here. We wanted to warn you."

Keeli wrapped the sheet around her body and stood up. "Warn us about what?"

"Your grandmother," Richard said. "She's gone apeshit. Real nuts. When she found out that you had escaped, and that your fang here had been trying to get into the tunnels, she wanted to send Trackers out."

"Shit."

Michael looked at her. "Trackers?"

"They're usually reserved for criminals—ferals and exiles who need to be brought in for control. Judgment." Keeli's throat burned. "If she brings me in like that, she'll discredit me in front of all the clans. No one will ever respect or trust me."

"She smelled scared," Suze said, quiet.

"Pissed off," Richard corrected her.

"Scared," Suze insisted, "and pissed off."

"Either way," Richard said, "you need to get out of here. The other Alphas challenged her about the Trackers, but we left as soon as we heard the word. I don't know if the old lady has this address, but if she does and sends them out, they'll come here first."

"The Alphas challenged her?" Keeli could not imagine it.

"Hargittai, especially."

The phone rang. Everyone looked at each other.

"It's the middle of the night," Keeli said. "Who calls you in the middle of the night?"

The phone continued to ring. They all stared at it. Michael frowned, and finally answered.

"Jenkins," he said, a moment later. Keeli sighed.

Michael's brow furrowed. "Are you sure? Yes? All right. Thanks for calling. Yes, she's here. I'll tell her."

"What?" she asked, concerned by the look on his face.

"There's been another murder," he said, hanging up the phone. "A vampire. The body was found outside Maddox territory, but it's the same kind of kill. Less careful, though. This time there were bite wounds. The techies found DNA traces. Vampire and werewolf."

Keeli shook her head. "It's him, Michael. The man we fought tonight is our killer."

"And how do you explain the divergent vampire and werewolf DNA?"

260

"I can't, but it has to be him."

"What's going on?" Richard asked, hugging Suze close to his side. Keeli noticed he held the briefcase. Quick hands—she hadn't even observed him move.

"You remember that guy you told us about, the one who freaked you out so much you decided to join a clan? He came after us tonight."

Suze sucked in her breath. Her eyes glittered large in her pale face. "How are you alive?"

"Luck," said Michael. "How much do you know about this person?"

"Nothing." Richard's jaw tightened. His eyes looked far too old for his face. "Or everything. When you live on the street, the things you hear get exaggerated. But this guy . . . he popped up about a month ago. Likes to sing. Likes to kill."

"What does he kill?" Keeli asked, remembering a low voice telling her that humans and wolves were off-limits to hunger. She saw Suze blink, noted the way Richard suddenly looked at her face, alarmed.

"Suze," he said, as though to stop her, but she ignored him.

"Fangs," she whispered, looking at Michael. Richard grabbed her arm. "We didn't see the actual murder, but it was afterwards, when he was done and standing over the body."

Michael closed his eyes. Keeli stared. "Why the hell didn't you tell us this earlier? Didn't you know about our investigation? The crimes we were trying to solve?"

Richard looked uncomfortable. "We knew. We just didn't think it was related."

"You are lying," Michael said.

Suze swallowed hard, her gaze darting between Keeli and Michael. She looked afraid, and it bothered Keeli because Suze's fear had a familiar taste, a recognizable face, and she said, "Who told you not to give us this information?"

"It wasn't just you," Suze whispered. "We weren't supposed to tell anyone. We weren't even supposed to mention that we'd seen him. But you got us on a roll and we forgot, and then it was too late. When you didn't ask the right questions, we kept our mouths shut."

"Who told you to do this?" Keeli asked, knowing the answer, and dreading it—fearing it.

"The Grand Dame," Richard said. "She said that we had seen a demon, and that it was dangerous to speak about them. That we could voodoo ourselves in a bad way if we did."

"And she knew you had seen this individual murder a vampire?"

"We told her," Richard said, his eyes haunted. "We told her everything."

Michael touched Keeli's hand, and she said, "What was she thinking? What was she trying to do to us?"

"I do not know." He looked troubled. "But we need to find this man before he kills again."

Michael went to the bed and began dressing. His movements were quick, sharp and efficient. "Keeli and I need to go out for a while. You two can stay here if you like."

"Michael," Keeli said. The look he gave her was grave, but tinged with compassion.

"We have no time. We need answers, fast."

She nodded, steeling her heart—shoving down the lonely ache that filled her chest when she thought of her grandmother. No more tears. Not until she had answers. Not until she knew exactly what was going on.

Richard and Suze huddled together in the kitchen while Keeli dressed. They said, "We'll stay for a bit," and Michael nodded without comment and led Keeli out onto the fire escape. No one said good-bye. Richard shut the window and pulled the blind down behind them.

The sky was dark, though Keeli glimpsed the edge of dawn in the sky. She floated on the scent of roses. Michael wrapped her in a tight hug.

"Where are we going?" she asked him, clutching his shoulders.

"Jenkins," he said. "But really, I just wanted to be alone with you."

Her smile felt weak, and faded quickly as she said, "So we know who our murderer is."

Michael hesitated. "Maybe."

"Maybe?"

"It seems too convenient. And Richard and Suze said themselves that they didn't actually see the murder. We need more facts. Evidence."

"I think you need a signed confession before you'll be satisfied," Keeli said.

He shook his head. "I am completely convinced that the werewolves had nothing to do with the murder. But that does not mean this . . . this man . . . is wholly responsible. He said that he was being watched. Perhaps even given orders."

"You think he belongs to the humans?"

"Humans built the mechs. He could be another kind of creation."

"He was starved," Keeli said. "Emotional and irrational. I think he was even afraid for me. He didn't trust himself. For good reason, I guess." She hesitated, remembering the shame in his voice, his broken apology. "You told me he wanted to know if a vampire could ever love a werewolf."

Michael kissed her hands. "When I saw the blood on his body, and realized it was you he spoke of, I wanted to kill him. Perhaps I should have. Another person is dead."

"Compassion always strikes at strange moments. You were thinking of yourself. What could have been. What was."

"I recognized myself. In his words and hunger. Though in some ways, he is worse than me. He has some control, but still he chooses to kill."

"We need to find out why. But if there's no helping him . . ."

"I will do it," Michael promised.

"You won't be alone," she said, and when he looked at her, solemn and dark and so serious, she realized that she might be the first to ever say so, the first to ever offer Michael something like friendship, love. She touched his cheek, the golden tattoo. "I think it's time you stopped wearing this."

"No," he said softly. He covered her hand. "I don't run, either. Even when I want to."

Keeli smiled, sad, and kissed his cheek. "I know. That's what I love about you."

Chapter Eighteen

Because dawn was so near, Michael suggested they walk or take a cab to Jenkins's crime scene. He did not want to fly. He had been taking too many risks at night as it was. The gift of flight was not much help if it only got him shot down by a mech or some other human operative. He did not want to risk Keeli.

Although it seemed that simply being together was risk enough.

He watched her as they walked. She tried to pretend nothing was wrong, but he could taste her pain, see it in the line of her shoulders. He touched her, pulled her close to his side. They stumbled down the street, an odd four-legged creature.

"We need to be careful now," she said. "If my grand-mother sends out the Trackers, they'll be looking for my scent. They're good, Michael. They can hunt almost any-thing."

"Not us," he said. "I won't let them hurt you, Keeli."

She shook her head, eyes lost in shadow, dim and gray. "She hates me, Michael. Or loves me. I don't know which anymore. I'm not sure I care. It took her a long time to let me spread my wings, to go topside to find a job. Getting that waitress gig at Butchie's was a big deal. My one big step. She was always so afraid of something going wrong—that I would turn out like my father, maybe. And now it's happened. I didn't mean it to, but it has, and she's trying to protect me by ruining my life."

"Maybe you should go home," he suggested quietly. "Talk to her. She will understand in time, and then you and I—"

"I'm not giving you up," Keeli said, fierce. Michael was shocked to see tears in her eyes. "I don't understand what we've got, but it means something to me. It means more to me than anything has in a long, long time, and I'm *not* letting go. I won't."

"All right," he breathed. "There is your answer, then. We will fulfill our obligations by finding this murderer, and then we will go. We will make another home, in another city, far from here."

She looked so pale, but her mouth set in a stubborn line and her gaze was steady, unafraid. "Is it ever that easy, Michael?"

"No," he said. "But we'll be together. I would rather have that than an easy life."

Keeli smiled. "I think I love you more now than I did ten minutes ago."

"That's a good sign. I would not want you to grow tired of me." He grabbed her hand and kissed her palm.

They walked several blocks through his neighborhood before Keeli saw a cab. She jumped up and down, waving her hands. Michael did not think the yellow car would stop for them: a pink-haired waif in rough black clothes, or the tall man beside her who no doubt looked strange wearing a hat and sunglasses in the dark.

But the cab did stop. Keeli threw herself inside.

Their driver's name was Emanuel. He had a gentle voice, a gentle demeanor, and he told Keeli and Michael in no uncertain terms that it was unsafe for "two nice young people" like them to be out and about on such dangerous streets.

Because Michael was not feeling particularly nice—and because both their appearances were probably the antithesis of what most normal people considered wholesome—Emanuel's comment made him shake his head. It was obvious the driver had no idea what he was carrying in his cab. Keeli laughed outright—and that was good, wonderful, that she still could laugh, that she could set aside her troubles long enough to see the absurdity of their situation.

"We were visiting a friend," she said, as Michael looked out the window. In the distance, he saw the multicolored signal lights of the Crimson Light district emblazoning the cloudy sky.

Michael thought of Walter Crestin, and of his own promise to Emily. Despite their new theories about the murderer, it wouldn't hurt to still go to The Bloody Pulp to ask questions, as well as to look for any vampire who carried a silver cross-shaped knife, and had a reputation for attacking werewolves and their women.

Emanuel noticed where Michael's gaze strayed. "We will be passing through that place. It is a faster route to where you want to go. If you don't like, we will try another."

Michael shrugged. "Faster is good."

"We're going to pass through the Crimson Light district?" Keeli looked out the window. "I've never been there."

Michael was unsurprised. Wolves generally stayed away from places where vampires frequented, and the entire four-block quarter of the city was all about the fangs. Michael knew they were getting close when he saw crowds of tired teenyboppers, rich kids doing their rebel thing, walking en masse down the dirty sidewalks, heading home before the dawn after a night of hard partying and attempts to skank the attention of immortals. A deep booming bass pulsed through Michael's chest. The nightclubs closed at dawn, but then, only for humans. Vampires were always welcome, no matter the time of day.

"You like the vampires?" Emanuel guided the cab around several limos parked illegally in their lane. Michael watched a chauffeur hold open a door; an impossibly long leg emerged from the darkness.

Keeli glanced at Michael, an amused smile on her lips. "Not especially. But I'm trying not to be so judgmental. You?"

"I do not like any of them," Emanuel said fiercely. "Vampires, werewolves. They are dangerous. You see these children, walking so free amongst the monsters? They do not know how close they are to losing their souls."

"And you think all werewolves and vampires are the same?"

Emanuel shrugged. "Back in Venezuela the lines are more clear. We know what we are to them, and that is food. We do business with the vampires and the werewolves because it is necessary, but we do not trust ourselves to them. Not like this." He waved a hand at the bright lights, the advertisements streaming a glitter of alluring images, all of them promising sex and youth.

"I can see your point," Michael said, unable to feel offended. It was the truth: humans *were* food. For vampires, by necessity. For werewolves, by accident. And yet, to be human, to regain and aspire to the essence of idealized humanity, was the secret goal of most vampires. Perhaps the werewolves, too.

They told Emanuel to let them out when they were still

several blocks away from the address Jenkins had given Michael. Dawn threaded the sky. Michael tugged down the brim of his hat.

Keeli watched the cab's taillights disappear around the block. "I feel as though I should be angry at him. I guess if I had heard him yesterday, I would be mad. But we're all the same, Michael—humans, werewolves, vampires. It's just that our hang-ups are all aimed at different people. Even me . . . I still can't bring myself to like most vampires."

"I'll try not to be too wounded."

She gave him a strange look. "Doesn't it ever bother you, not liking your own kind? Isn't that the same as not liking yourself?"

"I don't always like myself," Michael said, the words rising, honest, from his throat. "I have done terrible things, Keeli. I am . . . not a good man."

"Liar. You want to be. You said so."

Michael turned away and walked down the street. Keeli followed him, but he did not look at her.

"Michael." She grabbed his arm. "Stop."

"You said it yourself. You don't like vampires. And why should you? We *are* monsters, Keeli. When we kill, it is for pleasure. It is a choice we make."

"That choice was taken away from you. Have you killed since then? Have you?"

"No," he whispered. "But in that time, I murdered more people than most vampires could ever dream to brag on."

"I'm sorry," she said.

"I don't want your pity."

"Fuck you. I'm sorry for those people who died."

"And you think I'm not?"

"I think you feel more sorry for yourself." She stood with her hands on her hips, stubborn and bright and hot.

"Snap the hell out of it, Michael. And don't try and tell me all this verbal self-immolation is because you deserve it. That's crap. If you really hated yourself that much, you would be dead by now. You'd be a fucking mess on the side of the road."

He almost argued with her, but he knew she was right. He did not have the energy to stand up for a losing case.

"Are you ever diplomatic?" he asked, weary.

"You should know the answer to that question."

"I do not want to fight with you about this," he said.

"I don't want to fight, either." Keeli leaned against his chest, small and warm. "But I won't take hypocrisy, especially from you. Because why the hell did you start investigating these murders in the first place? Why is this alliance so important? You told me once. Was that a lie?"

"No," he said, frustrated. "I would never lie to you, Keeli. It's just . . ." He balled up his hands, fighting for words that should not have been difficult to say, but were, that hurt. "You are not my first friend," he finally told her. "But you are my best, Keeli. The closest. And when I talk to you, I tell you everything. Do you understand? I let you see everything. All my weaknesses, my fears. If I am a hypocrite, then fine. That is me. I love myself and hate myself and that is the way it will be until I die. And if I cannot . . . if I cannot go on about these things to you, then who can I?"

"No one," she said immediately, softly. "I'm your girl, Michael. I always will be."

The effortless quality of her words made his breath catch. "You accept me? Even what you dislike?"

"I'm here," she said, her eyes flashing bright with promise, challenge. "If you can accept my crap, I sure as hell can love yours."

Shocking. He did not know what to say, how to express his relief, and so he kissed her, crushing her body close—

closer—and her arms snaked around his neck, tugging his mouth hard against her mouth. He shuddered at the taste of her, wild and sweet, and he briefly wondered if it was still dark enough, the streets still empty enough, to take her—right there—on the sidewalk, against the building they stood beside. And he thought, *yes*, and lifted them off their feet, drifting up, up, until he pressed her against brick, between two large apartment windows, his hand sliding up under skirt, peeling away underwear. Keeli made a soft sound and wrapped her legs around his hips.

He took her in the dawn light, above the street, and every slick hot thrust brought him closer to some unspoken trust, the culmination of riotous need that had nothing to do with lust, and everything to do with the desire to be in her skin, as close to her soul and heart as flesh would allow. Wild, running wild—in his blood was the steppes, those cold dawns of empty grassland, and she was that freedom to him, that humanity he had given up, lost, and if he ever lost Keeli—and oh, how had this happened—he really would lie down and die. . . .

"Michael," she gasped, digging her nails into his shoulders. She threw back her head, and Michael barely managed to cushion her skull with his palm before it slammed into the brick wall. She groaned, her face contorting, and Michael increased his rhythm, her body rising, tightening, and he emptied himself into her as she cried out, writhing violently against him. She pulsed around his body, a slow long throb of satiation.

"I love fighting with you," she murmured breathlessly. Michael drew her closer into his body. He kissed her neck, scraping his teeth against her skin.

"That was not a real fight," he said, as she shivered.

"Never mind," she murmured. "Let's do it again."

So they did.

* * *

"What we just did was illegal," Keeli said, still blushing. She readjusted her T-shirt as they approached the yellow police tape, which divided the not-so-crowded sidewalk and the milling men and women in uniform. They were in the bar district, a section of town Keeli had walked through the night before. Most of the bars were closed; Keeli had to step around several men passed out on hard stoops that reeked of vomit. The scent made her stomach lurch, stealing away the warm tingle she'd had ever since Michael brought her back down to earth.

Jenkins saw them coming. He said several sharp words to a tall dark woman who looked like Sheila. She glanced at Keeli and Michael, nodded, and then moved off to speak with the other officers. Within minutes, the scene cleared of people.

"I guess everyone needed a cigarette break," Jenkins said, as he met them at the flimsy barrier.

"Sure," Keeli said. "How convenient they won't see their boss allow an unauthorized viewing of a dead body."

He shrugged. "See no evil, hear no evil. Not that there's much left to view at this point."

"We may have a lead," Michael said, discreetly smearing on more sunscreen as Jenkins led them to the vampire's body. Keeli smelled the drying corpse long before it came into view. A large black tarp covered a lump in the middle of the sidewalk.

"God, I hope so." Jenkins pointed at the covering. "There you go. No witnesses. Or least, no one who is willing to talk."

Keeli crouched beside the covered body. The smell was musty, tinged with blood, meat. Sort of like a dusty closet in a butcher shop.

The vampire looked like she smelled, except there was

not much left of her, and what was still solid had lost all its gruesome qualities. Keeli felt like she was ogling a mummy.

She took a deep breath and let the tarp drop down. Backed away, checking the air, trying to catch the faint remnant of anything that stirred memory. After a moment, a scent—familiar and warm—filled her head. For some reason, she thought of Hargittai, but that was not right; this was also different, alien, and she said, "He was here, Michael."

"Who was here?" Jenkins looked at them both. "You said you had a lead. Is this it?"

"We might know who your murderer is," Michael said, hesitant.

"Actually, we don't," Keeli clarified. "But he's not a werewolf."

"He's not a vampire, either."

Jenkins blinked. "Well, what is he?"

Michael and Keeli looked at each other. Jenkins sighed. "Can you at least tell me what he looks like?"

"We don't know." Keeli threw up her hands when Jenkins glared at her. "He wore a mask."

"But he's not human," Michael said, possibly staving off Jenkins's next question. "He could fly."

Jenkins closed his eyes. "You guys are killing me here."

"It gets better." Keeli stepped close, dropping her voice to a whisper. "We think he works for the government."

Jenkins said nothing. Keeli could not read him; it was as though his entire expression were wiped clean away. His face looked like clay: unnerving, startling. Michael stared at Jenkins like he was seeing his friend for the first time. His lips tightened into a hard line.

"What do you know?"

Jenkins backed away, slow. "I'll call you, Michael."

"Jenkins."

"Don't ask me, man. Not now. I'll get back to you as soon as I can. Now get the hell out of here." He turned and walked away to one of the parked squad cars. Not a single backward glance. As soon as he reached the vehicle he got on the radio. Unease slithered up Keeli's spine.

Officers began trickling back onto the crime scene. They looked at Michael and Keeli with curious gazes. Dismissive, with a hint of suspicion.

Michael and Keeli left. The sky was the light blue of early morning; cars had their headlights turned off and traffic was thick. People shared the sidewalk, most of them dressed for work. Keeli tried not to be bothered by how out of place she looked, or the concentrated indifference of the people who refused to look at her face. She felt them watch her, though, from the corners of their eyes.

"Jenkins knew something. You think he's heard rumors?"

"If he has, they did not have anything to do with the murders. Jenkins would never let that stand."

"There was something, Michael. You saw that look on his face."

"Jenkins said he would call. I trust him to keep his word."

Keeli blew out her breath. She liked Jenkins, but didn't have as much faith in him as Michael did. Of course, she did not have much faith in anyone who worked for the government.

"Great," she said, deciding to go along with him. "What next?"

"I want to go to The Bloody Pulp. I should have gone before." Michael held up his hands when Keeli opened her mouth to protest. "It is possible that one of Walter Crestin's friends saw the murder. Perhaps, even, the men and women who go to that bar have heard rumors of this

274

man who attacked us. After all, they live much closer to the street than the rest of the vampires."

"Don't you think if vampires knew about this guy, they would have reported it by now?"

"You do not know *these* vampires. They belong to a lower class that is looked down upon by the rest of my kind. I suppose it is because they do not embrace the same desire to be human—or maybe the genetics of their making render them unsuitable to hold most positions in high vampire society. Either way, there is no love lost. The first six victims were from the higher classes. If anyone near the street heard rumors about their murderer, they would not be inclined to say anything."

"So why didn't we go there earlier?" Keeli asked.

Michael glared at her. "We've been a little busy."

"Yeah, okay." Keeli sighed. "So, you vampires are just assigned a job based on what your genes say you should do? That sounds kind of limiting."

Michael shrugged. "It works, for the most part."

"What does that say about you?"

"I am a special case. Malachai was of the warrior class, and I inherited some of that strength, the inclination to fight. I also inherited his inability to eat solid food. I learned later that the deficiency set him apart as something of a freak, but he was old and rich and powerful, and no one dared treat him different because of it. I was not so lucky. The cult of humanity, then and now, does not allow diversity in its expression."

"You mean, they treat you weird because you can't eat food?"

"It's one more strike against me," Michael admitted wryly. He glanced up at the sky and grimaced. "Now will be a good time to go back to the Crimson Light district. The Bloody Pulp will still be open to vampires, but the clientele will consist of only the most . . . committed. The ones who don't have anywhere else to go."

"I thought you were the only outcast."

"There are different levels," he said, with a twist of humor. "If a vampire—especially a made vampire—breaks the law or develops a reputation for being a troublemaker, their social circle grows smaller. And smaller."

"Until they end up living in bars? That's pretty small, Michael."

"You've never been to The Bloody Pulp," he said. "There's nothing small about it."

"I can't wait," she muttered.

Michael frowned. "You're not going."

"Right. You said that place is dangerous for you."

"In the past six months I've carried out three executions there. They won't be happy to see me again. I'm bad for business."

"And you don't see the logic of 'I'm going with you'?"

"No." Michael bent close. "Tensions are too high right now between vampires and werewolves. Between vampires and humans, too. I've never had two executions ordered within such a short period . . ." He stopped, as though he had said something wrong. Keeli peered at him.

"That's what happened the night we met. Your pager went off and you had to run. It was an execution, wasn't it?" She wished she could see past his dark glasses to his eyes. All she saw instead was her reflection. She looked distorted, frustrated.

"Michael," she said.

"I have been doing this for a long time," he said. "Please, Keeli. Let me do this my way. Alone."

His request hurt—not because he was asking her to stay behind, but that by doing so she would be unable to help him. They had shared so much, so fast, and the close intensity of their relationship—as though in all the world, they had only each other—made her desire to protect him all the more urgent.

He may be all I have left of friend or family. I may no longer have a clan.

Terror clutched her heart, but she forced down a deep breath and shook off the worst of her fear. Later—she would deal with that later. Right now, Michael needed her, whether or not he wanted to admit it. Yeah, like going into a place full of dangerous people who hated you was a smart move. Shit. They might as well go back to the underground.

"I'll stand outside the bar," she said firmly. "I won't go in. I'll just wait for you outside."

He stared at her, and she sensed his uncertainty, the urgency of time and duty pressing down on his shoulders. "If you get hurt," he began, and Keeli shook her head.

"I could get hurt just standing on this street. You know I'm being tracked. Please, Michael."

He gripped her shoulders. "You are making me insane."

"I've got it down to an art."

"Yes," he muttered, grabbing her hand and pulling her down the street. "You do."

"I'm confused," Keeli said. "Tell me why this neighborhood is still rolling high? It's broad daylight." She looked up at a gigantic billboard decorated with scantily clad women baring unnaturally large breasts. They all had fangs, and called themselves "Sex and Lies." Part of a strip club advertising vampire dancers. Keeli seriously doubted the women were vampires. A true fang would never do that kind of work. Own the club, maybe. Dance? On your grave, perhaps.

"It's the Crimson Light district. The tourists and fang-bangs love it, no matter what time of day it is."

"I guess so," she said. Techno blared out of stereos built

into the turned-off streetlights, beating out the rhythm of her quick walk; her heart strummed tight in her chest. Keeli gave herself to the wolf, coaxing it gently to the surface. Not so it would show, but to give her that extra edge. She ignored the scents of drugs and smoke, blood; excited chatter about a potential vampire sighting, cameras clicking.

She felt battered by sound, the uncomfortable awareness that she stuck out like a sore thumb. Not because she was a werewolf, either. She doubted anyone but a vampire could tell her apart, and there weren't any of those on the street. No, it was just that everyone around her was dressed sleek and clean, like they were all ready for a slam party even though it was morning in a town where night usually ruled the comings and goings of human fascination. Not so, here. Keeli felt like a crasher, some wannabe out for a look-see into the realm of the beautiful people. Pale, hungry, desperate people.

Not that the scenery matched the visitors. The city always looked better in the dark, and from what Keeli had seen earlier through the taxi window, the Crimson Light district was no different. The sidewalks, which in shadow blazed bright with color, now looked gray and filthy; the bar facades cheap, garish. Instead of alcohol or piss, Keeli smelled blood.

"So what's the story with The Bloody Pulp? Why is it the hot place for all the lowlifes?"

"No one asks questions and the blood is cheap and good. The management also allows a certain flexibility in the kinds of activities that go on. Most of them verge on the highly illegal."

"And your council lets places like this exist?"

"They have to. You can't kill too many of your own without just cause, and not expect trouble. The old ones are survivors. That's why our new leader, Fleur Dumont, is having difficulties. She's a member of the warrior class. Maybe one of the last. She wants to fight back, though smart. The negotiations between vampires and werewolves are because of her. If the elders in the Primary Assembly had their way, we would be massacring every human in sight. Or running."

"Moderation's on the not-so-happening side, huh?"

"They do not know the meaning of the word."

If Keeli had been by herself, she might have walked past the bar. Everything in this area looked the same in sunlight—featureless and gray—but Michael slowed and Keeli caught a wet, warm scent. Blood. Lots of it. He touched her arm and guided her into a small alcove that had steel bars screwed across the door window.

"Across the street," he said. "That's where I need to go."

Keeli looked. There was no bar sign, no indication that anything beyond pain and hostility existed past the barbed wire and concrete blocks surrounding a set of stairs that disappeared beneath the sidewalk into shadow.

"Cozy," she said. "You're an idiot."

"I'm well-armed."

"You're an idiot with a sword and a steel choker."

"Try to stay out of trouble," he said, running his fingers down her cheek. He kissed her. "I love you, Keeli."

"Whatever. Just watch your ass in there."

He smiled, and it was sweet—so sweet—that Keeli wanted to throw her arms around his body and hold him tight against her, tight enough to anchor his feet to the ground so he would not go into that awful place without her; but she loved him, knew him well enough to understand his determination, and so she did not move when he left her side and crossed the street, a dark figure in sunlight, gliding into the gray, the dirty, alone.

He descended the stairs and disappeared. Keeli leaned against the alcove wall and settled herself for a long wait.

Ten minutes passed. They were long, boring, minutes that consisted of watching cheap blondes in cheap dresses with cheap breast jobs stalk up and down the sidewalk in search of a fang fix. Their arms were riddled with teeth marks. They looked pale, anemic, their eyes too bright. Keeli pushed deeper into the alcove whenever they passed her. Not that they would be interested in a werewolf, but Keeli did not want to be the focus of such depressing addiction. Those girls embodied the most desperate desire for youth and immortality—the one perfect bite: the answer, the prayer.

Movement flickered at the corner of Keeli's eye. She peered beyond the alcove wall, studying the street—

—and then jerked back into hiding, heart hammering like a steel jack.

The profile she had just seen was all too familiar. A Maddox wolf. A Tracker.

Keeli closed her eyes. The Tracker was far away down the street, on the opposite end of where she and Michael had walked. Which meant that he still did not have her scent. If he just kept walking in the other direction, he might not pick it up at all. Or at least, she might have enough time to get away before he scouted the entire district.

Shit. Granny May must have overruled the others. And then, what? Sent them here? Because yeah, all the fangs take their new bangs to the Crimson Light district for a good time.

If he found her, it would be a hard fight. Trackers played dirty. They used tranquilizer weapons, stun rods, anything to incapacitate with the least amount of damage. Keeli didn't think she was prepared for that sort of thing. Superhuman rage was not so effective against a man with a tranq-dart.

Careful, she peered around the alcove wall. The Tracker had his back turned. He began walking down the street, a lean strong figure in nondescript jeans and a jacket with deep pockets that no doubt held his arsenal. Keeli watched him, and when he was far enough away and walking with enough intent that she didn't think he would turn around, she darted from the alcove and pelted full force across the street toward The Bloody Pulp's stairs. Yeah, let him catch her scent and follow her in there. Good luck. If she didn't get herself or Michael killed in the first five minutes, then maybe she would have a chance to see a Tracker come up against a room full of vampires. That would be a show—if he were actually stupid enough to follow her in.

Stupid like you. You are so screwed.

Keeli descended into darkness, encased by concrete and the overwhelming scent of blood. The stairs went deeper into the ground than she anticipated, and when she finally stopped in front of an iron door, rusty with damp and years, the blue sky felt very far away, and she felt very small.

Michael, please forgive me, for I cometh to crasheth thy party.

She tried the door. It was locked. Keeli banged her fist on the cold iron. A low buzz filled her ears and she glanced right. A small green light blinked, right beneath a tiny intercom.

"What," said a dry cool voice, "do *you* want?"

Shit, she thought, but words filled her mouth, sultry, and she said, "It's not what *I* want, sweet. I got a call for blood. *Different* blood."

"We've already got blood. No one here would place a call."

"You an expert on wants and needs? Don't think so. Come on, bravo. Open up your *hole*."

Silence. Terror wrapped hot fingers around Keeli's gut, but she stayed frozen with a half-smile on her face, trying desperately to pretend indifference.

The door clicked. Swung open an inch. A hard drum-beat filled her ears.

Keeli pushed the door open and walked into a pulsating darkness tinged with blue—blue shadows, blue furniture, everything blue—tinted lights set high in the walls and ceiling, pouring fey moonlight into the maw that counted as a room. Keeli had never seen so many vampires gathered in one place: men and women, smooth and young, with bloody glasses in their hands and hideous teeth flashing smiles.

Or rather, only some of them were smiling. She looked deeper, past the vampires nearest her, and caught the unmistakable wrinkle of deep concern rippling through the crowd nearest the bar. No one there looked happy.

Bingo.

Keeli moved toward the bar. A cold hand grabbed the back of her neck.

"Look what we have," said a booming voice. *"Werewolf."*

He might as well have called her a nun with a gun. A startled hush fell over the room, and dozens upon dozens of eyes stared and studied and judged.

"She told me she was here as blood," said another vampire, pushing close. He had the dry voice she had heard over the intercom, attached to a gaunt face that bore too many imperfections to be called handsome.

The hand on Keeli's neck tightened. "Is that so, wolf? You here to feed us? Maybe *all* of us?"

"My blood is for only one vampire," Keeli shot back. "And if he's not here, then I'm gone."

The gaunt vampire sidled close. "She smells like trash. Looks like trash."

"Maybe we treat her like trash?"

Keeli searched desperately for Michael. Near the bar, the vampires thinned out for just one moment. She looked hard, straining, and what she saw made her heart thud into her stomach.

The reason for the looks of concern had nothing to do with Michael. Or maybe everything. There was a vampire slumped against the bar counter. He did not have a head.

She was in a lot of trouble.

Chapter Nineteen

Viggo the doorman let Michael into The Bloody Pulp without fuss. Michael did not expect trouble from the skinny vampire, who liked to talk big but consistently folded under any hint of pressure. Marcus would be more of a problem, but that, also, was to be expected.

Just ask your questions and go. Go back to Keeli, before she changes her mind and comes in here after you.

Easier said than done. The resentment and fear he felt radiating from the crowd could have ridden the pulse of the room like its own music: hard and vicious. The Vendix was back, and that meant one of them was going to die. All of them deserved it; receiving the order was only a matter of time, borrowed time, playing in the belly of a bar, pretending to be immortal, when all it took was a phone call to bring down the hand of death.

Silence descended. Men and women peeled back from Michael's approach, trying to maintain dignity while pretending not to run for their lives. The last time Michael had been here there had been no warning, barely a glance. Walking, and then a flash of steel, the rolling thud of a lost head.

And yet, he knew that not one of these vampires would leave their sanctuary. Forget sunlight—all of them had enough sunscreen to protect themselves, and if not, the bar had its own supply. No, the answer rested in pride, arrogance. Everyone here had it in spades, and no one wanted to be the first vampire to admit weakness in the face of death. It was a strange code of honor that had grown up amongst the lower classes of vampire, but it also made Michael's job more dangerous, because that pride meant protection, for all of the men and women watching him wanted nothing more than his slow and painful death.

Michael made it to the bar without any trouble. He leaned against the blue counter, studying the human men and women strapped naked to the wall with blood taps running fine and clear from their wrists. There were eight humans, four of each sex. All of them were impossibly beautiful, with glazed eyes that stared blindly into the room. Marcus provided small doses of painkiller and marrow stimulant—not enough to taint the taste of blood, but just the right amount to dull the discomfort of the blood taps and leather straps. The men and women worked four-hour shifts, providing drinks to the customers. Marcus was the only one in control of the tap.

"Michael," said Marcus, waddling to a blond human whose breasts jutted out like hard balloons. He turned the tap at her wrist; blood raced through the attached tube into a crystal glass. The woman never flinched.

"Marcus." Michael watched him hand the glass to a lithe vampire who bared her teeth at the rim, inhaling so deeply it seemed she would feed herself on fumes.

"You come to kill?" Marcus leaned on the bar. His jowls

shook, but his eyes—black and small, remained steady, sharp. Michael tilted his head. Marcus had always been a mystery. He was rumored to be one of the most powerful vampires in the city, but it was an underclass power, the kind that came not from money, but from information and pure stubborn immorality.

"You've never asked me that question before," Michael said.

"You have a look about you. Something different from the other times you came to kill. Your sharp edge is not for death tonight." He shrugged. "But I could be wrong. So I ask. What is your answer?"

"No death. Not unless it is asked for."

Marcus smiled, humorless and cold. Michael sensed a shift in the air, a promise, and he ducked, whirling, just as a knife hacked into the bar top where he stood. Michael unsheathed his sword. The blade danced. The vampire's head hit the bar, bouncing once before rolling to the floor. Blood spurted from the slumped body, striking the pale men and women who scrambled to create distance. They wiped their faces, disgusted.

Michael cleaned his sword on the dead vampire's silk slacks. He looked at Marcus. "Any other points you'd like to make?"

Marcus shrugged. "The very young and newly made are so easy to manipulate. I knew you would kill him."

"Nice of you."

"Indeed."

"You come in for a drink?"

"Answers."

"Then *I* need a drink." Marcus turned the tap on a brunette. He mixed vodka into the blood, and then gestured for Michael to follow him. "Come. We go talk."

Michael glanced at the other vampires. None of them made eye contact. When he was sure that no one else planned on hacking him to death, he picked up his attacker's knife, stuck it in his belt, and followed Marcus through a door set off to the left of the bar.

The office was painted blue, filled with large, comfortable chairs and an uncluttered oak desk stuck in the corner beside a small armada of surveillance cameras.

Marcus sighed, slumping down in one of his recliners. Michael did not sit.

"I'm here because someone is murdering vampires."

Marcus laughed. "That is ironic."

"I suppose."

"No, you do not suppose. You know." Marcus traced his fat cheek, and then pointed at Michael's tattoo. "Murder is your calling, is it not?"

"It's what I do," Michael said, sliding into the game. He had never spoken like this with Marcus, though he knew from rumor and reputation that The Bloody Pulp's owner was shrewd, sharp as his years, with a fang pressed hard into the city's dark pulse.

Marcus sipped his drink. "The murders I know. Most of the dead were familiar faces."

"Walter Crestin was not the only one to come here?"

"Of course not." He smiled. "Even high-class vampires like to roll dirty, sometimes. Though do you know, none here believe the wolves are responsible for their deaths?"

"Who, then?"

"Why, you. You would make a perfect serial killer, Michael. Not a one doubts your ability to pull it off."

"I did not murder those men and women."

Marcus shrugged. "Perhaps it does not matter. Soon, the humans will be doing your job. Indiscriminately, too. And to think, there might come a day when our kind sing your praises as a gentle soul—sing, too, how you did not spare the rod to our spoiled blood-hungry children."

Michael suspected that Marcus took an inordinate

amount of pleasure in hearing himself speak. He said, "Did you see anyone with Walter Crestin the night he died? Any rumors on who—or what—killed him?"

"Plenty of rumors, Michael."

"Do not play games with me."

He smiled, sly. "No games. Just maybes and what-ifs. I will tell you this: Walter Crestin was not alone in the bar the night he died. He had a companion."

"Who?"

"I never learned his name. He came in here sometimes. Never stayed long. Walter talked to him before he died. Walter had a thing for men. Pretty boys. This one had red eyes. Demon-breed, maybe, but Walter did not care. He was too hungry for a taste of sweet."

"What did they talk about?"

"Oh, poor Walter. He liked to brag about the things he did to pinks, the humans. Sticking them the fang *just so*."

"Did he leave with this man?"

"Left, and never came back."

Michael took a deep breath. So. It seemed that all the clues truly did lead back to his mysterious attacker. "You said the other murdered vampires were familiar. Did any of them ever talk with the demon-breed?"

"As I said, he was here sometimes, but I think that was coincidence. Or not. It is difficult to remember. I do not know where he comes from."

"Can you remember the last time he came in?"

"The night Walter died. I have not seen him since. As I recall, he did not drink much, and when he did, it was not from the tap. He wanted water."

"That did not strike you as bizarre?"

"With his eyes? I did not want to antagonize him. Besides, not everyone's drink of pleasure is the same." He gave Michael a pointed look that slid sideways to the monitors. Michael followed his gaze.

At first he did not know what Marcus was trying to tell him, but he looked closer at a shot of the bar, and saw a tiny figure surrounded by vampires. A tiny black and white waif with short pixie hair. A large hand was clamped around her neck.

Michael ran to the door. It was locked. Marcus smiled.

"There is no key, Michael, so do not think of attacking me for one. The lock is voice activated; I must speak a code for it to open."

"Do it," Michael said, watching in horror as the large vampire holding Keeli's neck forced her to the ground. Her face contorted.

"Fascinating," whispered Marcus, staring at Michael. "I heard the rumor, but I did not think such a thing was possible. How deliciously perverted."

Snarling, Michael pounced on Marcus. He drew a knife on the vampire's throat, pressing the blade into the crease of his chin. "Open the door!"

"No," said Marcus, unafraid. "Not until you answer *my* question."

"Anything," Michael promised, watching the vampires in the bar descend on Keeli. Hair pushed through her skin; her cheeks shifted, bones rippling into the wolf. And still the vampire held her. Michael felt his life slipping away, the first true agony, worse than anything he had ever experienced.

Something that could have been compassion stirred deep within Marcus's eyes. "Ah," he sighed. "So you are vulnerable."

Rage blazed hot, burning, and Michael threw away the knife and slashed open the vampire's throat with his own fingernails. He dug his fingers into the wound, twisting. Blood spurted, hitting Michael's face. Marcus howled.

"Open the door!" He ripped his fingers out of the writhing vampire's throat.

"No!" Marcus gasped, blood frothing past his lips. "Not until you tell me how you killed Malachai."

Michael froze; his mouth tasted like ashes. No one had said that name to him in centuries.

"He had me too," Marcus ground out. "Longer than you. Only reason I have not killed you, paid for the job to be done right."

Michael felt like he was going to die. He tore his gaze away to look at the monitors. Keeli was fighting now; he watched her squirm free, slashing her claws through a knee. The vampire fell backwards, but there was another to take his place. Too many.

"I cut off his head," Michael croaked, looking back at Marcus. "I burned his body to ashes. He is *dead*. Now open that door before I do the same thing to you."

Marcus said the code. The door clicked open. Michael ran.

The office had been perfectly soundproofed because out in the bar the blast of anger, excitement, and blood lust was loud enough to feel in his chest. He threw himself up and over the crowd—caught sight of Keeli's pink hair, the blur of her body as she rolled across the ground.

"Keeli!" he shouted. She spun, light, the wolf in her sharp face, inhuman eyes blazing blue and gold. Her cheek bled, and her body shone slick with dark fur. She was the most beautiful thing he had ever seen in his life: wild and strong.

Blood covered her hands; several vampires were sprawled at her feet. Michael flew toward Keeli, stretching—she grabbed his hands and he hauled her off the ground. Vampires shot up after them; Keeli kicked one in the head. Michael slammed an elbow into a chest, whipping in a tight circle, spinning too fast for hands to catch hold. Keeli's hair tickled his chin, her body squashed flat against his own. She smelled like roses, blood, her heart flashing a quick sweet rhythm. Something hard hit his back.

Enough. He had to keep Keeli safe, no matter what, and this—*this*—could not be tolerated. Not anymore—not ever again.

He flew behind the bar, sliding into a dive that had him skinning his back, Keeli riding hard on his chest. The humans were finally awake; they stared down at Michael and Keeli with wide, startled eyes, and began struggling in their restraints.

"Michael!" Keeli gasped, but he barely heard her. He unsheathed his sword and jumped on top of the counter with a monster curling tight in his gut, vicious and hungry. Keeli touched his ankle.

High-class vampires touted their refinement, played at being human—the lower classes reveled in myth, the human expectation of desire and cruelty and blood. But it was all the same in the end, born or made. Their existence was founded on masks, worn tight in games and play, hiding the true face of the beast, the shadow on the soul that was both power and death.

No one was more familiar with that dark nature than Michael. No one else had been stripped down to that pure essence of vampire, where the human was dead, the conscience drowned in blood. None of the vampires in front of Michael knew what that meant—could even conceive of such darkness, no matter how much they desired to be a part of it. Rebels. Rogues. They were weak. Pathetic.

I will kill them all. I will kill them. For Keeli. For me. For all the people they have hurt or dream of hurting.

Keeli jumped up beside him. He expected her to try to calm him, but instead he heard a low growl, the scrape of claws. He glanced sideways and found her facing the vampires, more wolf than woman.

Ready to watch his back.

I love you, Keeli Maddox.

Marcus appeared in the doorway of his office. One hand clutched his neck; blood spilled over his fingers, staining his white shirt. He leaned against the thick frame, chest heaving.

"Stop it," he said. It took Michael a moment to realize Marcus was talking to the vampires in his bar. He staggered forward, trailing blood. He looked at Keeli.

"She is your friend," Marcus said.

"The best," Michael said, sensing Keeli stir beside him. "She never gives up on me."

Marcus turned to face the vampires. "Go away. Sit down and pretend you are clever. Do *not* bare fang to the wolf or you will answer to me."

"She's a dog," spat Viggo, wiping blood from his mouth. "A bitch. You gonna let that stand in here?"

Marcus hissed, terrible violence rippling through his thick face. His jowls shook. "Do you want to fuck with me today, Viggo?"

Even Michael did not want to fuck with Marcus now— not with that terrible brutality shadowing his face, transforming it into something terrifying and ancient.

Viggo slunk away into the blue shadows.

"You could have killed me," Michael said, voicing that awful, humbling, realization. "Back in your office. You're strong enough."

"I could have," Marcus agreed. "But we are both sons of Malachai, and that is an uncommon bond."

The bleeding slowed. Marcus peered up at Keeli, who stood straight and tall beside Michael. Her chest heaved; cuts and scratches dotted her body, barely visible beneath the dark fur and tattered clothing. Her sharp face was barely human. Michael reached for her hand and she gripped him hard.

"How very curious," Marcus murmured.

A shiver ran up Keeli's arm. She jumped off the bar counter, landing lightly on the balls of her feet with a wild grace that was both wolf and woman. Michael leapt after her and sheathed his sword. The floor was sticky with blood.

Marcus approached, slow. Behind him the humans, still strapped to the blue wall, watched with large uncertain eyes. Michael briefly considered cutting them down, but realized it would be a useless act. They could walk anytime they wanted; Michael knew that much about Marcus. Those humans hung there, night after night, because they *wanted* to be food on tap. Because for them, whoring out blood was better than whoring sex. Might pay better, too. Michael thought it was a toss-up.

Marcus glanced at Keeli, who stared back, defiant. "Michael. Did I give you the answers you needed?"

"Do you have more answers?"

"Not yet." A mysterious smile touched his pale lips. "And I suspect you might have more than me."

"Emily?" Keeli prompted.

Michael nodded. "We are also looking for a vampire who carries a silver knife with a hilt shaped like a crucifix. He likes to attack women, and the occasional werewolf."

Marcus paused. "If I see him, I will tell you."

"Will you really?" Keeli asked. Her face shifted back to full human, the fur on her arms receding. She looked past Marcus to the restrained humans. Her mouth twisted. "You don't really inspire a whole lot of trust."

"A vampire is only as good as his word," Marcus said. Keeli shook her head, unamused.

"Thank you for your help," Michael said, and then stepped close, savoring the taste of blood as his teeth cut into his lip. His hands felt sticky. Marcus did not move, not even when Michael touched his wounded neck and whispered, "If you ever put Keeli's life in danger again, I will kill you. I will do to you what I did to Malachai, and I will make it slow. Do you understand?"

"I understand that your word is as good as mine." Marcus shrugged. "Your wolf is safe from me."

Keeli touched Michael's hand and he pulled her close; he looked around the bar, through the blue haze at the vampires who had attacked her. They sat like statues, dark eyes set within pale faces that were detached, pitiless.

They are not all like this.

No, but it was easy to forget, to see only darkness. Perhaps it was so easy because Michael was intimately familiar with his own monster, the horrific face of his own heart.

Keeli stirred. "If you really mean it, that I'm safe from you, then show us the back door."

Michael tried not to show his surprise. Marcus merely tilted his head and gestured for them to follow. They walked through his office; Keeli glanced at the blood on the floor and looked at Michael. He shrugged.

The Bloody Pulp's back door was inside a closet filled with sunscreen and other sundries. Marcus tossed Michael a bottle, along with a package of wet-naps. Michael eyed them with some amusement; he broke open the package and cleaned his face. Tossed everything to Keeli. She wiped her hands.

Marcus said, "I am sorry."

Michael blinked. "For what?"

"For what was done to you. All of Malachai's children committed crimes, but you were the only one punished." He smiled, bitter. "And in some ways, you are the only one who has redeemed yourself."

"I do not feel redeemed."

Marcus shrugged. He unlocked the door at the back of the closet and opened it. Michael saw another closet, this one filled with cleaning supplies. Keeli slipped through and stood on the other side, waiting. Her pink hair stuck out in wild directions. Michael wanted nothing more than to find a quiet place and hold her. He felt so tired.

Marcus did not say good-bye, and Michael did not turn around as the door shut behind them. He wrapped Keeli tight in his arms. Relief made him weak.

"Rough," he said, voice muffled by her hair.

"Yeah." Keeli clutched his shoulders. She was shaking. "I shouldn't have come in, but there was a Tracker nearby. I'm sorry, Michael."

"There is no reason to be sorry." He moved just enough to look into her eyes. He studied the cut in her cheek. "Are you hurt anywhere else?"

She shook her head, swallowing hard. "I was in trouble. There were too many of them."

"You looked like you were doing fine."

Keeli briefly closed her eyes. "Fine. Yeah." She looked around the closet. "Where the hell are we?"

"We could open the door and find out," he suggested, and then kissed her smile. Keeli pushed against him, soft, and he felt her desperation in the way her lips moved, the hard suck and pull of her mouth.

I almost lost you, he wanted to say, but he let his body speak for him, and Keeli seemed to understand.

They opened the door and found themselves at the back of a very normal, and completely incongruous, health food store. Boxes of green tea and organic dried fruits covered the tables around them. Low-carb snacks, seeds, and seaweed lined the walls. Michael smelled incense.

"Whoa." Keeli stared at a rack full of herbal sexual aides. "Did we just cross into another universe?"

"Hello!" A pert little brunette with shells around her neck flounced toward them. "I didn't see you guys come in."

"Uh," said Michael, but the woman looked past him at the open closet door and giggled.

"Isn't that cute? I just started renting this space, and I still can't get over how much fun it is to have a"—her voice dropped to a whisper—"secret entrance. Were you guys just at the club? Marcus is *such* a sweetie pie. He said I should stop by some night and see his bar. I still haven't gotten around to it. Is it nice?"

"Um," said Keeli.

"Well, never mind. Feel free to look around. I'll be up front if you need anything."

They did not need anything. They left the store as quickly as possible, and stood outside, looking up and down the street.

"We're just on the other side of the Crimson Light district," Michael said. "The Bloody Pulp must back right up against this building."

Keeli shook her head and raised a hand to a cab. "Whatever. Did you find out anything before I crashed the party?"

Michael blinked back the memory of Keeli, alone and surrounded. "Apparently, our murderer liked to go to the bar. All the victims had some kind of presence there; slumming it, maybe. Which makes me think he was actively hunting them."

A cab pulled up to the sidewalk, responding to Keeli's wave. "I'd high-five you, but that would look tacky."

Michael opened the cab door. "Marcus implied that our man lured Walter away with promises of sex."

"Sounds fascinating," said the cabbie. Michael smiled, and gave the man his apartment address. They did not talk about the case again until they reached his building. The old brick facade looked more dilapidated and dirty than Michael ever remembered it being. He felt embar-

rassed, but when he looked down at Keeli, she was studying him with an intensity that stole his breath.

"What is it?" he asked.

"Just thinking how glad I am to be here with you," she
said. "It's a good feeling."

"You can say that, even after everything we've been
through?"

"Can't you?"

"Of course."

"Then why would I feel any different?"

Michael smiled. "I would never presume to predict
your emotions, Keeli."

That made her grin. She tucked her arm around his elbow and he led her down the alley, the back entrance to
his apartment. "Marcus thought our attacker was a demon. The red eyes. Apparently, he never drank blood
while he was at the bar. Only water."

Keeli shuddered. "If he won't touch humans, then I'm
not surprised water was his choice of beverage. What a
messed-up place."

"Maybe the perfect place to plan a murder," Michael
said.

"So . . . what? Our guy is a vigilante?"

"Some of the vampires who died were not known for
harming humans."

"But they were vampires, and if our murderer is working for a rogue element of the government—"

"It might not matter if they were good or bad," Michael
finished. "We are all the same, after all. Just monsters."

Keeli's brows furrowed. "He acted so hungry, Michael.
Almost vulnerable—in a lethal, psychopathic sort of way.
How could he have the control to sit down in a bar and
listen to conversation if he were that starved?"

"Maybe he has better control than we give him credit

for. I identified with him because of his words, because there was something familiar in the way he carried himself, but I was irrational when I committed my acts. This man is clearly not. He knows what he is doing, and has enough composure to plan—to stop himself, even. Like he did with us."

"And that was because we smelled like each other. Vampire and werewolf."

"Tell me," Michael whispered, "is it possible for a vampire to love a werewolf?"

Keeli smiled. "What did you tell him?"

"Nothing. But the next time he asks, I'll be ready."

"You think there's going to be a next time?" He simply looked at her, and Keeli sighed. "Yeah, I know. I just had to ask."

Michael pulled her into his arms and flew them up to his fire escape.

"Careful," she whispered. "There could be a Tracker in there."

"Or Richard and Suze," he said.

Michael set Keeli down, gently, but refused to release her from the loose circle of his arms. Ignoring the possibility of danger, he carefully broke off a white rose and stuck it behind her ear.

"Perfect," he said.

Keeli smiled. "You think you're going to charm my pants off?"

"You're not wearing pants." He patted her backside and hitched up her skirt. Keeli slipped out of his embrace. She took a deep breath, opened the window, and jumped into his apartment. Michael followed, but had to stop himself fast—Keeli stood perfectly still in front of him. She stared at the door, at the man leaning against it.

Chapter Twenty

"Hello," said Hargittai quietly. "I thought I would find you here, Keeli."

Michael gently pushed Keeli aside so he could get into his apartment. Richard and Suze were nowhere to be seen. The briefcase was gone.

He did not miss the way Hargittai's lips tightened, the hard pulse in his cheek.

"Why are you here?" Michael asked. "How did you find us?"

"The Grand Dame had your address. She was going to send a Tracker, but I convinced her to let me come instead."

Keeli stepped forward. Michael wanted to snatch her back, but he knew that if he made any move toward her, Hargittai might react badly. After what Celestine had told him last night, any response was possible.

"Alpha Hargittai," she said. "Please, I don't want to go back."

"It's for the best," he said, his voice as hard and dull as his eyes. "This won't last."

"Because it did not last for you and Celestine?" Michael shook his head. "Do not compare us."

Hargittai went very still. "How . . . ?"

"We overheard you last night," Keeli said, with more compassion than Michael had ever imagined she possessed. He watched Hargittai, and it seemed to him that the Alpha had trouble breathing. Muscles moved convulsively in his neck; his dead eyes suddenly blazed bright with pain.

"If you overheard," he said finally, his gaze darting to Michael, "then you know what Cel—what she said about *him*."

Keeli's chin jutted out. "Michael told me everything." Which implied she had already known the story before Celestine's revelation, but Michael was not going to lecture her about absolute and perfect truths. "It's not what you think."

"When you love someone, it never is."

Michael finally did step forward. "Celestine must have told you her own history. Did she ever mention a vampire named Malachai?"

Hargittai's eyes darkened. "She hated him. He made her. Tortured her."

"We shared the same master," Michael said. "He tortured all his made children, and there were many."

Hargittai hesitated. "All right. Fine. Perhaps I can see why your story might not be what I think. I'll give you that. But I do not know you, and I do not know how this can last. Keeli, your grandmother is furious. I do not agree with the way she treated you, but she is the Grand Dame. Her word is law."

"She's afraid for me. Too afraid to think straight. I didn't mean to make a bid for Alpha, but now that I have, she seems to believe the other leaders will try to murder me."

"History, repeating itself."

Keeli nodded. "Maybe it will. Maybe no one will tolerate a Grand Dame who has a vampire for her lover."

"You could rescind your bid. Explain it away as a mistake."

"I tried to tell her that, but she doesn't seem to care. She won't listen to me. All she can talk about is my relationship with Michael. She's terrified of how I'll be treated because of it."

"You have your own power now," Hargittai said. "You defeated an Alpha in battle."

"Power doesn't mean anything without respect," Keeli told him. "And I'm not looking to rule. I just want to live my life the way I want. I want . . . I want to be able to go home without being treated like a criminal. But if that can't happen—if my grandmother won't let me—then I'm out of here. I'll leave my clan."

"For him?" Hargittai said. "For a vampire, you would do this?"

"Wouldn't you have done the same for Celestine? Didn't you love her that much?"

Hargittai turned away. Keeli followed him, seeking out his face.

"Why did you do it?" she asked softly. "Why did you force that bid on me? Don't pretend. You knew what would happen when you said those things to Jas."

Hargittai threw back his shoulders. "At the time it seemed like the perfect opportunity. I respect Jas Mack, but he is not the right wolf for Grand Alpha. He is too . . . inflexible. He has no sense of what it means to deal with humans, to live topside. He is incapable of diplomacy outside our species, of any long-term planning that requires finesse. He knows it, too. He knows all these things, and still he pushes. All because of *her*."

"You cannot blame him for wanting to protect his wife," Michael said.

"Yes, I can." Hargittai clenched his fists. "In this, the clans must come first."

"And why do you think I would be any better?" Keeli pressed forward, her face an urgent mask of confusion and hunger. "Please. Why me? I don't know anything. Everyone's afraid of me."

"Some fear you, yes. But that is just ignorance. After what you did today . . . Keeli, do you have any idea how important that was? Not only did you unseat an Alpha and three of his men, but you did it without the support of your clan. You protected your wolves."

"It was the right thing to do."

"But you were the only one there who did it." Hargittai bowed his head, staring at his hands. "They respect you, Keeli. If not now, then later they will learn to respect you. They already respect the Maddox legacy. Of all the wolves, and all the bloodlines, yours is the oldest. The most powerful, both in character and instinct."

"Blood doesn't mean anything," she whispered. "The men who murdered my family taught me that."

"Blood alone does not mean anything," he agreed quietly. "But your strength is not just blood and a name. I have watched you ever since you were a child—all of us have—and you have what it takes to become a great leader."

"You are so full of shit," Keeli said, and it was clear to Michael that she was so lost in her own fear that she had forgotten who she was talking to. "I couldn't lead a pack of goats to water."

"Then why are we arguing about this?" Hargittai leaned forward, his gaze intense. Shrewd. "You are right: The actual bid was my fault. But you beat that Alpha, and you went along with everything I said. Why, Keeli? Why do that, unless deep down, you think you could lead the clans? Lead them well, even."

"My temper—," she began, but Hargittai shook his head.

"That is an excuse, something your grandmother should never have forced on you. She was so afraid you would turn into your father, she made sure you learned to be afraid, too."

Michael wrapped his arms around Keeli's shoulders and she leaned into him, warm and small. "I loved my father. He was a good man. He fought too much, but he was good to us."

"Yes," said Hargittai faintly. "Your mother was a good woman, too. They just made the wrong people angry."

Keeli shook her head. "It always comes down to anger. What to do with it, how to control it. How not to be an animal. I don't know if I'm ready to face up to that kind of thing on a large scale."

Michael turned her around to face him. "Perhaps you are not meant to lead the clans, but do not deceive yourself, Keeli. Do not denigrate your abilities. Do you have any idea what you've done, the strength it took to be here, with me? To make the sacrifices you have, all in the name of helping your people and mine? You are the rarest person I have ever met, and the wolves would be lucky to have you as their Grand Dame."

"You're only saying that because you like me."

"I *love* you. But love is not the same as truth, and Alpha Hargittai and I both know what you are capable of, even if you do not."

Keeli squirmed. Michael let her go, and she stood apart from both men, staring helplessly. "None of this solves the real problem. I can't go back to my grandmother. Not now, anyway. We're getting close to solving this crime, and if we can do that, we might be able to save the alliance."

Hargittai frowned. "The vampires are demanding full access to the underground in case of an emergency. They also want us to retrofit a good portion of the tunnels to suit their . . . needs. More luxury than survival, if you ask me."

"What are they offering in return?" Michael asked.

"Ten million dollars."

Keeli's eyes widened, but Michael shook his head. "That is too small a number. The Grand Dame should be asking for at least one hundred million."

"What?" Keeli looked incredulous. "There's no way they would pay that much."

"The vampires will pay what it takes, and trust me, they have the money. They have more than enough. And if they want the tunnels retrofitted, then they must pay for that in addition to any fees the wolves require."

Hargittai snorted. "The Grand Dame has not even talked price yet. She's still trying to get the vampires to compromise on their access to the underground. Or at least, she was. Fleur Dumont ordered the envoys to remain in the Maddox tunnels until an agreement is reached. Your grandmother was very displeased. She's refusing to talk to them until tonight. I think her disagreement with you has something to do with her decision."

"Tonight is the full moon. No one's going to be doing any talking."

"Exactly."

Keeli covered her face and groaned. "She planned this out perfectly. We are so screwed."

"No," Hargittai said, and there was something in his eyes that made Michael want to shake his head, plead silence, but it was too late—too late—and the Alpha moved close and whispered, "Not if you challenge her."

"I threatened her with that," Keeli said softly. "But I was angry. I didn't really mean it."

"And if it means saving the alliance?"

"Stop it." Keeli glared at him. "Why are you here?

Why are you saying these things to me? It's the same as treason."

"Wolves do not believe in treason. You know that, Keeli. We believe in survival. Survival at any cost. And right now, our survival depends on people like you and Michael. We have no time for pettiness. The humans say a rogue element was responsible for the recent attacks on the major vampire family, but what if that is a lie? We are not prepared for the possibilities."

Michael moved to the window. He soaked in the bright dazzle of his roses, thinking about the ephemeral qualities of beauty and pain. He said, "How did you meet Celestine?"

Hargittai's eyes narrowed. "It is none of your business."

"She's been a lawyer for fifty years. She must be very good by now. Did you go to her with a legal question, not knowing she was a vampire?"

A low growl emerged from the Alpha's throat. Michael continued looking at his roses. "Or maybe she was just curious and decided to slum it. Found more than she bargained for."

Keeli cried out. Michael ducked as Hargittai's fist slammed into the wall. The plaster cracked. The werewolf froze there, his hand embedded in the wall. Fur spiked through his skin.

"You still love her," Michael said, keeping his distance. "And you are here because you cannot stand to be so near, and not see her. Touch her. You want this alliance just as bad as anyone, and you want Keeli to be the next Grand Dame. But you're as selfish as Jas, even if your goals are completely different. You want all this because you think it will bring back Celestine. You want it because you think it will make a world where your relationship will be accepted, easy."

"That is not true," whispered Hargittai. "I believe Keeli is our best hope for Grand Dame."

"And if she is a Grand Dame who has taken a vampire as her lover, who proves such a thing is possible?"

Hargittai's jaw tightened. "Celestine and I were together for three months, and it was wonderful. Beautiful. I thought . . . I thought it would stay that way." His voice broke, dropping to a whisper. "There was no warning. One day she told me it was over, that our differences in age made it too difficult to love me—that she did not love me. But it was a lie. I could smell it all over her. She was afraid, terrified."

Keeli stepped close. "She didn't tell you why?"

Hargittai shook his head. He pulled his hand out of the wall and rubbed his knuckles. "I searched for her after that, but it was as though she never lived in the city." Michael felt the wolf's agony—tried to imagine what it would be like to lose Keeli in such a way. He found himself reaching out to her and almost closed his eyes in relief when she took his hand, held it tight.

"Someone found out," Hargittai said, glancing away from their joined hands. "She was forced to leave me. I know it."

Michael thought of Celestine, everything he knew of her, and said, "Celestine is too stubborn to be easily forced into anything. If she were threatened, then it had to be by someone she took very seriously, who had enough power to carry out the threat."

Like an elder in the Primary Assembly. In the Council. Michael remembered the menace in Frederick's voice, and wondered just how far such a thing could go—how much the elders would be willing to sacrifice to prevent a vampire and werewolf from living their lives together. What could be so terrible?

He also considered the possibility that Celestine really

had grown tired of Hargittai, but no—her words of the night before, the shaken confidence, the quavering of her voice—that could not be faked. Celestine had once been in love with a werewolf. Perhaps she still was.

"I am sorry," Hargittai said to Keeli. "Perhaps . . . perhaps Michael is right. Maybe I do want Celestine too much, but not at the cost of the clans. Keeli, at least consider it. Please. If you are brought back to the underground by force I will do my best to convince the other Alphas to hear your bid before the Grand Dame abdicates to Jas. It would be better, though, if you came of your own free will."

"To challenge her? She is my *grandmother*. I can't hurt her. I *love* her."

"Challenges between blood are not to the death, Keeli."

"She'll never submit, not in a million years. She's too afraid for me."

"Then you must hope she changes her mind about the vampires. Her anger toward you and Michael is affecting the negotiations."

Keeli looked miserable. Michael tugged her close, and gave Hargittai a hard look. The Alpha backed away, toward the door.

"Go home," said Michael. "Try to salvage the negotiations, if you can. Talk to Jas. Celestine, too. Try to find out why she left you."

"She won't tell me."

Michael smiled. "That might be for the best. She won't tell you anything if she still loves you. Whatever secret she's keeping, she still cares too much to let you hear it."

Hargittai frowned. "Just how well do you know her?"

"Not as well as I thought I did," Michael said. Keeli tried not to laugh, but her shoulders began shaking.

"This is not very funny," Hargittai said.

"Yeah," sighed Keeli. "But you weren't there the first time I met Celestine."

* * *

When Hargittai left, Michael drew Keeli to the bed. He took off her boots and made her lie down. He curled around her body. Keeli listened to his slow, even breaths, the rise and fall of his chest against her back. He felt safe and lean and strong. With his arms wrapped around her, she could imagine safety—imagine, too, that this feeling would last forever.

Poor Hargittai. Poor Celestine, too.

Exhausted, she closed her eyes and fell asleep.

She awoke to the sounds of voices. Michael, and someone else. Keeli rolled over and sat up. Jenkins stood just within the front doorway. The men stopped talking when they saw her move.

"What is it?" she asked, rubbing her eyes. Jenkins was in street clothes; he held a baseball cap in one hand and slapped it lightly against his thigh.

"I have some information," he said. He looked unhappy.

Keeli rested her elbows on her knees. She felt very glad she was still wearing all her clothes. "Spit it out, Jenkins. I have to pee."

The cop could not hide his smile. He shook his head. "Only you," he muttered. "Shit, Michael. You sure you want to keep her?"

"She makes me laugh."

"I bet." Jenkins looked at Keeli, and the smile died. "It goes like this, Keeli. Your murderer is not working for the government. Or at least, he's not working for the government in any official capacity. Actually, the government doesn't have anything to do with him. He's an outside contractor."

"I have no idea what you just said to me, but it sounds highly top secret."

"I get around," Jenkins said. "I used to be in the military and I've still got contacts, people who owe me favors. I just never would have thought what or who to ask if you hadn't pointed me in the right direction. So here, listen. It seems that some really ugly stuff has been going on in B-Ops, all if it run by a guy named Kippenham."

"Yes," said Michael. "We know about this."

Jenkins nodded, serious. "Yes. It was in the papers. Or part of it was. So, you won't be surprised to learn that he had some other projects on the side. Nonmilitary contracts. I can't tell you much about this vampire-killer, except that he's part of an ongoing private experiment."

She felt cold. "Experiment?"

"He's a true-blue lab tool. Been kept for the past sixteen years in a privately funded lab near the military base at LAX. Kippenham had an agreement with the person in charge."

Keeli was incredulous. "How did you get people to tell you all this?"

"I'm a likable guy. Also, Kippenham got himself killed. A little death makes everyone want to talk, especially if you know how to ask the right questions."

"All right," said Michael. "So we know where he is. Can you tell us *what* he is?"

"Sorry. All I know is that they're paying big money for this kid. They just recently began turning him loose." He swore, looking sick.

"Yeah," Keeli said softly. "Life's a bitch when everyone's trying to kill you."

"I suspected," Jenkins said. "But that's different from knowing. The word is that it's just a handful of people who organized this, but no one I talked to knows who they are—or if they do, they're too scared to talk."

"Which suggests power," Michael said. "And an agenda."

Keeli studied Jenkins's troubled face. "You realize, don't you? This is what we didn't want to talk about."

"I don't want to know," he said, holding up his hands. His entire body sagged. "Christ. This entire city is screwed. My kids—"

"You should get them out. You have family in the Midwest, right?" Michael asked. "Send them there. You and your wife, too. Just leave, Jenkins."

"You think it's that bad?"

"It could be," Michael said. "There's no way to know for certain. But vampires are dying, have already died, and certain measures—legal and otherwise—are being implemented that curb our freedoms. Werewolf freedoms, too. We are being edged out, Jenkins. Pushed. And one day soon, we will have to push back."

"And you weren't going to tell me." His voice got hard.

Keeli did not blame him for being angry. "You're a good man," she said, trying to make him understand. "But good men do stupid things."

"Like help people?" Jenkins said in a scathing voice. "Or try to stop racist attacks between three different species?"

"Yes," Michael said sadly. "Exactly that. This is bigger than you, Jenkins. It's bigger than all of us."

"If there's a fight, my guys might be called up against you."

"I know," he said, and Keeli could tell he hurt for it.

The same tragedy was written on Jenkins's face. He looked at Keeli, and it was a measuring gaze, sharp. But then his eyes softened, and he said, "Take care of him, will you? Watch his back."

"I will," she promised softly.

Jenkins nodded, running a hand through his spiky hair. "All right, then. Okay. I guess this may be it for a while." He handed Michael a piece of paper. "I've written down the exact location of your man. Getting him will be up to you. Completely off-the-record, too. I can't touch him. Not anymore. Word finally came down, Michael. We're supposed to cut off all relations. No more liaisons, no more investigation into paranormal crimes, period. None. We lay off, or else. Guess I know why, now."

"Jenkins," Michael began, but the man shook his head with a grim smile.

"Don't. Just . . . let's hope this thing blows over. That we can get back to our old lives." He hesitated, looking at Michael and Keeli. "Yeah, I know. Impossible."

Michael held out his hand. Instead of taking it, Jenkins grabbed Michael and wrapped him in a tight hug. He thumped the vampire's back, and reached for Keeli. She joined the two men, and for a moment they all clung to each other: vampire, werewolf, and human. Keeli felt something small break inside of her.

Nothing changes. It's always pain. Loss is the undeniable force, and afterward, death. Sometimes, death comes first. Either way, you're screwed.

"Be safe," Jenkins said, finally releasing them.

"You too," Keeli said, astonished to feel tears burning her eyes. "Get out of here, Jenkins. Go with your family and stay far away. Don't be here when the fighting starts."

"Maybe." He took a deep breath. "Don't know how fair that would be to the ones left behind. And maybe there's still a way to make things right. The only way to know is to try."

He left. Michael watched Jenkins walk down the hall, and shut the door.

"It's hard," Keeli said gently, reaching for his hand, "when you lose friends."

"It's harder when you don't actually lose them," Michael said, drawing her close.

"Yeah." She kissed his cheek, trying not to cry as she thought of her grandmother. "I guess I'm learning how hard that can be."

Chapter Twenty-one

They spread the piece of paper on the table and studied the information Jenkins had given them. There was not much, but it was enough.

Enough to know they were in deep trouble.

"That place is built like Fort Knox. No way in hell we're just walking in there. We're going to have to wait until he comes to us."

"If we wait for that, someone else could die," Michael said.

"It'll be the full moon tonight," Keeli reminded him. "You are going to change."

"I won't be able to help it. You'll have to . . . to keep me tied up. Chains are better. Collars. I don't have any here with me, though."

He looked so uncomfortable. Keeli leaned close and kissed him. "It's all right, Michael. Better restraints than having me run wild through the streets. I might hurt someone."

"You have no control at all?"

Keeli stared at the desk, her small pale hands. She recalled what it was like to look at her hands and see paws instead. The distorted view of the world—everything was larger, sharper, more intense. "There's some control, but the animal takes us. And we *are* animals during that time, Michael. You won't be able to trust me."

"I have trouble believing that."

Keeli touched his face, forcing him to look her in the eyes. "Don't think for an instant I won't hurt you. Love means nothing when the wolf has you. Wolves don't love. It's only instinct. Nothing more, nothing less."

"You are still inside the wolf, Keeli. You are still the woman."

"Not when the moon is full. Tonight, Michael, the woman is going to be the one sleeping. It's the price we pay."

He caressed her face, wrapped his hand around the back of her neck. His touch was cool, gentle. "You will be safe with me, I promise. I will watch over you tonight."

"No," she whispered, though it warmed her to hear him say so. "And I'm not the one who needs to be kept safe. Just . . . tie me up. Muzzle me. And then go out and solve this case."

"Not without you," he said.

"Michael, if we can't find this guy today—which seems very likely—that's just what you'll have to do. We can't let him hurt anyone else."

"Of course not. Which means we *will* find him before the moon rises. It's still afternoon. We have time."

Keeli closed her eyes. It was inevitable. He was finally showing his stubborn side.

Yeah, and it's only been two days. Of course, if that's the worst you ever say of him, you'll be counting your blessings.

Keeli sighed and flopped down on the bed, her heels dragging on the floor. She spread out her arms and stared, limp, at the cracked ceiling. Michael walked over and looked at her. He knelt between her legs. His fingers touched her ribs, tickling.

"I'm too young to die," she said, laughing weakly, trying to roll away from him. "Oh, God. Michael, I hope you have a good plan."

"I do," he said, unbuttoning her skirt. He kissed her belly, and Keeli stopped struggling. "I have a very good plan."

"Yeah? Tell me."

Michael smiled, and told her.

It was always alleys with them. Keeli thought it might be nice to one day sit down with Michael in the lobby of a posh hotel, or even on a grassy hill in a park. Go down to the beach for the sunset and some bloody margaritas.

Anything but this smelly, skanky piece of concrete that was shiny with greasy puddles and urine and other, more awful biological hazards to her health.

"This is part of your plan?" Keeli stared at the back of his head. She wondered if it was time to start kicking his ass.

Michael said nothing and she hurried to keep up with his long quick strides. They were still in his neighborhood, just a couple of streets down from his apartment, and this alley looked like a combination of war zone and garbage dump. Barbed wire laced the ground, which was thickly covered with loose trash: beer cans, used sanitary napkins, decaying food. Flies buzzed through the air; Keeli swatted at them, swearing.

"Michael!" she snapped. He glanced at her, but kept walking.

"We're close," he said. "Don't worry."

"I'm not *worried*," she muttered. "I just want to kill you."

She thought he laughed, but that would make him too stupid to live. She gave him more credit than that.

Less than a minute later, Michael did finally stop.

Right in front of a large rusty trash can. Keeli stood beside him.

"If Oscar the Grouch is in there, I'm leaving."

Michael smiled. He knocked on the battered lid.

God, yes. This is going to be the Sesame Street version of hell.

The trash can rattled. Keeli took a step back. The lid popped open, revealing a set of brilliant green eyes. Inhumanly pale and green.

Oh. Shit.

"What'sa?" rasped a low voice.

Michael's smile widened. Keeli blinked, completely taken aback by the charm that swept over his face, softening his hard angular features, easing the darkness in his eyes.

"Grindla," Michael said. "I've got a problem you can help me with."

Keeli looked back at the trash can and found those green eyes studying her. Intense, hungry. She took another step away before she could stop herself.

"Gotsa howl with you, M'cal. Strange now. Strange."

"She's a biddy, Grindla. Real bid like. Come now, let us in."

"Ai," whispered the rough voice. "Ai now, M'cal."

The lid sank back down. Michael waited a moment, and then pulled it off. Keeli edged forward. All she saw was darkness.

"That can has no fucking bottom," she said.

"It is Grindla's home," Michael said mildly. Keeli glared at him. She wanted to pull out her hair—that, or run away screaming.

"It's all right," Michael said, holding out his hand. "I've known Grindla for a long, long time. She's very friendly."

Keeli did not take his hand. Michael said, "Okay, she's a demon."

"Yes." Keeli remained very still. "I kind of figured that

out, when I saw the bottomless pit inside the trash can she calls home."

"Oh." Michael peered over the edge of the can. "I suppose that is rather distinctive. It's nothing to worry about, though. Grindla's nothing like other demons. You know, the banished ones. I'm not sure where she's from—or where she goes. But we're friends."

"M'cal?" Grindla's faint voice floated out of the darkness.

"We should go," Michael said, edging toward the can. "She doesn't like to keep her front door open for long periods of time."

"Gee. That's too bad."

"Keeli—"

"This is your plan?" She finally moved, shoving his shoulder. "You're getting a *demon* to help us? Are you an idiot?"

"Grindla has always been a good friend to me. Please, Keeli. Trust me on this. I know what I am doing."

Keeli sucked in her breath. Her gums ached from grinding her teeth. "I'm breaking up with you if she sucks my soul into hell."

"I don't think that's how it works."

"Says you." Keeli inched over to the trash can and peered over the edge. She winced, and looked away, fast. "I feel dizzy."

"I'll hold you the entire time. I won't let you go."

Keeli studied his face, taking in his genuine concern, the soft worry. She squeezed shut her eyes.

"Keeli?"

"I hate you," she muttered. "I can't stay mad when you look at me like that."

Michael wrapped his arms around her. He held her tight.

"Hold on to my neck." He kissed her brow. "I'll make this fast."

He picked her up. Keeli did not think they would fit through the opening of the trash can, but as Michael floated down into the darkness, nothing brushed her body. Just the whisper of cool air, the scent of damp. The sense of something large and immense hiding beyond the edge of shadow, ready to swallow them up.

And then it did.

When she opened her eyes, it took Keeli a moment to realize that she was not dead. Just stuck within a darkness so absolute, not even her werewolf vision worked. She could not see her hands, but she pressed them to her face to give herself some sense of presence. Some evidence that her body still existed. She patted her eyes; they really were open.

"Michael," she called out, ashamed at how her voice cracked. He did not respond.

"Curious." A low rasp emerged from the darkness, full-bodied, like a rough tongue against Keeli's ears. "Howl gotsa need for the v'pire."

"Grindla?" Keeli tried to reach for the wolf, but the beast slept and could not be wakened. The heart of her, cut off. Real fear laced Keeli's gut; sweat broke out on her back, beneath her breasts.

"M'cal says you be a biddy, but M'cal does'no have no biddy gals. Strange, strange." The last was whispered, so close that Keeli whirled, lashing out with her fists. Her hands cut through air.

"Heart beatin' like a lil' lamb." Keeli heard a loud sniff, the wet slurp of a very long tongue. "Tasty. Sweet to suckle."

"Stay away," Keeli warned, trying to sound strong.

"You in m'home, howl-biddy. No thing you can do till m'ready."

"Where is Michael? What have you done with him?"

Keeli smelled sulfur—reared back as something wet licked her cheek. Low laughter filled the air.

"Fear tastes good. So does M'cal. You want him, howl-biddy? Want him bad?"

"Yes," she breathed, fear thrumming through her heart, which hammered like a wild thing.

"Ai," sighed Grindla. "Ai, then. Gotsa pay a price, then. Big one."

"Anything," she said. "I'll pay anything. Just don't hurt him."

"You pay with y'life, howl? How's that for a b'gain?"

Keeli went very still, lost in the possibilities, the irony. "Yes," she said, wishing she could make her voice louder, braver. She sounded like a lost child. "Yes, I would pay that."

And suddenly she felt him there, his scent filling her nose like the most perfect bouquet—better than roses—and she sagged against his body with his arms wrapped tight around her shoulders. She could not see him, but it was Michael, and that was enough. She could hate herself later for being so weak.

"Keeli," he murmured. "Sorry. I am so sorry. I did not know."

"You heard."

"Grindla made sure of it."

Light appeared—a bright shaft shaped like a door. Keeli saw a shadow just on the edge of that light, bumpy and small, with waving limbs in all the wrong places. She looked at Michael and found his face terrible: violent, harsh.

"I trusted you, Grindla." Keeli felt the anger in his voice, his razor-sharp shame. "I promised Keeli she would be safe here, and you betrayed me. Broke my word."

"I be your biddy, too," Grindla said, rasping soft. "Had t'be sure of the howl. Long journey you got, M'cal. Gotsa know your true biddys."

"I thought *you* were my biddy, but you made the woman I love bargain for a life that was in no danger!" Michael drew out a long, harsh breath. "Will you make her pay, Grindla? Will you?"

"In time, everyone gotsa pays. Howl's no different."

"Grindla!" Michael held Keeli so tightly she had trouble breathing. Or maybe that was just fear. Hers and his. She felt him shaking.

The waving limbs stilled, lowered. "Ai now, M'cal. Ai. Rest easy. Long as you be around, no thing will happen to her."

Which was not entirely comfortable wording, from Keeli's point of view. Michael, apparently, didn't think so either.

"Promise me you won't hurt her. You or any other demon. Promise me, Grindla."

Grindla moved close, but her back was still to the light, and Keeli could not make out her features. "Ai, M'cal. Ai. I promise."

Michael finally began to relax. Keeli did not, but she kept her mouth shut. She had already done enough talking to last a lifetime—however long that turned out to be. She was not sorry, though. Not for anything.

I would do it again if I had to.

Yes, and wasn't that a startling truth to discover about herself?

"You be needing m'help, M'cal? That why you be here?"

Michael did not let go of Keeli. His arms felt impossibly strong. "We need to go into a place where we do not belong. There is a murderer there."

"You goin' to do a job on this murder-boy?"

"Talk," Michael said. "Help him, if he deserves it. Kill him, if he needs it."

Keeli thought Grindla smiled. She hoped not. It was a disturbing sight.

"Ai," rasped the demon. "Ai, now. I can help you with that. A little talk, a little murder. Tell me where, M'cal. Give me a place."

Michael told her, and Grindla laughed. She sounded like a brick scraping a rusty washboard. She stepped away from the light, her limbs waving, braiding air.

"Go." Her chin pointed at the light. "Go and find your murder-boy."

"Grindla."

"I be waiting for you, M'cal. You, too, Keeli-girl. My new howl-biddy."

Like hell. You're a psycho demon bitch.

"Yes," rasped Grindla cheerfully, as Michael tugged Keeli toward the light. "I be just that."

They stepped through the light into a small red room. The room contained a bed, a desk covered by books, and a tiny closet. Posters covered the red walls, from movies, musicals. Music played softly: an opera, a classic recording of *Aida*.

"She did send us to the right place, didn't she?" Keeli tried not to let her voice shake, but it was impossible. She wanted to lie down on the bed she stood beside and suck her thumb. Michael, grim-faced, pulled her tight against his chest.

"I trusted her," he whispered. "I am so sorry, Keeli. You were right to be suspicious."

"You're a good guy," Keeli replied, her voice muffled by his chest. "And she said she was doing this to protect you. I guess if we'd been friends for a hundred years, I'd like you enough to do the same."

"That's no excuse."

"No," she said. "But she's a demon. They probably do things differently." *Shit, yes. And I'll tell her that, the next time she reads my mind.*

Michael drew in a shaky breath; Keeli would never admit it, but she got a perverse thrill from seeing him so torn up about losing her. It made her feel just a little better about offering up her life on a plate.

She studied the room. "Some experiment. Besides the overabundance of color, this looks pretty normal. Not like a lab at all."

Michael frowned, going to the desk. "Keeli, come look at this."

Keeli joined him. There were files stacked in neat piles. Each one had a name attached, as well as black and white photos, most of them taken from a distance. "This one has Walter Crestin's name on it."

Keeli checked out his photo. Walter Crestin had been a skinny white vampire with a shaved head. There was a red "X" through his face. She flipped through the pages inside his file.

"These notes are handwritten. Recently dated, too. Says here that 'target has confessed to multiple crimes against humans, in particular, young boys.'"

Keeli set down his file and thumbed through the others. Froze.

"Michael," she whispered, heart thundering. "Oh, God."

Her hand shook. He took the file from her and stared grimly at his name, a snapshot of his back. He was standing in his kitchen. The file contained a clear plastic bag. Inside the bag was a swath of cotton stained with dried blood.

"The hunter becomes the hunted," he whispered. "But why? What would any rogue element in the human government want to kill me?"

Keeli flipped through some more files, frowning at the things she read. "Not all of these vampires are dead. Either he's choosing his targets, or he's been given them."

"Who else?"

"There's a billionaire philanthropist in this file, and a strip club owner in another. All kinds, Michael. Some of them are not very nice people."

"Including me?" His voice was cold. She scowled.

"You know what I mean."

"Yes," he said. "I do."

"He's executing them," Keeli said, still watching Michael's eyes, the emotions shifting wildly through his face. He was trying so hard to wear a mask, and it hid nothing from her. "Or assassinating. These are specific targets, you included."

"He said I was supposed to die."

"He told me he had someone to find."

They stared at each other. Keeli felt sick.

"I suppose this is what the vampires I hunt feel like," Michael said. "This man and I are both executioners. Assassins. We have jobs."

He thumbed the books on the table. "Joseph Campbell, Machiavelli, Gandhi . . . these are not the books I expected."

Keeli tugged on his sleeve. "Michael, don't compare yourself to this man."

"Why not? I see so much of myself in him. Maybe too much. I am not sure I like the reflection."

"I don't know," Keeli said, turning around to look at the room. "He doesn't seem to be living so bad. Not like an experiment at all."

Shouts suddenly erupted outside the room. There was no time to run and no place to hide. Keeli did not know the signal they were supposed to use to get Grindla to pick them up.

"Michael," Keeli said. The door opened.

The first things she saw were red eyes in a stunningly handsome face, attached to a stunningly perfect naked body. And then perfection fell to his knees, hard, screaming as a thick black rod slammed into the small of his back, sliding down between his buttocks. Keeli heard the sound of cooking flesh—smoke rose from the tip of the rod as it trailed a path to his left hip. Two men in white jumpsuits flanked him. One man held the rod. The other had a clipboard.

No one seemed to see Michael or Keeli, who stood less than two feet away.

"Careful," said the man with the clipboard. "We need him to heal fast."

"He always does," said the other, smiling. He pushed a button in the rod and the young man screamed again, rolling on his side. Keeli took a step; Michael grabbed her arm.

The man with the stun rod knelt and seized a fistful of hair. "You like that, Eric? Feel good? You want some more?"

Eric said nothing. Keeli could not believe how young he looked—barely a man—but there was no youth in his eyes. Hard, resigned, and achingly lonely. No fear. Just calm expectation.

His captor lifted up the stun rod and began shoving it into Eric's mouth. This time, Michael moved. Keeli stopped him just as the other human dropped his clipboard and hauled up his companion.

"Are you an idiot? That could burn away his tongue."

"I thought you wanted to check his regenerative abilities."

"No permanent damage! I have kids to send to college, man. I need this job."

"Yeah." He kicked Eric in the stomach. "But she did tell us to teach him a lesson." He knelt again and forced the young man to look up at him. Blood dribbled from the corner of his mouth. "You learn your lesson, freak?" He jammed the stun rod into Eric's ribs, making the young man scream. "Or do you need a little more?" He dragged the rod down to Eric's genitals.

Keeli wanted to gag. She leaned against Michael, holding back her own cries as Eric writhed, screaming until his voice broke.

"Come on. Stop that. You're enjoying it too much."

"Damn straight. This one's the worst of both worlds. If I can't get my own fang or dog, I'll take him."

"No. I'm pulling rank. Get the hell off him. He has to be able to function for tonight's assignment. The target is still loose."

"Spoilsport."

The two men were still arguing when they left the room. They never spared a backward glance for the young man sprawled naked on the floor. Beyond the open doorway, Keeli glimpsed a long white hall, cold and sterile.

As soon as the door closed, Michael and Keeli rushed to Eric's side. Keeli touched his cheek. Eric's eyes flew open. His nostrils flared.

"You," he croaked. "I know those scents."

"Shhh," whispered Keeli.

"I don't see you, I—get away from me." Eric rolled onto his side. He tried to stand, and would have fallen if Michael had not caught him.

"Don't," Eric said. "They're watching me."

Keeli looked around the room. She did not see any cameras, but had no doubts they were there. She thought of the files she and Michael had been looking at, and wondered if that had shown up on any monitors as floating paperwork. She didn't know how far Grindla's demon voodoo extended.

Eric stumbled to his bed, collapsing hard on the mattress. He curled up in a fetal position, facing the wall. Michael and Keeli crouched near his head. She watched his sweat-slick body shiver, and noticed for the first time a fine web of scars across his back and shoulders. She followed the trail of old wounds until they disappeared around his raw pink hip.

He looked completely human except for his eyes, and that same strange scent tickling her nose: alien, yet familiar. Keeli thought she should recognize it.

"I don't know why you're invisible," Eric murmured, shivering, "and I don't care. How did you find me? Why are you here? To hurt me? Kill me?"

"We want to know who you are," Michael said.

"We want you to come with us," Keeli added. The words slipped out before she could stop herself, but in that breathless moment, after it was too late, she suddenly did not care about repercussions or past crimes. Something terrible was happening here, something awful being done to this young man, and what she was seeing, feeling, did not add up to a coldhearted killer. Or if it did, he had been made this way—*taught* these things—and she could not allow it to continue.

Give him a chance, any chance, to redeem himself. To start over. And if he can't—if murder really is all he's capable of— then you'll take care of him. You'll do what has to be done.

"Come with you?" His eyes drifted shut. He fumbled for a cover and yanked it over his hips. "No place for me. I'll hurt people. I'm an animal."

His words slurred. Keeli wondered what else had been done to him, if he was drugged. Michael said, "You are not an animal, but you are a murderer. You killed all those vampires. You would have killed us. Me. That is why we are here."

"A vampire and werewolf together," he breathed, as though he hadn't heard Michael call him a murderer. His voice was soft, musical, and weary. "You smelled like sex. Still do. She always told me that was impossible. That it had to be rape."

"What are you talking about?" Michael asked immediately. "Who told you such things?"

"She told me vampires and werewolves hate each other. Told me . . . told me they wouldn't accept me. No one would. No . . . love."

Keeli saw something strange on the edge of Eric's elbow. She bent close, peering at the inner part of his arm. Needle tracks riddled the flesh. She looked down, farther, and saw old burns on his wrist. She checked his neck and saw the same thing.

"Michael, he's been doped up. And here—these look like silver burns."

"Silver." Michael sat back on his heels. "Silver only burns werewolves."

Keeli's breath caught.

"Check his teeth," she whispered. Michael stared; comprehension filled his eyes.

"You do not think . . ."

"Do it," she said.

Eric's eyes were half-open, but there was little life in them as Michael reached around and pulled back his upper lip. Michael sucked in his breath.

"Keeli."

"I see them."

Michael pulled back his hand. "It is impossible."

Keeli shook her head. She thought about all those condoms they should have used. And suddenly, everything made perfect, terrible, sense. She knew why he seemed so familiar.

"Michael," Keeli said. "He's not a lab experiment. I know who his parents are."

"Grindla," Michael whispered. "Get all of us out of here."

Chapter Twenty-two

Eric did not struggle when Michael carried him through the portal. Keeli heard alarms blare just before she stepped through—apparently, someone did notice Eric floating off his bed and disappearing—but the red room vanished behind her before she saw anyone come in after them.

Grindla's home no longer resembled an oubliette. Rough stone walls arched over Keeli's head; shallow holes pitted the large expanse of floor. The room looked like someone had taken a large mallet and beaten the crap out of a cave.

Michael lay Eric down on a narrow stone platform that could have been a bed, but looked more like an archaic examining table. Keeli gazed at his slack face, taking in the dark hair, the fine high cheekbones and strong jaw.

"Celestine's hair used to be this color," Michael said. "Blue black. She shaved it off because it was Malachai's favorite thing about her."

"You see the resemblance now?" Keeli asked. "It was the scent that got me. I finally realized why it was so familiar. He smells like Hargittai. Not quite the same, but too close to be anything but blood."

"Celestine was pregnant. That must be the reason she left him."

"And what? She abandoned her baby? Gave him to the government? Look at him! He's so young."

Michael shook his head. "We need to talk to her. Hargittai, too. They need to know they have a son."

Eric stirred, whimpering. Keeli touched his shoulder. After a moment, he quieted.

"He's been tortured, Michael. Maybe for his entire life. How does someone recover from that without permanent damage?"

"You don't," he said quietly. "Sometimes you don't recover at all."

Keeli heard cloth rustle; she and Michael turned. A beautiful woman stood behind them. She wore loose yellow silks that perfectly complimented her tousled red hair and green eyes.

"Grindla," Michael said. Keeli blinked. Grindla noticed Keeli's surprise, and smiled. Her teeth were perfect, white.

"I can be many things," she said, and even her voice was different, fluid and feminine. The demon approached the table; Michael carefully edged Keeli aside until he stood between her and Grindla. His hand dropped back for one moment and Keeli grabbed it. He squeezed once, then let go.

Grindla studied Eric, trailing her fingers through the air above his body. She closed her eyes. Shivered.

"Would you like me to wake him?"

Michael studied Eric's face. "How will he react?"

"With fear, but that is to be expected. He has been raised by that emotion."

Keeli sensed his hesitation. "We need to talk to him,

Michael. We need to know if he can be helped, whether he'll continue killing."

"We will not get that from one conversation," Michael said.

"*I* will." Grindla smiled, and it was still disturbing, no matter how different she looked. "Ask him the right questions, and I will tell you what his true heart says."

Keeli did not want any more of Grindla's help, but she had to admit it was tempting to take advantage of the demon's powers.

"More than tempting," Grindla said, looking into Keeli's eyes. "You do not have time for anything else."

"No trickery," Michael warned.

Remorse flickered through her face. "Let this be my apology, M'cal. For the sake of our friendship, please let me do this."

He hesitated. Keeli touched his cool hand. "She's right. We don't have time."

His jaw tightened. "All right. But Grindla—"

"In this you can trust me, M'cal. I promise you."

Promises or not, Eric would be waking on his own soon enough. Keeli heard his heartbeat quicken, his breathing grow shallower.

Michael remained silent. Grindla placed her hands on Eric's cheeks. His eyes snapped open. Bright, with the same hues as a ruby backlit by fire. For a moment he stared at them, and then sat up—a blur—his hands striking out toward Michael and Keeli.

Grindla hissed a word. Eric froze in mid-lunge. Keeli glimpsed the faint outline of tentacles around the demon's body, but then the illusion returned.

"Let me go," Eric said, and Keeli remembered his great strength, the speed at which he could move. She wondered what other traits of the wolf and vampire he had inherited.

"Will you kill us?" Michael stepped close. His face was a mask: cool, calm, devoid of anything resembling emotion. His voice was just as dry, but commanding. "You are supposed to kill me, but you stopped once before. Will you again, this time? We need to talk."

Eric peered at them, and Keeli tried to reconcile this defiant young man with the confused shadowy figure who had attacked her in an alley, who'd begged her to run because he could not control himself. In that alley had been a monster, terrible and lonely and broken. Something here was not right—she could taste the difference in attitude, the clarity of his gaze. It was like being in front of a completely different person.

"If you let me go," Eric said, "I won't attack you. Not unless you try to hurt me."

Keeli glanced at Grindla, who nodded. She released Eric. He began shivering.

"Michael." Keeli tugged on his sleeve. "Give him your coat."

The coat was too small for Eric, but he accepted it without complaint and wrapped himself tight. His feet swung off the stone table. Keeli looked at his ankles, the burns in his flesh.

"Did those men we see do that to you?" She pointed.

Eric's legs stopped swinging. "Only recently. I wasn't cooperating."

"Cooperating," Michael echoed. "With the murder of vampires and werewolves?"

"It wasn't murder," Eric said, grim. "It was execution. Punishment."

"But you're so young," Keeli said, appalled.

"You called me the enemy." Michael stepped close, and Keeli felt his desperation, his hunger to understand this young man—this boy—who was so much like himself. "I have seen my file. I know you were spying through my window, planning your kill. Why? Why did you call me 'food'? Did humans teach you such things?"

"Turnabout is fair play," Eric said harshly, though Keeli saw the glimmer of uncertainty in his eyes. "Karma. Vampires treat humans as food. It's time someone showed them what it feels like."

"But you are one of us!" Michael grabbed him by the shoulders. Eric wrenched away and rolled off the table. Anger contorted his face.

"One of you? I'm not *anything* like you. I'm not . . . I'm not anything at all."

"We know who your parents are." Keeli stepped forward, dodging Michael's attempt to pull her back. She walked to Eric, watching his surprise mingle with distrust. "Your father is my friend. Your mother is Michael's friend." Which was a bald-faced lie, but now wasn't the time for semantics. "Their names are Hargittai and Celestine, and they loved each other very much."

She might have sucker-punched him for the way he looked at her—distraught, flustered, stunned—but when he staggered back, hugging himself, she also saw his youth, the echo of a dream flaring to life within his eyes.

"You're lying," he whispered.

"We can take you to them. Right now."

"Keeli," Michael warned.

"Eric needs to see his parents," she said, "and his parents sure as hell need to see him."

"He does not believe you." Grindla swayed near, intently watching Eric. "He wants to, but he has been taught that he was conceived from rape, that his mother abandoned him for that reason. For being an abomination."

"What are you?" Eric whispered.

"Something far stranger than a little hybrid." Grindla smiled and touched Eric's face. He shied away, but the demon followed, gently stroking his cheek. "There is no such thing as abomination, no such thing as a person who should not exist. We are here, young Eric. All of us, together."

"Not all of us. You're all monsters."

"So what does that make you?" Keeli asked.

"The worst . . . the worst of both worlds."

"Or the best," Michael said. "You have not been given the chance to discover that for yourself."

"I'm a murderer. A cannibal."

"He is lying," Grindla said, still caressing him. "He never ate the flesh of the men and women he killed. He did, however, take some blood last night. He was too hungry not to."

Eric finally pulled away. "Stop."

"No." Michael's arm snaked around Keeli's waist and she leaned into his side, grateful for his touch, for the way Eric's expression changed, watching them. "No, Eric. We must resolve this now. I need to know why you did those things. What was in your heart when you killed."

"Survival," Grindla said, and Michael gave her a hard look.

"Let him talk," he said. His voice was gentler than his eyes.

They all stared at Eric, who watched them with a peculiar defiance that gave Keeli the impression of a man hanging from a cliff by his fingernails. Eric was still fighting—screaming on the inside—with the world beneath his body, ready to swallow up his heart.

"I don't know you," he said. "I don't trust you. I get beat up at the lab, but at least I know what they want. You two are strangers, and what you're telling me does not make sense."

"That's frightening, isn't it?" Keeli shook her head. "Yeah, why the hell should you trust us? Shit. We're not asking for miracles here. Just the fucking truth. I think you owe us that much. You did try killing us, after all."

Shame fluttered through his eyes. "I stopped."

"You didn't stop when you murdered all the others."

"They were vampires. My assignments. I had to kill them."

"Bullshit. You're a vampire. A werewolf. Should you die, too?"

"Maybe," he said. "Maybe that's all I'm good for. Death."

"You learn that in your fancy lab? Did all your nice teachers drill that into your head with their stun rods and silver and drugs? You think they made you take it up the ass to help your self-esteem?" Keeli shrugged off Michael's arm and stalked forward, feeling the wolf stir within her body, the thunderous presence of her anger. She rolled it on her tongue: hot, fierce.

"If that's all you're good for," she rasped, "then tell us now. Tell us. If the only thing in your heart is death, and all you want to do is keep killing, then let's start here. Do it right this time. Kill me."

"Keeli!" Michael grabbed her arm. "What are you doing?"

"Ending this, one way or another. I want the truth, Michael. I want *his* truth." Still struggling against Michael's grip, she turned to look at Eric. "You're strong enough. One good blow. Do it."

"No," he breathed, and right then, Keeli knew she had him. Knew with absolute certainty that the game was done.

"Why not?" she asked, still hot in her skin. "Tell me *why*."

"Because I don't want to." Eric sucked in his breath. "I don't want to hurt you. I don't want to kill."

"And the others? Why, Eric? Why them?"

"I had to." He backed away, shaking his head. "You don't understand. For the past year they've been training me. Hardening me. They want me to be a weapon, an assassin. This was just the practice run."

Keeli grabbed his chin and forced him to look into her eyes. "You're different from last night. Last night, you were an animal. You could barely function. You said you were hungry."

"They don't feed me anymore," he whispered. "And they pump me full of drugs before sending me out. The cocktail enhances my hunger. Lowers inhibitions. Alters my . . . personality."

Michael touched Keeli's shoulder. She released Eric. "Grindla says you didn't eat your victims. She called it a show. And we saw your files, the research you did."

"Practice. They—she—gave me the targets, told me to go out and do reconnaissance. I think she wanted to see if I could move amongst vampires without them realizing what I am. Making them look like they had been eaten, though . . . that was my idea. I wanted her to believe my control was gone, that she had the upper hand."

"Who is doing this to you?" Michael asked. "You speak of more than one person, but there is also a woman."

Eric looked down at his hands. He turned them palms up, and Keeli watched fur push through his skin—quick, sleek, and silver. "I don't know her name, but I spent my entire life in that lab, in that building. It's all I know. She hired people to raise me, and sometimes I saw her. Through glass. She talked to me through glass. Read me stories, sometimes. Told me things. Gave me music, encouraged me to sing. She said . . . she said, she liked to hear me sing. Sometimes she visited when the people came to run their tests. And then last year she said I was outliving my usefulness." His voice wavered; his eyes grew distant. "So she gave me away to the men and they turned me into something useful."

Eric looked at Michael. "I received your file yesterday morning. You were a priority case. Last night was the deadline for your hit. But I couldn't finish the job. I botched it. Thought I could make up for it by completing another assignment, but she was still furious."

"Furious enough to torture you?"

"I don't listen well," Eric said softly. "That's why they've been using a new cocktail. The effect is stronger. Makes it hard to control the monster. Music . . . the music she gave me helps me concentrate, so I tried that."

She remembered his ghostly voice, so lovely and strange. "You sang. To distract the beast."

"It didn't work. She was mad about that, too." A bitter smile touched his lips. "Good thing you fight dirty."

Grindla reached for him. Eric slithered from her touch, shaking his head. "No, don't. Don't . . . touch me. I don't like it."

Silence reigned over the room; Keeli listened to their heartbeats mingle, the harsh sound of Eric's breath. He closed his eyes.

"I talked," he said. "I told you what I've done. What are you going to do with me now? What's the punishment for murder in cold blood?"

Michael walked to Eric and grabbed his hand. He placed the young man's palm over the tattoo glittering hard and golden in his cheek. "This is *my* punishment," he said. "For all the people I murdered when I was tortured and starved. I will not do the same to you."

Eric tore his hand away from Michael's tattoo. He rubbed his palm. "What then? Are you going to kill me?"

Michael smiled, grim. "Like you, I also execute vampires. But at least you can say you were raised to be a weapon against them. I have no such excuse. I do the job because I think it needs to be done, and because I am paid to do it. Of the two, I think I am the worse man."

"Do they accept you?" Eric asked, still rubbing his hand.

"No," Michael said. "But they need me."

"They won't need me. They won't accept me. Not unless . . . there are others?"

The hope in his face took Keeli's breath away. She felt hit in the heart by his youth, the elusive breathlessness that was still innocent, full of dreams. She wondered how he could be capable of such optimism, but even as she grasped that thought, she realized the silence had gone on too long; shadows passed through Eric's red eyes, a slow descent into something still and hard and lonely.

"Never mind," he said.

"Are you ready to go?" Keeli asked.

"Go where? Back to the lab? A vampire firing squad?"

"I was thinking more in terms of my home, but if you prefer those other places, I'm sure Grindla could arrange something."

"I am sure I could," Grindla said.

"You live with other werewolves?" Eric looked suspicious. "How will they treat me?"

"Like shit," Keeli said. "Some of them might even hate your guts. Could be they'll try to kill you."

"You're not convincing me to come."

Keeli shrugged. "I'm being honest. You may never fit in. But let me ask you something: What do you prefer? Making your own home, free to screw up your life any way you want—or being stuck with a bunch of sadists who screw up your life for you? I know what I chose."

"Freedom?"

"No." Keeli smiled, thinking of how that was both lie and truth: freedom was always a matter of perspective. "I chose *him.*"

Michael glanced down at her, startled. Keeli smiled.

Her cheeks felt red, but that was good—she was glad she was the kind of girl who hadn't forgotten how to blush.

Eric stared at them, lost. "You never answered my question."

"We will not kill you," Michael said, tearing his warm gaze away from Keeli's warmer face.

"No, not that one. The other. Do you love her?"

"With all my heart," Michael said.

Eric closed his eyes. "Then I'm ready. Take me to my parents."

Chapter Twenty-three

Michael did not want to take Eric to the underground. He most certainly did not want to return there with Keeli. The reception she might receive frightened him; he could not bear to see her suffer for their relationship, but—

It is done. She made her choice, and you made yours. The best you can do now is fight for her—for her right to live at your side, with respect and dignity. You know she would do the same for you.

Yes. Keeli never ran. The least he could do was be as strong. After all, what had he sacrificed to be with her? Nothing. Keeli was the one who had made the great leap, the blind flight of faith.

Grindla opened the portal: a blaze of white light. Eric stood beside her, dressed in green silks. With the young man's dark hair pulled away from his face, the resemblance to his parents was clear: Celestine's gaze, sharp and keen, set in Hargittai's fine angular face. The way Eric held himself belonged to his mother—the way he walked, all wolf. Keeli leaned against Michael, studying the young man.

"It's incredible," she said.

"Yes," he said, trying to imagine what their own child might look like. He needed to start buying condoms.

Grindla gestured for them to draw near. "The portal will take you into the underground."

"Can we enter through my grandmother's rooms?"

"If you like." Grindla touched Keeli's cheek. An odd smile flitted on her lips. Before Keeli could pull away, the demon leaned forward to kiss her on the mouth. Michael felt power wash over his body; for one moment he was afraid. But Keeli blinked, puzzled and unhurt, and said, "What the hell was that?"

"A well wish for a good howl-biddy." Light rippled through Grindla's eyes.

"Right." Keeli looked suspicious.

Michael took her hand. With his other, he reached out toward Eric. "Are you ready?"

"No," he said.

Michael smiled. "Good."

Grindla trailed her fingers across Eric's chest, tracing a design. "You are always welcome here. Simply call my name."

"Thank you." Eric hesitated, and then wrapped Grindla in a clumsy hug. Grindla smiled. When he released her, she turned to Michael.

"You are still my friend," he said, in response to the question in her eyes. He was rewarded with a sigh.

"Be safe," she said.

And then light enveloped him, blinding, and he lost his body to a great empty expanse that made his mind brittle. He had no mouth to scream, no arms to flail, but he felt his soul fall—fall too fast—and then the light disappeared and he was on his back in a warm golden room with a fire on his left, a young man on his right, and a pink-haired waif on his chest.

"Hello," Keeli said.

"Hello," Michael replied. He kissed her nose.

"We have company," she told him.

"I know." He looked sideways and up, up into the stunned faces of werewolves and vampires. The Grand Dame's sitting room was crowded, bodies packed in between luxurious furnishings and glowing candles. The air smelled like incense. Classical music played softly. Michael wondered what time it was. Moonrise would mark the end of this gathering.

Hargittai stood nearby, with Jas and several other wolves beside them. They were clean, dressed in formal attire. Celestine sat on a plush velvet footstool on the opposite side of the room. She looked tense, her flawless brow slightly furrowed.

The Grand Dame was not in the room.

"Where's my grandmother?" Keeli asked, as Hargittai helped her stand.

"She received an urgent call that she did not want to take in front of the envoys. She should be back soon."

"What is going on?" Frederick pushed himself out of a deep leather chair. He stopped when he saw Michael. Celestine floated to her feet. She stared at Eric.

"We need to talk in private," Keeli said to Hargittai, ignoring the envoy leader. She glanced at Celestine and said, "You need to be there, too."

Frederick looked at Celestine. "What do you know about this?"

"Nothing," she said, but there was a look in her eye that Michael had never seen before: a crack in the steel; pale vulnerability. Hargittai swayed toward her.

Frederick's mouth tightened with displeasure. Michael leaned close, and in a deadly quiet voice, said, "Do not speak what you are thinking. Do not even dare breathe it. There is more going on here than you can imagine, and if

342

you have any desire to save this negotiation, then you will do exactly what I say. Is that clear?"

A hush fell upon all the vampires in the room: shocked, fearful. Frederick's eyes narrowed. "You dare speak to me that way?"

"I could dare much more than that," Michael told him. "Maybe I will start with you."

Fury twisted Frederick's face, but Michael felt movement against his back, and he turned just enough to see the werewolves sidle close. It was pitiful how outnumbered the vampires looked within the small confines of the Grand Dame's sitting room. Every gathered werewolf was tall and strong, with the bearing of an Alpha. A smile haunted the corner of Hargittai's mouth. Jas looked very grave.

"So it was not just a petty rumor," Frederick said, looking past Michael at Keeli. "You are with the wolves, now."

"I am with the woman I love," Michael said. "And if that means the wolves, so be it."

Celestine made a small sound. At first Michael thought it was in response to what he had said, but when he looked, he found her staring at Eric. Eric returned her gaze, steady and strong. A good act—Michael caught a glimmer of insecurity, desperate hunger. To come face to face with the mother and father he had only dreamed of—to look them in the eyes and not flinch, not weep or beg . . .

Celestine made another noise; it sounded like a whimper. Hargittai reached for her elbow and she flinched.

"Don't." Eric's composure slipped. He choked on his voice. "Don't touch her."

Hargittai frowned. Celestine drew away from him, swaying toward Eric. Looking at her face was like seeing a picture of perfect tragedy: grief and loss, her eyes full with agony. Michael had never seen anything so terrible

343

in his entire life, and that it was Celestine suffering—Celestine with her sharp mouth, her callous heart—merely made the moment more heartbreakingly bizarre. She was completely oblivious to everyone in the room.

"It can't be," she breathed, still staring at Eric. "No."

"Celestine?" Hargittai whispered. She shook her head, reaching out to touch Eric's face. The young man's breath caught; he stood, frozen, as Celestine peered into his eyes. Everyone was frozen, caught up in the tragic peculiarity of the moment.

A moan burst from Celestine's mouth. Her face crumpled; her entire body sagged in on itself. Eric caught her against his chest and gently lowered them both to the ground, cradling her in his lap. Hargittai fell to his knees beside them.

"Your eyes," Celestine sobbed, curling in on herself. "Oh, God. No one else could have eyes like yours."

"What did you do to her?" Hargittai seized Eric's shoulder. He pulled back his other arm, hand closing into a fist. Michael grabbed him around the chest. Keeli scrambled to impose her body between the Alpha and Eric.

"No!" she cried. "No, you can't. This is your son, Hargittai. Your *son*."

Her voice shocked the room into one giant wheeze; gasps, the struggle for breath. Bewilderment surged from one body to the next; dancing confusion. Hargittai stopped struggling.

"But that's impossible. That's—" He looked at Celestine. She lay there, staring at him, tears racing down her flawless cheeks. Hargittai choked, falling backward against Michael. Trembling, he breathed, "Why didn't you tell me?"

"I couldn't," Celestine whispered. "They said they would kill you. That if I ever spoke to you again, they would kill us both."

"Who?" Hargittai's voice cracked on that word.

The door to the Grand Dame's rooms opened. The old woman appeared, her silver hair loose and wild, her silk robes reflecting firelight. She looked at Michael and Keeli, and then her gaze fell upon Eric.

No, Michael thought, watching her eyes. *Oh, no.*

Eric stared. He whispered, "You."

The Grand Dame smiled.

Her grandmother's smile had to be one of the most sinister things Keeli had ever seen in her life, and she stood there, struck dumb as she tried to reconcile that face—that reaction—to Eric's simple "you."

You. As in, I know you. As in, I am shocked to see you here. As in—

"Why the hell does Eric know you?" Keeli asked her grandmother.

No one breathed as the Grand Dame glided into the room. Even the vampires seemed rooted, frozen in their shock. Everyone watched the old woman as she moved close, and only Michael stirred, placing himself in front of Keeli.

"This is unfortunate timing," said the Grand Dame, looking down at Eric. "Inevitable, but unfortunate. You should have stayed in your room."

"We kidnapped him," Keeli said, and then, "Holy shit. Oh, my God. What have you done?"

"What I had to do," she said, flashing a hard look. Cold—Keeli felt so cold staring into her grandmother's face, which could have belonged to a stranger. Eric looked afraid, and—*she talked to me through glass, read me stories*—Keeli recalled a stun rod burning a trail through his skin—*until last year she said I was outliving my usefulness*—in his balls, because he had to be punished—*so she gave me away to the men*—punished—*and they turned me into something useful*—for not killing Michael, and—oh.

Oh.

Frederick made a sound of protest; he looked ugly with distress. "You told Marakova the child was dead. You promised—"

Celestine cried out, lurching clumsily from Eric's lap. Hargittai and son grabbed her waist, holding her back from the envoy leader. "You knew? All this time—"

"I was Dumont's advisor," Frederick snapped. "Of course I knew. All four leaders of the Great Houses knew about your disgrace. And all of them—all of them—agreed that the best recourse would be to rid you of the child. And so we did." He stared at the Grand Dame. "Or at least, that is what we were promised."

"Yes," said the Grand Dame. "The poor vampires did not have the stomach to do it themselves, all those years ago. But me, the Grand Dame, a Maddox—I was already a dog to them. An animal. And animals have no conscience, do we?"

Hargittai snarled, and Keeli jumped between him and the Grand Dame. "All of you out," she ordered. "Jas, take the envoys into the hall. The rest of you, please—I know you are Alphas and above this, but please guard the vampires. Make sure they do not leave."

"This negotiation is finished," Frederick hissed.

"No," Keeli snapped, getting right up in his face. "It has just fucking started. So unless you want to go home and tell your new leader that you lost this alliance because we found out some of you vampires have been paying people to kill your children, you had better keep your mouth shut, go out in that hall, and sit tight until I come get you. Got that?"

"You are not the Grand Dame Alpha," Frederick said,

staring down his nose at Keeli. "You are a small little wolf with no authority. Why should I listen to you?"

"Because if you do not," Michael said quietly, "I will hurt you."

"No," Keeli said. "*I'll* hurt you. Now get the hell out of here."

"Stay where you are," said the Grand Dame. "That is not your order to give, Keeli."

"Isn't it?" Keeli asked, making her decision. She looked at Hargittai and Jas, at all the Alphas watching her. "Then I challenge you, Grand Dame Alpha Maddox. I challenge you."

It was like all the air got sucked out of the room; everyone held their breath, staring at the Grand Dame and Keeli. She willed herself not to falter, to stay strong under the power of her grandmother's shocked gaze, but it was difficult—the most difficult thing she had ever done—not to crumble and say *I'm sorry* and *Please, love me again, please.* But she kept her face strong, her mouth set, and she swallowed down the words, stamped out the pain and longing, because her grandmother had gone too far. Too far, and it was not right.

"Keeli," her grandmother breathed, and then gazed around the room, studying the faces of her wolves. Keeli did not know what was in their eyes, only that a great chill seemed to fall upon her grandmother's narrow shoulders and that the woman's mouth twisted down into a frown. The Grand Dame turned back to Keeli and said, "I accept. I accept your challenge, Keeli Maddox."

What have you done? Oh, no. What have you done?

"Leave us," said the Grand Dame to everyone, still looking at Keeli. "Now."

This time, Frederick did not protest. He led the vampires out of the room into the corridor. The wolves followed, Jas in the lead. He glanced at Keeli, and in his eyes was resignation. He looked too tired to feel angry.

Hargittai and Celestine made no move to leave. Neither did Michael or Eric. When the door closed behind the last Alpha, everyone stared at the Grand Dame.

And then Hargittai reached out and pulled Celestine into a quick hard kiss that was desperate, reckless—and returned with equal passion.

"Celestine," he murmured, and looked at Eric. He leaned forward to grab the young man's face. The two men stared into each other's eyes, nostrils flaring.

"My son," Hargittai whispered. "I didn't know."

"I believe you," Eric breathed. His hands flexed around Celestine's shoulders and waist. She raised a shaky hand and brushed his cheek.

"You were the reason I had to leave your father," she said. "And I hated you for that. Hated, and loved. The love was stronger."

"Then why did you give me up?" Eric's voice shook. "I spent my entire life in a lab, being treated as an experiment. Being taught that I was a monster. Told that the only way I could exist is because my mother was . . . was raped."

"No," Hargittai said, shooting the Grand Dame a hate-filled glance. "No. We loved each other. I still love her."

Celestine's eyes flashed. "Do not say that. It is too dangerous." She struggled against Eric, and he helped her sit up. "You have to go," she told her son. "You have to run and hide. They stole you from my womb before you were ready. They said you were dead. They will try to kill you if they know you are still alive."

The Grand Dame shook her head. "Your son is not so easy to kill, Celestine. Why do you think the vampires wanted him dead? Why there is opposition to an alliance between our two peoples?"

Celestine hissed.

The Grand Dame raised her hands. "I did what I had to," she said. "The vampires came to me when they learned of your relationship with Hargittai. They told me you were pregnant. The elders said they were giving me the courtesy of knowing they would be 'handling the problem.' I told them to let me manage it. I said it was my right, because the baby was also a werewolf. They agreed. They were more than happy to give me the child to kill. I made them pay for it, too. Pay well. And then I used the money to raise your son."

"He was being tortured when we found him," Michael said, his eyes dark with menace. "Those are silver burns on his body. He has permanent scars. His arms look like they belong to a junkie. Is that how you raise a child?"

The look she shot him was pure venom. "He would not have been punished if he had done his job."

"To kill me?" Michael asked quietly. He looked at Hargittai and Celestine. "Your son has been raised to be an assassin. Your son has been taught to kill vampires."

Hargittai stood. Eric grabbed his hand. "No," he said. "She was good to me. Don't hurt her."

"Good to you? How can you say that?"

"Because anyone else would have killed me." He looked at the Grand Dame. "I was nothing more than an investment to her, but that was something, at least. And maybe . . . maybe sometimes she liked me."

"I did," said the Grand Dame softly. "I liked you very much, Eric."

"Then why did you let them hurt him?" Keeli asked, drawing near.

Pain moved through the Grand Dame's face. "Because Eric is right when he calls himself an investment. Up until a year ago he was not using his full potential. I spoiled him—all that time, letting him breathe easy, have his childhood—and when I did need him, when all I required was an expression of his true nature, he balked. Refused. And so I had him punished. I fixed his inhibitions. It is quite amazing what money can buy, and what the government was willing to pay in order to see him mature into a . . . useful member of society."

"You bitch," Celestine said. "I am going to kill you."

"Really." The Grand Dame's eyes cooled. "You, who did not fight for the love of your wolf. You, who did not fight for your child."

Celestine jerked. "The Council would have killed Hargittai."

"Maybe," said the Grand Dame. "Probably. But you did not even try to defy them. You took the easy path, and simpered the years away as a lackey to the man who oversaw the removal of your child from the womb."

Keeli stared at her grandmother, incredulous. "You're telling her she should have fought harder? When I fought back, you tried to kill Michael!"

"My blood," Michael said. "I got it on your body. You took a sample and gave it to Eric for my scent. For my taste."

The Grand Dame nodded. "I was too late to stop what happened to Hargittai and Celestine, but I refuse to see the same hardship for my granddaughter. If you and she continue, a child is inevitable. And if that happens, if she is forced . . ." Her voice broke. She took a deep breath. "To lose your child is a pain I could not bear to see her endure."

"You made me endure it," Celestine said.

"You were not strong enough to endure the truth. To make the sacrifices necessary to keep him. That you did not fight for your wolf told me that much. Keeli, however, *is* strong enough. And that frightens me."

Keeli wanted to scream. "Why did you do it? Why have you done any of this?"

"Money," Michael said, thoughtful. Eric nodded slowly.

"Money is power," said the Grand Dame, quiet. "And money is the one thing we werewolves lack. The one thing we need. And you, Keeli, know that I will do anything to keep our people safe. Anything."

Keeli did know this. She just had never imagined that her grandmother would go so far.

"I made deals with the government. A man named Kippenham. He and his scientists were fascinated with the idea of a hybrid. Many things they learned from Eric went into developing the mech program—the perfect alignment of disparate parts into one body. And then, a year ago, Kippenham contacted me about other benefits. Favors. If I could provide him with another weapon against the vampires, he promised to keep the werewolves out of any upcoming conflict. He promised not to hurt us."

"You trusted him?" Keeli asked, appalled.

"Of course not. I was buying us time, Keeli. Time to expand the tunnels, to build a better infrastructure that would keep us safe if the city above went to pieces. I was trying to make us self-sufficient. Agreeing to negotiate with the vampires was part of that. The money we could get from an alliance with them would make us secure."

"But at the same time you were taking contracts on the lives of vampires," Michael said.

"And being paid for it. All the money went into the clan trust account."

Keeli blinked. "The morning after Crestin's death, I saw a note on your desk. Fifty thousand dollars was deposited into the clan account."

"I have five more contracts waiting," Eric said, standing.

"They're worth over one million dollars," said her grandmother. "Crestin was pennies. Practice for Eric."

"But he made a mistake," Michael said. "He left behind some DNA."

"Crestin took me by surprise," Eric said. "He fought well."

"And making the kills look like a werewolf was involved?" Keeli asked her grandmother. "Didn't you think that would cause us trouble?"

"Kippenham promised his protection. He had contacts, influence with the city government. And I knew that as long as there was no hard evidence left behind, the politicians would be unwilling to call for a roundup. Especially for the murder of vampires."

"Kippenham is dead," Celestine said. "We killed him."

"I know." Her face darkened. "I wish you hadn't done that."

Keeli sat down on the chair in front of the fire. She stared at the flames; Michael touched her shoulders. She listened to the shift of bodies, the rustle of cloth, and thought of the vampires and werewolves beyond the door, waiting for something, some conclusion and answer.

"We can't tell the vampires that Eric has been assassinating them," Keeli said, turning in the chair. "They'll want him dead, and then they'll turn on the wolves."

Eric shook his head. "I committed crimes. They deserve the truth."

"They do not deserve anything of the sort," Hargittai said.

"I agree." Celestine touched her son's cheek, and then drew her hand away as though burned. Keeli looked up at Michael.

He said, "All they know is that the Grand Dame did not kill the child. They have no idea what she used him for."

"All right." Keeli studied her grandmother, who watched Michael's hands on her shoulders. "We'll keep it that way. But things are going to change. Someone needs to pay for these crimes."

"Keeli," the Grand Dame began, and then stopped. Someone knocked on the door. Jas poked his head in.

"Moonrise will be soon." He glanced at Michael. "You'll need to keep an eye on our guests, what with Dumont ordering them to stay until the negotiations are complete."

Keeli stifled her surprise. Jas trusted Michael to do something important? Michael squeezed Keeli's hand and said, "Hasn't anyone informed her of this new situation?"

"Frederick is convinced that the Assembly doesn't give a damn who leads. Any will do. They just want results."

"Jas," the Grand Dame said, gliding past. A chill swept over Keeli's body, the urge to recoil. "Do you still wish to be Alpha?"

He hesitated, and in his eyes Keeli saw the desire, the dream—defiance hot in his blood. But then he swallowed, hard, and shook his head. The Grand Dame bowed her own.

"Prepare the ring," she said, and her voice was bitter, sad. "Prepare the wolves. We have a challenge."

The challenge ring was accessible only through a trapdoor in the main corridor of the Alpha core. A ladder led down, deep into shadow. The Grand Dame descended first, with Jas above her. The other Alphas hung back.

"We have no time," said Hargittai. "Are there rooms we can use?"

Keeli pointed at all the doors lining the hall within the Alpha core. "Those rooms are unoccupied. You can use them."

The gathered Alphas did not move. With the vampires beside them, they gazed steadily at Keeli and then Michael, Celestine, and finally, Eric.

"So that's what happens when we screw each other?" Leroux pointed at Eric. Hargittai growled. Leroux raised his brow and looked at Keeli. His eyes were calm. "It could be worse," he said.

"Yeah," said one of the women standing behind him. "He could look like you."

The wolves laughed out loud. Leroux closed his eyes, a smile touching his crooked lips. Eric stared at them all, a look of wonder on his face, and Keeli thought, *Yes, this is going to work. Somehow, we will make this work.*

The vampires did not laugh. They did not smile. But Celestine had her head thrown back and she stared at them, defiant, one pale hand wrapped tight around her son's. Maybe bald was a good look on a woman, Keeli decided. Especially when she stopped being a bitch for just one minute.

"You all better go," Keeli said to Hargittai. "You need to get locked down."

Hargittai looked at Eric. "Do you shift during full moon?"

"I can control it," Eric said. "I'll be fine."

Hargittai rested his hand on the young man's shoulder. "I cannot wait to find out more." He reached past his son and grabbed Celestine. He kissed her, long and deep, ignoring the vampires and werewolves shifting uncomfortably around them. Her face flushed crimson. Keeli glanced at Michael. He wore an odd expression, confused and disturbed. She could not imagine what he was thinking.

"This is disgusting," Frederick muttered.

"Right." Keeli pointed at the ladder. "After you."

The vampires descended into the darkness. They refused the ladder, floating down one after the other. The Alphas peeled away to find sanctuary for the moonrise; Hargittai went with them.

"Be safe," he said to Keeli, before he loped down the hall.

Which part of me? she wondered. *Body or soul?*

Michael's lips brushed the top of her head. She took a deep breath, and climbed down the ladder.

There were no lights; the challenge ring was used so seldom that no one had wired it for electricity. Light was unnecessary, though. Everyone there could see perfectly in the dark.

The Grand Dame was already in the ring, a deep circular pit surrounded by thirty-foot-high concrete walls. Keeli looked down at her grandmother and kicked off her shoes. Vampires lined the edge of the pit. Ironic. The only witnesses to this challenge would be the very people werewolves distrusted most.

Keeli jumped into the pit, easily absorbing the impact of her fall. The sand was soft, cool beneath her bare feet. Keeli sank her toes into it, testing her balance. Her body tingled.

"The moon is rising," Jas cried, already climbing the ladder to the Alpha core, escaping the ring. "Hurry!"

Keeli stripped off her clothes, tossing them away. Her grandmother did the same. They stared at each other, and Keeli felt her heart break.

"Please," Keeli said.

"You've made your choice." The Grand Dame's voice wavered. "This is the way it has to be, the way it has been done since the first wolf. I will not abdicate to you, Keeli. Never. I could never live with myself if it cost you your life."

"The wolf will be on us both," Keeli reminded her. "What if you kill me?"

A sad smile touched the Grand Dame's lips. "We both know the outcome of this fight, Keeli."

Keeli did not know the outcome, but the look in her grandmother's eyes made her afraid. She could taste the old woman's resignation like a cold stone, heavy on her tongue.

She tore her gaze away and looked up at the pit's edge. Michael stood there, Erik and Celestine at his side with the vampire envoys spread out around them, watching everything with varying expressions of fascination and contempt. All the wolves were locked away in their rooms or chained in the halls. The only two who remained free were Keeli and her grandmother, and at the end of the night, just one would be left standing.

Michael jumped into the air and alighted beside Keeli. He touched her face.

"I love you," he said. "Carry that with you tonight, if you can."

She nodded, unable to speak. She rubbed her arms. Felt the beginnings of fur. Moonrise. The full moon, pulling beast from humans.

Keeli forced her throat to work. "Get away from me."

Michael kissed her—hard, quick—and flew into the air.

Keeli did not watch him leave. Her lips burned from his kiss—burned as flesh pulled, stretching back over shifting bone—pulling low, pulling in—muscles bunching tight, against her ribs, her hips. Her lower back ached; Keeli gritted her teeth, growling as bone gathered and pushed out—and suddenly she was on all fours, writhing in the sand, hugging back the pain, the fire in her gut, and she opened her mouth to scream and all she heard was a high whine, a whimper that was animal—wolf. . . .

She closed her eyes for just a moment. When she opened them, the world was different. Different, similar—scents bright and alluring—but after a moment, none of that mattered.

There was another wolf in the ring with her.

She had a vague sense of unease, a—*no, do not hurt her, please, please*—but the other wolf bared teeth, snarling, and she forgot words, thought, as adrenaline rushed through her body, responding to the instinct to live.

The wolf attacked—a hard feint that took Keeli off balance so that she stumbled—too slow—teeth razing her ribs, cutting through fur, flesh—pain bright as memory, striking—*please no, not this, you cannot*—so that she flipped on her side, rolling as the wolf crashed down on her chest, rolling tight to cover her throat, hot spit flecking her muzzle, and still she did not fight, did not struggle for blood, because something—*you love her*—dulled her reactions.

The wolf snapped at Keeli's exposed belly, biting through the soft spot to blood. Agony—Keeli howled, ripping her body free from those teeth with a sharp turn that had her trailing crimson in the sand. Fury tangled with pain—killing reservations, killing everything—and she drove her body into the other wolf, snapping, tearing, and she tasted blood—hot, bright from the throat—*I am sorry*—and her jaws tightened, piercing, and the wolf below her cried out, cried—*love*—and Keeli stopped in the middle of the kill, stopped on the cusp of drinking death, and shouldered the shuddering wolf down into the sand. She relaxed her jaw and then slouched down, still and heavy and quiet, on the gasping body. She scented blood, saw it run thick and crimson.

Keeli rested her head on the wolf's shoulder, and listened to their heartbeats mingle.

Chapter Twenty-four

Michael was there when Keeli opened her eyes. She felt sticky and sore and very human. The full moon had come and gone. Sand filled her mouth; the taste of old blood. She spat, rolled over. Hit another body, pale and wrinkled.

Keeli scrabbled to her knees. Michael crouched beside her as she reached out to her grandmother, pressing her cheek to the old woman's breast. She listened to the slow steady rhythm of her heart, the rise and fall of her chest. Her throat was pale, perfect. The sand around her head was stained red.

A sob tore from Keeli's throat. She fell away from her grandmother, weeping, and Michael wrapped her in his arms, whispering, kissing her cheeks, her tears.

"I thought I killed her," Keeli rasped. "Oh, God. If I had killed her—"

"You didn't," Michael whispered, rocking her. "I watched you, Keeli. I watched you stop. You controlled the wolf."

Memory filled her, faint: fur and hot blood, rolling,

sharp pain. She said, "I was an animal, Michael."

"No," he said, smiling. "You were Keeli Maddox, Grand Dame Alpha."

Rustling from above drew her attention; the edge of the pit was filled with werewolves. Werewolves crowded to peer down, jostling for a view. Silent, except for the movements of their bodies. For a moment, Keeli felt afraid. All her grandmother's warnings swarmed into her heart, immense and terrible. She wondered if this was what her father had felt, in that moment before his death. So small, inferior and weak.

Michael pulled back from Keeli. She stood on her own, but kept her hand wrapped tight around his. She looked at the wolves—found the vampire envoys far behind them, looking weary and wary. Keeli turned in a circle to meet all their gazes. She saw Jas, Hargittai—even Richard and Suze—face upon face of the familiar. And then, as one, they bowed their heads to her.

"Greetings," said a dry voice near Keeli's feet. Her grandmother stared up at her with a sad, tired pride. "Greetings to the new leader of Maddox, the new leader of all the clans of Crimson City. Grand Dame Alpha Keeli Maddox."

Hours later, Keeli found herself in her grandmother's rooms, sitting in a pea-colored chair in front of the fireplace. Her grandmother sat in the other chair, a steaming cup of tea in her hands.

"So," she said, sipping the brew.

"So," Keeli said. She studied her fingernails. No more grease to worry about; after today, she wasn't going to have time to waitress. Guess she'd have to call Jim and let him know. He might care.

"I still love you," said her grandmother. Keeli studied those clear blue eyes, the stubborn mouth. She tried to imagine herself becoming that woman, making those same decisions.

"I love you too," Keeli said. "But I hope to God I don't make the mistakes you did."

A slow smile touched her grandmother's mouth. "I hope so, too. I also hope you learn what it means to make the hard decisions, the sacrifices to the heart and soul. I hope, one day, that you understand me."

Keeli gave her a noncommittal shrug. "Eric will be moving to Hargittai's clan. I'll need your help shutting down that lab, getting rid of the paper trail."

"My cooperation in return for your silence?"

"Something like that. The clans don't need the scandal."

"The clans need the money."

"We'll get it another way."

Displeasure sparked in her grandmother's eyes; it made Keeli's hair curl, but she reminded herself of blood and sand. She kept her gaze strong, true—and her grandmother looked away first.

Silence pressed down on them. Keeli tried to remember all the good moments, the sweetness of their relationship, and found she could not. Maybe time would return those feelings. She thought of Michael, too, and those were the only memories that felt good on her heart.

"Why do you hate the vampires?" she asked.

"I don't hate them, Keeli. I simply do not trust them. They have been arrogant for too long, believing themselves full of glory, expecting the good life. The good life has to be earned."

"So you were punishing them? Is that what this was all about? All the killings, treating Eric like he was less than human?"

"No, I was not punishing them. I was teaching them how to be controlled. I was teaching them what it is like to be hunted. The vampires have forgotten what that is like.

They have forgotten what it is like to be prey. Eric . . . Eric was my tool, my weapon."

"Your investment."

"I do care for him," she said quietly. "There were times when I almost revealed his existence, when I would look at Hargittai and see Eric in his face and think, yes, now is the time. But I did not tell him, and I let Eric think that he was unloved and alone, because it made him easier to control. He knew I wanted to control him. He knew what our relationship was. I did not pretend to him on that."

"Are you trying to make yourself feel better?"

"Maybe." Her grandmother smiled. "But the past cannot be changed, and I am not certain I would do anything different."

"Nothing?"

The ex-Grand Dame looked away. "Perhaps I would not have turned on Michael. Perhaps . . . perhaps I was wrong about him. Or not. Love makes people do very strange things, Keeli. Love for clan, for family."

"Love for a vampire."

"Yes."

Someone knocked on the door. Keeli turned as it opened. Michael entered, with Hargittai and Eric close on his heels. The young hybrid looked nervous; a light sheen of sweat covered his forehead. He swallowed hard when he saw the Grand Dame. Hargittai showed no emotion at all. His was a dead gaze, merciless and empty. A heart devoid of compassion.

Keeli could not blame him.

"Ah," whispered the Grand Dame. She looked at Keeli. "I was unaware we were expecting guests."

Keeli said nothing. She had been expecting them. All of this—the sitting, the talking—was nothing more than a prelude to the final act. Keeli's one last chance to speak with her grandmother face to face. Alone, as blood. As family.

Hargittai said, "Did you truly think you would escape this unpunished?"

The Grand Dame still stared at Keeli. She met her grandmother's gaze, unflinching. Not easy. She wanted to weep and scream.

"No," said the old woman finally. "No, I suppose I should not have thought that. What will it be, then? An execution? Quiet, in the shadows? Will you let your vampire do the dirty work for you? What a fine choice in men, Keeli. What a good girl I have raised. It is always a fine thing to love and be loved by those who will turn and kill you."

"Stop," Keeli said, her temper rising. "You don't deserve to talk to me that way. Not after what you've done."

"And I do not deserve to die," said the old woman. Her fingers curled like claws around the armrest of the chair. Fur poked through her skin. Keeli felt Hargittai and Michael move; she held up her hand and they stopped. The Grand Dame watched them obey her, vampire and werewolf, and Keeli felt that vision burn a hole into her grandmother's heart.

"Who do you think you are?" Keeli asked softly, and to say those words felt like her own little death, the final stab. "Who do you think you are, to murder and deceive?"

"I was the Grand Dame," the woman said coldly. "It was my right—my *prerogative*—to do all that was in my power to help the clans. And if you, my dear, plan on leading them with any success, you will quickly learn to do the same."

"Being Grand Dame is my highest responsibility," Keeli said quietly. "I will give my life to it, if necessary. But I will never break the covenant between myself and the wolves. I will never deceive them, as you have done. I will never shame them with indiscriminate murder, as you have, or steal their children to raise as soldiers, commodities."

A high flush stained the Grand Dame's cheeks. "Just wait," she whispered. Hateful. "Wait until that moment when you must choose. See what sacrifices you make, and *then* lecture me."

Hargittai snarled. Eric caught him by the arm and swung his father around so that they stared into each other's eyes. It was uncanny, seeing the two of them together. The resemblance was undeniable, and not just in appearance, but in spirit.

Eric looked past his father at the Grand Dame. "You're not going to die."

"Eric," Hargittai began, but his son gave him a hard look. "I can't be cruel," he said softly. "She needs to know."

Eric walked to the Grand Dame and knelt before her. They stared into each other's eyes. Keeli held her breath. She felt Michael draw near; he touched the back of her neck.

The Grand Dame said, "So. You are free now."

"Yes," said Eric. "And I forgive you."

The Grand Dame raised one fine eyebrow. "That is big of you."

"Don't," he said. "Don't try to belittle what I'm giving you. You saved my life. You raised me. You gave me books and music. You gave me the tools I needed to resist the commands of the men you sold me to. For that, I will always be grateful."

"I made you kill," said the Grand Dame. "Surely you cannot forgive me for that."

"I forgive you," said Eric. But his gentle voice turned cold, soft. "I forgive you, so I can forget you. You have no power now. You are worth nothing. Old wolf, old heart. Your only legacy will be a sour taste in the mouths of those who once loved you."

"I thought you were not going to be cruel," said the Grand Dame, and Keeli sensed—for the first time—a sliver of real pain. Heartache in the old woman.

"The truth *is* cruel." Eric glanced at Keeli. "You taught *her* that, didn't you?"

The old woman's breath caught. Keeli did not give her a chance to respond—she could not bear to hear what her grandmother would say. It was already difficult enough.

"I am exiling you," Keeli said, gripping her teacup so hard her knuckles turned white. "You will leave this room. You will leave this city. And you will never come back."

Horrible to say, perhaps even more terrible to hear. It took the Grand Dame a moment to find her voice, to control herself enough to speak with dignity. "You said you needed my help."

"Nothing that cannot be done remotely." Keeli struggled to maintain her cool. "I and a few others will know where you are. You'll have a phone. Some money. You won't go hungry."

"And if I do not cooperate?"

"I will come for you," Hargittai said, and there was no mistaking what he would do. The Grand Dame stared at him.

"I think I would rather die than leave this city," she said.

"That is certainly an option," Hargittai agreed. "You betrayed us all, May. Perhaps my son can forgive you, but I cannot. All those years, defending you . . ." He shook his head. "You disgust me."

The Grand Dame blinked, speechless. She turned away from Hargittai, and the helplessness in her eyes—the shock—was unbearable.

Keeli felt she was ripping her own heart out—like *she* was the betrayer. In a sense, she was—but that was just something she would have to live with if she wanted to keep the clans safe. Her grandmother could not be allowed to stay. Keeli did not trust her. Her voice was still too powerful, the backlash of her crimes too great. An alliance with the vampires might be achieved with the Grand Dame's presence, but it would not last. A clean start was needed. A new beginning.

It is justice, she thought. *Merciful justice, if only she knew what the others wanted.*

"The car is ready," Hargittai said to Keeli. "We can take her now."

The Grand Dame did not need Keeli to tell her; she rose from the chair, still dignified and elegant, her despair becoming anger. She turned that wrathful gaze on Keeli, and then it was as though all her strength and vibrancy transformed into something more than a bitter heart.

"I will not worry about you," she said quietly. "Not one bit. You've learned your lessons very well indeed."

"Granny May—"

"No," she said. "Don't. Maybe I deserve this. Maybe I deluded myself. I just . . . did not want to hear it from you."

There was a knock on the door. Eric answered it. Celestine stood there, Frederick at her side. The cold hard features of her face softened when she looked at her son—a remarkable transformation. Keeli still couldn't believe that such a hateful person could ever love—and not just love, but love outside her kind.

Why couldn't you do the same? Keeli wanted to ask her grandmother. *Why did it have to come to this?*

"Are you ready?" Celestine asked, and it seemed like a question more for her son than Keeli.

"Are you coming with us?" Eric asked.

"Oh, yes." Celestine smiled, cold, at the old Grand Dame. "I would not miss this trip for all the world."

Keeli did not envy her grandmother, but she thought it was appropriate: Forced to sit in a car with the family she had destroyed. They would be driving quite a distance. Keeli wondered who would get the backseat with her grandmother.

Frederick looked at everyone in the room with varying expressions of unhappiness and confusion. Keeli hoped he stayed confused. It was all right for him to know her grandmother was going away—just not the reasons why. If the vampires ever found out she had ordered the murders, that Eric *was* the murderer . . .

Secrets. I suppose this is my first lesson in them.

"Good-bye," Keeli said to her grandmother.

Her grandmother said nothing; she turned and walked from the room. Hargittai looked at Keeli, hesitating. Keeli shook her head. No, nothing he could say would make this better. Nothing in the world could do that. She would be living with this day for the rest of her life.

Michael touched her hand. "I am here," he breathed, in a voice only she could hear. She nodded, swallowing hard.

Eric and Hargittai followed the Grand Dame from the room, Celestine between them. Frederick stayed.

The door closed. For a moment Keeli was a little girl again, sitting in her grandmother's lap, rocking and rocking, being held in the safety of strong warm arms.

Never again. Never again.

Frederick stirred, breaking the spell of memory. Keeli wondered how long she had been standing there, staring at the door.

"I do not know what just happened," Frederick said imperiously. "But I can tell you right now that I do not care for your attitude. I can't imagine we'll get much accomplished."

Keeli crossed her arms. She was not in the mood to be insulted.

"What do the vampires want from us?"

"Tunnels," he said.

"Why do they want the tunnels?"

His eyes narrowed. "We want them in case we need sanctuary against the humans."

"And will this be sanctuary for all the vampires? Every single one of you in the city?"

"If need be."

"Then I'm going to need some things in return, Frederick. If the vampires won't give them to me, we don't need to talk again. These are nonnegotiable conditions."

"I thought you said the negotiations were just beginning."

"I did. This is the beginning. This is also the end."

Frederick's mouth tightened. "What do you want?"

"One hundred million dollars. In addition to that fee, the vampires must also pay for complete renovations of the entire underground."

"That is outrageous."

"That is the deal. If you think about it, I'm sure you'll agree that it makes sense. The tunnels are not currently prepared to withstand an attack from human forces. If you want to use them, you will have to fix them—and fix them *well*."

Frederick gritted his teeth. "What else?"

"Real estate," Keeli said. She knew she was pushing the limits of Frederick's patience, but she was the Grand Dame Alpha now, and if she were going to screw the pooch, she might as well go all the way.

"Real estate," he echoed.

"I want Michael's neighborhood," Keeli said, and was pleased to see Michael blink, surprised. "The entire neighborhood. All the buildings. Everything. Free and legal and clear."

"He lives in a trash heap," Frederick said.

"But it'll be our trash heap," Keeli said. "That's what I want in return for access to the underground."

"The former Grand Dame refused us full access."

Yes. The former Grand Dame had also been playing games.

"If you agree to my terms, you can have full access—but you'll also take responsibility for the behavior of your vampires. If anyone breaks our laws—if even one fang scrapes the body of a werewolf or human—there will be no mercy. None. I will not tolerate fighting between our two peoples. I will not tolerate violence. I will not tolerate name-calling or patronizing behavior."

"You do not tolerate much at all."

Keeli smiled. "You need us more than we need you, Frederick. What's it going to be?"

"I cannot give you an answer now. I need to consult with Fleur and the other leaders."

Keeli pointed at the phone. "Consult. Michael and I will wait over here for their answer."

Frederick had the intelligence not to ask her if she was really serious; he picked up a phone and moved to a corner of the room. Keeli and Michael sat on the floor in front of the fire. She leaned against his shoulder. She needed to be near him. Her heart still hurt.

"I called Jenkins," he said. "He gives his best to the new Grand Dame."

"I bet. Did he have any news?"

"Nothing. I told him not to expect any more bodies. He told me not to say another word. He didn't want to hear it."

"See no evil, hear no evil. I like him."

"He's a good man. A good friend. He said his superiors closed the case completely. There's no more talk about roundups." Michael wound his fingers around Keeli's hand. "There's something else."

"Uh-oh."

"Marcus contacted me. He found Emily's attacker. He's holding him for me at the bar."

"Shit."

"I told Jas."

"Fuck."

"I am sorry," Michael whispered. "But I made a promise."

"Yeah, I know. I want to be there, Michael."

He kissed her hand. Behind them, Frederick hung up the phone.

"I need two hours," he said, and his patronizing attitude was gone. "Dumont is consulting with the others."

"Fine." Keeli stood. "That'll give us time to take care of some business."

The vampire's name was Kenneth. Michael did not bring him to the underground. He brought Kenneth to an abandoned building where Emily and Jas waited with Keeli. Michael knew they had the right vampire, because when Emily saw his face, she turned away, shaking. Jas shook, too. His scar stood out in sharp relief against his red face. He looked ready to kill.

"Emily," Michael said. "Are you ready?"

She straightened slowly. Turned around and took off her hat. Michael felt Kenneth go very still under his hand. Kenneth had a gag in his mouth. He was handcuffed to the stairs so he could not fly away. He made a small sound in his throat. At first Michael thought it was laughter, but then he looked into the vampire's eyes, and realized it was a whimper.

Emily took a deep breath. She looked into Kenneth's face, and her gaze was determined, cool.

"I brought tools," Michael said, gesturing at the bag of sharp things on the floor. "I even have his dagger if you prefer the original." He felt Keeli give him a sharp look.

"Yes," said Emily. "Please."

Michael gave her the silver dagger. She fingered the

crucifix-shaped hilt, and pressed it between her breasts as though in prayer. Jas watched her, distraught.

"She is going to hurt you now, Kenneth," Michael told the vampire, in a voice loud enough for everyone to hear. "She is going to cut your face."

Emily's steps faltered.

"She is going to slip your knife under your thick blond hair. She is going to cut *just so* and pull off your scalp. She is going to cut you slow."

Emily stopped walking. Started moving again.

"She is going to make you scream."

Emily stood in front of Kenneth.

"Do you remember me?" she asked softly. Kenneth nodded. Michael did not see remorse in his eyes, but he did see fear. Emily saw it, too. She took a deep breath. She touched Kenneth's face and pressed the dagger against his cheek. Pushed in. Kenneth closed his eyes and whimpered. Blood trickled from the cut. Michael watched Emily's face. Behind her, Keeli and Jas stood breathless.

Emily looked at Michael. Her eyes were stricken.

"I don't want this," she said. "I don't want to be like him."

"That's good," Michael said. "No one wants you to be like him, either."

He held out his hand and Emily gave him the knife. She walked back to Jas and Keeli. Jas gave Michael a look that was a mixture of gratitude and respect, and then he gathered up his wife and escorted her away.

Keeli met his gaze. She nodded, solemn, and then followed her friends out of the building.

She knows me and still she loves me. Michael did not understand such a blessing, only that it was the rarest of miracles, sweet and good.

Michael turned back to Kenneth. He tapped the vampire's dagger against his thigh. And then proceeded to tell Kenneth exactly why the Assembly had ordered his execution.

Keeli waited for Michael on the fire escape outside his apartment, drinking in the scent of roses. The sun was setting; she glimpsed gold, the shadowed blush of purple. It was very pretty. She imagined herself standing here every night—imagined, too, other wolves, on other fire escapes, watching shadows gather. It was a good feeling.

Michael drifted down from the sky. He wrapped his arms around her.

"Emily does not have to worry anymore," he said quietly.

"That's good," she said. "With this new money we're getting from the vampires, we'll be able to afford to pay for her reconstructive surgery."

"They agreed to the terms?" He sounded amused; perhaps a little surprised.

"All of them. Either I'm really good, or they're really desperate."

"Both, I suspect. Do the Alphas know?"

"Yup. Dumont and the other vampire leaders will be coming to the underground tomorrow to sign the papers."

"So. We have an alliance."

"We do." She turned to look at him. "There's still going to be trouble, you know. Wolves and vampires aren't going to get along just because of a piece of paper. And then there's Eric to think of. What he is, everything he's gone through. What he could become."

"Hargittai will take care of him. Celestine, as well. I hope."

"I hope," Keeli muttered darkly. "I hope my grandmother keeps her nose clean. I hope I can learn to lead as well as she did."

"Better," Michael said. "Aim better."

"Yeah." She studied his face, the pale line of his perfect

jaw. "And then there's us. It's not going to be easy."

"I know." He ruffled her hair, smiling. "But I love you despite all your trouble."

"I'll die before you do," she said. Michael's smile faded.

"I have considered that, Keeli. It does not make me love you any less."

She nodded, still dissatisfied, but unable to explain why. Michael caught her chin. "Do you remember Grindla, what she did to you?"

Keeli flushed. "She kissed me."

"Demons give strange gifts, and there was power when she touched you. I should ask her what her intentions were." She scowled, and he laughed, low. "I mean, it's possible we might be together longer than you think."

"Huh." She scratched her chin. "That could be a long time. You're still young by vampire standards, right?"

"I suppose," he said.

"Then what should we do with all that time?"

Michael's lips twitched. He patted her backside.

"You must be the horniest man I have ever met."

He laughed outright. "That is something I have never been called."

"Horny? What a shock. Bet you had the women crawling all over you." She stopped. "Never mind. I really don't want to know."

"That's probably for the best," he said, which instantly piqued Keeli's curiosity. She kept her mouth shut, though. Some things were better left unsaid.

Some things, but not all.

"I love you," she said.

Michael bent close, pale and cool and lean. He smelled like freedom, and when he kissed her, Keeli imagined she could fly.

"Let's find a cloud," she said.

And they did.

Carnival Pride℠
April 2 - 9, 2006.

7 Day Exotic Mexican Riviera Itinerary

DAY	PORT	ARRIVE	DEPART
Sun	Los Angeles/Long Beach, CA		4:00 P.M.
Mon	"Book Lover's" Day at Sea		
Tue	"Book Lover's" Day at Sea		
Wed	Puerto Vallarta, Mexico	8:00 A.M.	10:00 P.M.
Thu	Mazatlan, Mexico	9:00 A.M.	6:00 P.M.
Fri	Cabo San Lucas, Mexico	7:00 A.M.	4:00 P.M.
Sat	"Book Lover's" Day at Sea		
Sun	Los Angeles/Long Beach, CA	9:00 A.M.	

ports of call subject to weather conditions

For booking form and complete information
go to **www.AuthorsAtSea.com** or call **1-877-ADV-NTGE**

Complete coupon and booking form and mail both to:
**Advantage International, LLC,
195 North Harbor Drive, Suite 4206, Chicago, IL 60601**